W9-CRJ-761

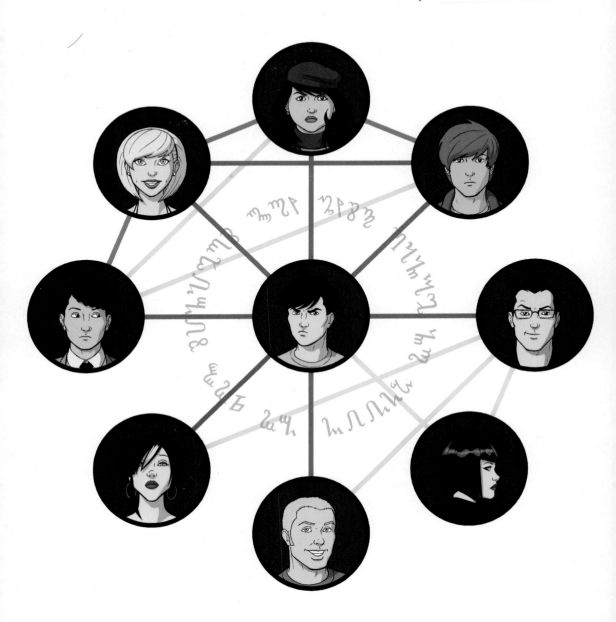

WITHDRAWN

PHON●GRAM
THE SINGLES CLUB

KIERON GILLEN & JAMIE McKELVIE

written by
KIERON GILLEN

art & lettering by
JAMIE McKELVIE
art assistance by JULIA SCHEELE

colors by
MATTHEW WILSON

collection design by DREW GILL

IMAGE COMICS, INC.
Robert Kirkman – Chief Operating Officer
Erik Larsen – Chief Financial Officer
Todd McFarlane – President
Marc Silvestri – Vice-President
Jim Valentino – Vice-President
Eric Stephenson – Publisher
Corey Murphy – Director of Sales
Jeff Boison – Director of Publishing Planning & Book Trade Sales
Jeremy Sullivan – Director of Digital Sales
Kat Salazar – Director of PR & Marketing
Emily Miller – Director of Operations
Branwyn Bigglestone – Senior Accounts Manager
Sarah Mello – Accounts Manager
Drew Gill – Art Director
Jonathan Chan – Production Manager
Meredith Wallace – Print Manager
Briah Skelly – Publicity Assistant
Randy Okamura – Marketing Production Designer
David Brothers – Branding Manager
Ally Power – Content Manager
Addison Duke – Production Artist
Vincent Kukua – Production Artist
Sasha Head – Production Artist
Tricia Ramos – Direct Market Sales Representative
Jeff Stang – Digital Sales Associate
Emilio Bautista – Administrative Assistant
Chloe Ramos-Peterson – Administrative Assistant
IMAGECOMICS.COM

PHONOGRAM, VOL. 2: THE SINGLES CLUB

Third printing. January 2016. ISBN: 978-1-60706-179-3. Published by Image Comics, Inc. Office of publication: 2001 Center Street, Sixth Floor, Berkeley, CA 94704. Copyright © 2016 Kieron Gillen & Jamie McKelvie. Originally published in single magazine form as PHONOGRAM: THE SINGLES CLUB #1-7 by Image Comics. All rights reserved. PHONOGRAM, its logos, and all character likenesses herein are trademarks of Kieron Gillen & Jamie McKelvie, unless expressly indicated. Image Comics® and its logos are registered trademarks and copyright of Image Comics, Inc. All rights reserved. No part of this publication may be reproduced or transmitted, in any form or by any means (except for short excerpts for review purposes) without the express written permission of Kieron Gillen & Jamie McKelvie or Image Comics, Inc. All names, characters, events, and locales in this publication are entirely fictional, and any resemblance to actual persons (living or dead) or entities or events or places is coincidental or for satirical purposes. Printed in the USA. For information regarding the CPSIA on this printed material call: 203-595-3636 and provide reference #RICH–660828.

Representation: Law Offices of Harris M. Miller II, P.C. (rights.inquiries@gmail.com).

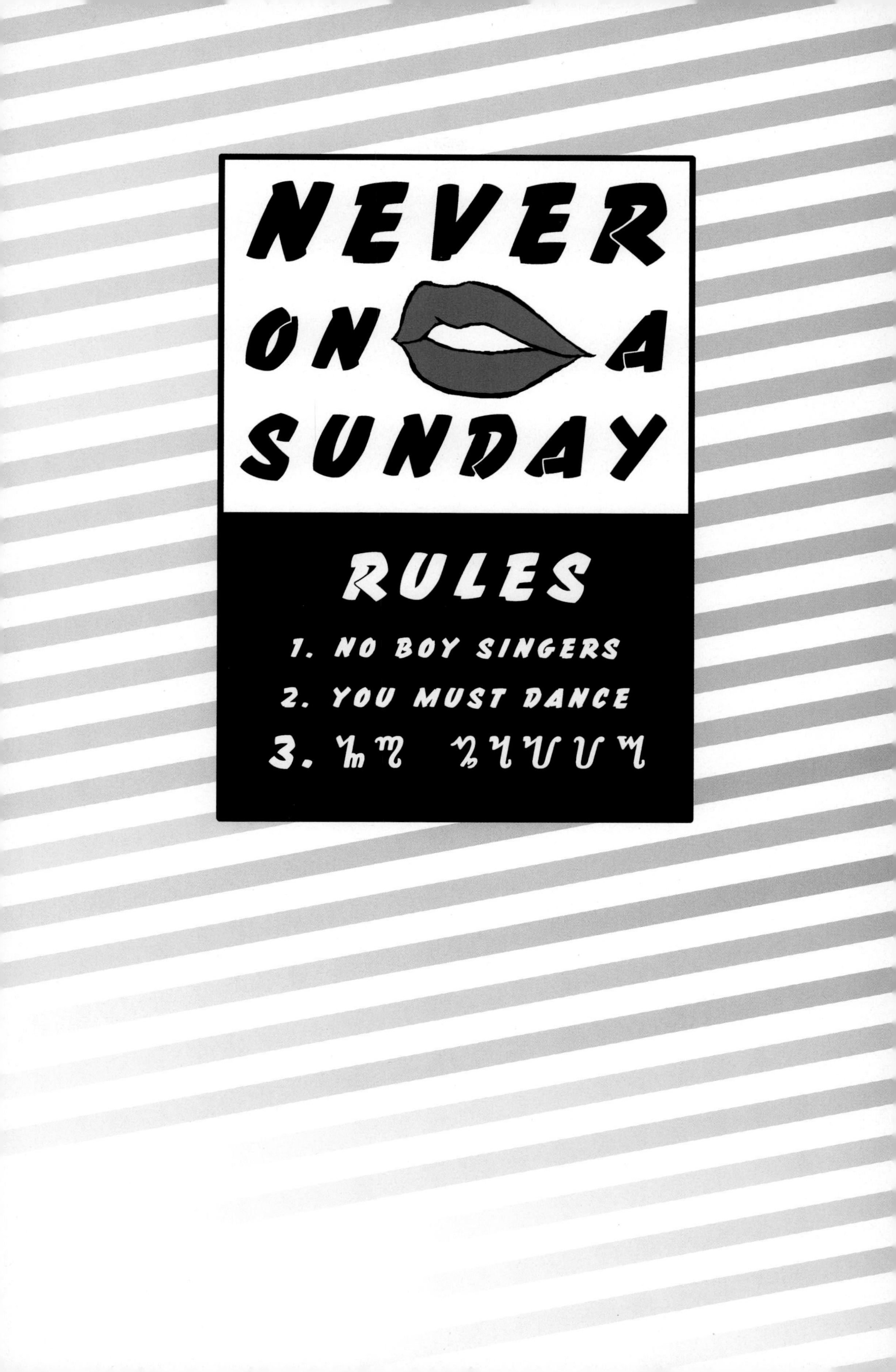
NEVER
ON A
SUNDAY
RULES
1. NO BOY SINGERS
2. YOU MUST DANCE

To Chrissy and Hannah and Nayoung

PHONOGRAM THE SINGLES CLUB

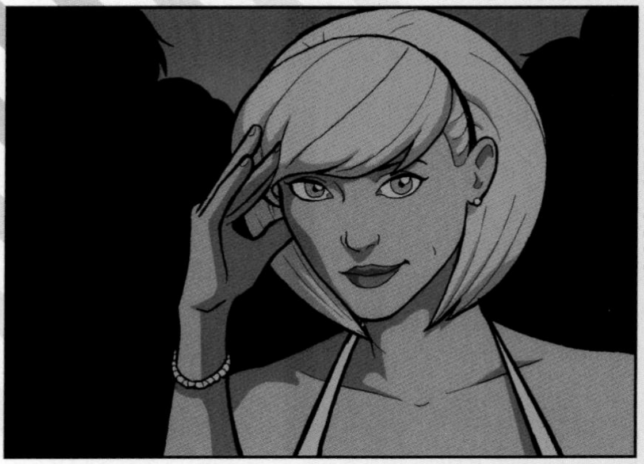

1. PULL SHAPES

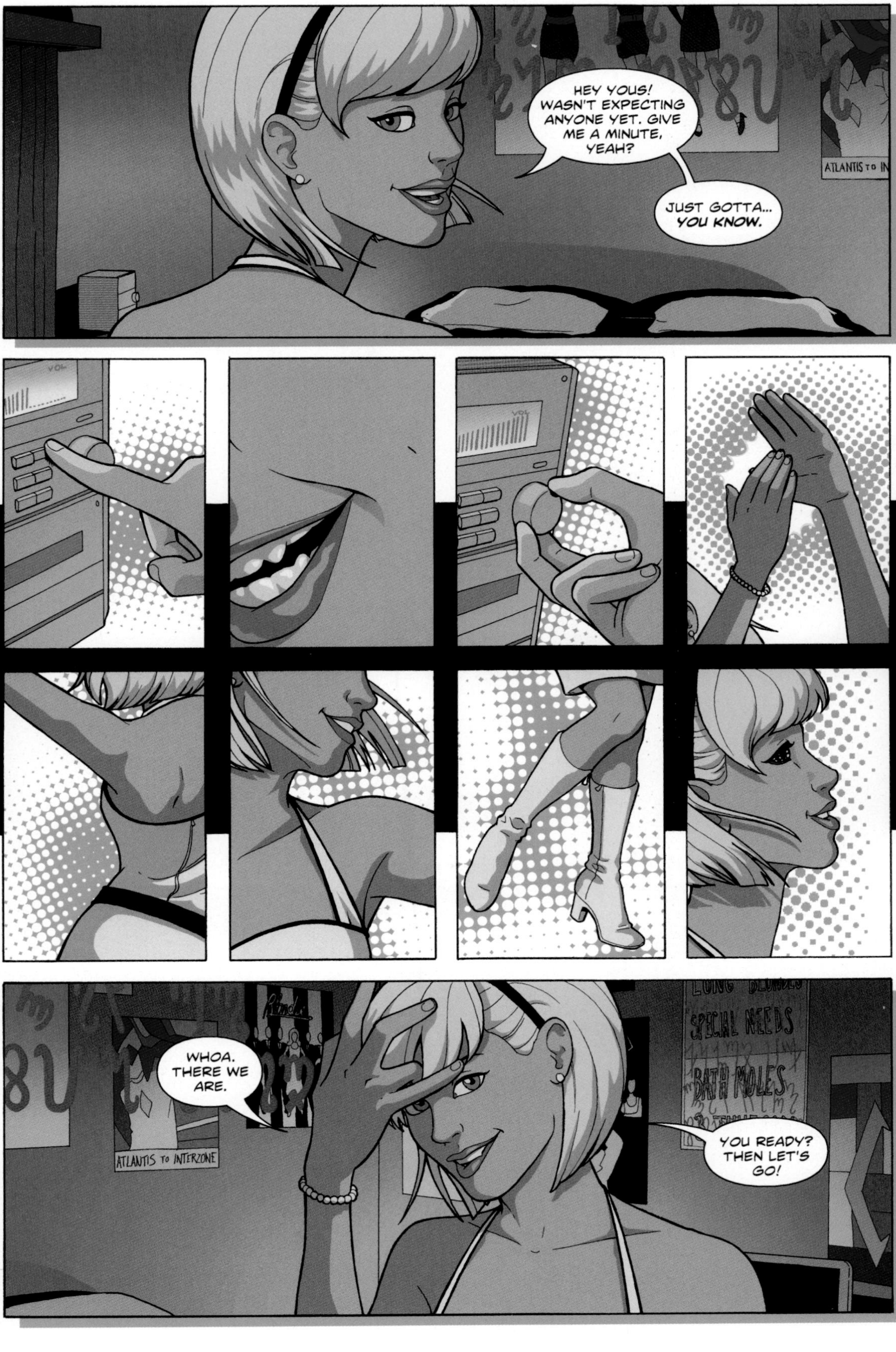
HEY YOUS! WASN'T EXPECTING ANYONE YET. GIVE ME A MINUTE, YEAH?
JUST GOTTA... *YOU KNOW.*
WHOA. THERE WE ARE.
ATLANTIS TO INTERZONE
SPECIAL NEEDS
BATH MOLES
YOU READY? THEN LET'S GO!

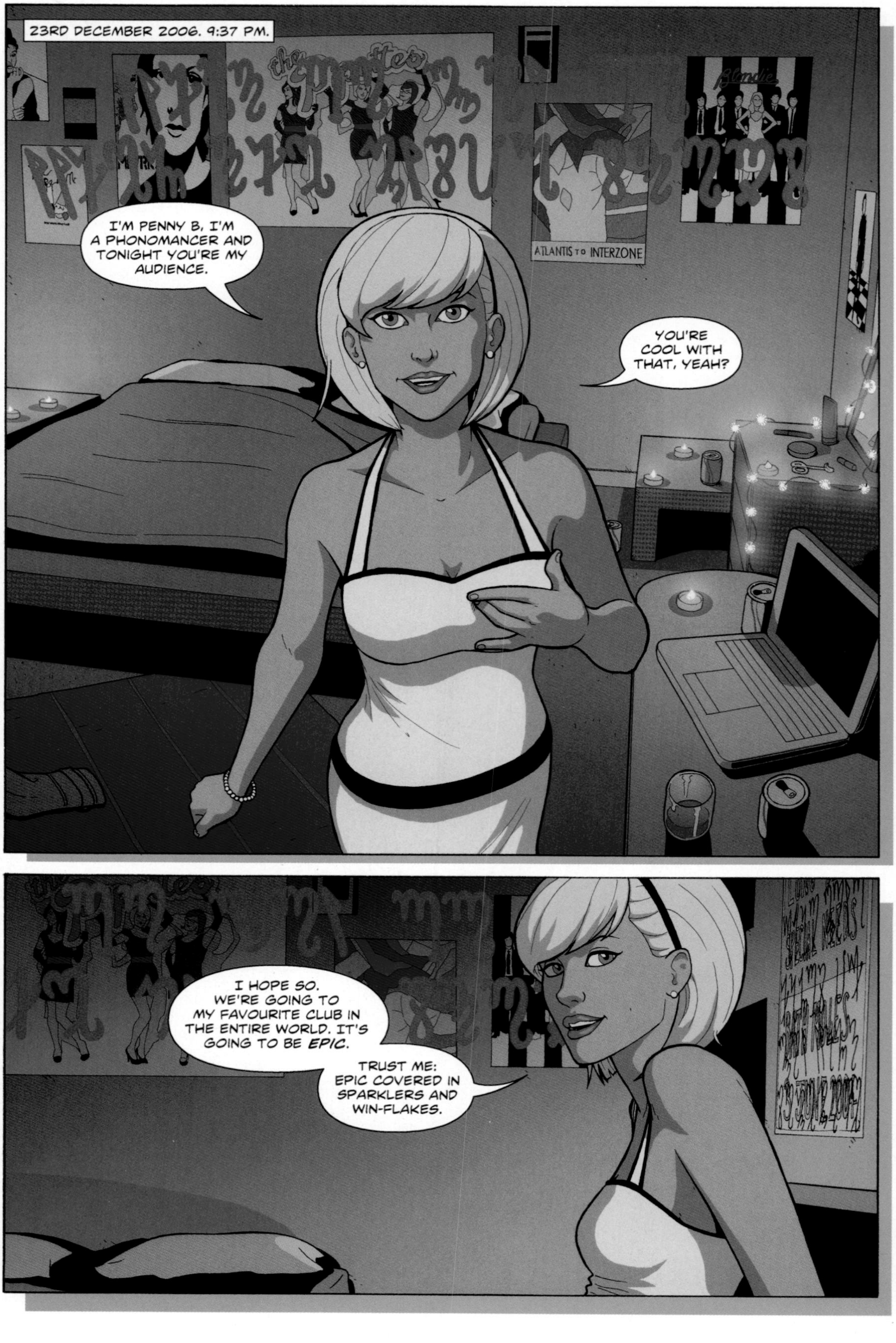
23RD DECEMBER 2006. 9:37 PM.
I'M PENNY B, I'M A PHONOMANCER AND TONIGHT YOU'RE MY AUDIENCE.
YOU'RE COOL WITH THAT, YEAH?
I HOPE SO. WE'RE GOING TO MY FAVOURITE CLUB IN THE ENTIRE WORLD. IT'S GOING TO BE *EPIC*.
TRUST ME: EPIC COVERED IN SPARKLERS AND WIN-FLAKES.

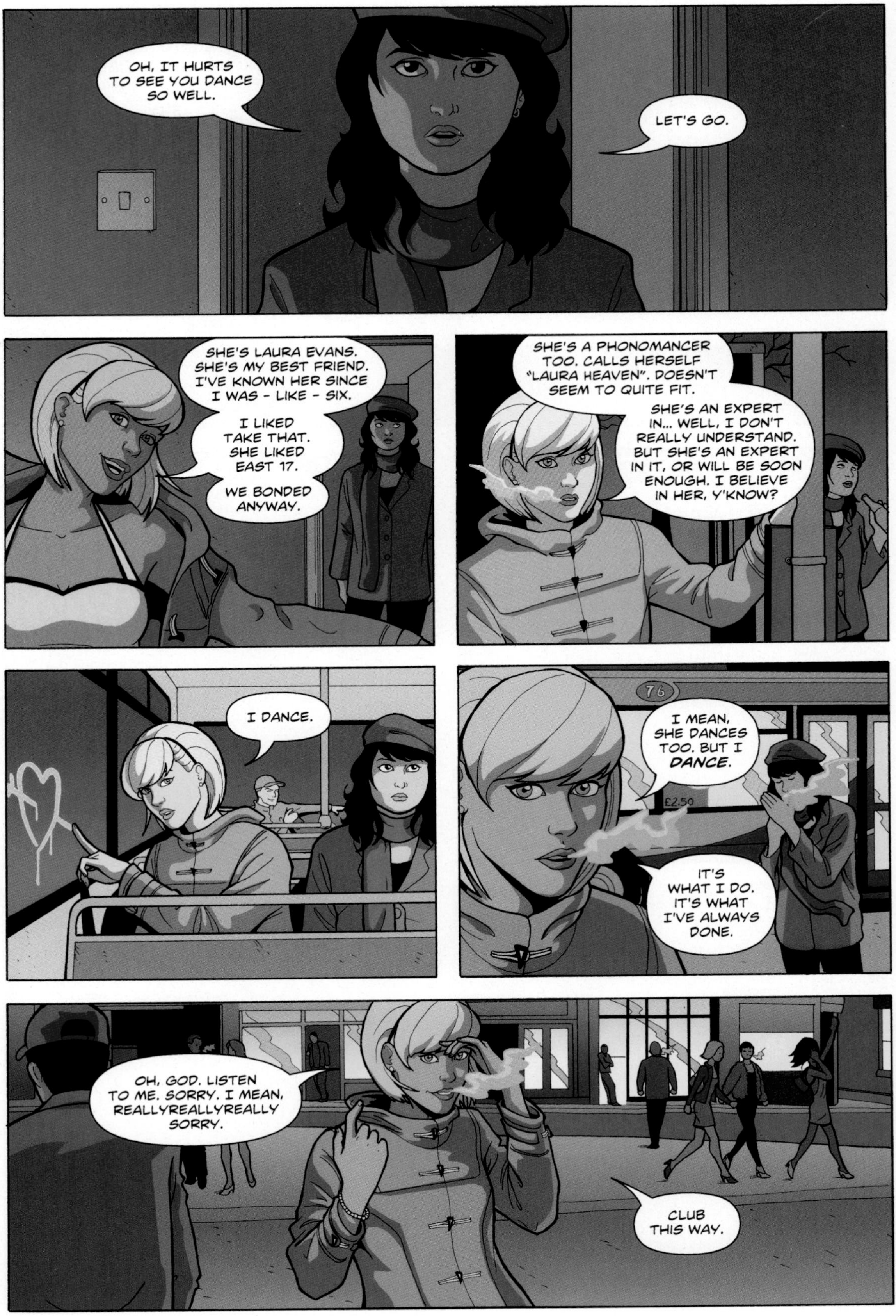
OH, IT HURTS TO SEE YOU DANCE SO WELL.
LET'S GO.
SHE'S LAURA EVANS. SHE'S MY BEST FRIEND. I'VE KNOWN HER SINCE I WAS - LIKE - SIX.
I LIKED TAKE THAT. SHE LIKED EAST 17.
WE BONDED ANYWAY.
SHE'S A PHONOMANCER TOO. CALLS HERSELF "LAURA HEAVEN". DOESN'T SEEM TO QUITE FIT.
SHE'S AN EXPERT IN... WELL, I DON'T REALLY UNDERSTAND. BUT SHE'S AN EXPERT IN IT, OR WILL BE SOON ENOUGH. I BELIEVE IN HER, Y'KNOW?
I DANCE.
76
I MEAN, SHE DANCES TOO. BUT I *DANCE*.
£2.50
IT'S WHAT I DO. IT'S WHAT I'VE ALWAYS DONE.
OH, GOD. LISTEN TO ME. SORRY. I MEAN, REALLYREALLYREALLY SORRY.
CLUB THIS WAY.

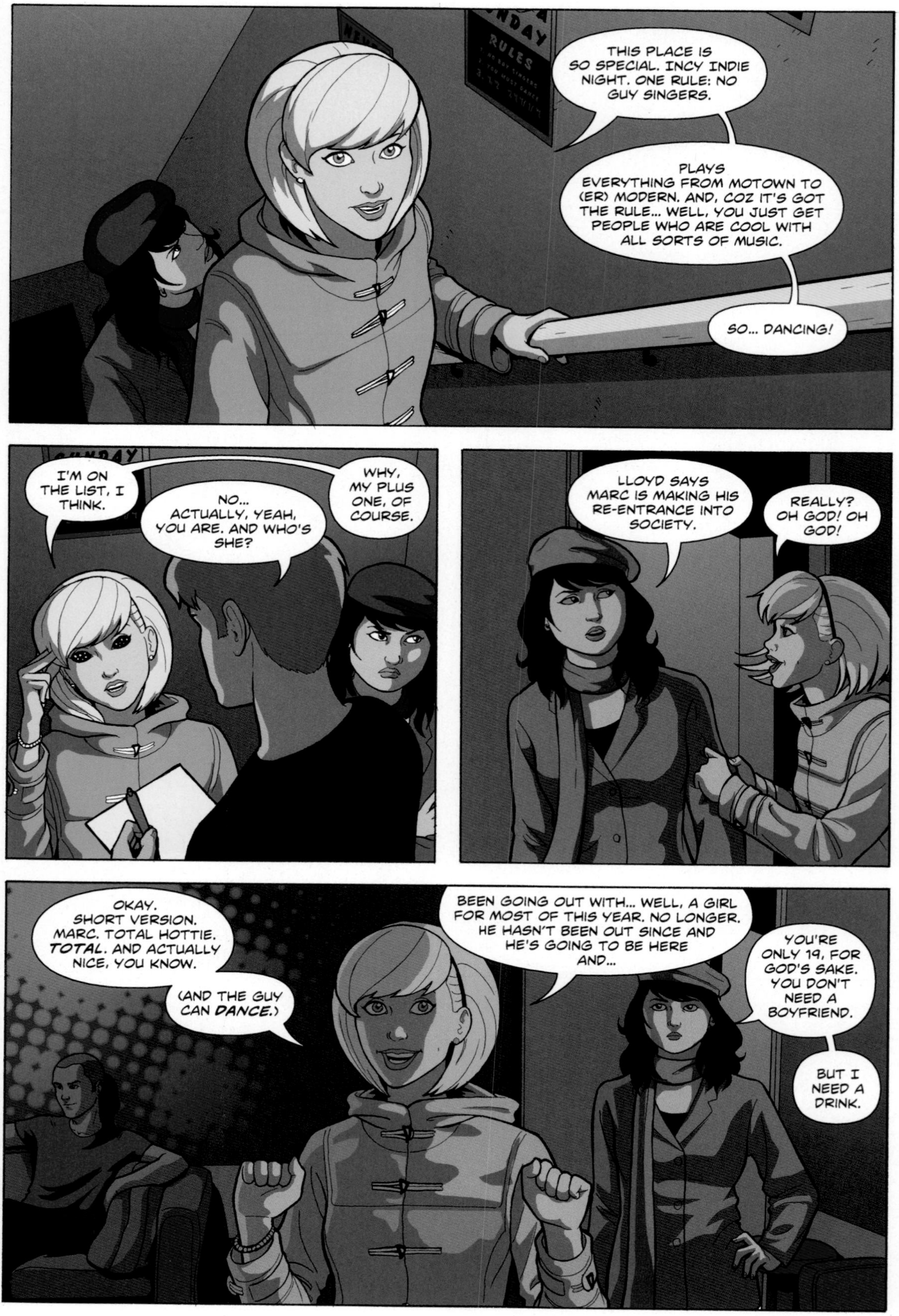
THIS PLACE IS SO SPECIAL. INCY INDIE NIGHT. ONE RULE: NO GUY SINGERS.
PLAYS EVERYTHING FROM MOTOWN TO (ER) MODERN. AND, COZ IT'S GOT THE RULE... WELL, YOU JUST GET PEOPLE WHO ARE COOL WITH ALL SORTS OF MUSIC.
SO... DANCING!
I'M ON THE LIST, I THINK.
NO... ACTUALLY, YEAH, YOU ARE. AND WHO'S SHE?
WHY, MY PLUS ONE, OF COURSE.
LLOYD SAYS MARC IS MAKING HIS RE-ENTRANCE INTO SOCIETY.
REALLY? OH GOD! OH GOD!
OKAY. SHORT VERSION. MARC. TOTAL HOTTIE. *TOTAL*. AND ACTUALLY NICE, YOU KNOW.
(AND THE GUY CAN *DANCE*.)
BEEN GOING OUT WITH... WELL, A GIRL FOR MOST OF THIS YEAR. NO LONGER. HE HASN'T BEEN OUT SINCE AND HE'S GOING TO BE HERE AND...
YOU'RE ONLY 19, FOR GOD'S SAKE. YOU DON'T NEED A BOYFRIEND.
BUT I NEED A DRINK.

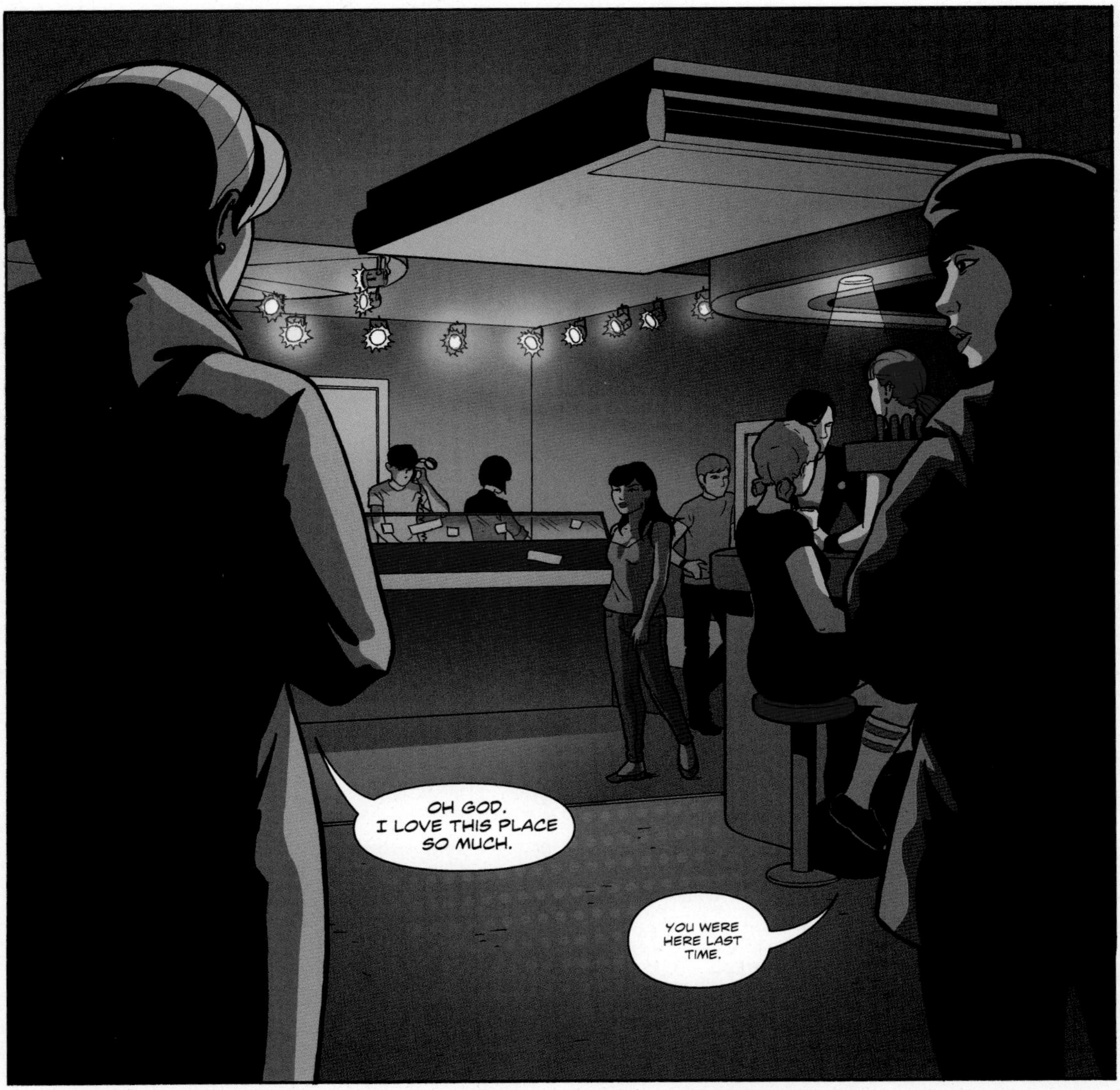
OH GOD. I LOVE THIS PLACE SO MUCH.
YOU WERE HERE LAST TIME.

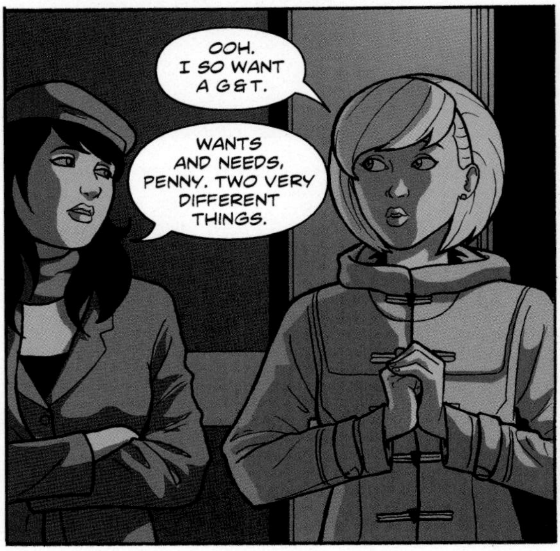
OOH. I SO WANT A G&T.
WANTS AND NEEDS, PENNY. TWO VERY DIFFERENT THINGS.

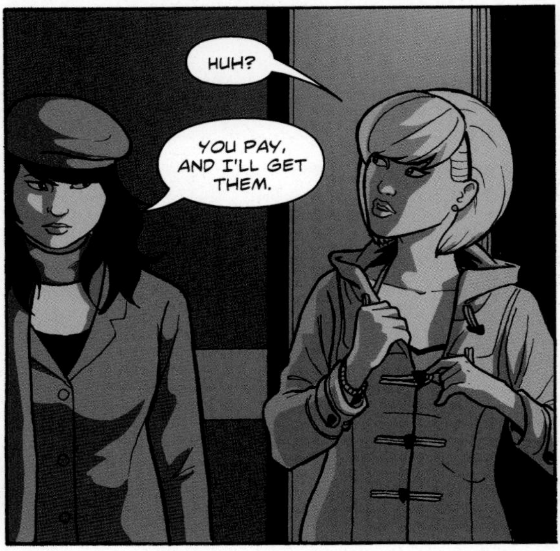
HUH?
YOU PAY, AND I'LL GET THEM.

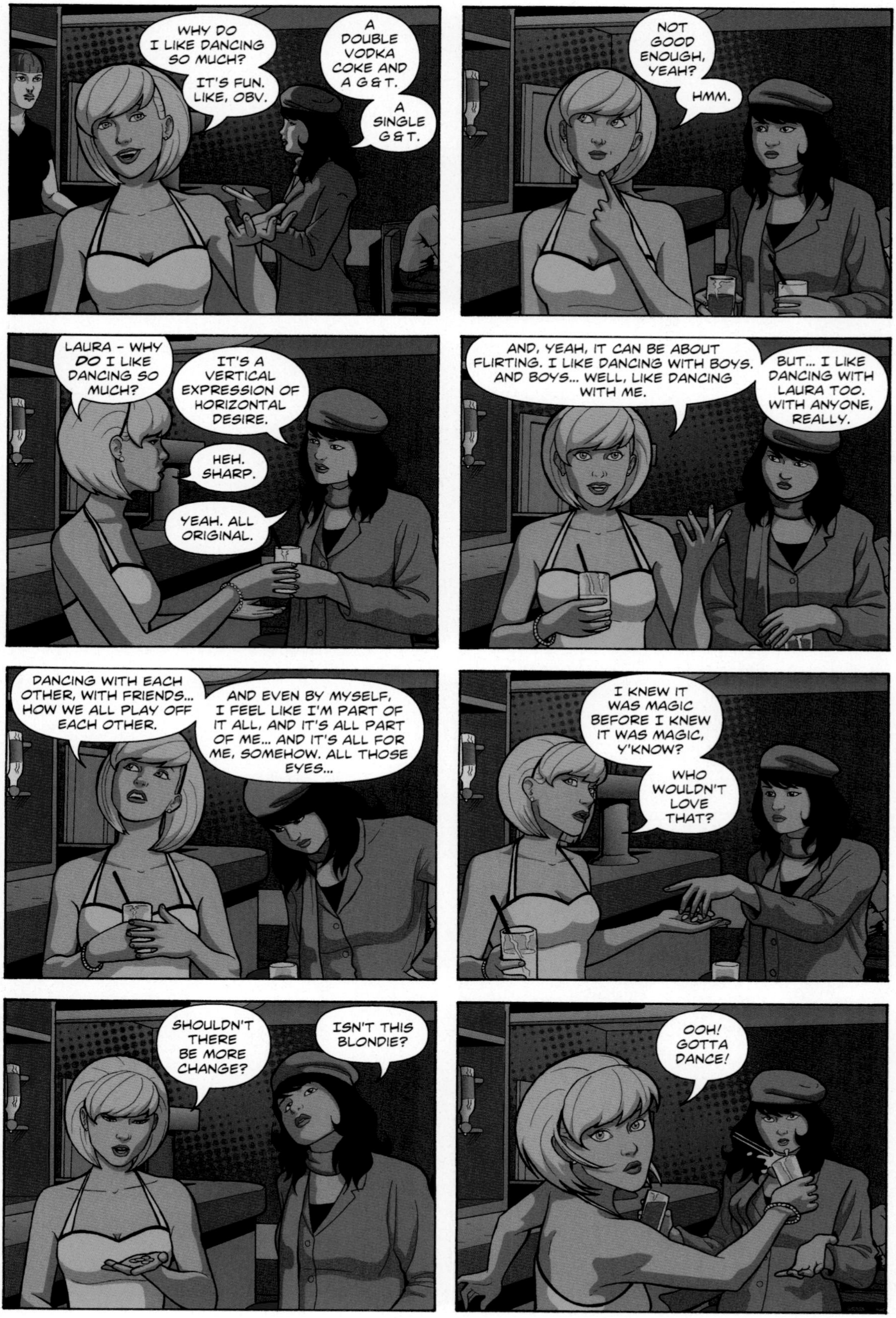
WHY DO I LIKE DANCING SO MUCH?
IT'S FUN. LIKE, OBV.
A DOUBLE VODKA COKE AND A G&T.
A SINGLE G&T.
NOT GOOD ENOUGH, YEAH?
HMM.
LAURA – WHY *DO* I LIKE DANCING SO MUCH?
IT'S A VERTICAL EXPRESSION OF HORIZONTAL DESIRE.
HEH. SHARP.
YEAH. ALL ORIGINAL.
AND, YEAH, IT CAN BE ABOUT FLIRTING. I LIKE DANCING WITH BOYS. AND BOYS... WELL, LIKE DANCING WITH ME.
BUT... I LIKE DANCING WITH LAURA TOO. WITH ANYONE, REALLY.
DANCING WITH EACH OTHER, WITH FRIENDS... HOW WE ALL PLAY OFF EACH OTHER.
AND EVEN BY MYSELF, I FEEL LIKE I'M PART OF IT ALL, AND IT'S ALL PART OF ME... AND IT'S ALL FOR ME, SOMEHOW. ALL THOSE EYES...
I KNEW IT WAS MAGIC BEFORE I KNEW IT WAS MAGIC, Y'KNOW?
WHO WOULDN'T LOVE THAT?
SHOULDN'T THERE BE MORE CHANGE?
ISN'T THIS BLONDIE?
OOH! GOTTA DANCE!

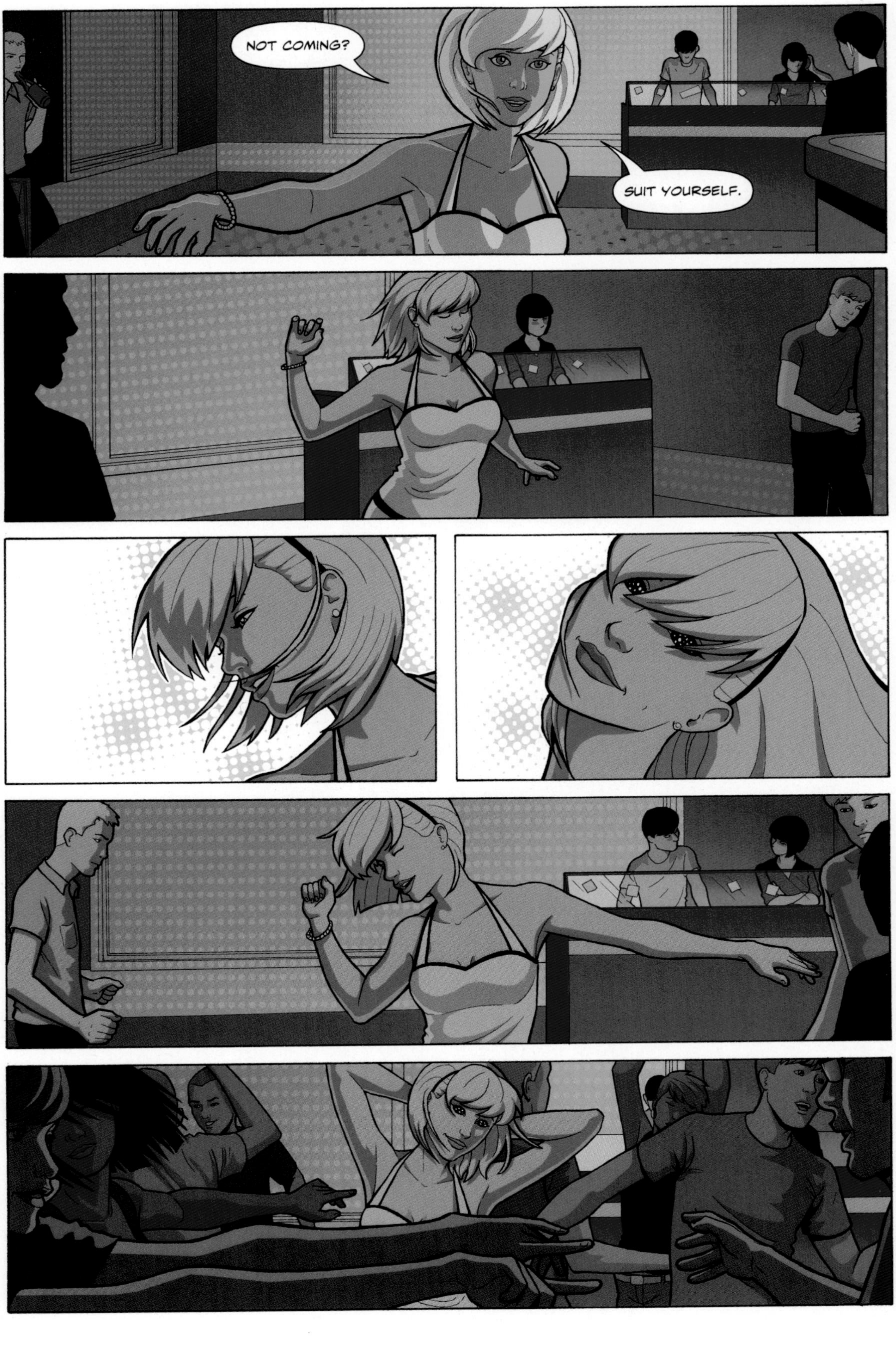
NOT COMING?
SUIT YOURSELF.

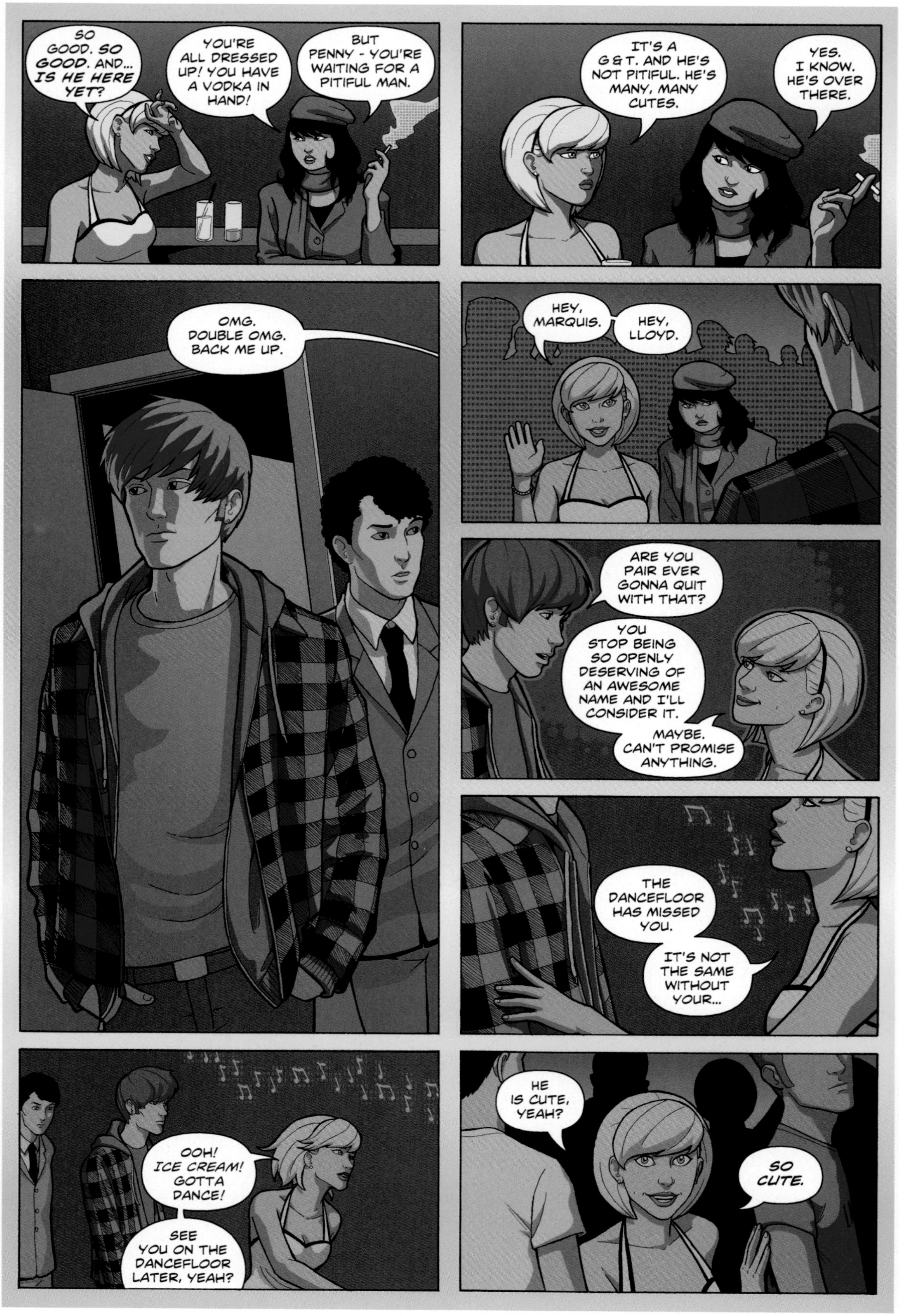
SO GOOD. SO GOOD. AND... IS HE HERE YET?
YOU'RE ALL DRESSED UP! YOU HAVE A VODKA IN HAND!
BUT PENNY - YOU'RE WAITING FOR A PITIFUL MAN.
IT'S A G & T. AND HE'S NOT PITIFUL. HE'S MANY, MANY CUTES.
YES. I KNOW. HE'S OVER THERE.
OMG. DOUBLE OMG. BACK ME UP.
HEY, MARQUIS.
HEY, LLOYD.
ARE YOU PAIR EVER GONNA QUIT WITH THAT?
YOU STOP BEING SO OPENLY DESERVING OF AN AWESOME NAME AND I'LL CONSIDER IT.
MAYBE. CAN'T PROMISE ANYTHING.
THE DANCEFLOOR HAS MISSED YOU.
IT'S NOT THE SAME WITHOUT YOUR...
OOH! ICE CREAM! GOTTA DANCE!
SEE YOU ON THE DANCEFLOOR LATER, YEAH?
HE IS CUTE, YEAH?
SO CUTE.

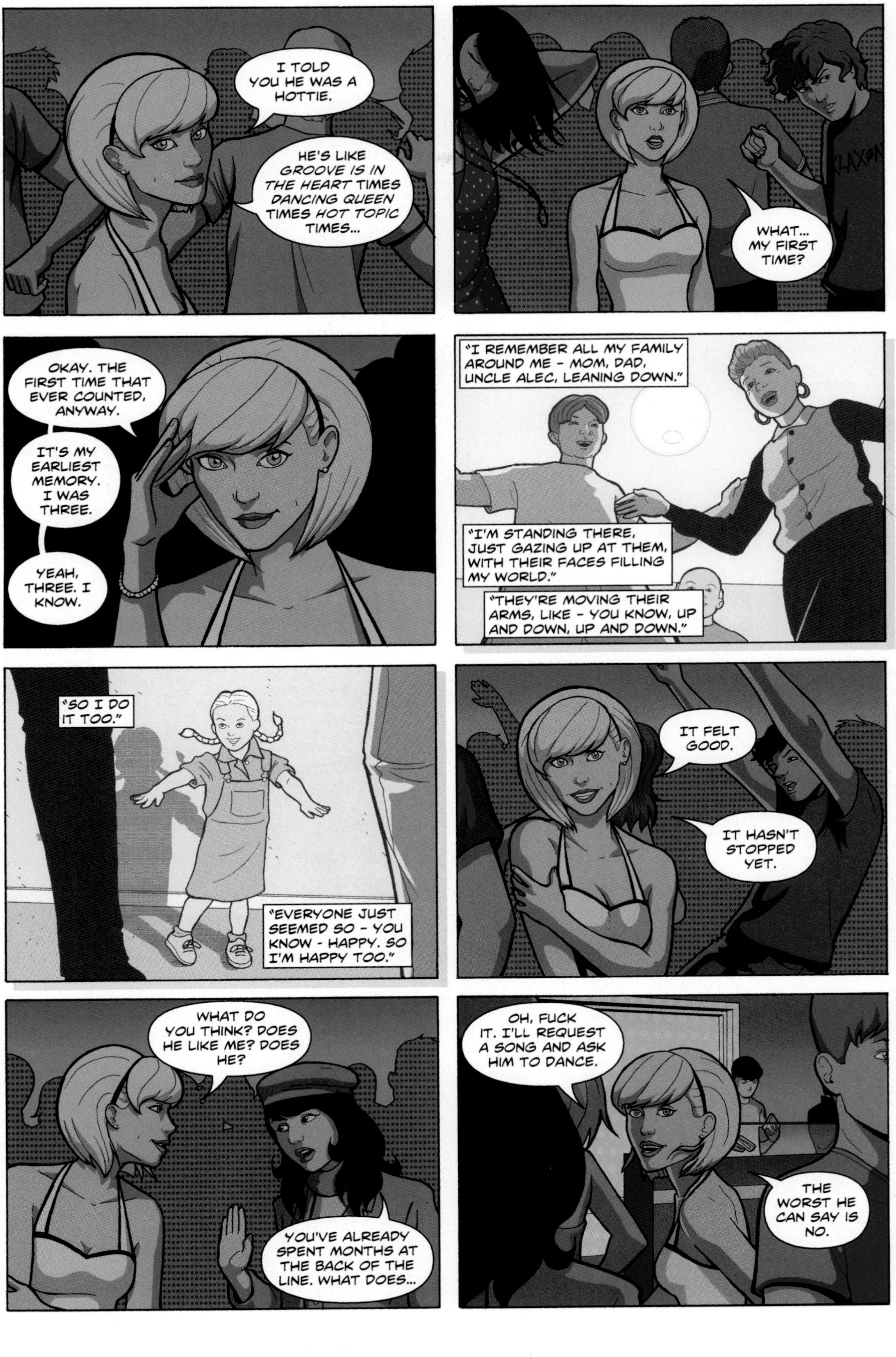
I TOLD YOU HE WAS A HOTTIE.
HE'S LIKE GROOVE IS IN THE HEART TIMES DANCING QUEEN TIMES HOT TOPIC TIMES...
WHAT... MY FIRST TIME?
OKAY. THE FIRST TIME THAT EVER COUNTED, ANYWAY.
IT'S MY EARLIEST MEMORY. I WAS THREE.
YEAH, THREE. I KNOW.
"I REMEMBER ALL MY FAMILY AROUND ME - MOM, DAD, UNCLE ALEC, LEANING DOWN."
"I'M STANDING THERE, JUST GAZING UP AT THEM, WITH THEIR FACES FILLING MY WORLD."
"THEY'RE MOVING THEIR ARMS, LIKE - YOU KNOW, UP AND DOWN, UP AND DOWN."
"SO I DO IT TOO."
"EVERYONE JUST SEEMED SO - YOU KNOW - HAPPY. SO I'M HAPPY TOO."
IT FELT GOOD.
IT HASN'T STOPPED YET.
WHAT DO YOU THINK? DOES HE LIKE ME? DOES HE?
YOU'VE ALREADY SPENT MONTHS AT THE BACK OF THE LINE. WHAT DOES...
OH, FUCK IT. I'LL REQUEST A SONG AND ASK HIM TO DANCE.
THE WORST HE CAN SAY IS NO.

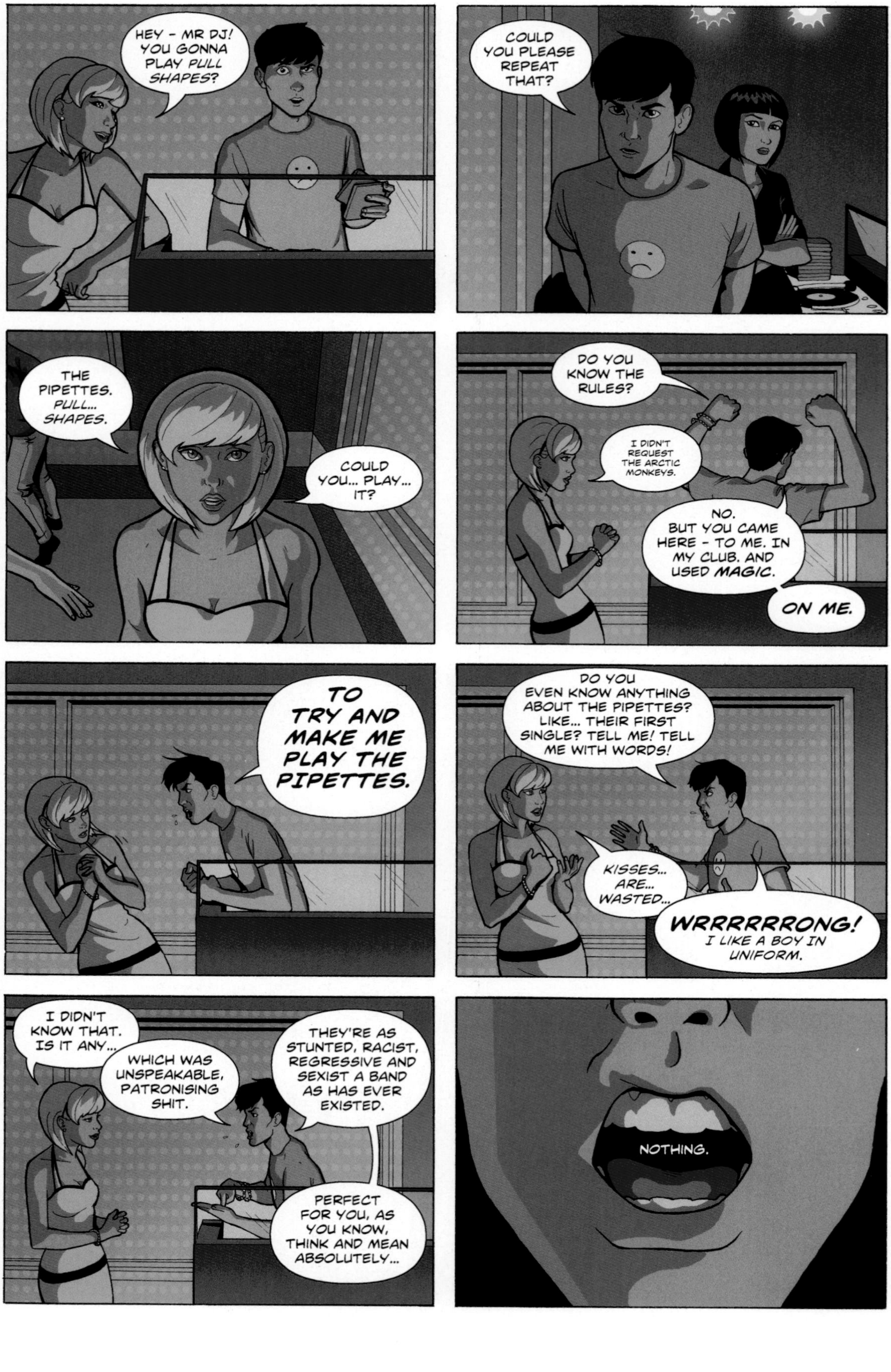
HEY – MR DJ! YOU GONNA PLAY PULL SHAPES?
COULD YOU PLEASE REPEAT THAT?
THE PIPETTES. PULL... SHAPES.
COULD YOU... PLAY... IT?
DO YOU KNOW THE RULES?
I DIDN'T REQUEST THE ARCTIC MONKEYS.
NO. BUT YOU CAME HERE – TO ME. IN MY CLUB. AND USED MAGIC.
ON ME.
TO TRY AND MAKE ME PLAY THE PIPETTES.
DO YOU EVEN KNOW ANYTHING ABOUT THE PIPETTES? LIKE... THEIR FIRST SINGLE? TELL ME! TELL ME WITH WORDS!
KISSES... ARE... WASTED...
WRRRRRRONG! I LIKE A BOY IN UNIFORM.
I DIDN'T KNOW THAT. IS IT ANY...
WHICH WAS UNSPEAKABLE, PATRONISING SHIT.
THEY'RE AS STUNTED, RACIST, REGRESSIVE AND SEXIST A BAND AS HAS EVER EXISTED.
PERFECT FOR YOU, AS YOU KNOW, THINK AND MEAN ABSOLUTELY...
NOTHING.

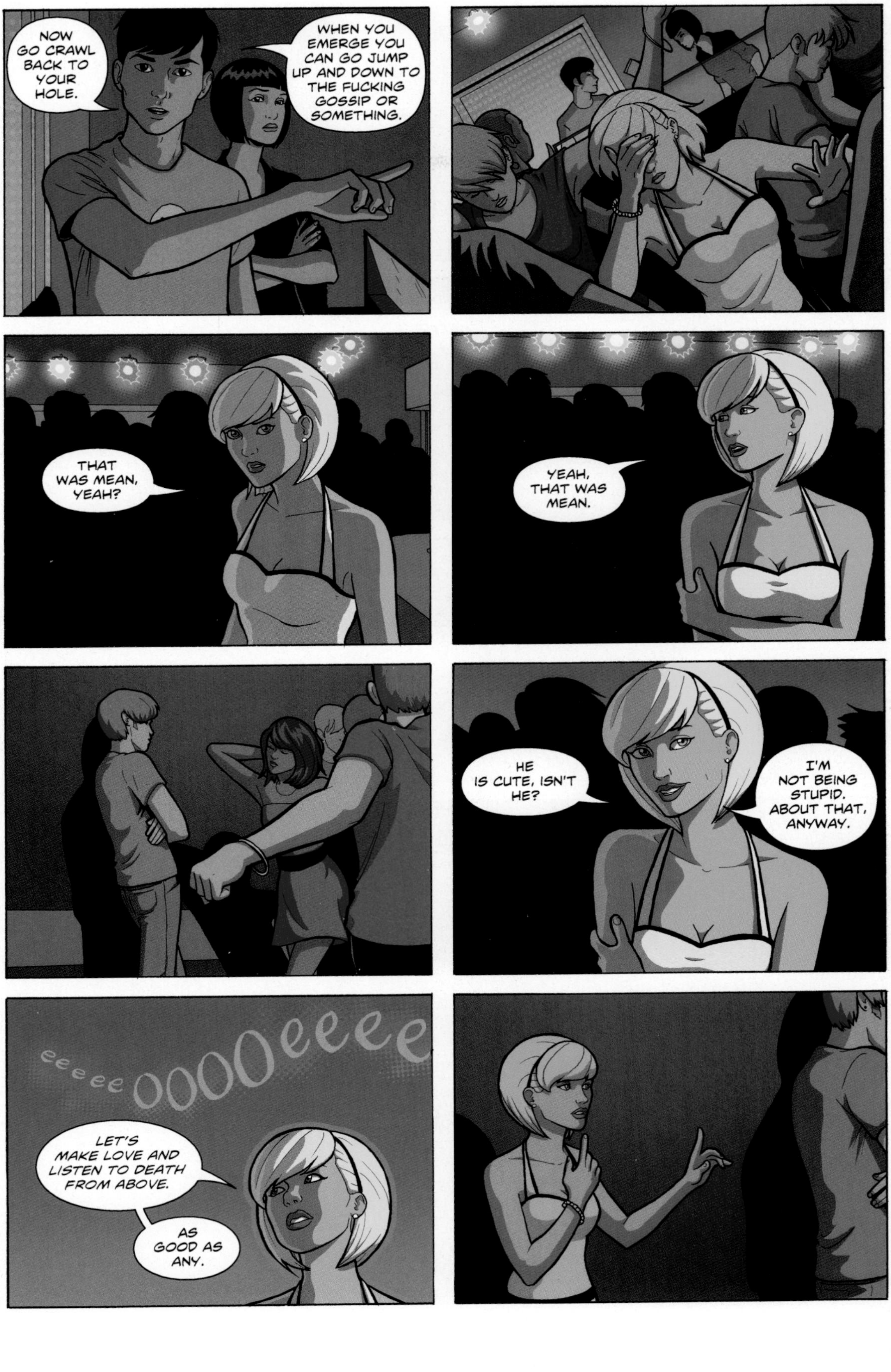
NOW GO CRAWL BACK TO YOUR HOLE.
WHEN YOU EMERGE YOU CAN GO JUMP UP AND DOWN TO THE FUCKING GOSSIP OR SOMETHING.
THAT WAS MEAN, YEAH?
YEAH, THAT WAS MEAN.
HE IS CUTE, ISN'T HE?
I'M NOT BEING STUPID. ABOUT THAT, ANYWAY.
eeeeeOOOOeeee
LET'S MAKE LOVE AND LISTEN TO DEATH FROM ABOVE.
AS GOOD AS ANY.

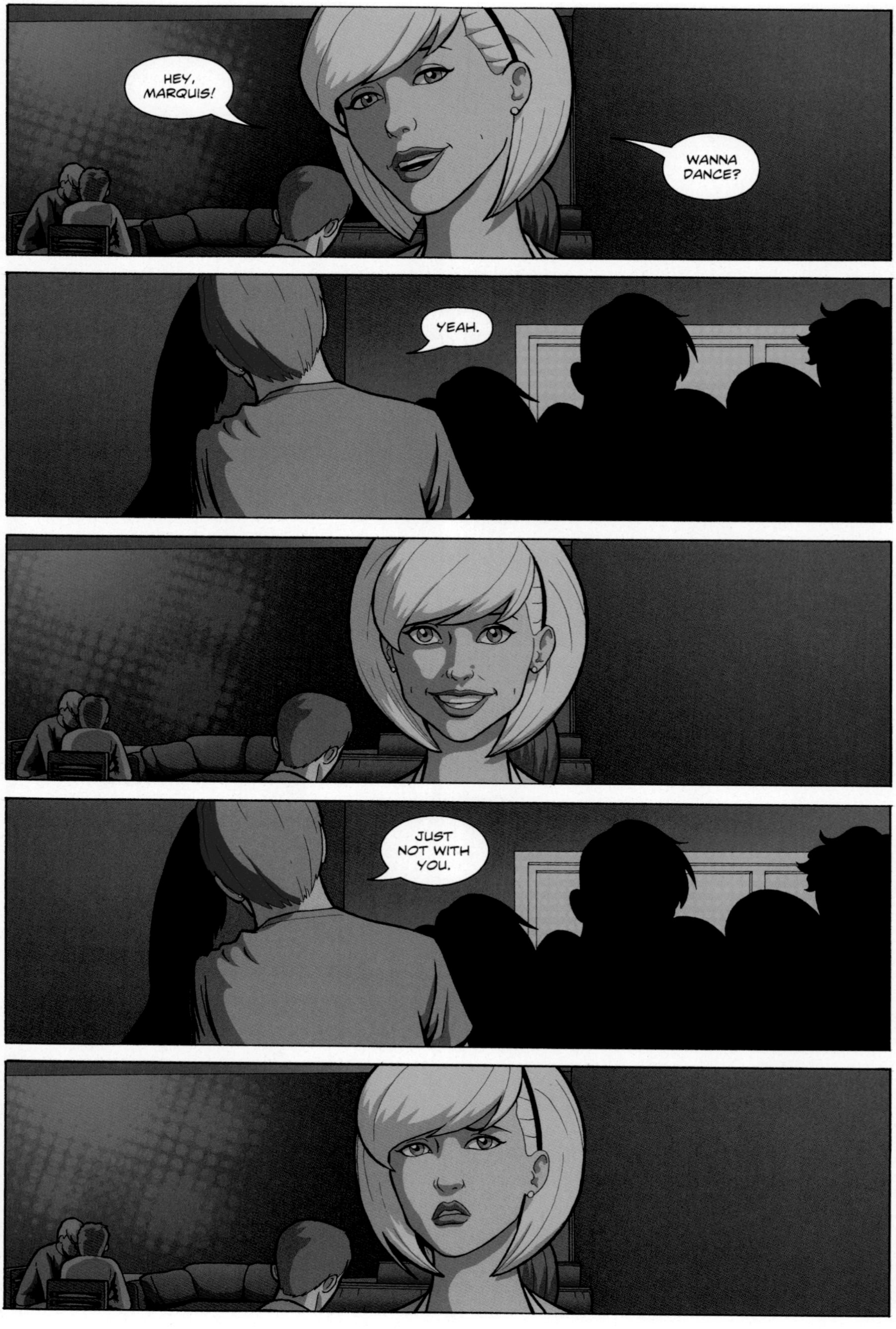
HEY, MARQUIS!
WANNA DANCE?
YEAH.
JUST NOT WITH YOU.

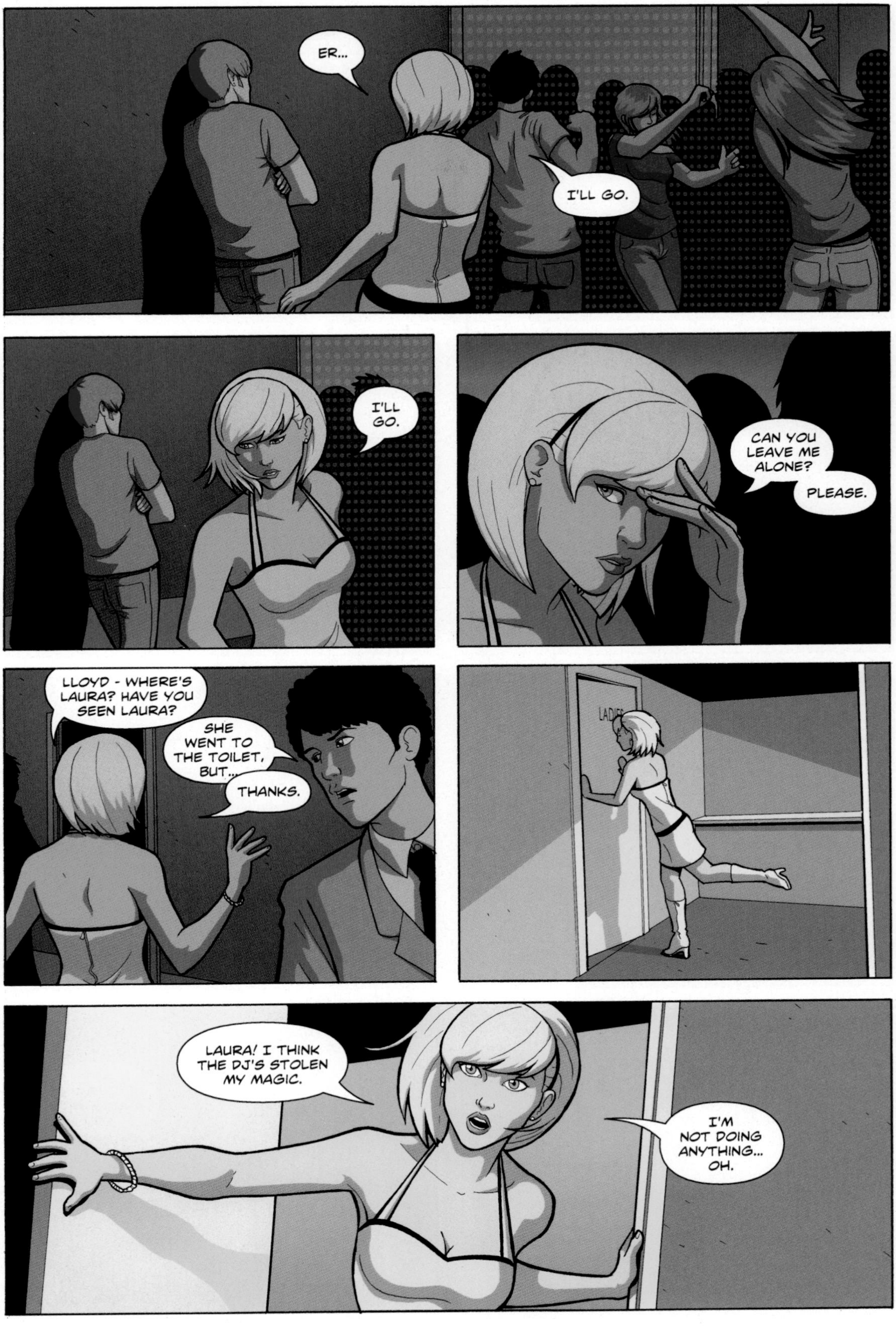
ER...
I'LL GO.
I'LL GO.
CAN YOU LEAVE ME ALONE?
PLEASE.
LLOYD - WHERE'S LAURA? HAVE YOU SEEN LAURA?
SHE WENT TO THE TOILET, BUT...
THANKS.
LADIES
LAURA! I THINK THE DJ'S STOLEN MY MAGIC.
I'M NOT DOING ANYTHING... OH.

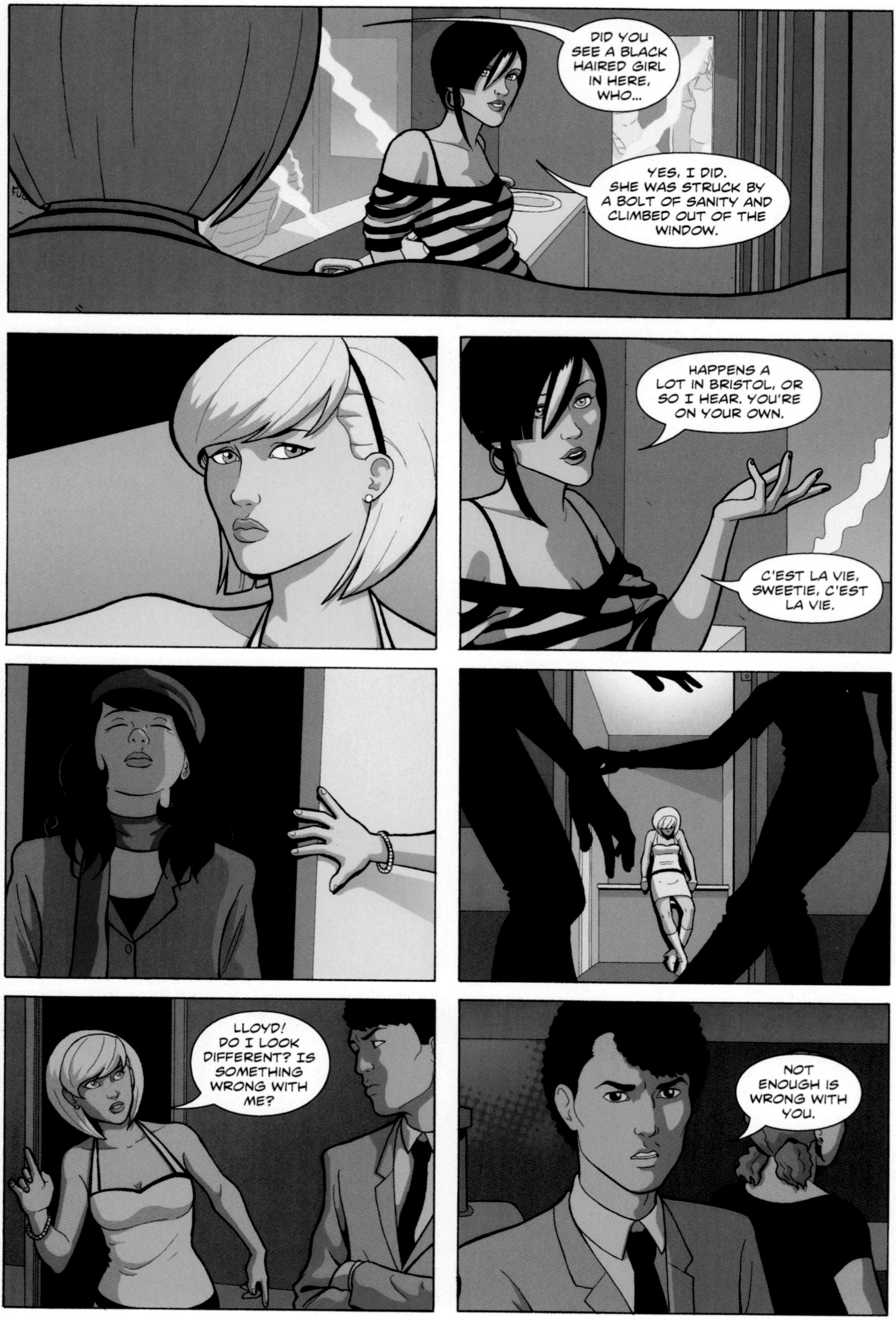
DID YOU SEE A BLACK HAIRED GIRL IN HERE, WHO...
YES, I DID. SHE WAS STRUCK BY A BOLT OF SANITY AND CLIMBED OUT OF THE WINDOW.
HAPPENS A LOT IN BRISTOL, OR SO I HEAR. YOU'RE ON YOUR OWN.
C'EST LA VIE, SWEETIE, C'EST LA VIE.
LLOYD! DO I LOOK DIFFERENT? IS SOMETHING WRONG WITH ME?
NOT ENOUGH IS WRONG WITH YOU.

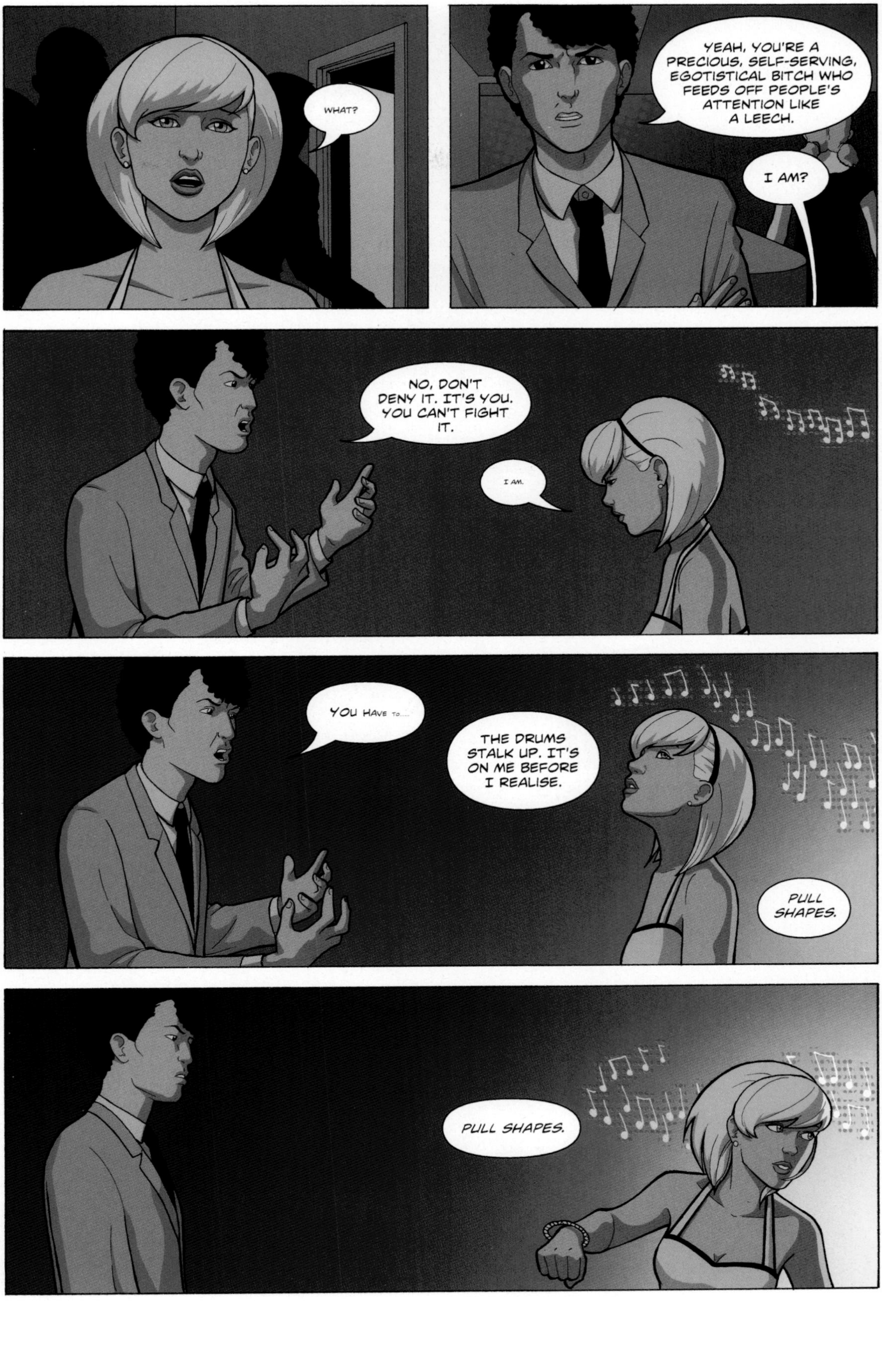
WHAT?
YEAH, YOU'RE A PRECIOUS, SELF-SERVING, EGOTISTICAL BITCH WHO FEEDS OFF PEOPLE'S ATTENTION LIKE A LEECH.
I AM?
NO, DON'T DENY IT. IT'S YOU. YOU CAN'T FIGHT IT.
I AM.
YOU HAVE TO....
THE DRUMS STALK UP. IT'S ON ME BEFORE I REALISE.
PULL SHAPES.
PULL SHAPES.

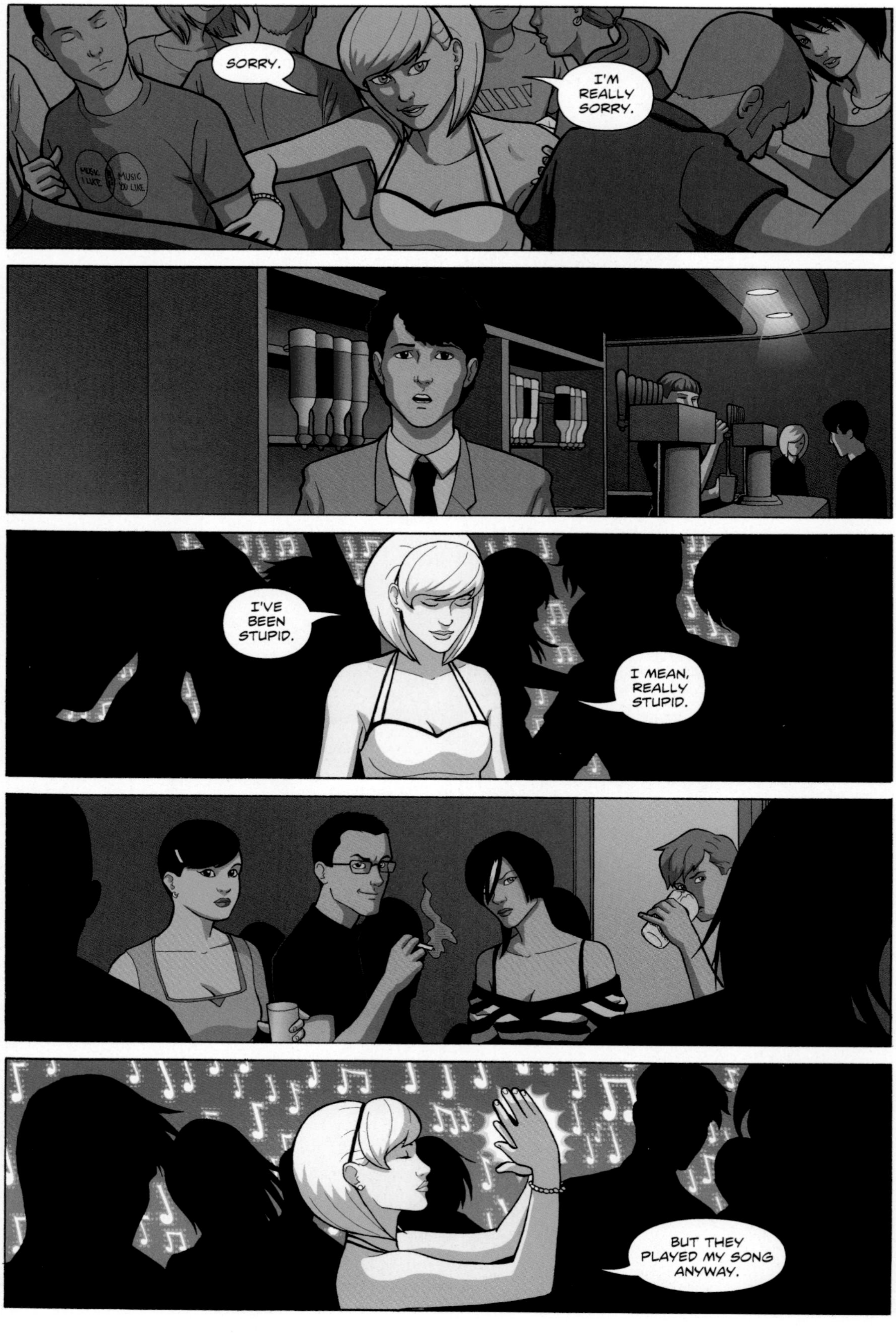
SORRY.
I'M REALLY SORRY.
MUSIC I LIKE
MUSIC YOU LIKE
I'VE BEEN STUPID.
I MEAN, REALLY STUPID.
BUT THEY PLAYED MY SONG ANYWAY.

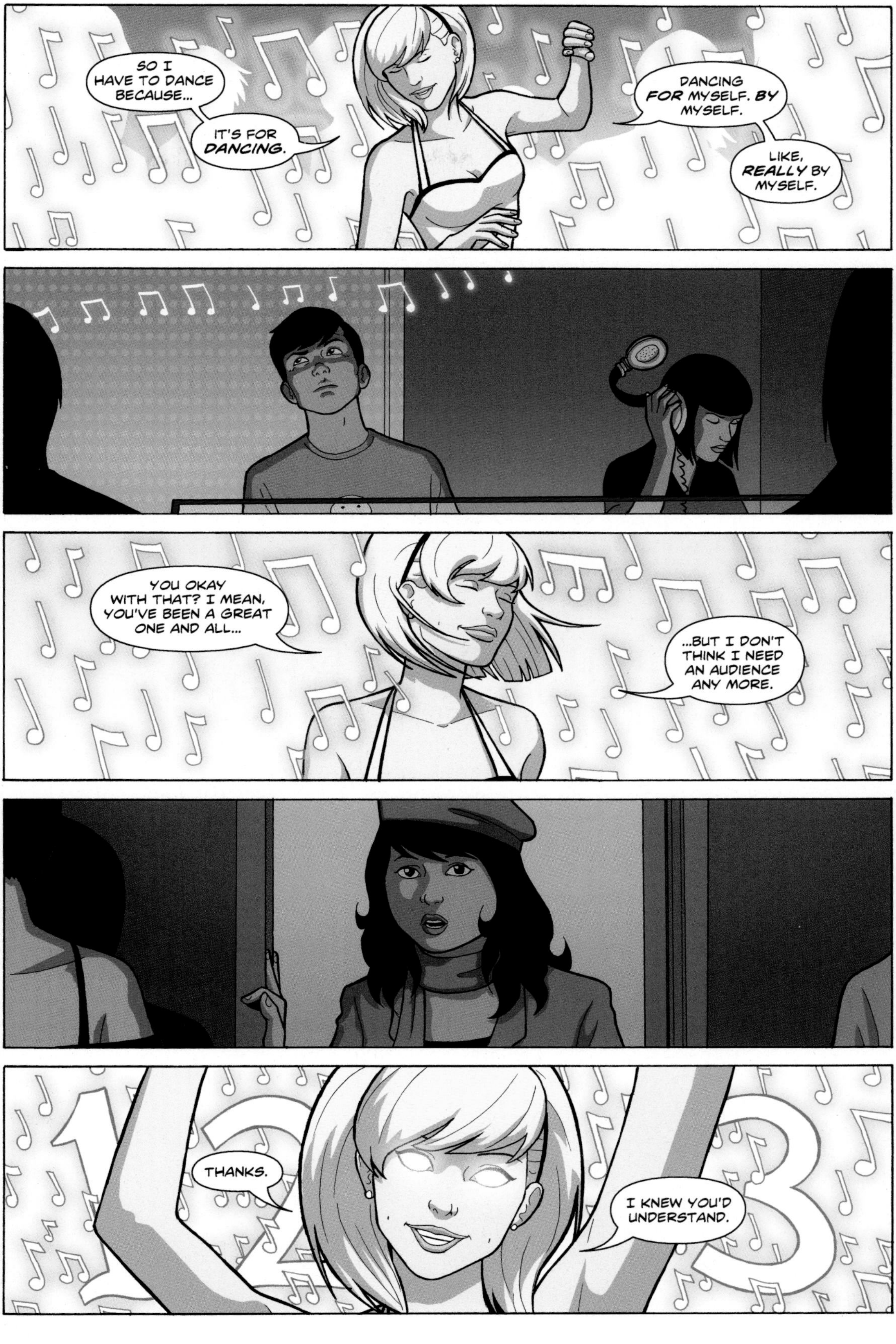
SO I HAVE TO DANCE BECAUSE...
IT'S FOR DANCING.
DANCING FOR MYSELF. BY MYSELF.
LIKE, REALLY BY MYSELF.
YOU OKAY WITH THAT? I MEAN, YOU'VE BEEN A GREAT ONE AND ALL...
...BUT I DON'T THINK I NEED AN AUDIENCE ANY MORE.
THANKS.
I KNEW YOU'D UNDERSTAND.

PULL SHAPES

GILLEN / McKELVIE / WILSON

PHONOGRAM

THE SINGLES CLUB

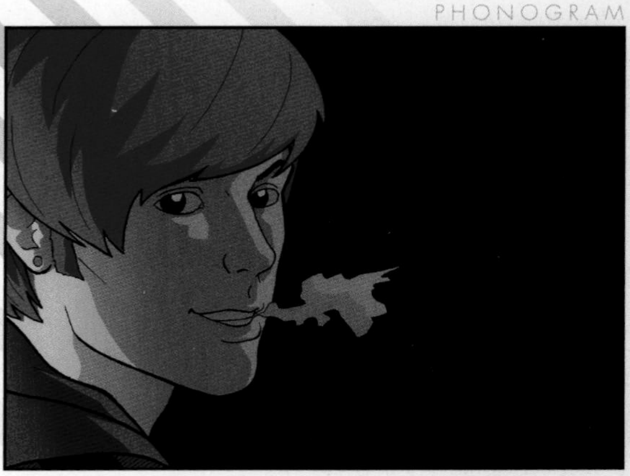

2..WINE AND BED AND MORE AND AGAIN

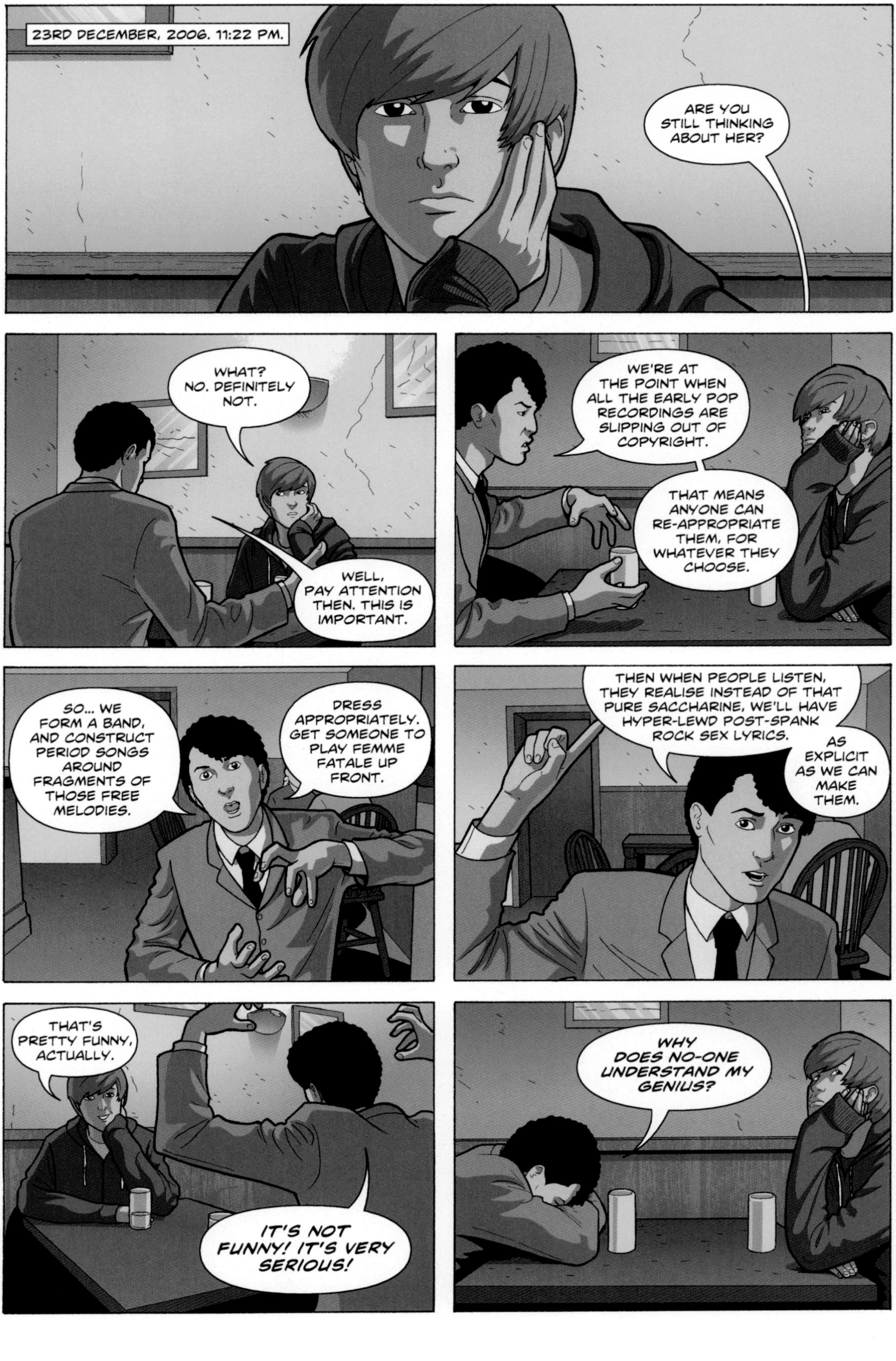
23RD DECEMBER, 2006. 11:22 PM.
ARE YOU STILL THINKING ABOUT HER?
WHAT? NO. DEFINITELY NOT.
WELL, PAY ATTENTION THEN. THIS IS IMPORTANT.
WE'RE AT THE POINT WHEN ALL THE EARLY POP RECORDINGS ARE SLIPPING OUT OF COPYRIGHT.
THAT MEANS ANYONE CAN RE-APPROPRIATE THEM, FOR WHATEVER THEY CHOOSE.
SO... WE FORM A BAND, AND CONSTRUCT PERIOD SONGS AROUND FRAGMENTS OF THOSE FREE MELODIES.
DRESS APPROPRIATELY. GET SOMEONE TO PLAY FEMME FATALE UP FRONT.
THEN WHEN PEOPLE LISTEN, THEY REALISE INSTEAD OF THAT PURE SACCHARINE, WE'LL HAVE HYPER-LEWD POST-SPANK ROCK SEX LYRICS.
AS EXPLICIT AS WE CAN MAKE THEM.
THAT'S PRETTY FUNNY, ACTUALLY.
IT'S NOT FUNNY! IT'S VERY SERIOUS!
WHY DOES NO-ONE UNDERSTAND MY GENIUS?

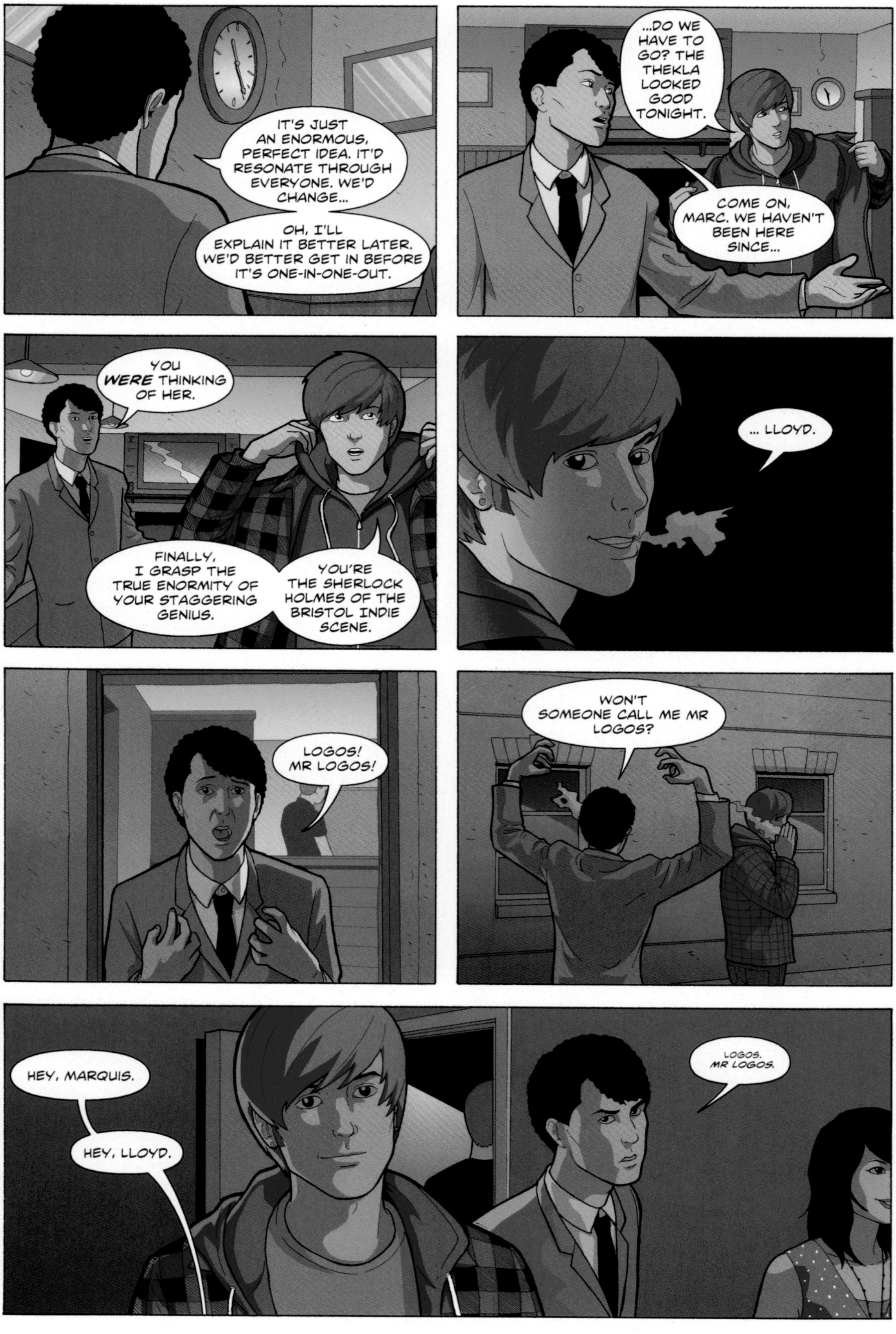
IT'S JUST AN ENORMOUS, PERFECT IDEA. IT'D RESONATE THROUGH EVERYONE. WE'D CHANGE...
OH, I'LL EXPLAIN IT BETTER LATER. WE'D BETTER GET IN BEFORE IT'S ONE-IN-ONE-OUT.
...DO WE HAVE TO GO? THE THEKLA LOOKED GOOD TONIGHT.
COME ON, MARC. WE HAVEN'T BEEN HERE SINCE...
YOU WERE THINKING OF HER.
FINALLY, I GRASP THE TRUE ENORMITY OF YOUR STAGGERING GENIUS.
YOU'RE THE SHERLOCK HOLMES OF THE BRISTOL INDIE SCENE.
... LLOYD.
LOGOS! MR LOGOS!
WON'T SOMEONE CALL ME MR LOGOS?
HEY, MARQUIS.
HEY, LLOYD.
LOGOS. MR LOGOS.

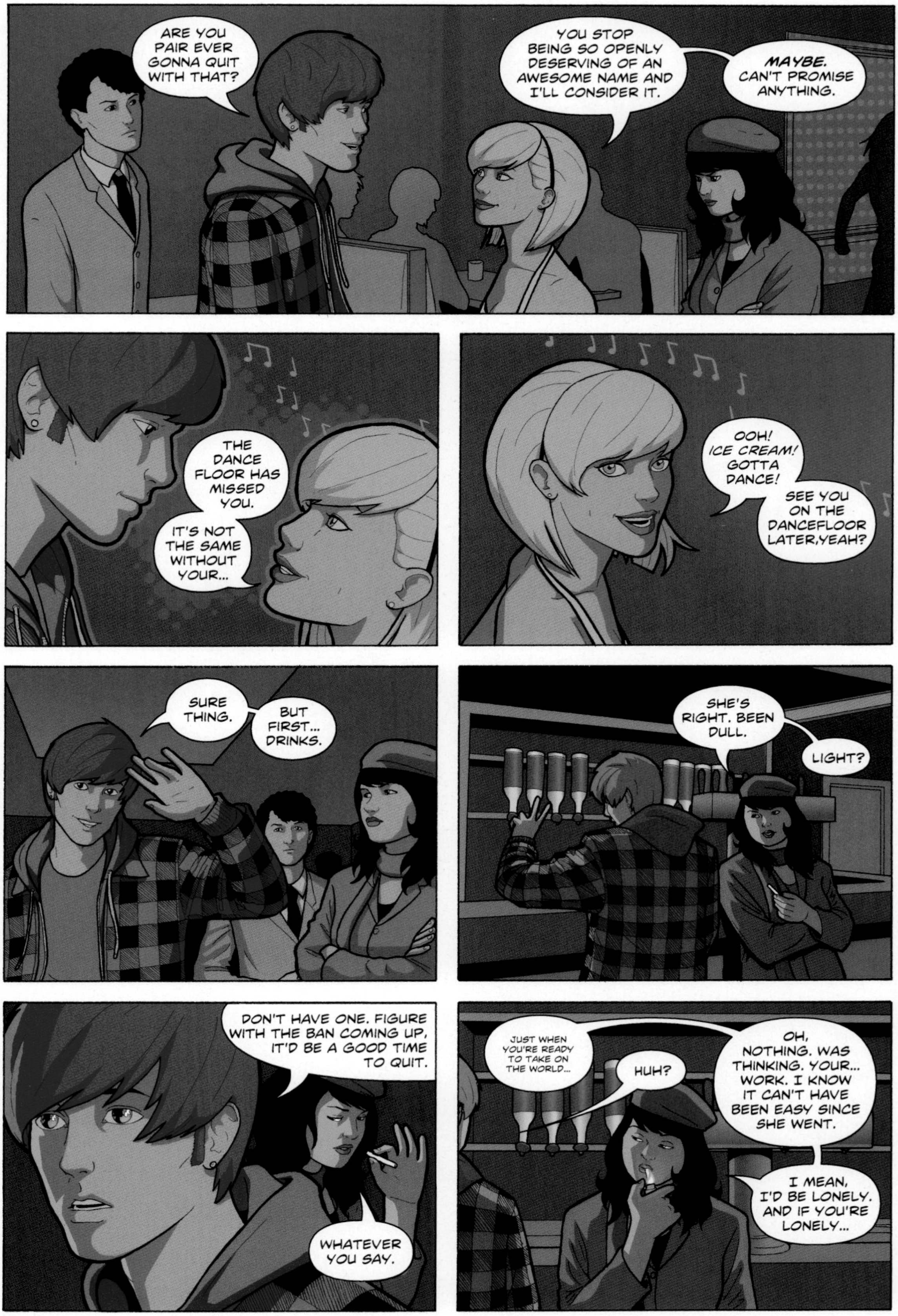
ARE YOU PAIR EVER GONNA QUIT WITH THAT?
YOU STOP BEING SO OPENLY DESERVING OF AN AWESOME NAME AND I'LL CONSIDER IT.
MAYBE. CAN'T PROMISE ANYTHING.
THE DANCE FLOOR HAS MISSED YOU.
IT'S NOT THE SAME WITHOUT YOUR...
OOH! ICE CREAM! GOTTA DANCE!
SEE YOU ON THE DANCEFLOOR LATER,YEAH?
SURE THING.
BUT FIRST... DRINKS.
SHE'S RIGHT. BEEN DULL.
LIGHT?
DON'T HAVE ONE. FIGURE WITH THE BAN COMING UP, IT'D BE A GOOD TIME TO QUIT.
WHATEVER YOU SAY.
JUST WHEN YOU'RE READY TO TAKE ON THE WORLD...
HUH?
OH, NOTHING. WAS THINKING. YOUR... WORK. I KNOW IT CAN'T HAVE BEEN EASY SINCE SHE WENT.
I MEAN, I'D BE LONELY. AND IF YOU'RE LONELY...

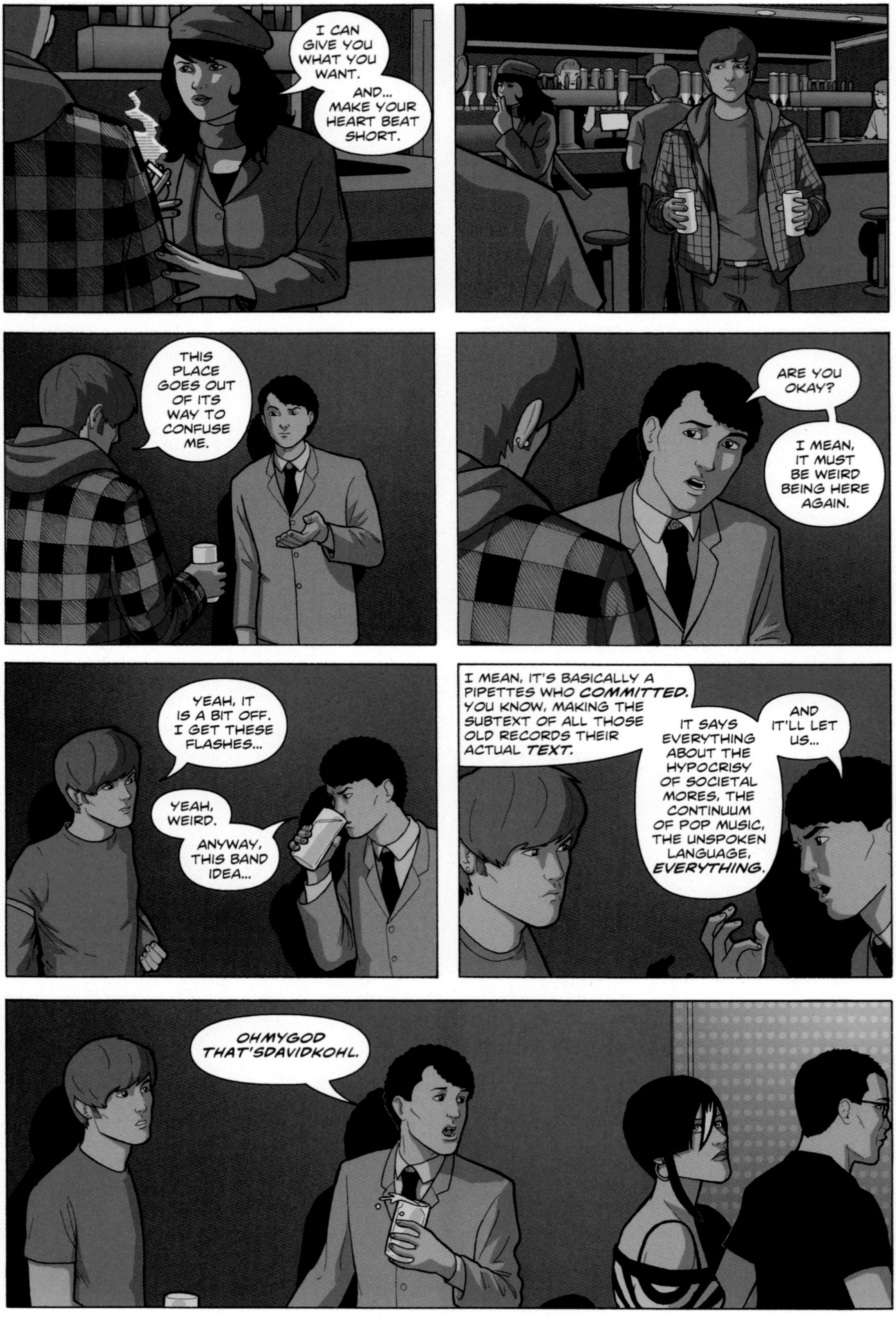
I CAN GIVE YOU WHAT YOU WANT.
AND... MAKE YOUR HEART BEAT SHORT.
THIS PLACE GOES OUT OF ITS WAY TO CONFUSE ME.
ARE YOU OKAY?
I MEAN, IT MUST BE WEIRD BEING HERE AGAIN.
YEAH, IT IS A BIT OFF. I GET THESE FLASHES...
YEAH, WEIRD.
ANYWAY, THIS BAND IDEA...
I MEAN, IT'S BASICALLY A PIPETTES WHO COMMITTED. YOU KNOW, MAKING THE SUBTEXT OF ALL THOSE OLD RECORDS THEIR ACTUAL TEXT.
IT SAYS EVERYTHING ABOUT THE HYPOCRISY OF SOCIETAL MORES, THE CONTINUUM OF POP MUSIC, THE UNSPOKEN LANGUAGE, EVERYTHING.
AND IT'LL LET US...
OHMYGOD THAT'SDAVIDKOHL.

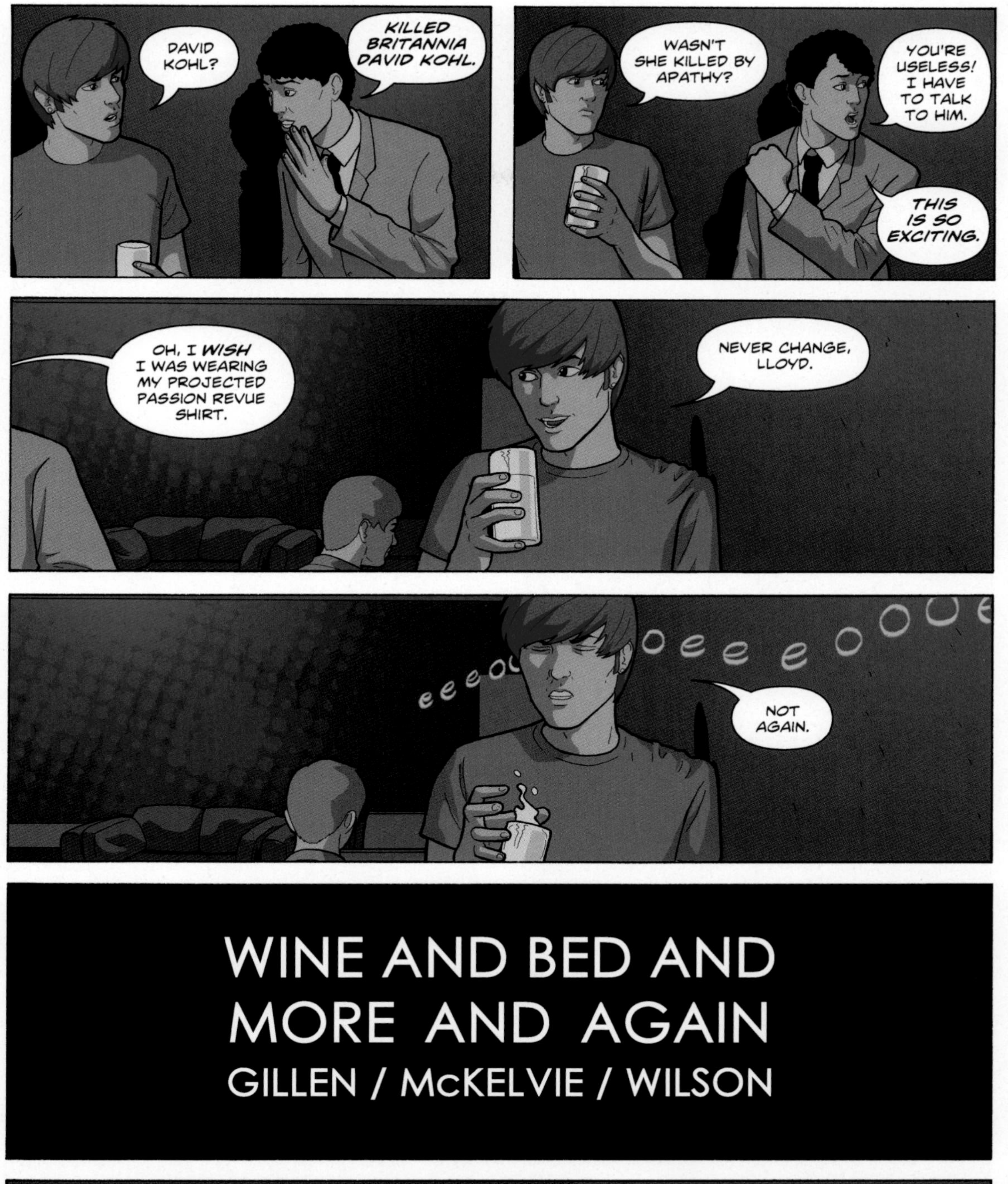
DAVID KOHL?
KILLED BRITANNIA DAVID KOHL.
WASN'T SHE KILLED BY APATHY?
YOU'RE USELESS! I HAVE TO TALK TO HIM.
THIS IS SO EXCITING.
OH, I WISH I WAS WEARING MY PROJECTED PASSION REVUE SHIRT.
NEVER CHANGE, LLOYD.
NOT AGAIN.

WINE AND BED AND MORE AND AGAIN

GILLEN / McKELVIE / WILSON

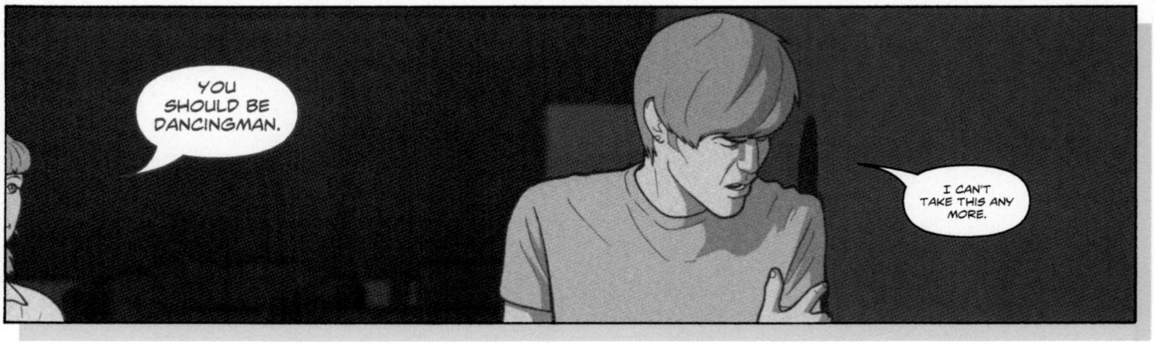
YOU SHOULD BE DANCINGMAN.
I CAN'T TAKE THIS ANY MORE.

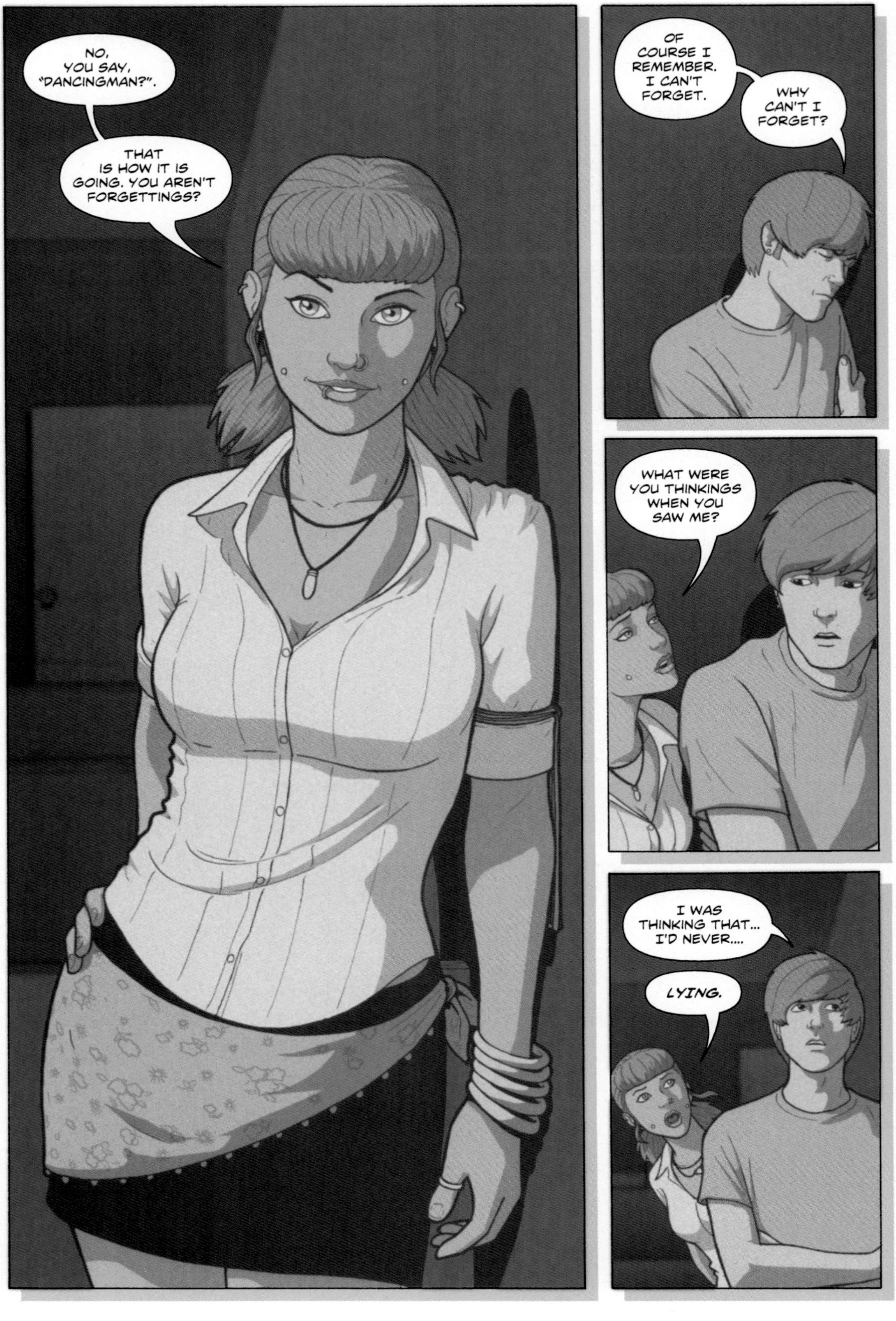
NO, YOU SAY, "DANCINGMAN?".
THAT IS HOW IT IS GOING. YOU AREN'T FORGETTINGS?
OF COURSE I REMEMBER. I CAN'T FORGET.
WHY CAN'T I FORGET?
WHAT WERE YOU THINKINGS WHEN YOU SAW ME?
I WAS THINKING THAT... I'D NEVER....
LYING.

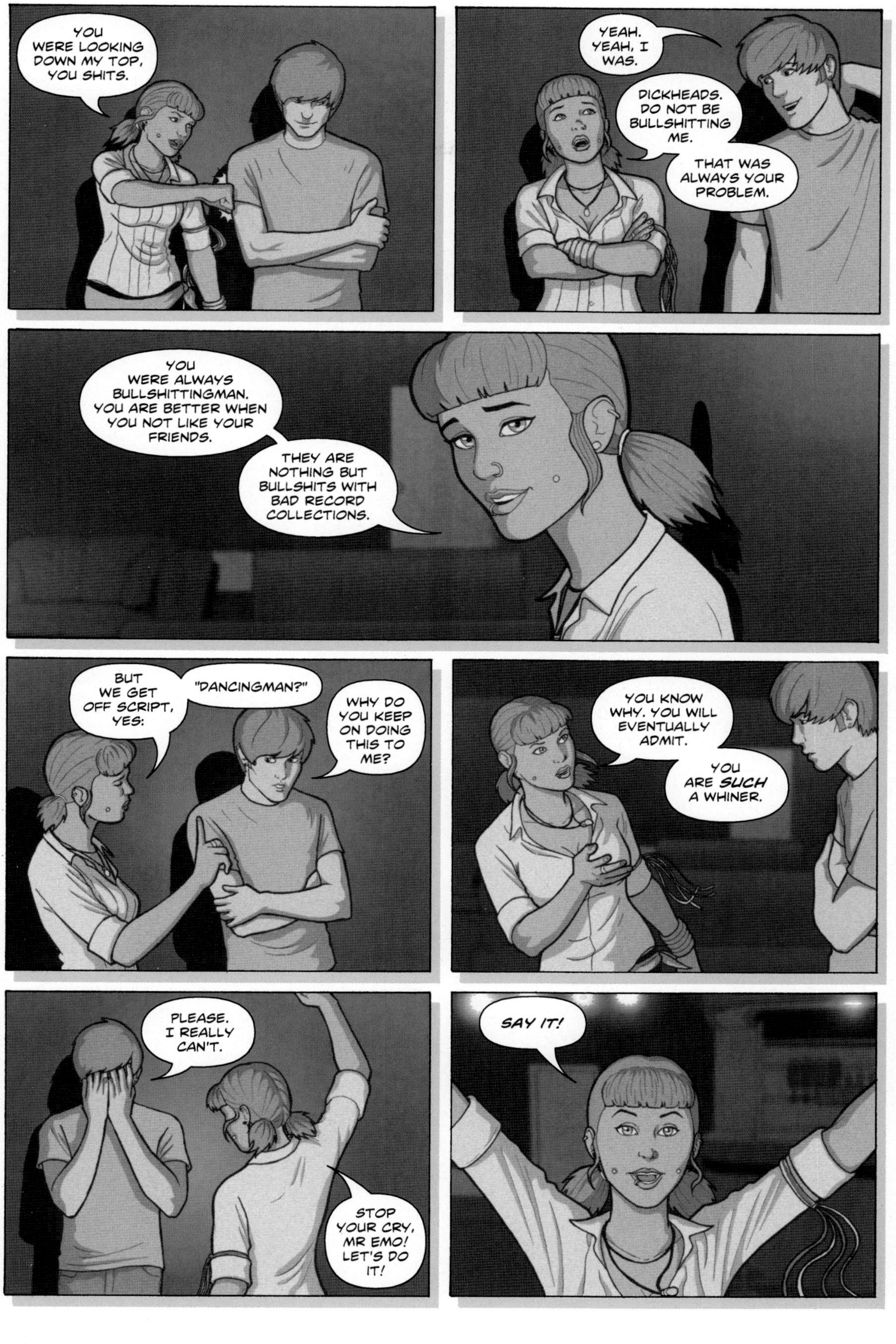
YOU WERE LOOKING DOWN MY TOP, YOU SHITS.
YEAH. YEAH, I WAS.
DICKHEADS. DO NOT BE BULLSHITTING ME.
THAT WAS ALWAYS YOUR PROBLEM.
YOU WERE ALWAYS BULLSHITTINGMAN. YOU ARE BETTER WHEN YOU NOT LIKE YOUR FRIENDS.
THEY ARE NOTHING BUT BULLSHITS WITH BAD RECORD COLLECTIONS.
BUT WE GET OFF SCRIPT, YES:
"DANCINGMAN?"
WHY DO YOU KEEP ON DOING THIS TO ME?
YOU KNOW WHY. YOU WILL EVENTUALLY ADMIT.
YOU ARE *SUCH* A WHINER.
PLEASE. I REALLY CAN'T.
STOP YOUR CRY, MR EMO! LET'S DO IT!
SAY IT!

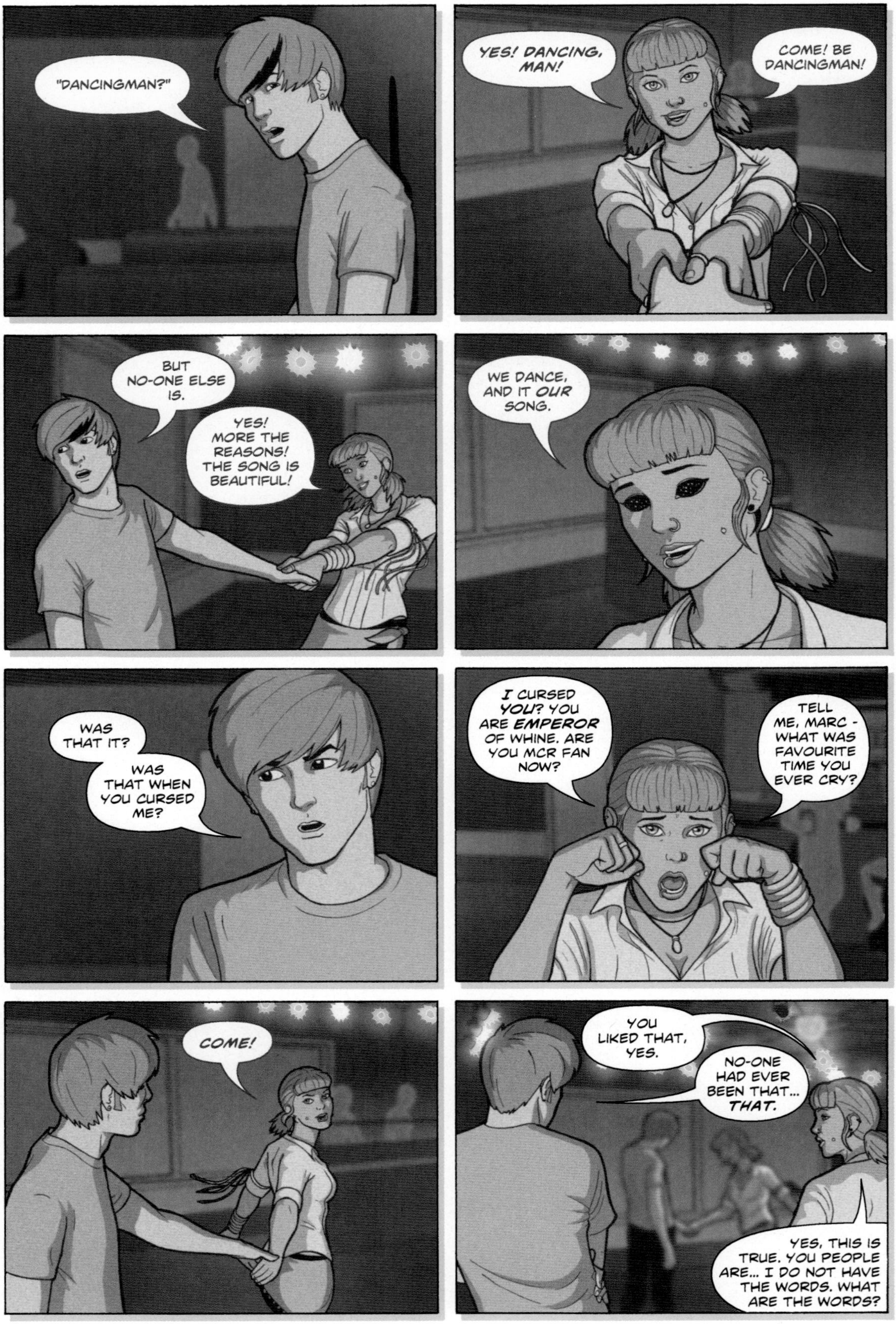
"DANCINGMAN?"
YES! DANCING, MAN!
COME! BE DANCINGMAN!
BUT NO-ONE ELSE IS.
YES! MORE THE REASONS! THE SONG IS BEAUTIFUL!
WE DANCE, AND IT OUR SONG.
WAS THAT IT?
WAS THAT WHEN YOU CURSED ME?
I CURSED YOU? YOU ARE EMPEROR OF WHINE. ARE YOU MCR FAN NOW?
TELL ME, MARC - WHAT WAS FAVOURITE TIME YOU EVER CRY?
COME!
YOU LIKED THAT, YES.
NO-ONE HAD EVER BEEN THAT... THAT.
YES, THIS IS TRUE. YOU PEOPLE ARE... I DO NOT HAVE THE WORDS. WHAT ARE THE WORDS?

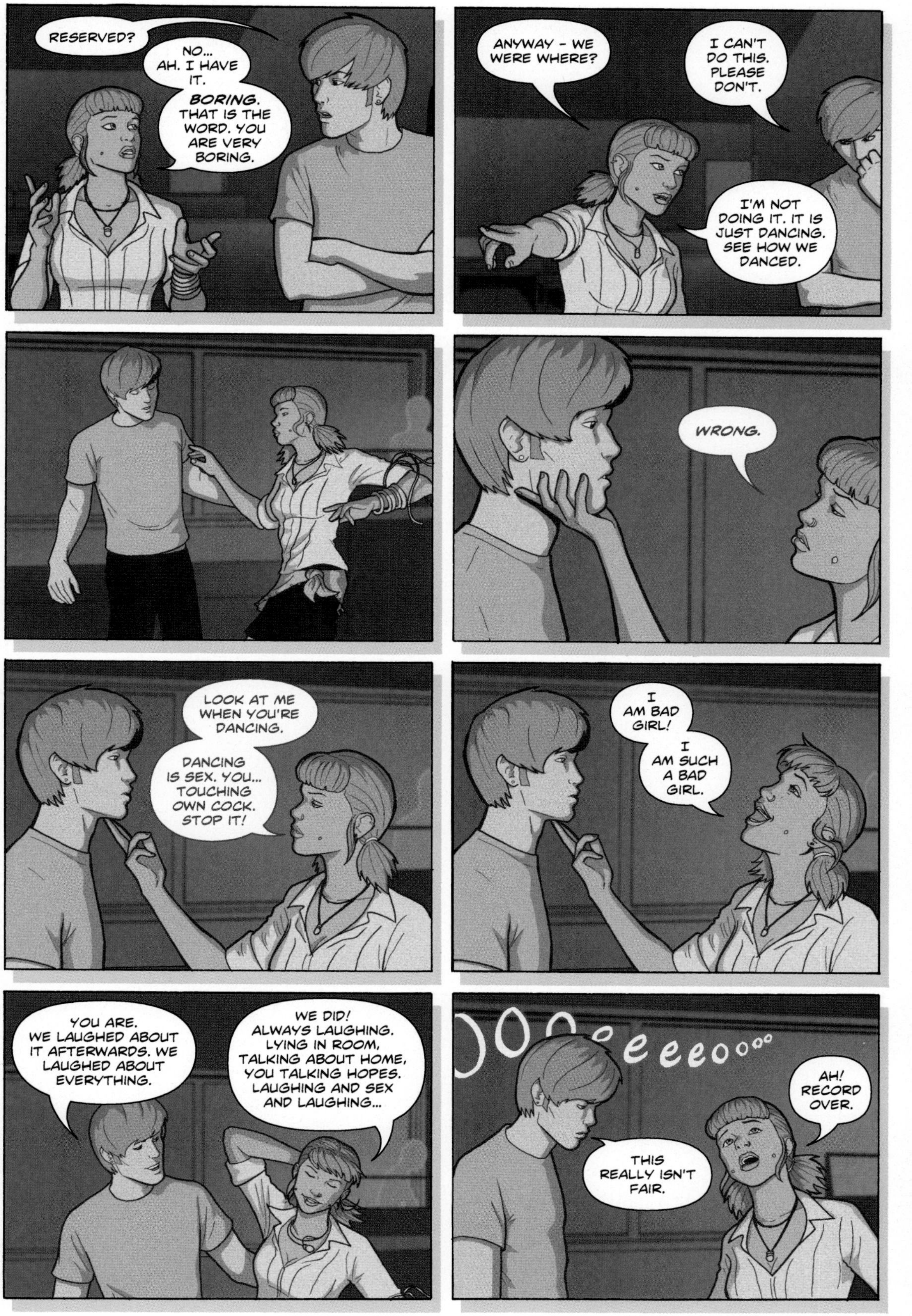
RESERVED?
NO... AH. I HAVE IT. **BORING**. THAT IS THE WORD. YOU ARE VERY BORING.
ANYWAY - WE WERE WHERE?
I CAN'T DO THIS. PLEASE DON'T.
I'M NOT DOING IT. IT IS JUST DANCING. SEE HOW WE DANCED.
WRONG.
LOOK AT ME WHEN YOU'RE DANCING.
DANCING IS SEX. YOU... TOUCHING OWN COCK. STOP IT!
I AM BAD GIRL!
I AM SUCH A BAD GIRL.
YOU ARE. WE LAUGHED ABOUT IT AFTERWARDS. WE LAUGHED ABOUT EVERYTHING.
WE DID! ALWAYS LAUGHING. LYING IN ROOM, TALKING ABOUT HOME, YOU TALKING HOPES. LAUGHING AND SEX AND LAUGHING...
OOOeeeeooo
AH! RECORD OVER.
THIS REALLY ISN'T FAIR.

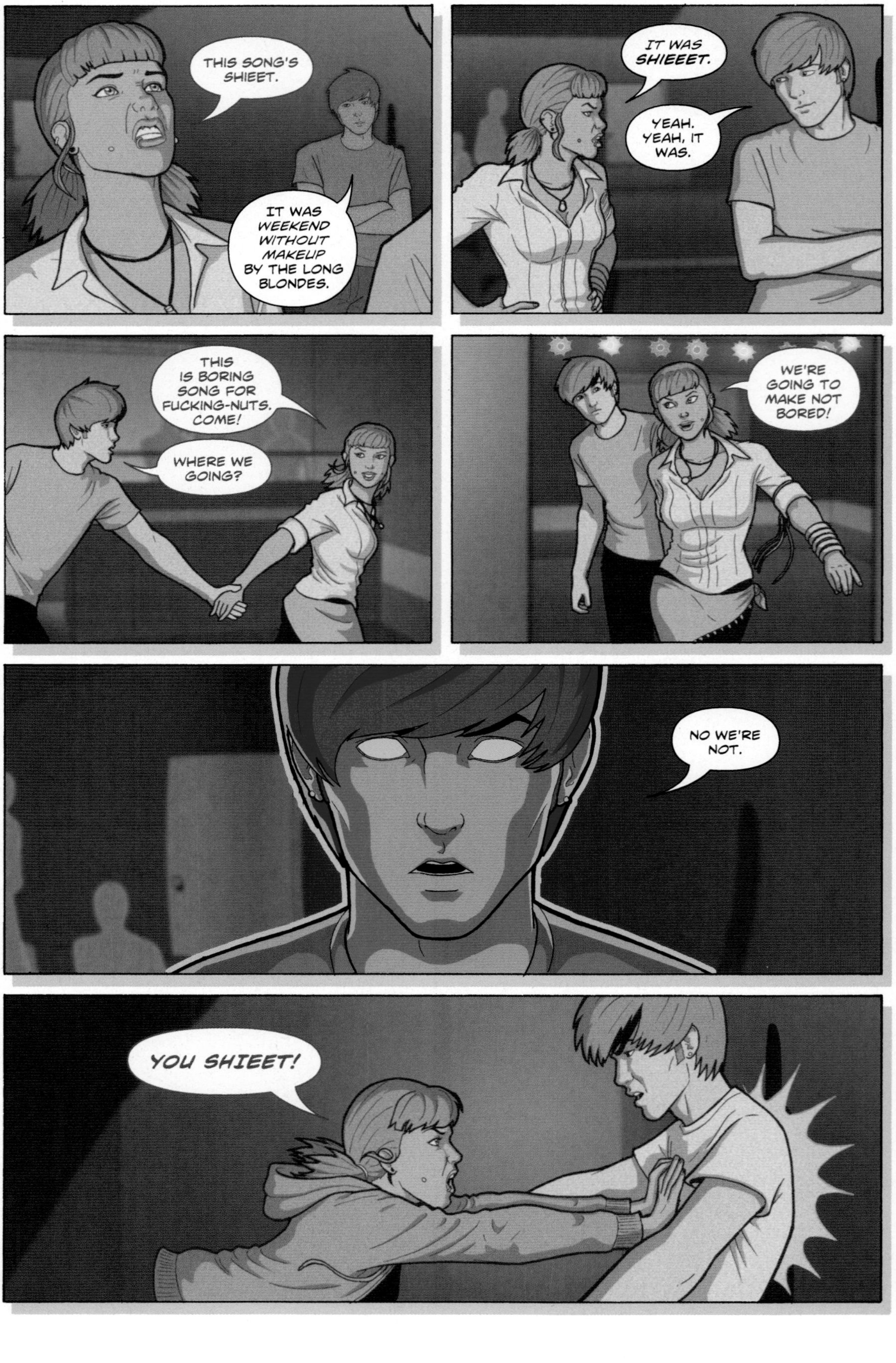
THIS SONG'S SHIEET.
IT WAS WEEKEND WITHOUT MAKEUP BY THE LONG BLONDES.
IT WAS SHIEEET.
YEAH. YEAH, IT WAS.
THIS IS BORING SONG FOR FUCKING-NUTS. COME!
WHERE WE GOING?
WE'RE GOING TO MAKE NOT BORED!
NO WE'RE NOT.
YOU SHIEET!

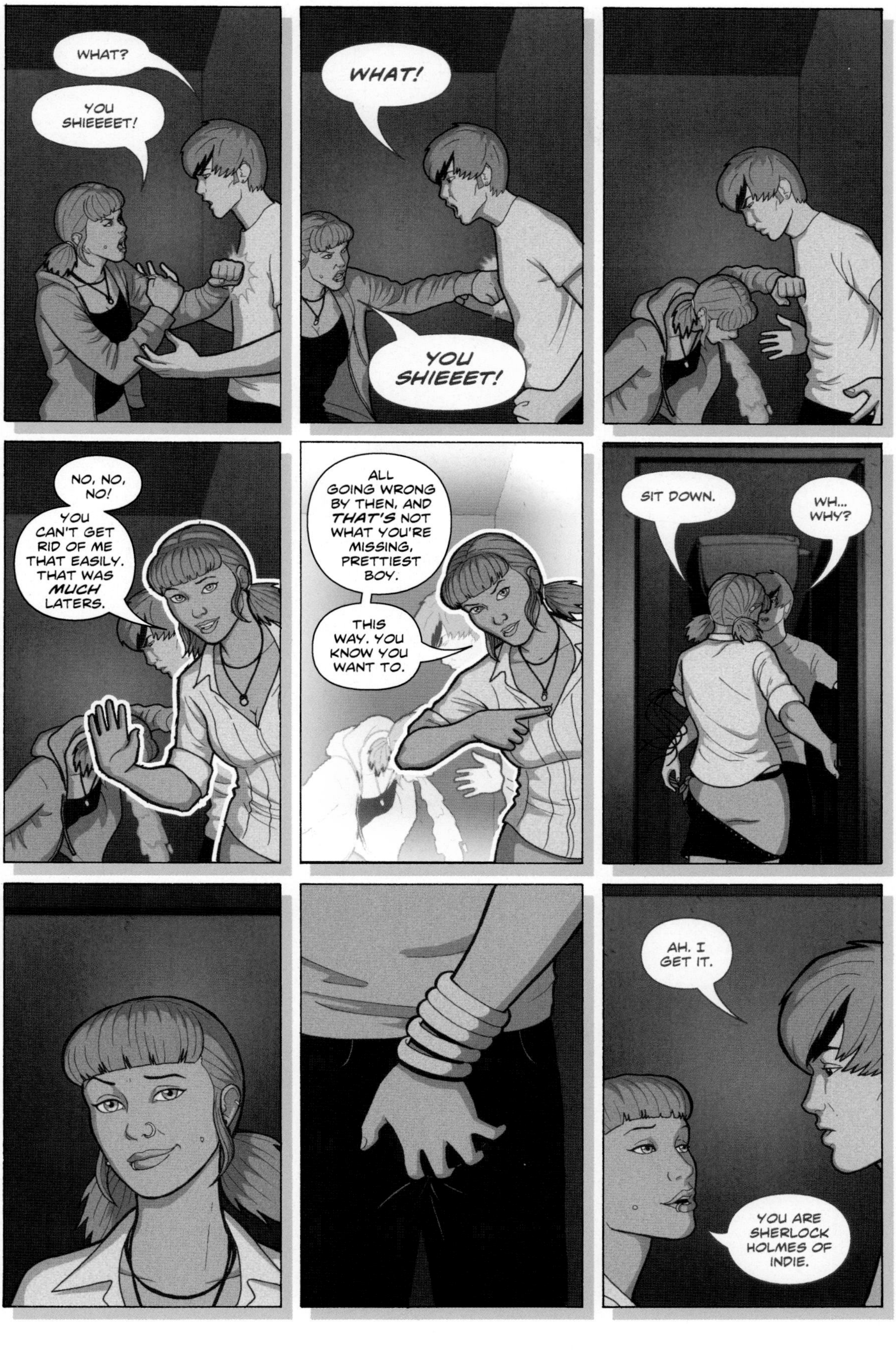
WHAT?
YOU SHIEEEET!
WHAT!
YOU SHIEEET!
NO, NO, NO!
YOU CAN'T GET RID OF ME THAT EASILY. THAT WAS MUCH LATERS.
ALL GOING WRONG BY THEN, AND THAT'S NOT WHAT YOU'RE MISSING, PRETTIEST BOY.
THIS WAY. YOU KNOW YOU WANT TO.
SIT DOWN.
WH... WHY?
AH. I GET IT.
YOU ARE SHERLOCK HOLMES OF INDIE.

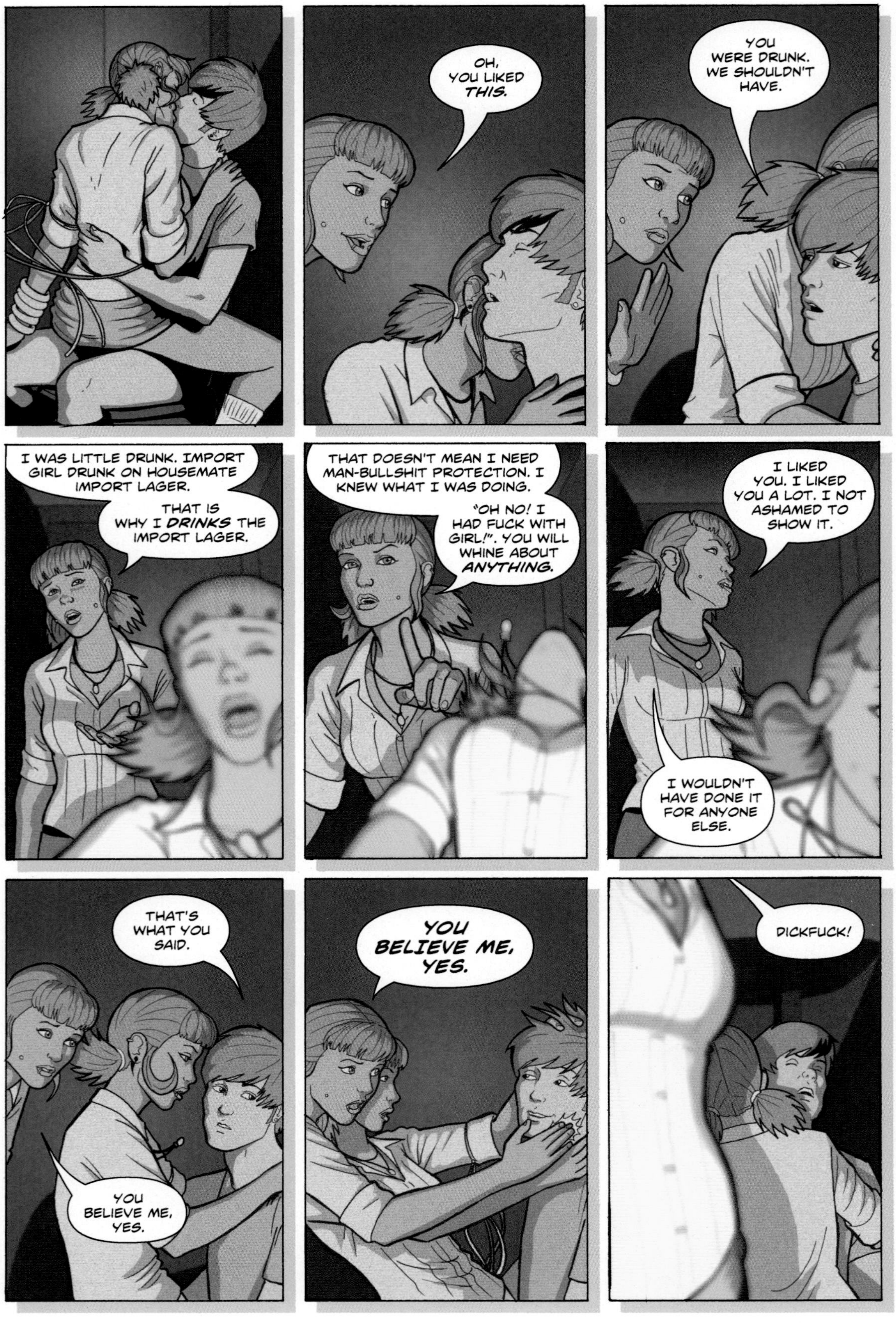
OH, YOU LIKED *THIS.*
YOU WERE DRUNK. WE SHOULDN'T HAVE.
I WAS LITTLE DRUNK. IMPORT GIRL DRUNK ON HOUSEMATE IMPORT LAGER.
THAT IS WHY I ***DRINKS*** THE IMPORT LAGER.
THAT DOESN'T MEAN I NEED MAN-BULLSHIT PROTECTION. I KNEW WHAT I WAS DOING.
"OH NO! I HAD FUCK WITH GIRL!". YOU WILL WHINE ABOUT ***ANYTHING.***
I LIKED YOU. I LIKED YOU A LOT. I NOT ASHAMED TO SHOW IT.
I WOULDN'T HAVE DONE IT FOR ANYONE ELSE.
THAT'S WHAT YOU SAID.
YOU BELIEVE ME, YES.
YOU BELIEVE ME, YES.
DICKFUCK!

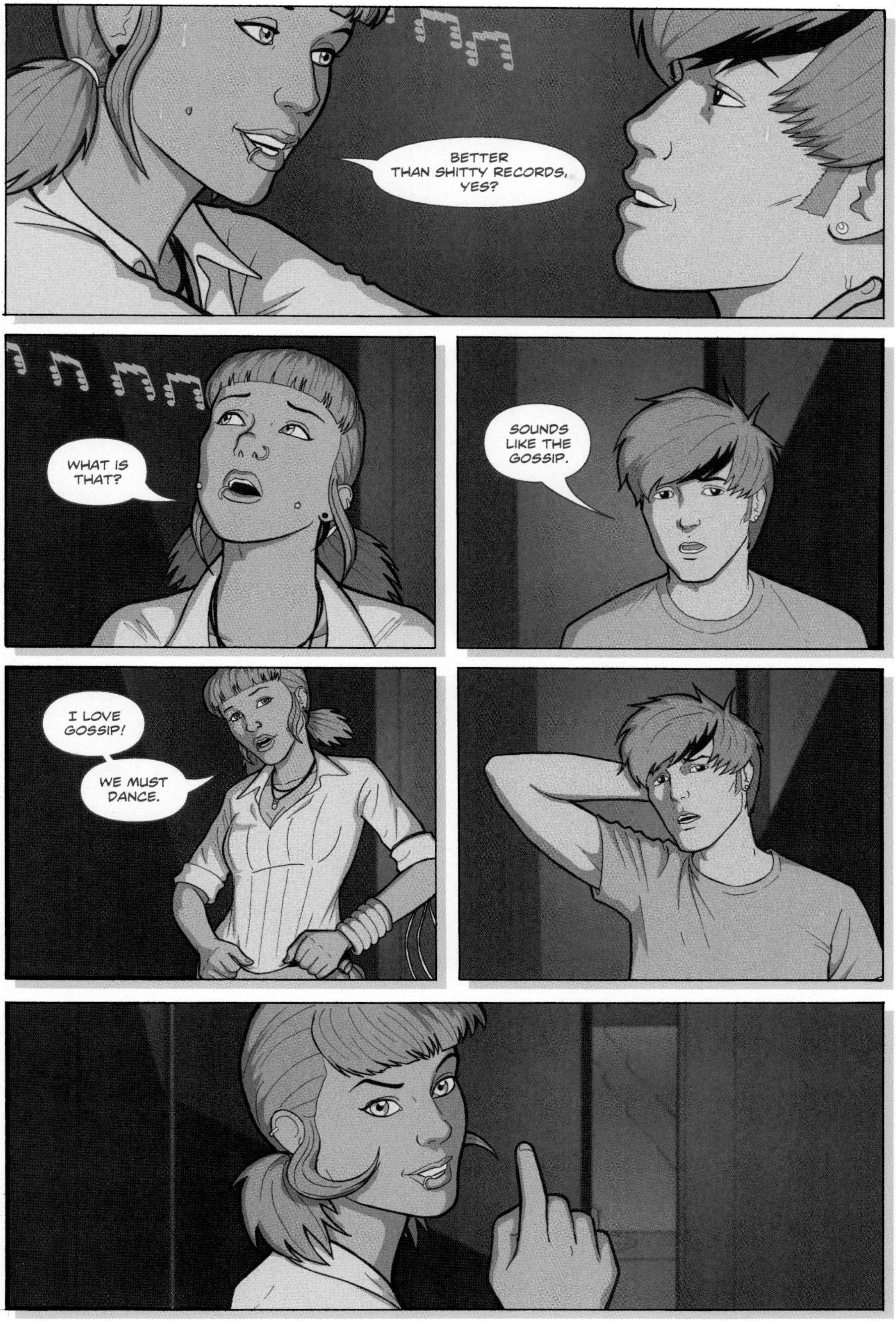
BETTER THAN SHITTY RECORDS, YES?
WHAT IS THAT?
SOUNDS LIKE THE GOSSIP.
I LOVE GOSSIP!
WE MUST DANCE.

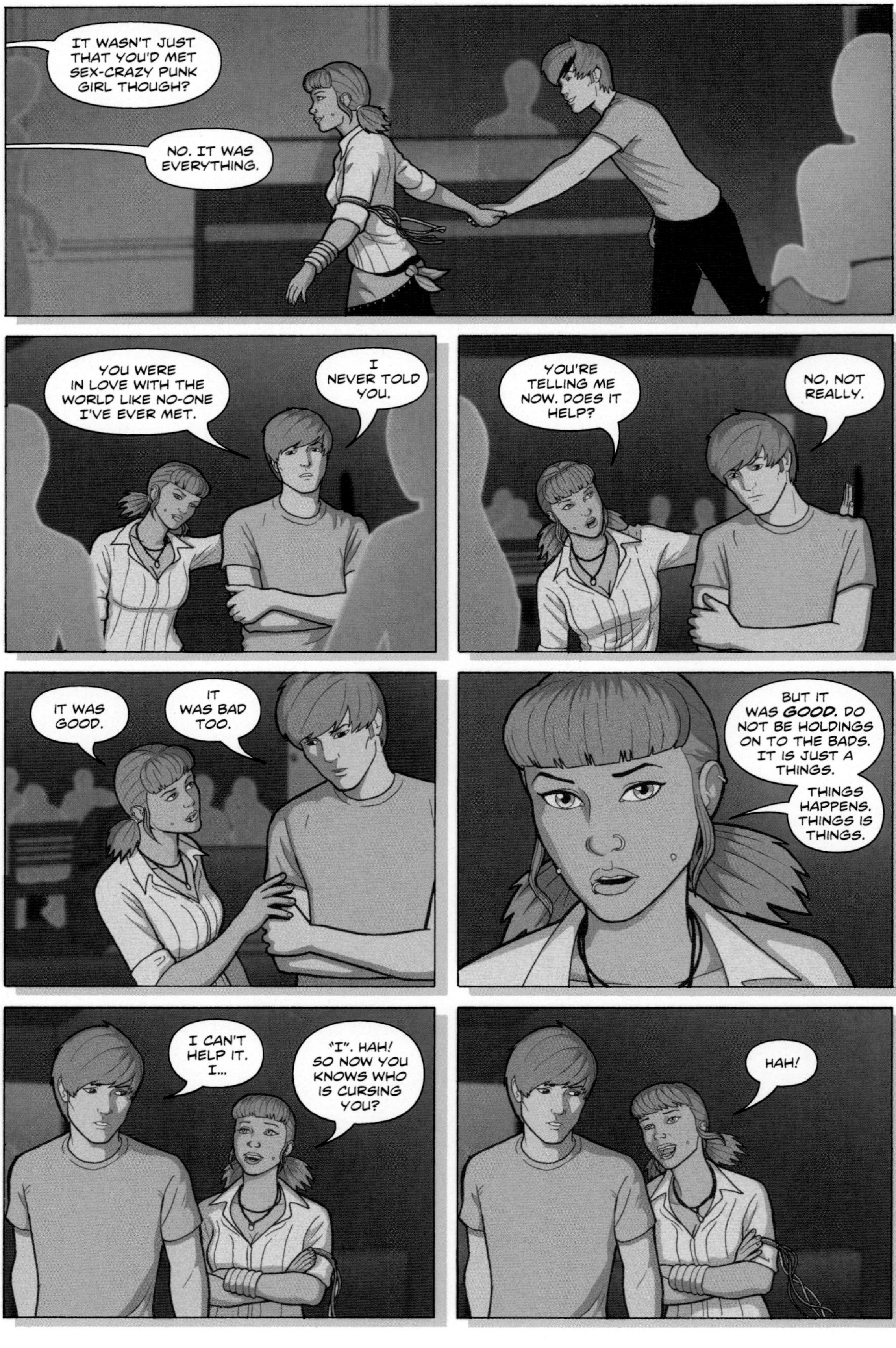
IT WASN'T JUST THAT YOU'D MET SEX-CRAZY PUNK GIRL THOUGH?
NO. IT WAS EVERYTHING.
YOU WERE IN LOVE WITH THE WORLD LIKE NO-ONE I'VE EVER MET.
I NEVER TOLD YOU.
YOU'RE TELLING ME NOW. DOES IT HELP?
NO, NOT REALLY.
IT WAS GOOD.
IT WAS BAD TOO.
BUT IT WAS **GOOD.** DO NOT BE HOLDINGS ON TO THE BADS. IT IS JUST A THINGS.
THINGS HAPPENS. THINGS IS THINGS.
I CAN'T HELP IT. I...
"I". HAH! SO NOW YOU KNOWS WHO IS CURSING YOU?
HAH!

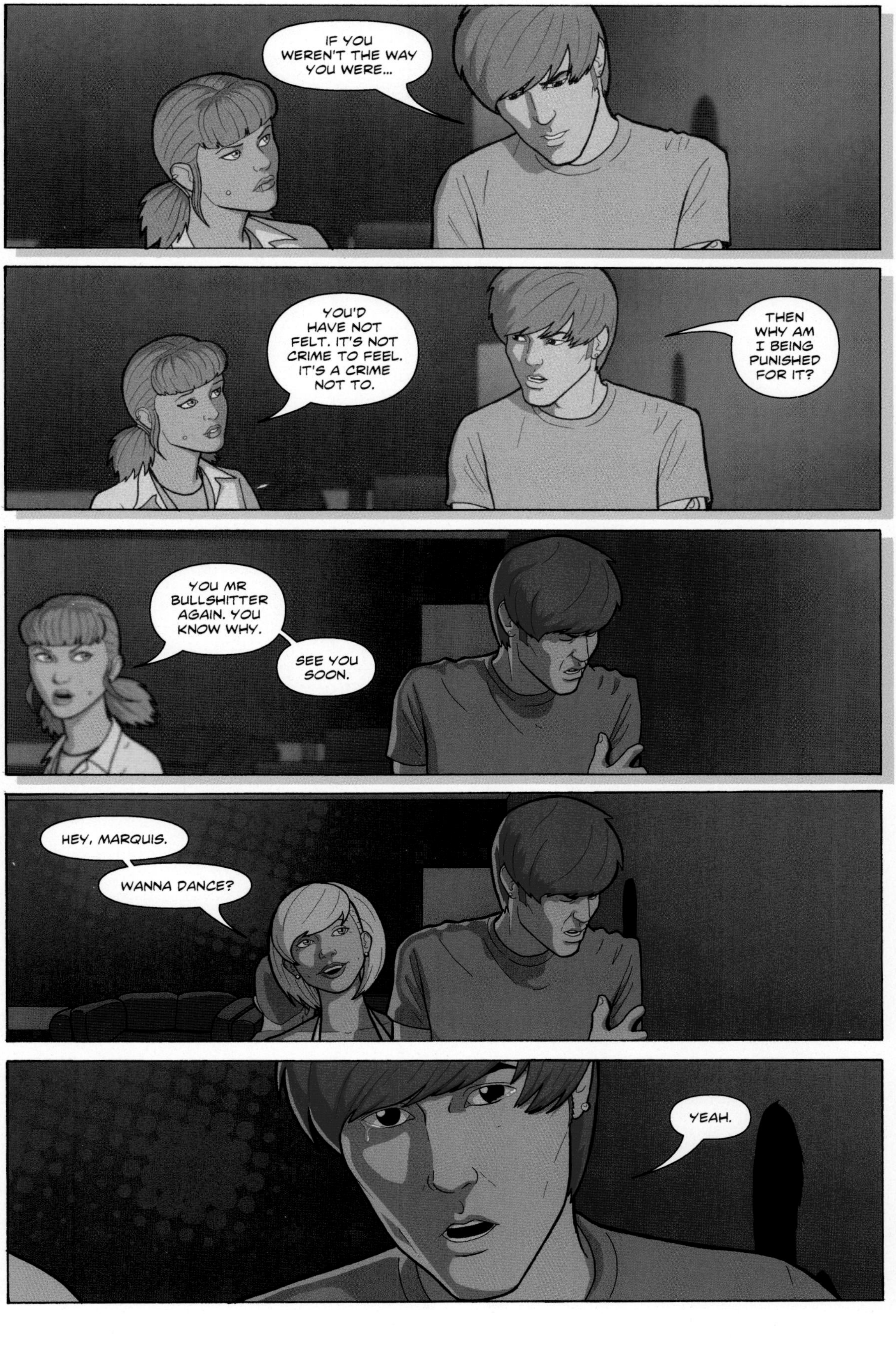
IF YOU WEREN'T THE WAY YOU WERE...
YOU'D HAVE NOT FELT. IT'S NOT CRIME TO FEEL. IT'S A CRIME NOT TO.
THEN WHY AM I BEING PUNISHED FOR IT?
YOU MR BULLSHITTER AGAIN. YOU KNOW WHY.
SEE YOU SOON.
HEY, MARQUIS.
WANNA DANCE?
YEAH.

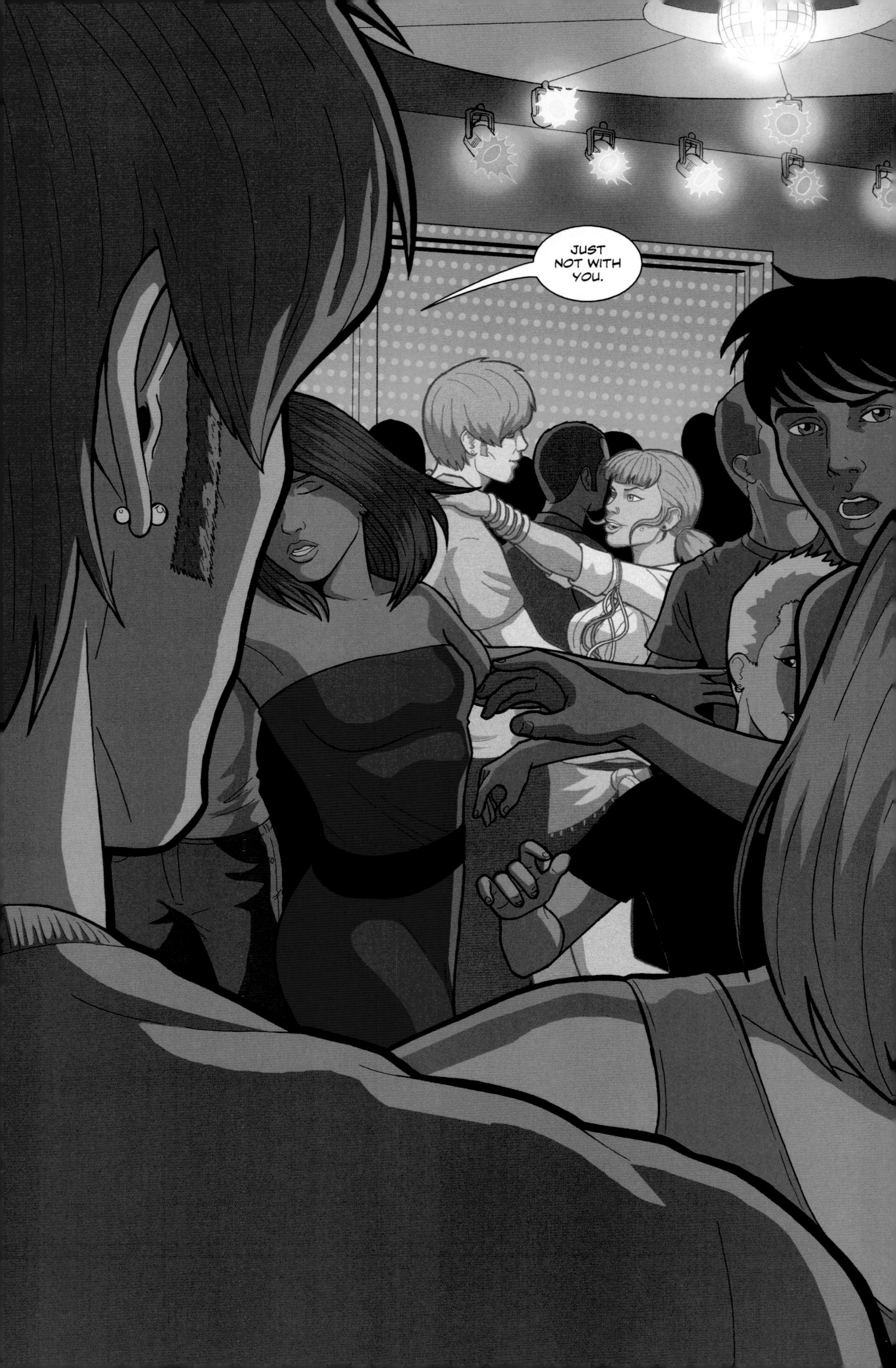
JUST NOT WITH YOU.

PHONOGRAM

THE SINGLES CLUB

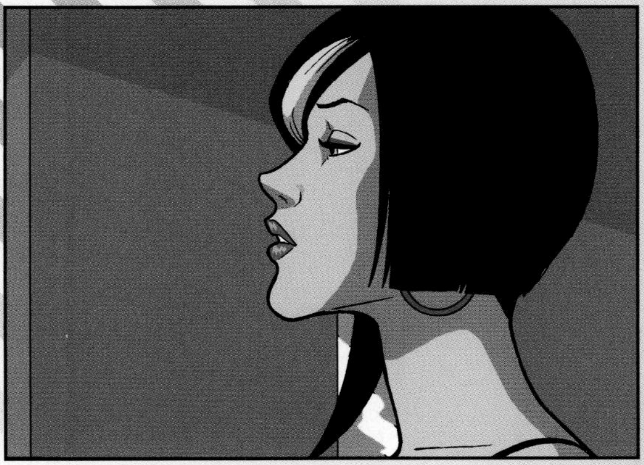

3. WE SHARE OUR MOTHERS' HEALTH

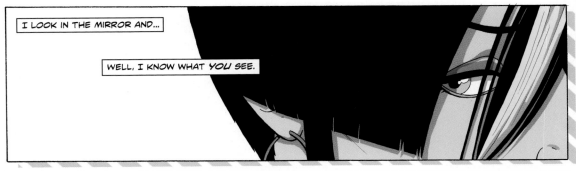

I LOOK IN THE MIRROR AND...

WELL, I KNOW WHAT *YOU* SEE.

MAYBE A WOMAN. MAYBE A GIRL.

OR A WOMAN NOT AFRAID TO DRESS LIKE A GIRL, AND KNOW SHE CAN STILL PULL IT OFF.

BODY TIGHT FROM LONDON GYMNASIUM AND LONDON DANCEFLOOR.

ATTITUDE AT THE FURTHEST POINT AWAY FROM INSECURITY'S SUBURB.

LIPS... AH. YES.

GET OUT OF MY HEAD, RIGHT NOW.

DAVID.

DAVID KOHL.

WHY ARE YOU TAKING ME TO AN INDIE NIGHT?

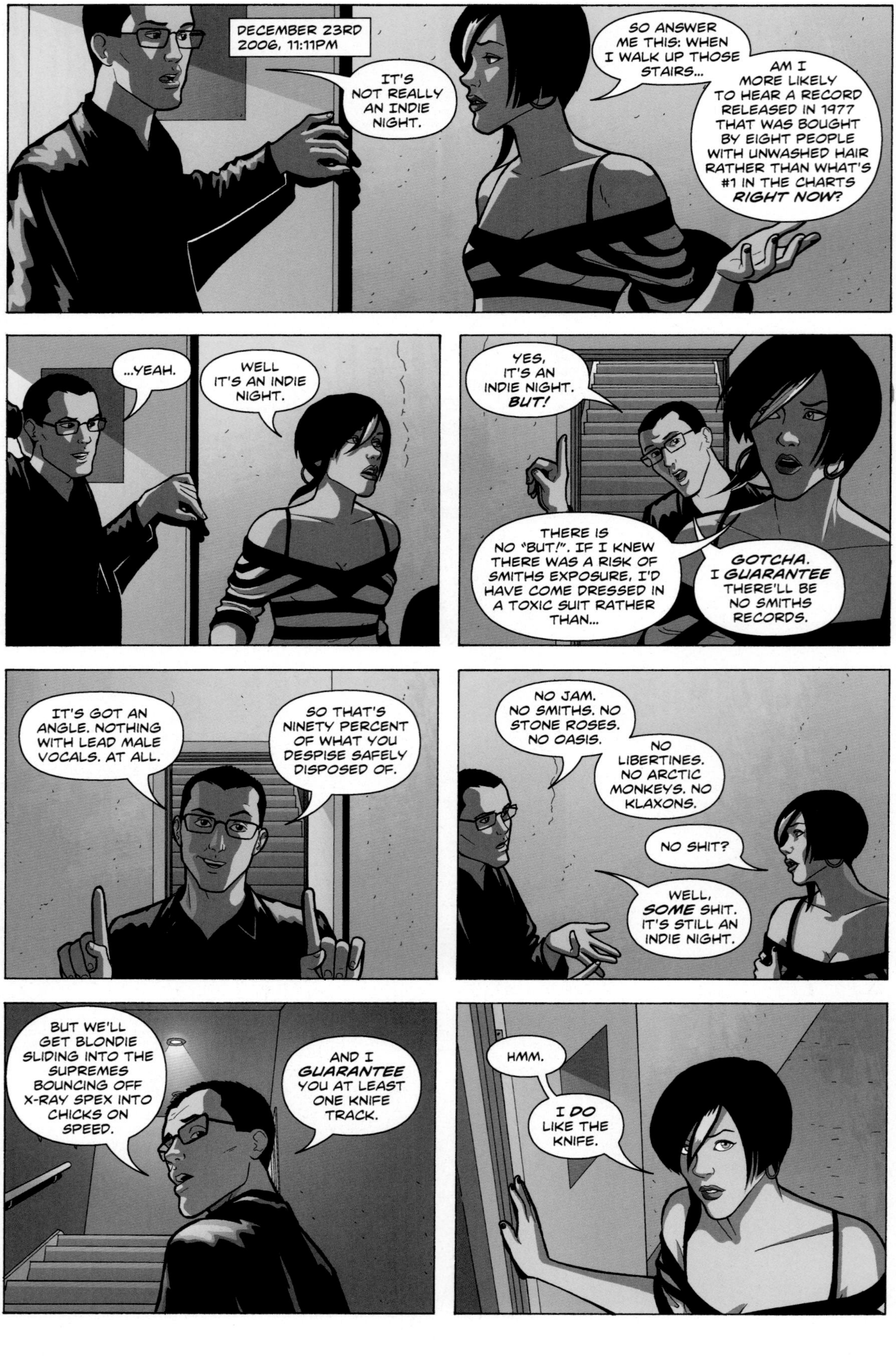
DECEMBER 23RD 2006, 11:11PM
IT'S NOT REALLY AN INDIE NIGHT.
SO ANSWER ME THIS: WHEN I WALK UP THOSE STAIRS...
AM I MORE LIKELY TO HEAR A RECORD RELEASED IN 1977 THAT WAS BOUGHT BY EIGHT PEOPLE WITH UNWASHED HAIR RATHER THAN WHAT'S #1 IN THE CHARTS RIGHT NOW?
...YEAH.
WELL IT'S AN INDIE NIGHT.
YES, IT'S AN INDIE NIGHT. BUT!
THERE IS NO "BUT!". IF I KNEW THERE WAS A RISK OF SMITHS EXPOSURE, I'D HAVE COME DRESSED IN A TOXIC SUIT RATHER THAN...
GOTCHA. I GUARANTEE THERE'LL BE NO SMITHS RECORDS.
IT'S GOT AN ANGLE. NOTHING WITH LEAD MALE VOCALS. AT ALL.
SO THAT'S NINETY PERCENT OF WHAT YOU DESPISE SAFELY DISPOSED OF.
NO JAM. NO SMITHS. NO STONE ROSES. NO OASIS.
NO LIBERTINES. NO ARCTIC MONKEYS. NO KLAXONS.
NO SHIT?
WELL, SOME SHIT. IT'S STILL AN INDIE NIGHT.
BUT WE'LL GET BLONDIE SLIDING INTO THE SUPREMES BOUNCING OFF X-RAY SPEX INTO CHICKS ON SPEED.
AND I GUARANTEE YOU AT LEAST ONE KNIFE TRACK.
HMM.
I DO LIKE THE KNIFE.

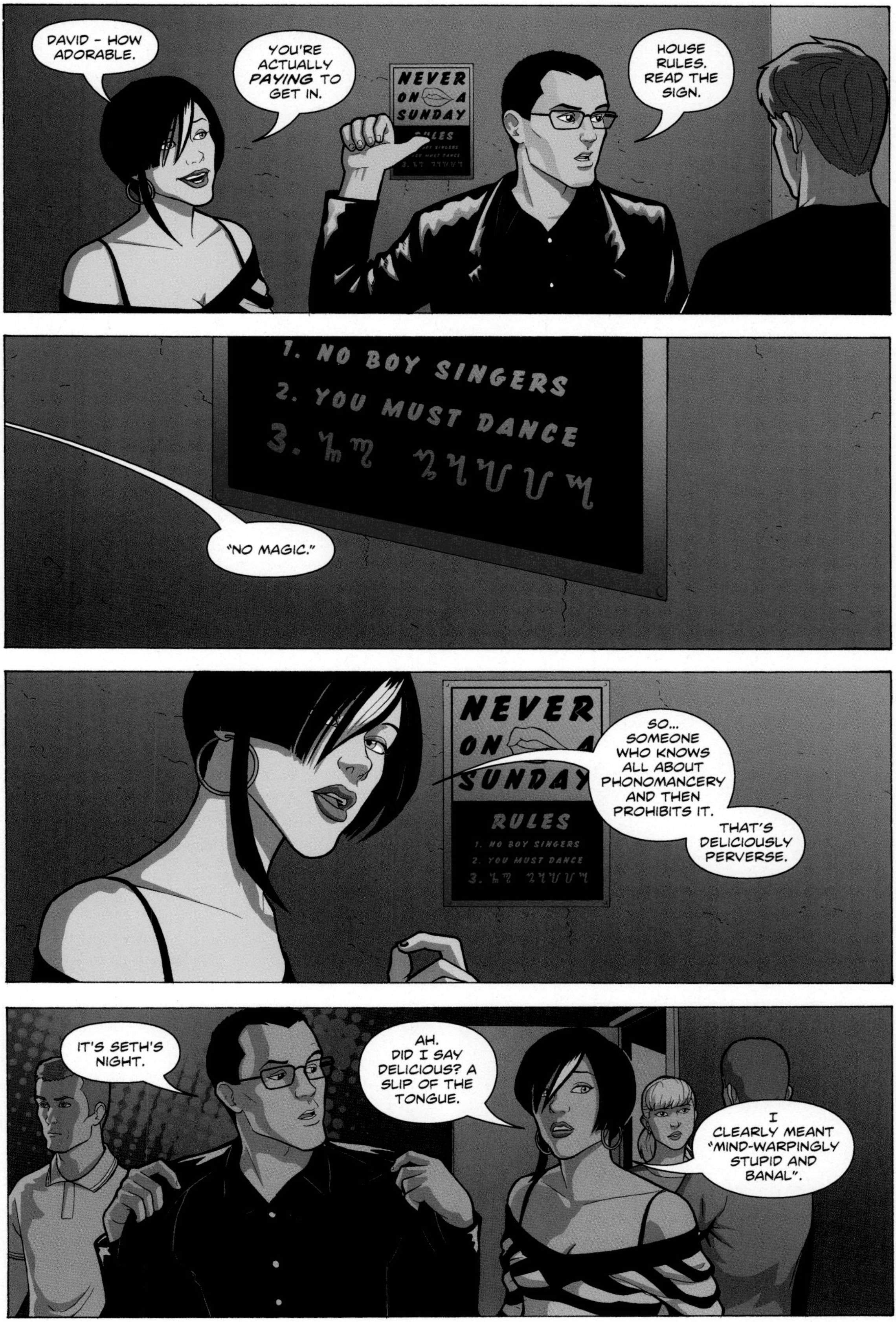
DAVID - HOW ADORABLE.
YOU'RE ACTUALLY *PAYING* TO GET IN.
NEVER ON A SUNDAY
RULES
HOUSE RULES. READ THE SIGN.
1. NO BOY SINGERS
2. YOU MUST DANCE
"NO MAGIC."
NEVER ON A SUNDAY
RULES
1. NO BOY SINGERS
2. YOU MUST DANCE
SO... SOMEONE WHO KNOWS ALL ABOUT PHONOMANCERY AND THEN PROHIBITS IT.
THAT'S DELICIOUSLY PERVERSE.
IT'S SETH'S NIGHT.
AH. DID I SAY DELICIOUS? A SLIP OF THE TONGUE.
I CLEARLY MEANT "MIND-WARPINGLY STUPID AND BANAL".

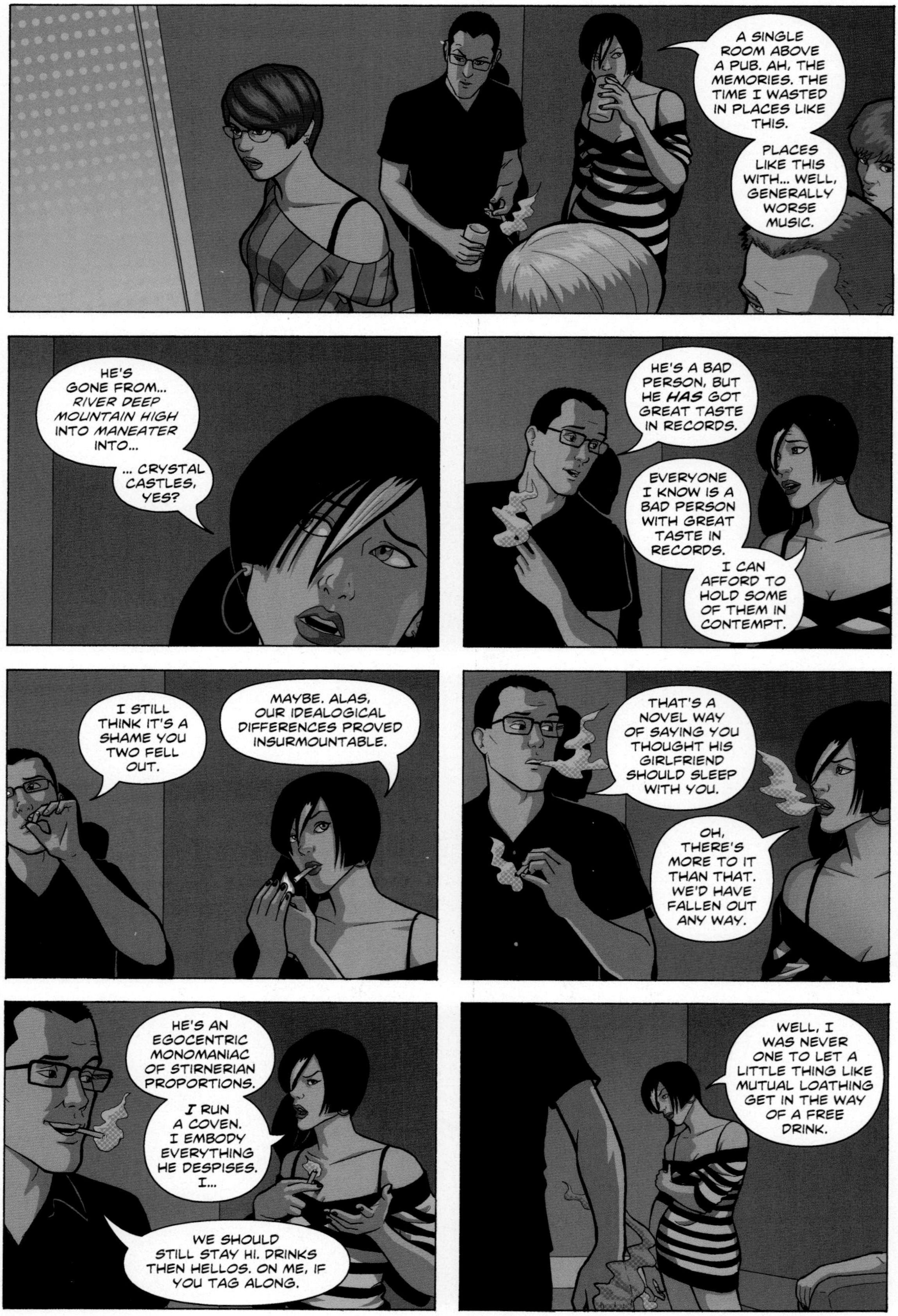
A SINGLE ROOM ABOVE A PUB. AH, THE MEMORIES. THE TIME I WASTED IN PLACES LIKE THIS.
PLACES LIKE THIS WITH... WELL, GENERALLY WORSE MUSIC.
HE'S GONE FROM... *RIVER DEEP MOUNTAIN HIGH* INTO *MANEATER* INTO...
... CRYSTAL CASTLES, YES?
HE'S A BAD PERSON, BUT HE ***HAS*** GOT GREAT TASTE IN RECORDS.
EVERYONE I KNOW IS A BAD PERSON WITH GREAT TASTE IN RECORDS.
I CAN AFFORD TO HOLD SOME OF THEM IN CONTEMPT.
I STILL THINK IT'S A SHAME YOU TWO FELL OUT.
MAYBE. ALAS, OUR IDEALOGICAL DIFFERENCES PROVED INSURMOUNTABLE.
THAT'S A NOVEL WAY OF SAYING YOU THOUGHT HIS GIRLFRIEND SHOULD SLEEP WITH YOU.
OH, THERE'S MORE TO IT THAN THAT. WE'D HAVE FALLEN OUT ANY WAY.
HE'S AN EGOCENTRIC MONOMANIAC OF STIRNERIAN PROPORTIONS.
I RUN A COVEN. I EMBODY EVERYTHING HE DESPISES. I...
WE SHOULD STILL STAY HI. DRINKS THEN HELLOS. ON ME, IF YOU TAG ALONG.
WELL, I WAS NEVER ONE TO LET A LITTLE THING LIKE MUTUAL LOATHING GET IN THE WAY OF A FREE DRINK.

HI SETH. HI SILENT GIRL.

WHY IF IT ISN'T DAVID KOHL, SAVIOUR OF THE INDIE UNIVERSE!

AND WHO'S THIS YOU'VE BROUGHT WITH YOU?

WHY, IT'S THE *MOST EVIL WOMAN IN THE WORLD!*

ISN'T THAT *AMAZING!*

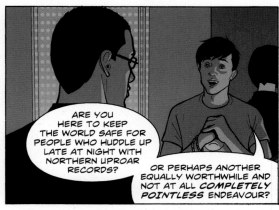

ARE YOU HERE TO KEEP THE WORLD SAFE FOR PEOPLE WHO HUDDLE UP LATE AT NIGHT WITH NORTHERN UPROAR RECORDS?

OR PERHAPS ANOTHER EQUALLY WORTHWHILE AND NOT AT ALL *COMPLETELY POINTLESS* ENDEAVOUR?

IF SOMETHING TURNS UP, YEAH, PROBABLY. IF IT DOESN'T, THOUGHT I'D HAVE A BIT OF A DANCE.

BETTER. WE ARE ALL ABOUT THE DANCING.

ANY REQUESTS, MR. DK?

THE BOILER BY THE SPECIALS?

I'M SURE THAT'S A VERY FUNNY THING TO SAY TO ANYONE WHO KNOWS YOUR OLD-MAN MUSIC, BUT YOU'RE JUST GOING TO HAVE TO MAKE DO WITH KENICKIE. AND YOU'LL *LIKE IT.*

YEAH. I WILL.

WHAT ABOUT LITTLE MISS FRATRICIDE?

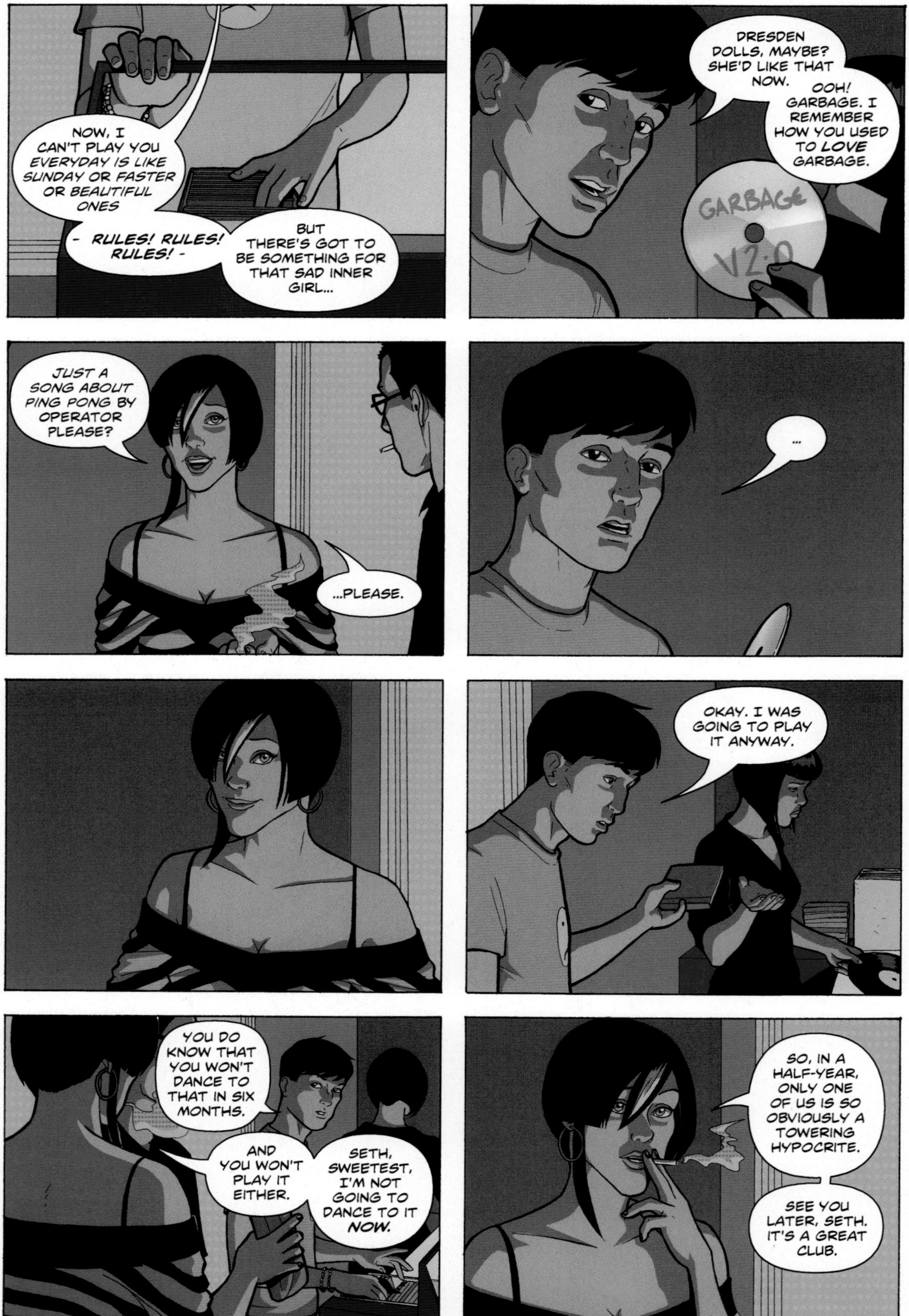
NOW, I CAN'T PLAY YOU EVERYDAY IS LIKE SUNDAY OR FASTER OR BEAUTIFUL ONES
- RULES! RULES! RULES! -
BUT THERE'S GOT TO BE SOMETHING FOR THAT SAD INNER GIRL...
DRESDEN DOLLS, MAYBE? SHE'D LIKE THAT NOW.
OOH! GARBAGE. I REMEMBER HOW YOU USED TO LOVE GARBAGE.
GARBAGE V2.0
JUST A SONG ABOUT PING PONG BY OPERATOR PLEASE?
...PLEASE.
...
OKAY. I WAS GOING TO PLAY IT ANYWAY.
YOU DO KNOW THAT YOU WON'T DANCE TO THAT IN SIX MONTHS.
AND YOU WON'T PLAY IT EITHER.
SETH, SWEETEST, I'M NOT GOING TO DANCE TO IT NOW.
SO, IN A HALF-YEAR, ONLY ONE OF US IS SO OBVIOUSLY A TOWERING HYPOCRITE.
SEE YOU LATER, SETH. IT'S A GREAT CLUB.

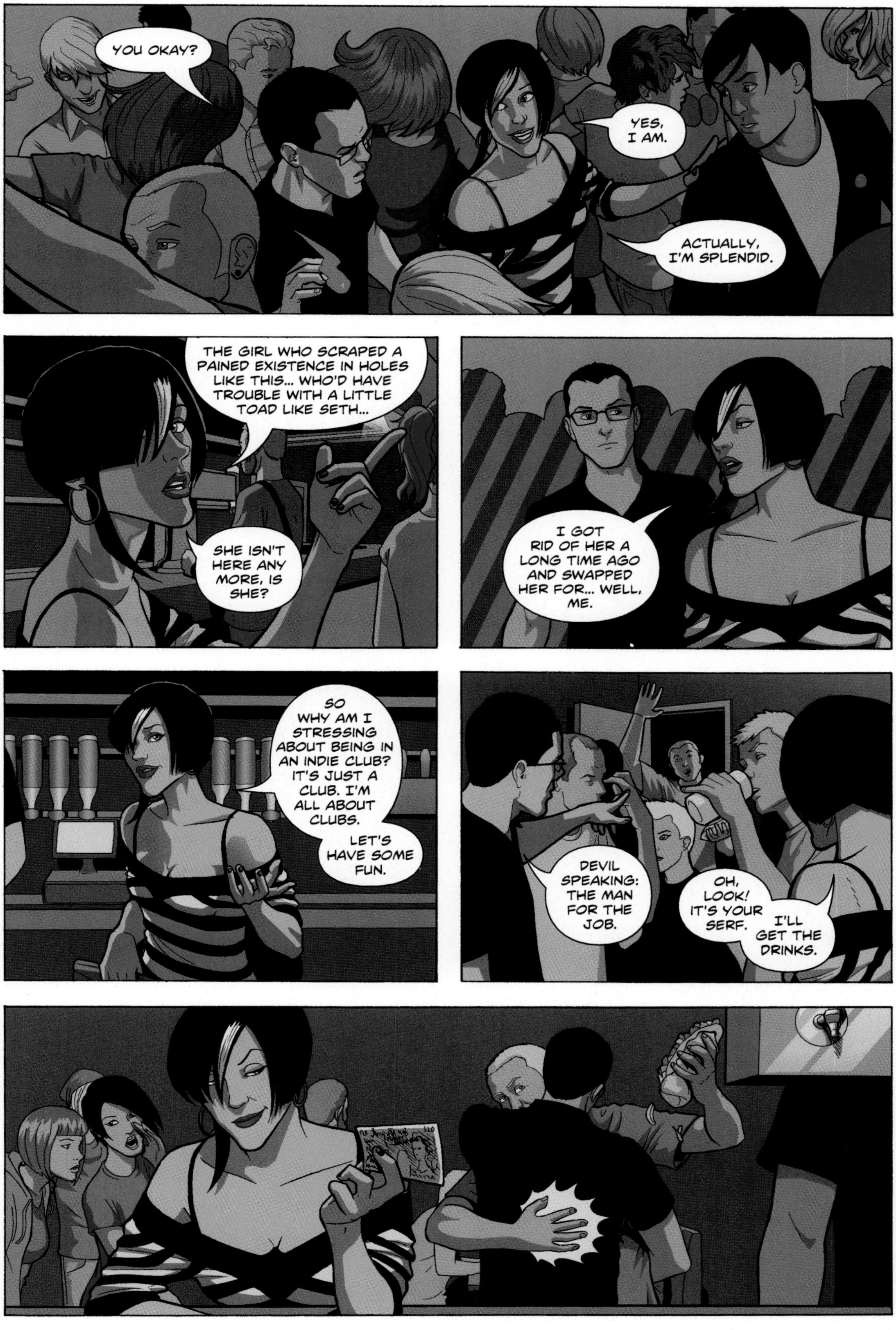
YOU OKAY?
YES, I AM.
ACTUALLY, I'M SPLENDID.
THE GIRL WHO SCRAPED A PAINED EXISTENCE IN HOLES LIKE THIS... WHO'D HAVE TROUBLE WITH A LITTLE TOAD LIKE SETH...
SHE ISN'T HERE ANY MORE, IS SHE?
I GOT RID OF HER A LONG TIME AGO AND SWAPPED HER FOR... WELL, ME.
SO WHY AM I STRESSING ABOUT BEING IN AN INDIE CLUB? IT'S JUST A CLUB. I'M ALL ABOUT CLUBS.
LET'S HAVE SOME FUN.
DEVIL SPEAKING: THE MAN FOR THE JOB.
OH, LOOK! IT'S YOUR SERF.
I'LL GET THE DRINKS.

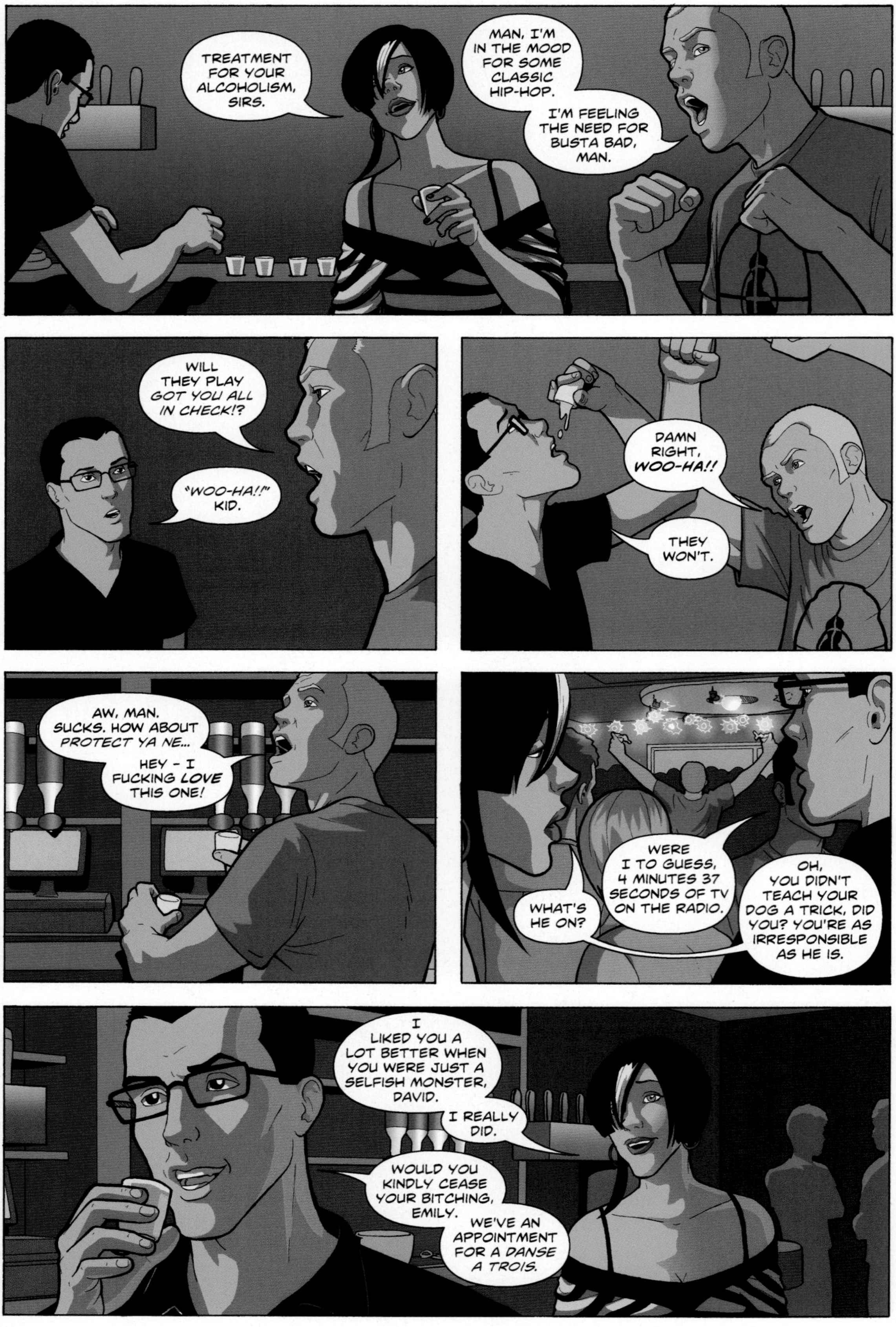
TREATMENT FOR YOUR ALCOHOLISM, SIRS.
MAN, I'M IN THE MOOD FOR SOME CLASSIC HIP-HOP.
I'M FEELING THE NEED FOR BUSTA BAD, MAN.
WILL THEY PLAY *GOT YOU ALL IN CHECK!?*
"WOO-HA!!" KID.
DAMN RIGHT, ***WOO-HA!!***
THEY WON'T.
AW, MAN. SUCKS. HOW ABOUT *PROTECT YA NE...*
HEY - I FUCKING ***LOVE*** THIS ONE!
WHAT'S HE ON?
WERE I TO GUESS, 4 MINUTES 37 SECONDS OF TV ON THE RADIO.
OH, YOU DIDN'T TEACH YOUR DOG A TRICK, DID YOU? YOU'RE AS IRRESPONSIBLE AS HE IS.
I LIKED YOU A LOT BETTER WHEN YOU WERE JUST A SELFISH MONSTER, DAVID.
I REALLY DID.
WOULD YOU KINDLY CEASE YOUR BITCHING, EMILY.
WE'VE AN APPOINTMENT FOR A *DANSE A TROIS.*

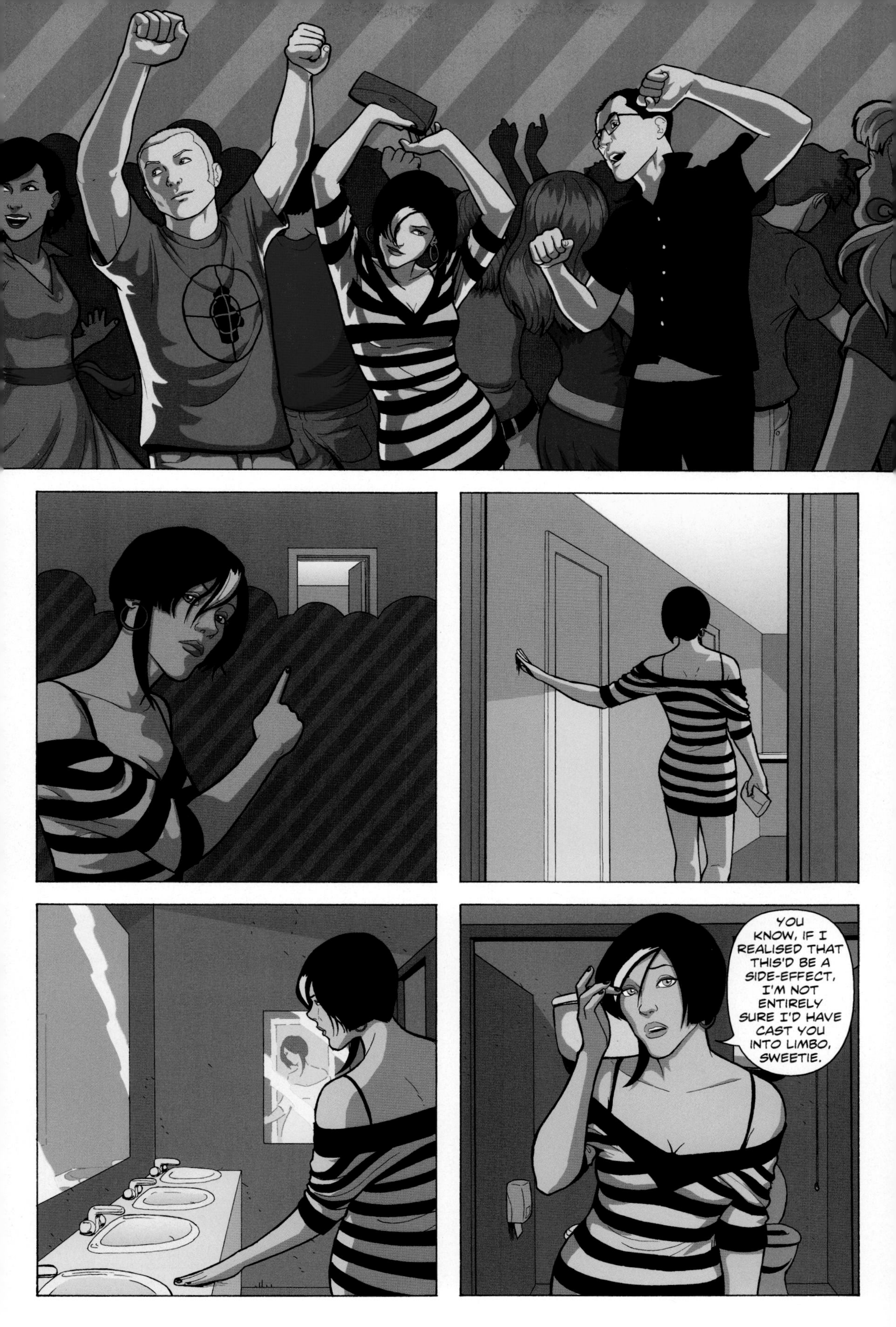
YOU KNOW, IF I REALISED THAT THIS'D BE A SIDE-EFFECT, I'M NOT ENTIRELY SURE I'D HAVE CAST YOU INTO LIMBO, SWEETIE.

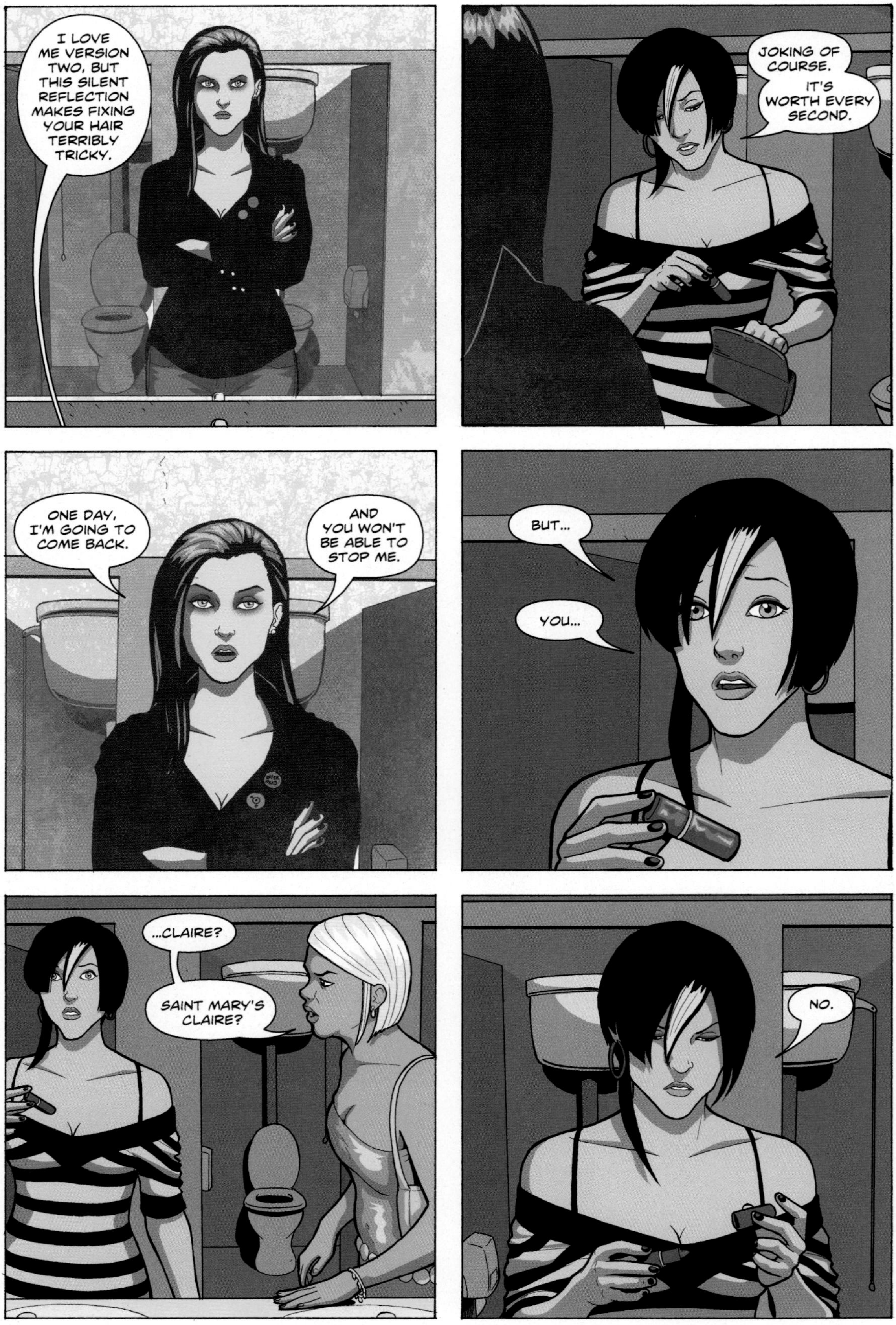
I LOVE ME VERSION TWO, BUT THIS SILENT REFLECTION MAKES FIXING YOUR HAIR TERRIBLY TRICKY.
JOKING OF COURSE.
IT'S WORTH EVERY SECOND.
ONE DAY, I'M GOING TO COME BACK.
AND YOU WON'T BE ABLE TO STOP ME.
BUT...
YOU...
...CLAIRE?
SAINT MARY'S CLAIRE?
NO.

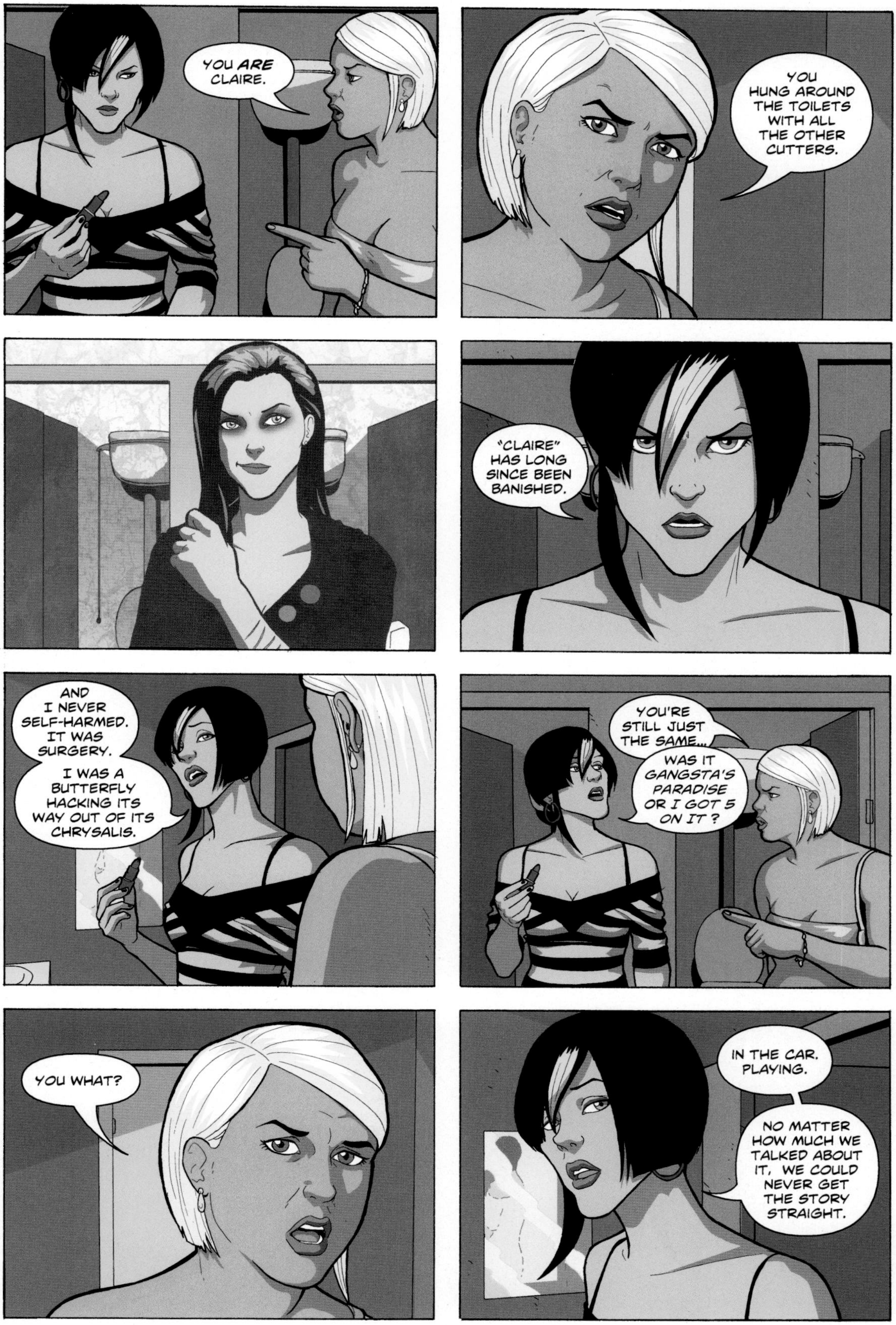

YOU *ARE* CLAIRE.
YOU HUNG AROUND THE TOILETS WITH ALL THE OTHER CUTTERS.
"CLAIRE" HAS LONG SINCE BEEN BANISHED.
AND I NEVER SELF-HARMED. IT WAS SURGERY.
I WAS A BUTTERFLY HACKING ITS WAY OUT OF ITS CHRYSALIS.
YOU'RE STILL JUST THE SAME...
WAS IT GANGSTA'S PARADISE OR I GOT 5 ON IT ?
YOU WHAT?
IN THE CAR. PLAYING.
NO MATTER HOW MUCH WE TALKED ABOUT IT, WE COULD NEVER GET THE STORY STRAIGHT.

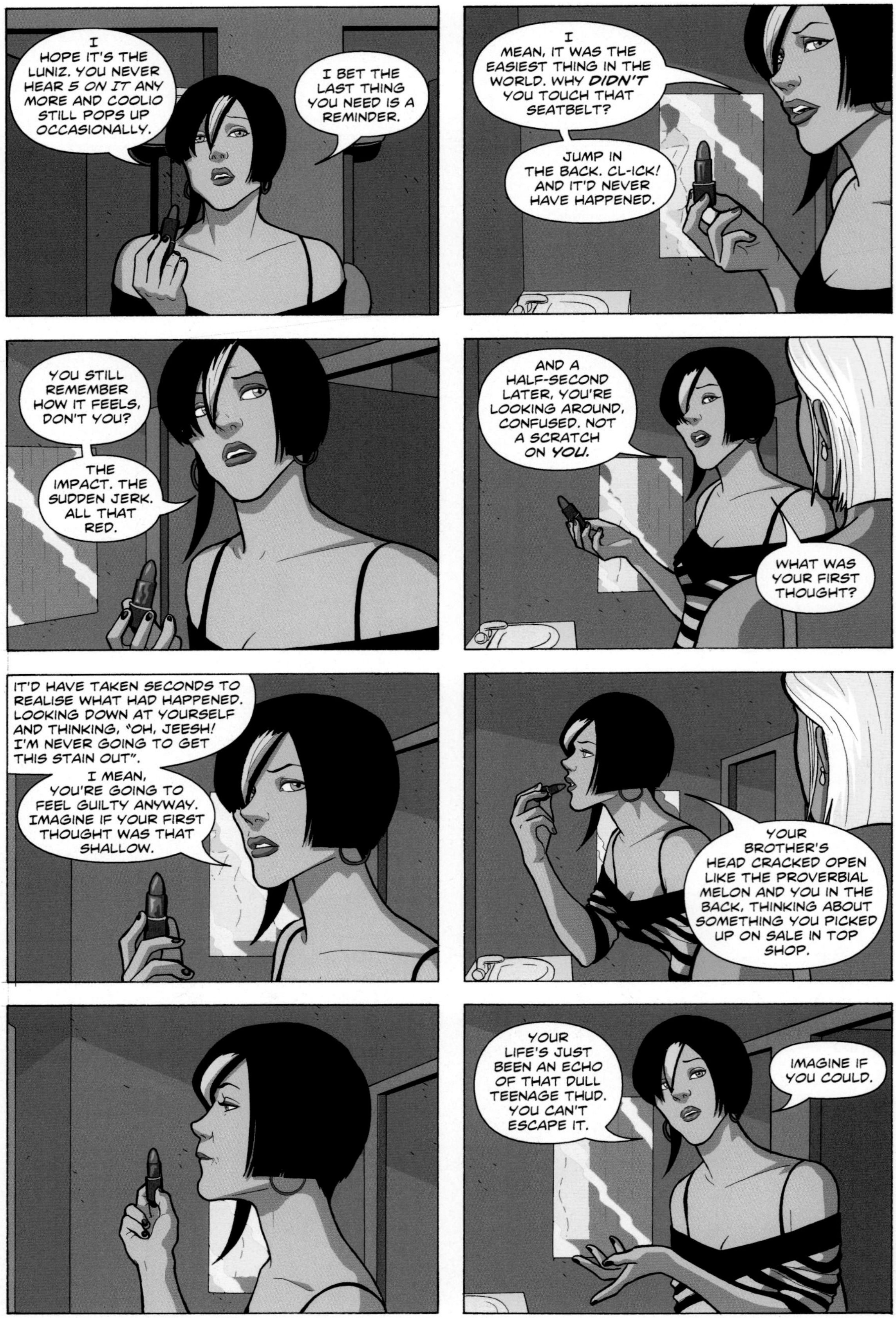
I HOPE IT'S THE LUNIZ. YOU NEVER HEAR 5 ON IT ANY MORE AND COOLIO STILL POPS UP OCCASIONALLY.
I BET THE LAST THING YOU NEED IS A REMINDER.
I MEAN, IT WAS THE EASIEST THING IN THE WORLD. WHY DIDN'T YOU TOUCH THAT SEATBELT?
JUMP IN THE BACK. CL-ICK! AND IT'D NEVER HAVE HAPPENED.
YOU STILL REMEMBER HOW IT FEELS, DON'T YOU?
THE IMPACT. THE SUDDEN JERK. ALL THAT RED.
AND A HALF-SECOND LATER, YOU'RE LOOKING AROUND, CONFUSED. NOT A SCRATCH ON YOU.
WHAT WAS YOUR FIRST THOUGHT?
IT'D HAVE TAKEN SECONDS TO REALISE WHAT HAD HAPPENED. LOOKING DOWN AT YOURSELF AND THINKING, "OH, JEESH! I'M NEVER GOING TO GET THIS STAIN OUT".
I MEAN, YOU'RE GOING TO FEEL GUILTY ANYWAY. IMAGINE IF YOUR FIRST THOUGHT WAS THAT SHALLOW.
YOUR BROTHER'S HEAD CRACKED OPEN LIKE THE PROVERBIAL MELON AND YOU IN THE BACK, THINKING ABOUT SOMETHING YOU PICKED UP ON SALE IN TOP SHOP.
YOUR LIFE'S JUST BEEN AN ECHO OF THAT DULL TEENAGE THUD. YOU CAN'T ESCAPE IT.
IMAGINE IF YOU COULD.

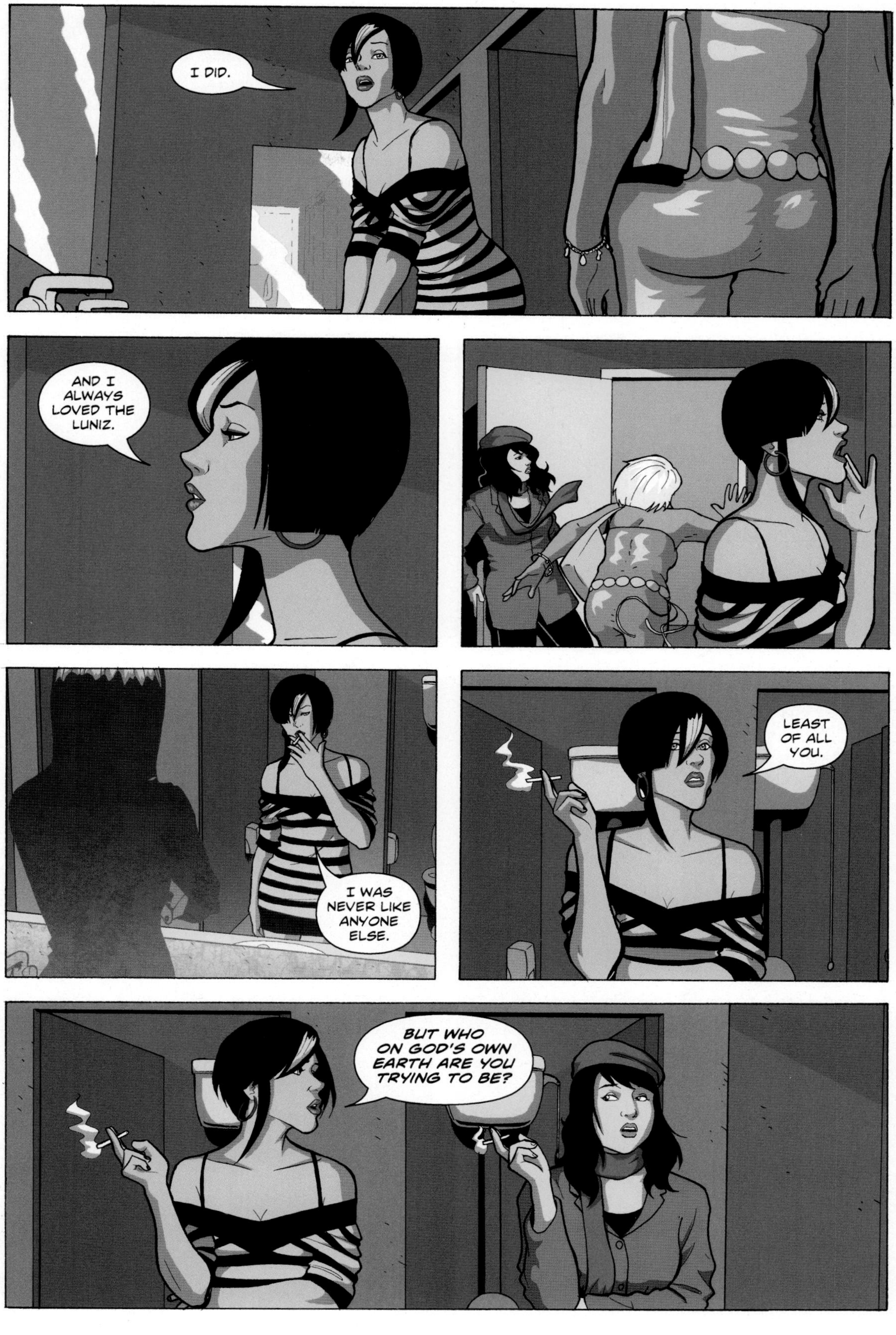
I DID.
AND I ALWAYS LOVED THE LUNIZ.
I WAS NEVER LIKE ANYONE ELSE.
LEAST OF ALL YOU.
BUT WHO ON GOD'S OWN EARTH ARE YOU TRYING TO BE?

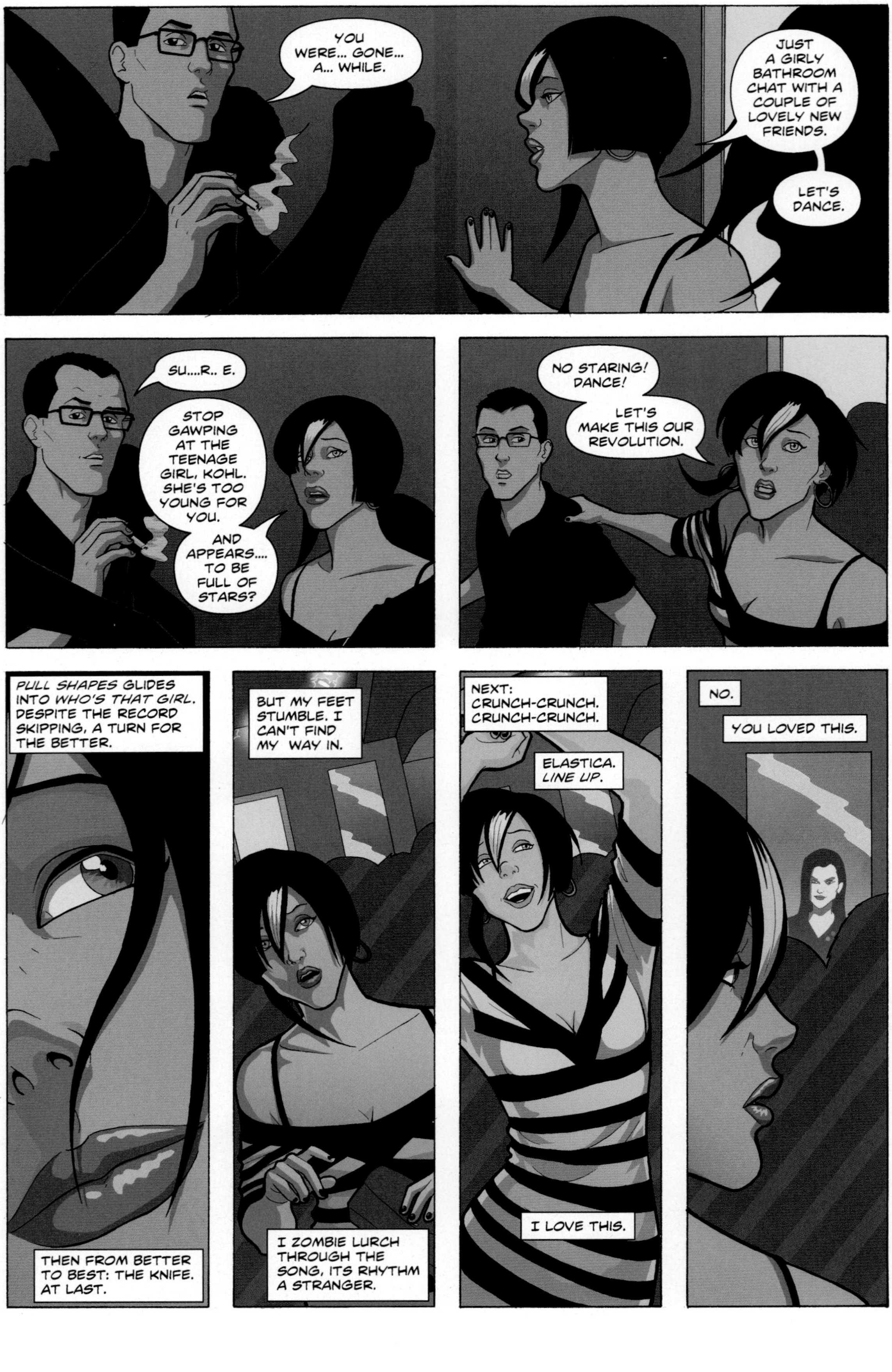
YOU WERE... GONE... A... WHILE.
JUST A GIRLY BATHROOM CHAT WITH A COUPLE OF LOVELY NEW FRIENDS.
LET'S DANCE.
SU....R.. E.
STOP GAWPING AT THE TEENAGE GIRL, KOHL. SHE'S TOO YOUNG FOR YOU.
AND APPEARS.... TO BE FULL OF STARS?
NO STARING! DANCE!
LET'S MAKE THIS OUR REVOLUTION.
PULL SHAPES GLIDES INTO *WHO'S THAT GIRL*. DESPITE THE RECORD SKIPPING, A TURN FOR THE BETTER.
THEN FROM BETTER TO BEST: THE KNIFE. AT LAST.
BUT MY FEET STUMBLE. I CAN'T FIND MY WAY IN.
I ZOMBIE LURCH THROUGH THE SONG, ITS RHYTHM A STRANGER.
NEXT: CRUNCH-CRUNCH. CRUNCH-CRUNCH.
ELASTICA. *LINE UP*.
I LOVE THIS.
NO.
YOU LOVED THIS.

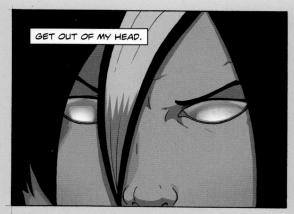

GET OUT OF MY HEAD.

EMILY - YOU OKAY?

TOO CLOSE TO HOME, DAVID. TOO CLOSE...

I MOVED OUT A LONG TIME AGO. I LEFT NO FORWARDING ADDRESS FOR A REASON.

WHICH REALLY ONLY LEAVES ONE COURSE OF ACTION.

HAVE SEX WITH THE LEAST APPROPRIATE PERSON HERE.

AH - A LIKELY CANDIDATE.

NEVER DO THIS TO ME AGAIN.

SORRY, LUV, I NEED A LITTLE WORD WITH THAT GUY.

WELL, MAYBE YOU DO. BUT YOU NEED TO ASK YOURSELF A QUESTION.

DO YOU *REALLY* WANT A WORD WITH THAT GUY OR WOULD YOU *RATHER* HAVE REALLY SPLENDID SEX?

YOU WANT TO FUCK? FOR REAL?

DO I LOOK LIKE THE SORT OF GIRL WHO'D OFFER SEX TO A TOTAL STRANGER?

...YEAH?

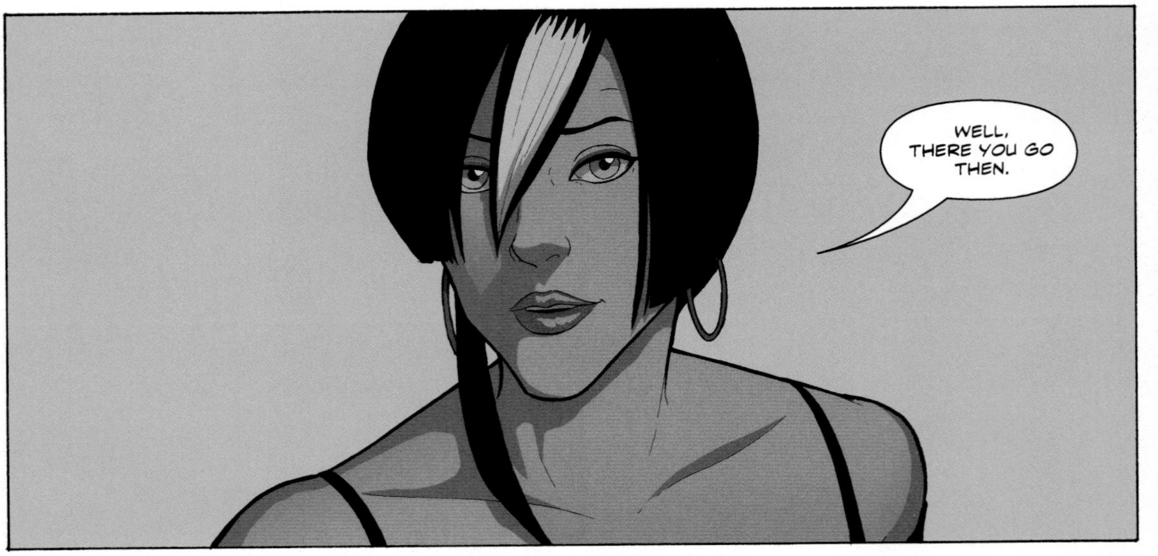
WELL, THERE YOU GO THEN.

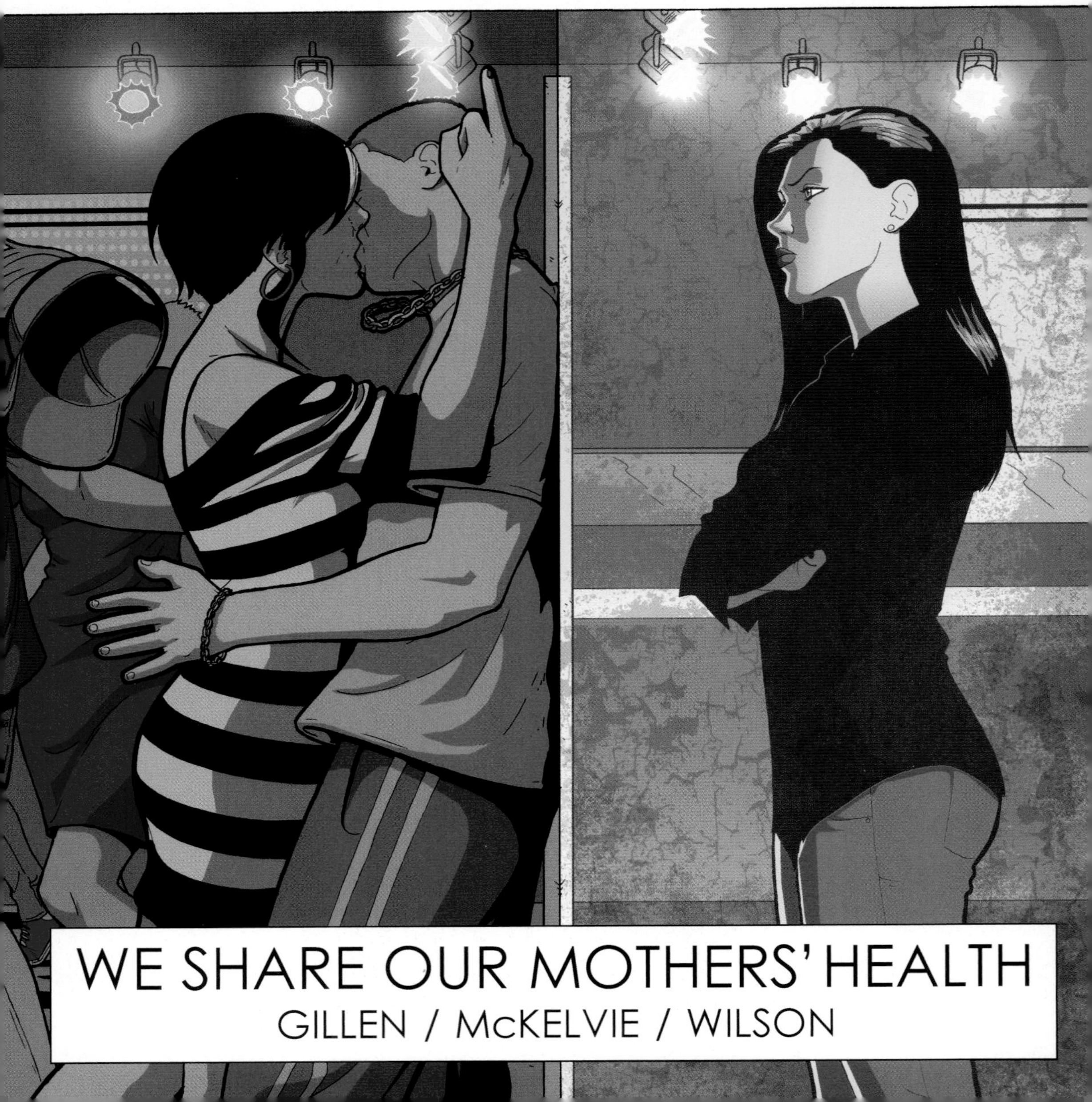
WE SHARE OUR MOTHERS' HEALTH
GILLEN / McKELVIE / WILSON

PHONOGRAM THE SINGLES CLUB

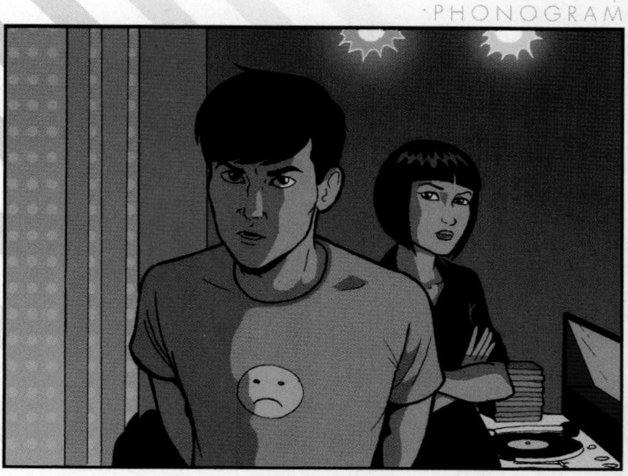

4. KONICHIWA BITCHES

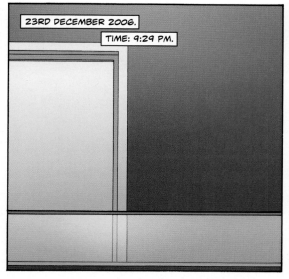

23RD DECEMBER 2006.
TIME: 9:29 PM.

HNNGH!

GAHH!

HEY, SILENT GIRL.

HI, SETH.

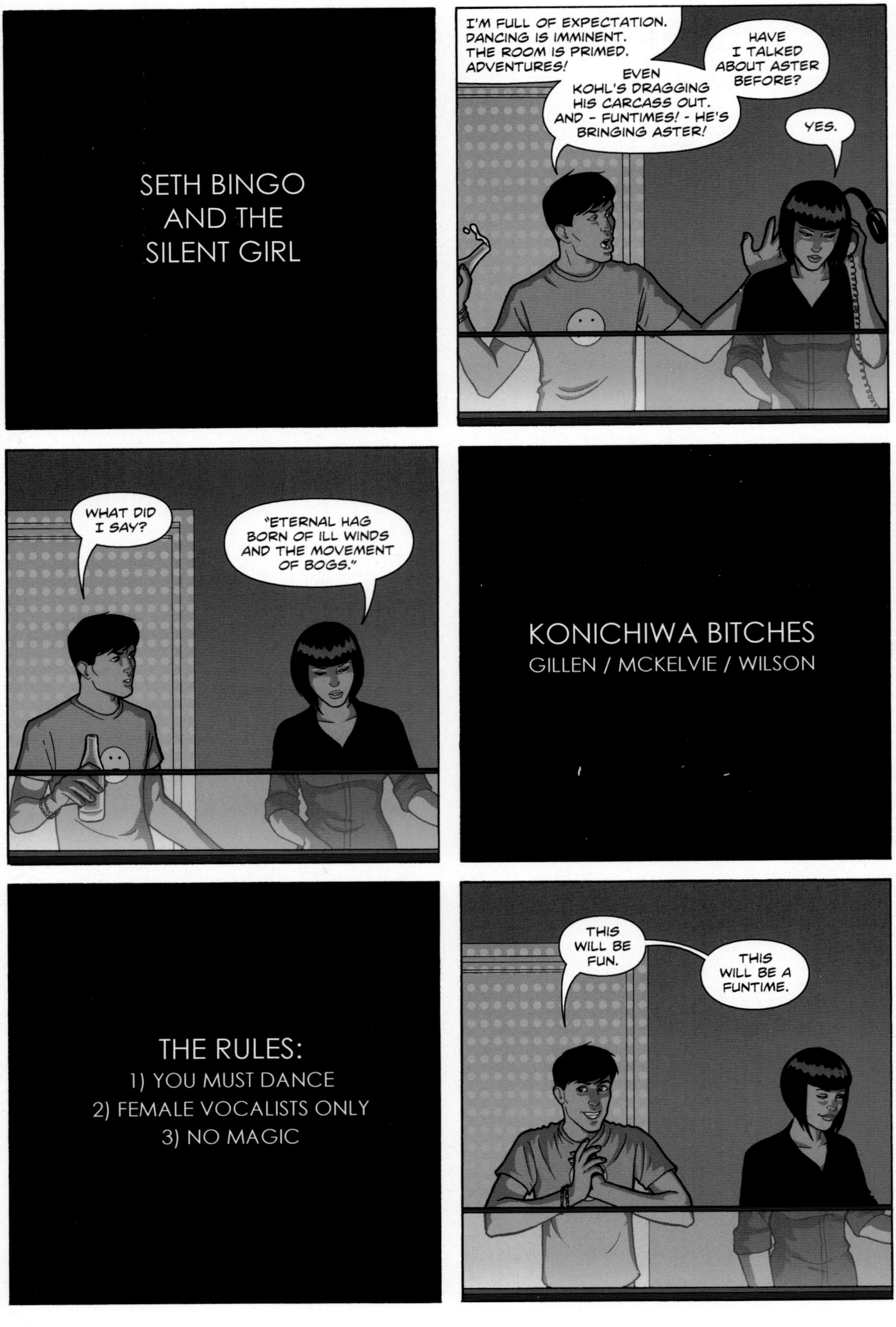
SETH BINGO AND THE SILENT GIRL
I'M FULL OF EXPECTATION. DANCING IS IMMINENT. THE ROOM IS PRIMED. ADVENTURES!
EVEN KOHL'S DRAGGING HIS CARCASS OUT. AND - FUNTIMES! - HE'S BRINGING ASTER!
HAVE I TALKED ABOUT ASTER BEFORE?
YES.
WHAT DID I SAY?
"ETERNAL HAG BORN OF ILL WINDS AND THE MOVEMENT OF BOGS."
KONICHIWA BITCHES
GILLEN / MCKELVIE / WILSON
THE RULES:
1) YOU MUST DANCE
2) FEMALE VOCALISTS ONLY
3) NO MAGIC
THIS WILL BE FUN.
THIS WILL BE A FUNTIME.

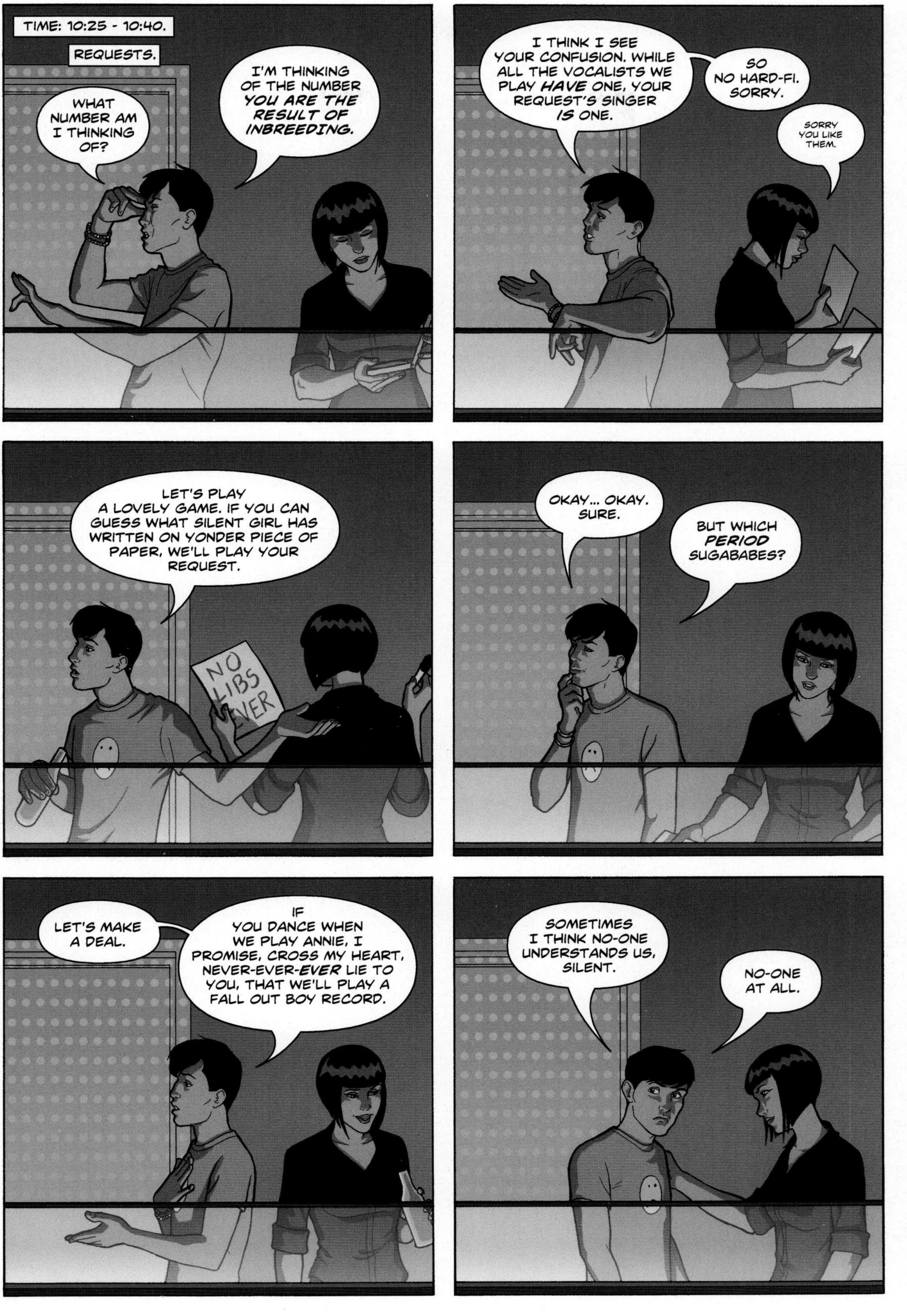
TIME: 10:25 - 10:40.
REQUESTS.
WHAT NUMBER AM I THINKING OF?
I'M THINKING OF THE NUMBER YOU ARE THE RESULT OF INBREEDING.
I THINK I SEE YOUR CONFUSION. WHILE ALL THE VOCALISTS WE PLAY HAVE ONE, YOUR REQUEST'S SINGER IS ONE.
SO NO HARD-FI. SORRY.
SORRY YOU LIKE THEM.
LET'S PLAY A LOVELY GAME. IF YOU CAN GUESS WHAT SILENT GIRL HAS WRITTEN ON YONDER PIECE OF PAPER, WE'LL PLAY YOUR REQUEST.
NO LIBS EVER
OKAY... OKAY. SURE.
BUT WHICH PERIOD SUGABABES?
LET'S MAKE A DEAL.
IF YOU DANCE WHEN WE PLAY ANNIE, I PROMISE, CROSS MY HEART, NEVER-EVER-EVER LIE TO YOU, THAT WE'LL PLAY A FALL OUT BOY RECORD.
SOMETIMES I THINK NO-ONE UNDERSTANDS US, SILENT.
NO-ONE AT ALL.

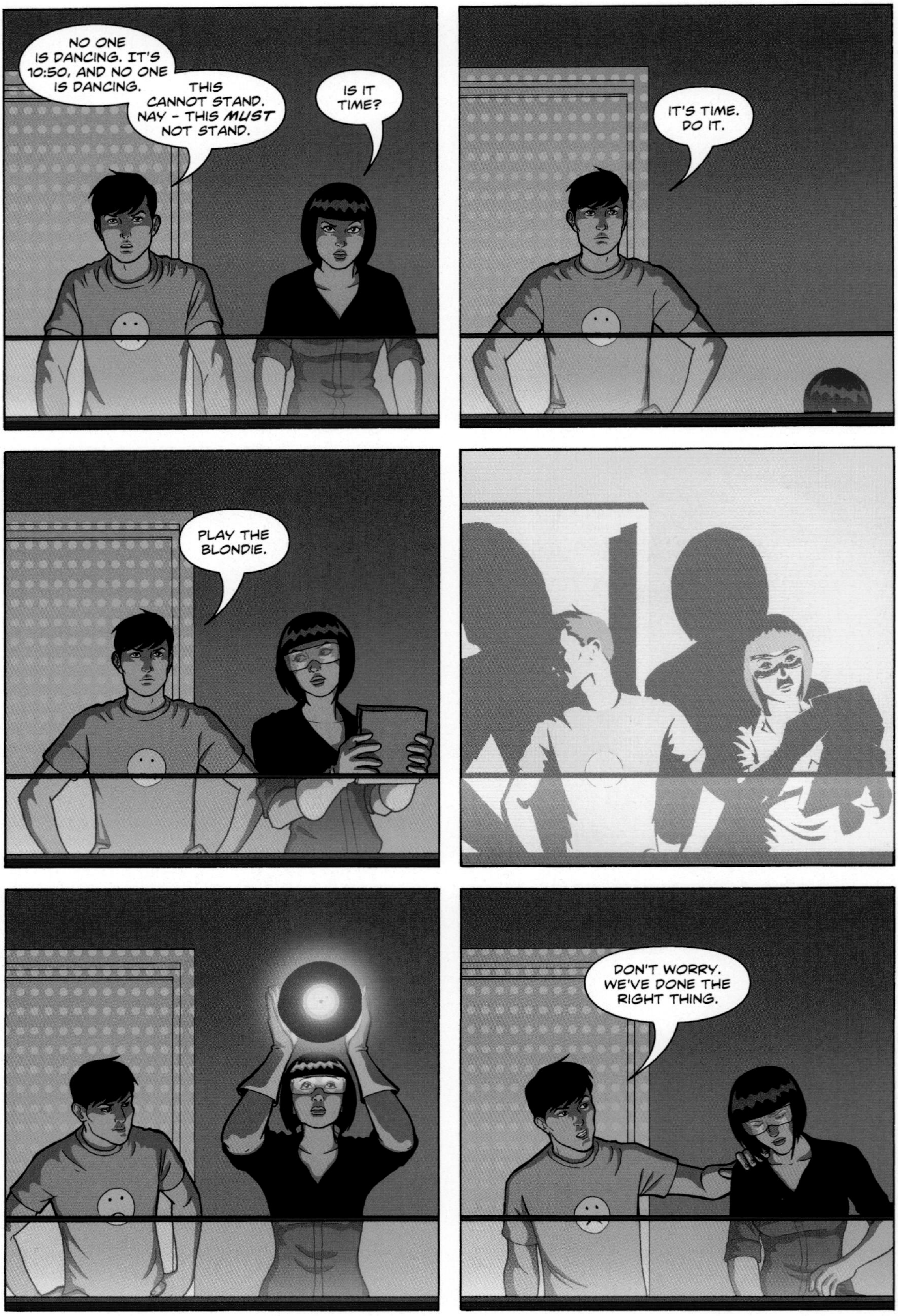
NO ONE IS DANCING. IT'S 10:50, AND NO ONE IS DANCING.
THIS CANNOT STAND. NAY - THIS *MUST* NOT STAND.
IS IT TIME?
IT'S TIME. DO IT.
PLAY THE BLONDIE.
DON'T WORRY. WE'VE DONE THE RIGHT THING.

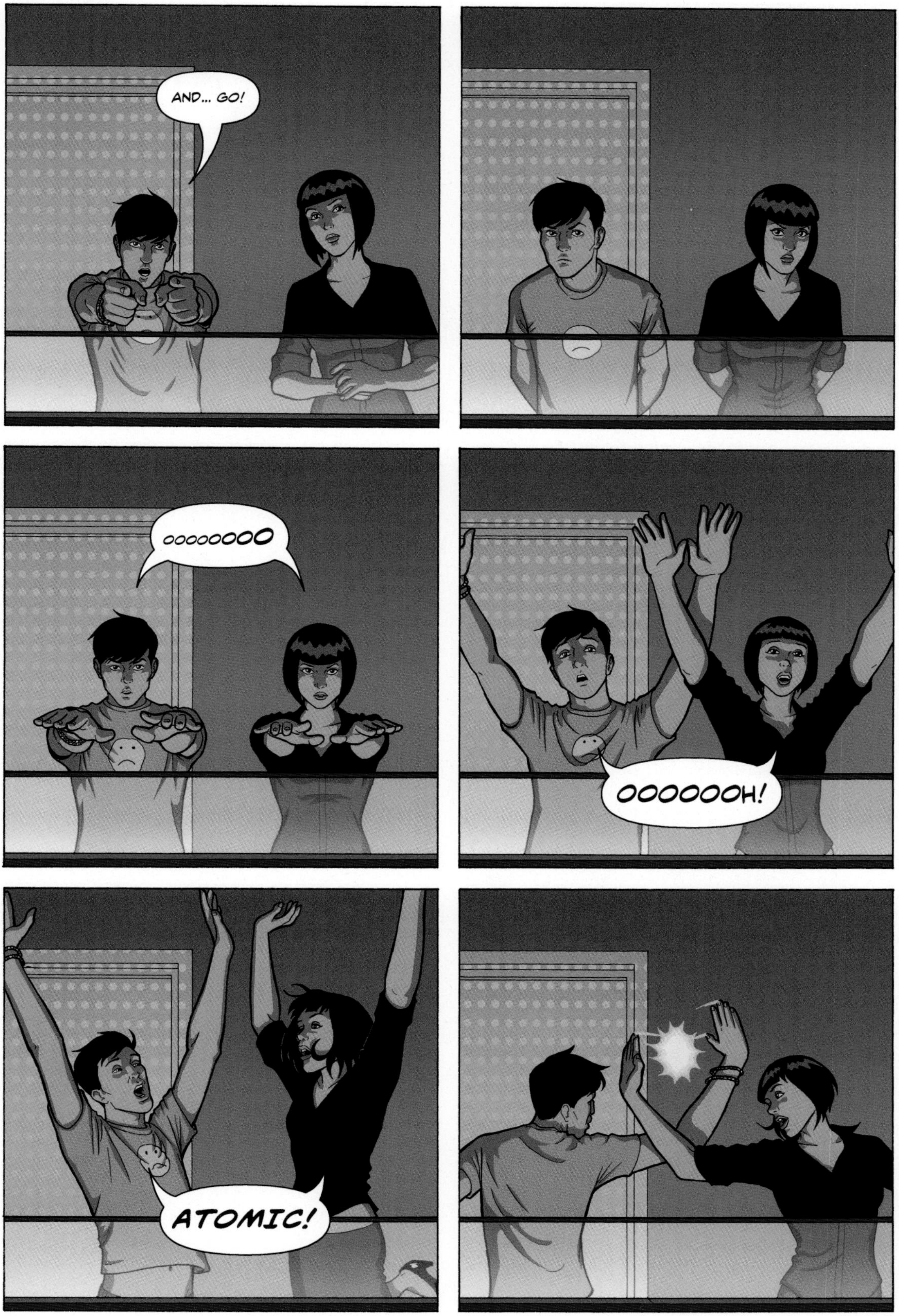
AND... GO!
OOOOOOOO
OOOOOOH!
ATOMIC!

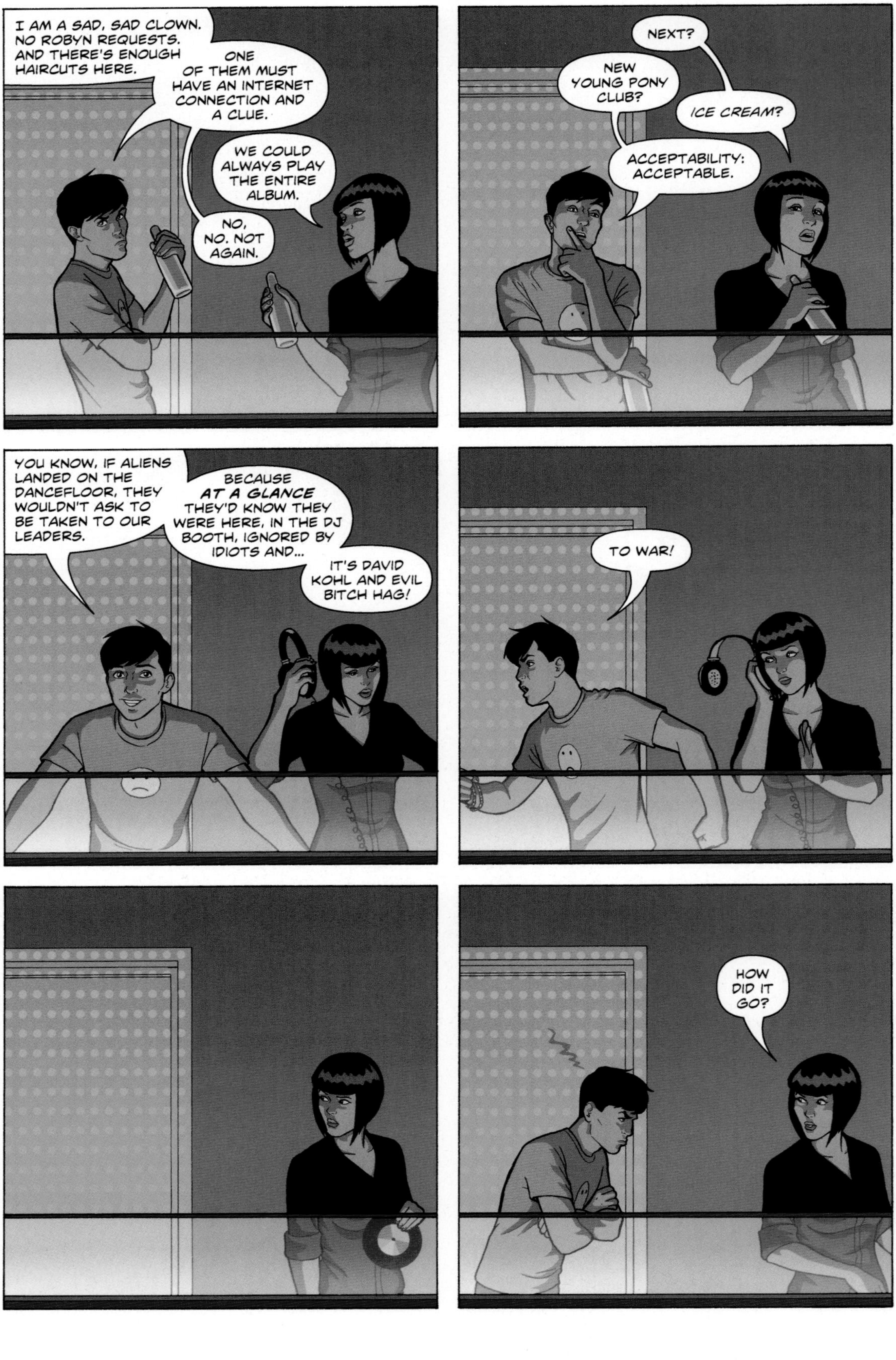
I AM A SAD, SAD CLOWN. NO ROBYN REQUESTS. AND THERE'S ENOUGH HAIRCUTS HERE.
ONE OF THEM MUST HAVE AN INTERNET CONNECTION AND A CLUE.
WE COULD ALWAYS PLAY THE ENTIRE ALBUM.
NO, NO. NOT AGAIN.
NEXT?
NEW YOUNG PONY CLUB?
ICE CREAM?
ACCEPTABILITY: ACCEPTABLE.
YOU KNOW, IF ALIENS LANDED ON THE DANCEFLOOR, THEY WOULDN'T ASK TO BE TAKEN TO OUR LEADERS.
BECAUSE *AT A GLANCE* THEY'D KNOW THEY WERE HERE, IN THE DJ BOOTH, IGNORED BY IDIOTS AND...
IT'S DAVID KOHL AND EVIL BITCH HAG!
TO WAR!
HOW DID IT GO?

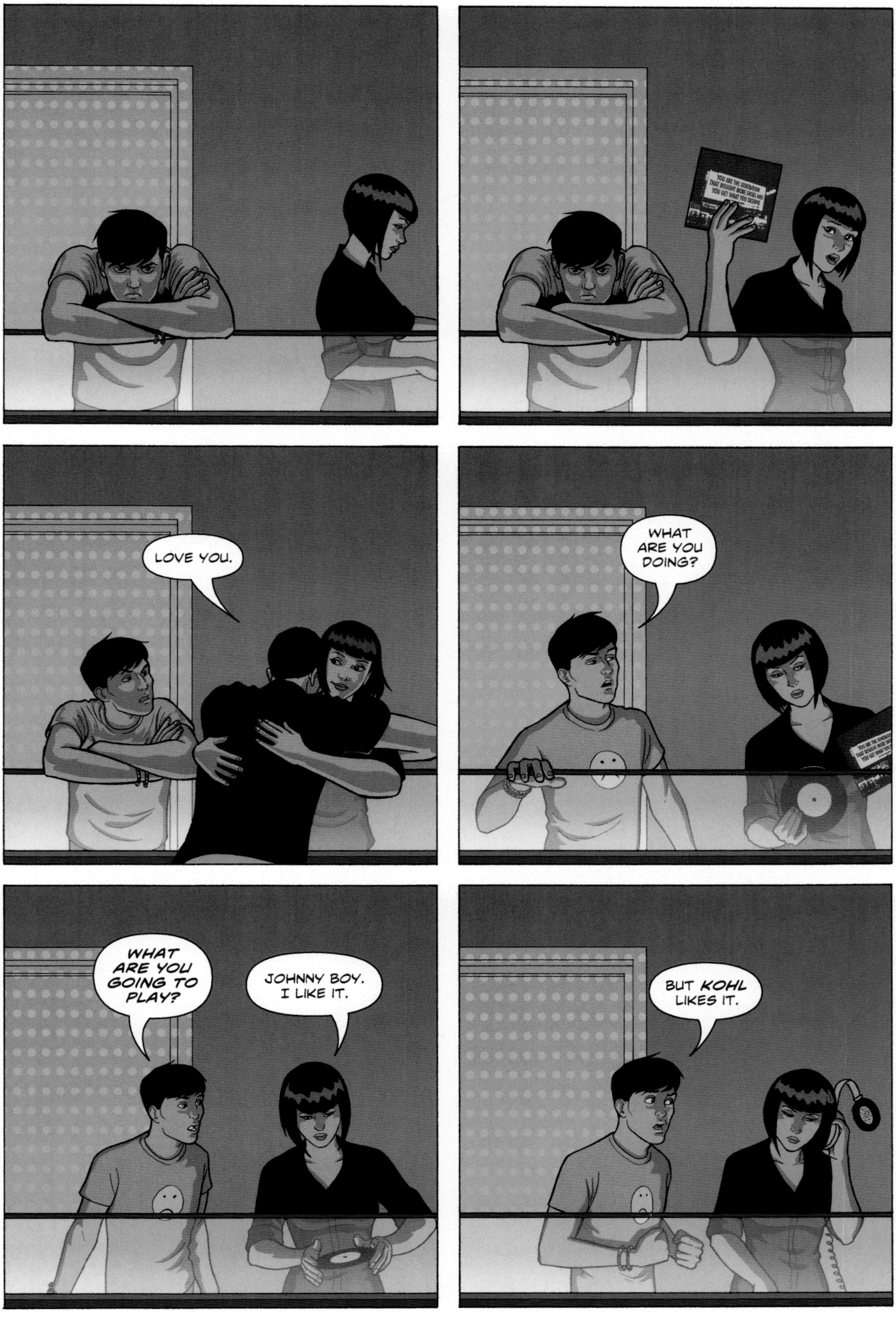
YOU ARE THE GENERATION THAT BOUGHT MORE SHOES AND YOU GET WHAT YOU DESERVE
LOVE YOU.
WHAT ARE YOU DOING?
WHAT ARE YOU GOING TO PLAY?
JOHNNY BOY. I LIKE IT.
BUT KOHL LIKES IT.

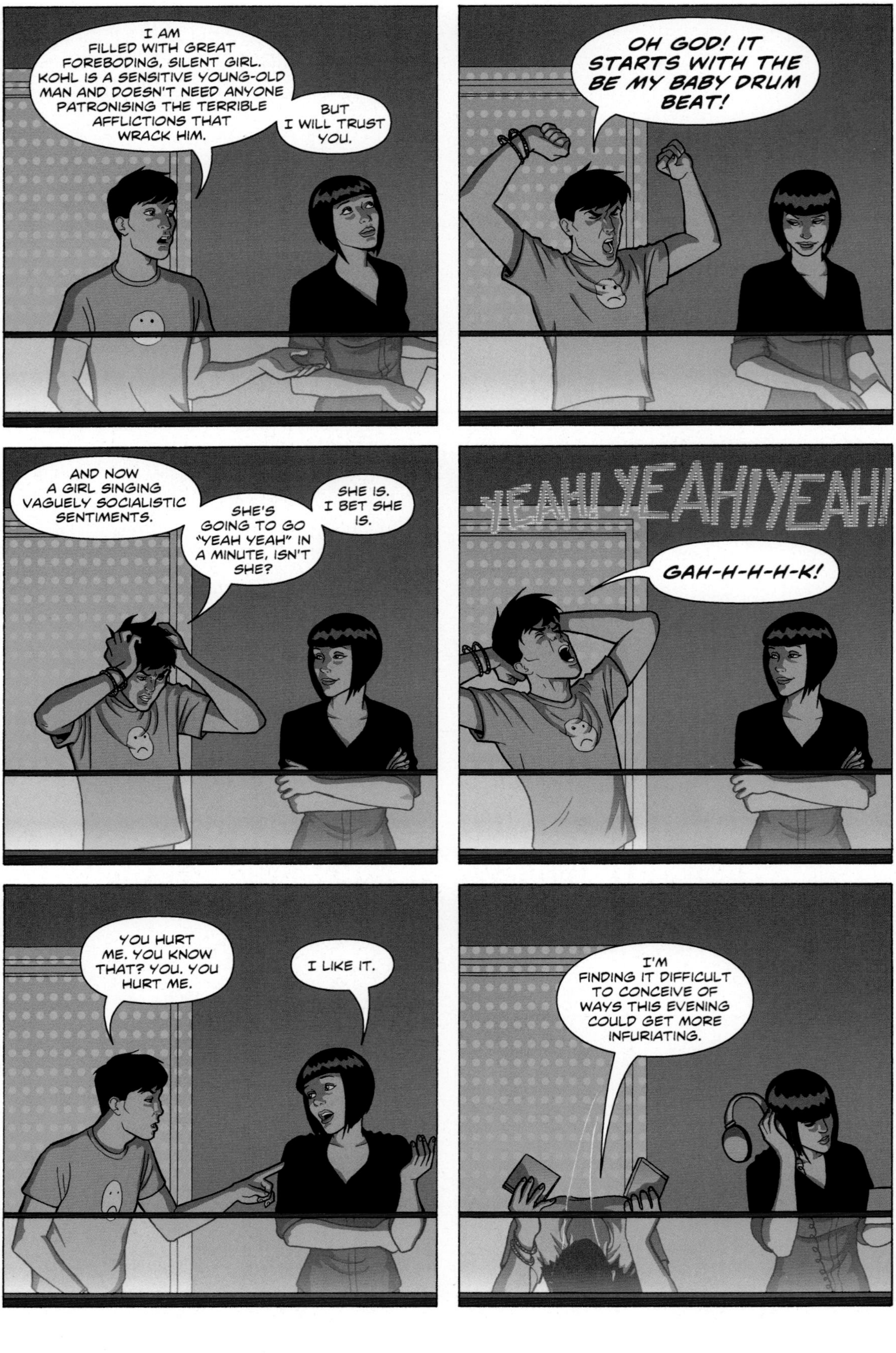

I AM FILLED WITH GREAT FOREBODING, SILENT GIRL. KOHL IS A SENSITIVE YOUNG-OLD MAN AND DOESN'T NEED ANYONE PATRONISING THE TERRIBLE AFFLICTIONS THAT WRACK HIM.
BUT I WILL TRUST YOU.
OH GOD! IT STARTS WITH THE BE MY BABY DRUM BEAT!
AND NOW A GIRL SINGING VAGUELY SOCIALISTIC SENTIMENTS.
SHE'S GOING TO GO "YEAH YEAH" IN A MINUTE, ISN'T SHE?
SHE IS. I BET SHE IS.
YEAH! YEAH! YEAH!
GAH-H-H-H-K!
YOU HURT ME. YOU KNOW THAT? YOU. YOU HURT ME.
I LIKE IT.
I'M FINDING IT DIFFICULT TO CONCEIVE OF WAYS THIS EVENING COULD GET MORE INFURIATING.

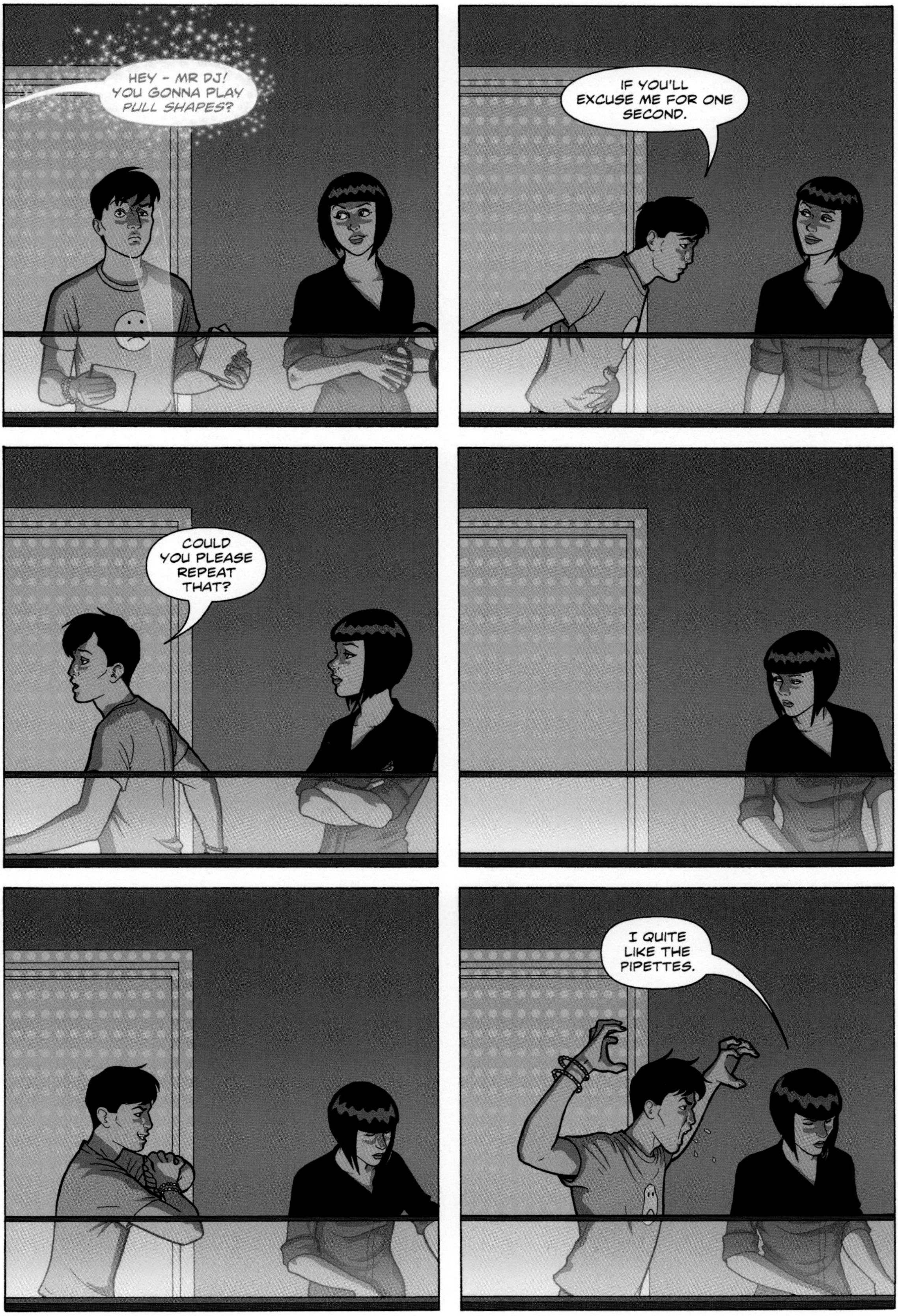
HEY - MR DJ! YOU GONNA PLAY PULL SHAPES?
IF YOU'LL EXCUSE ME FOR ONE SECOND.
COULD YOU PLEASE REPEAT THAT?
I QUITE LIKE THE PIPETTES.

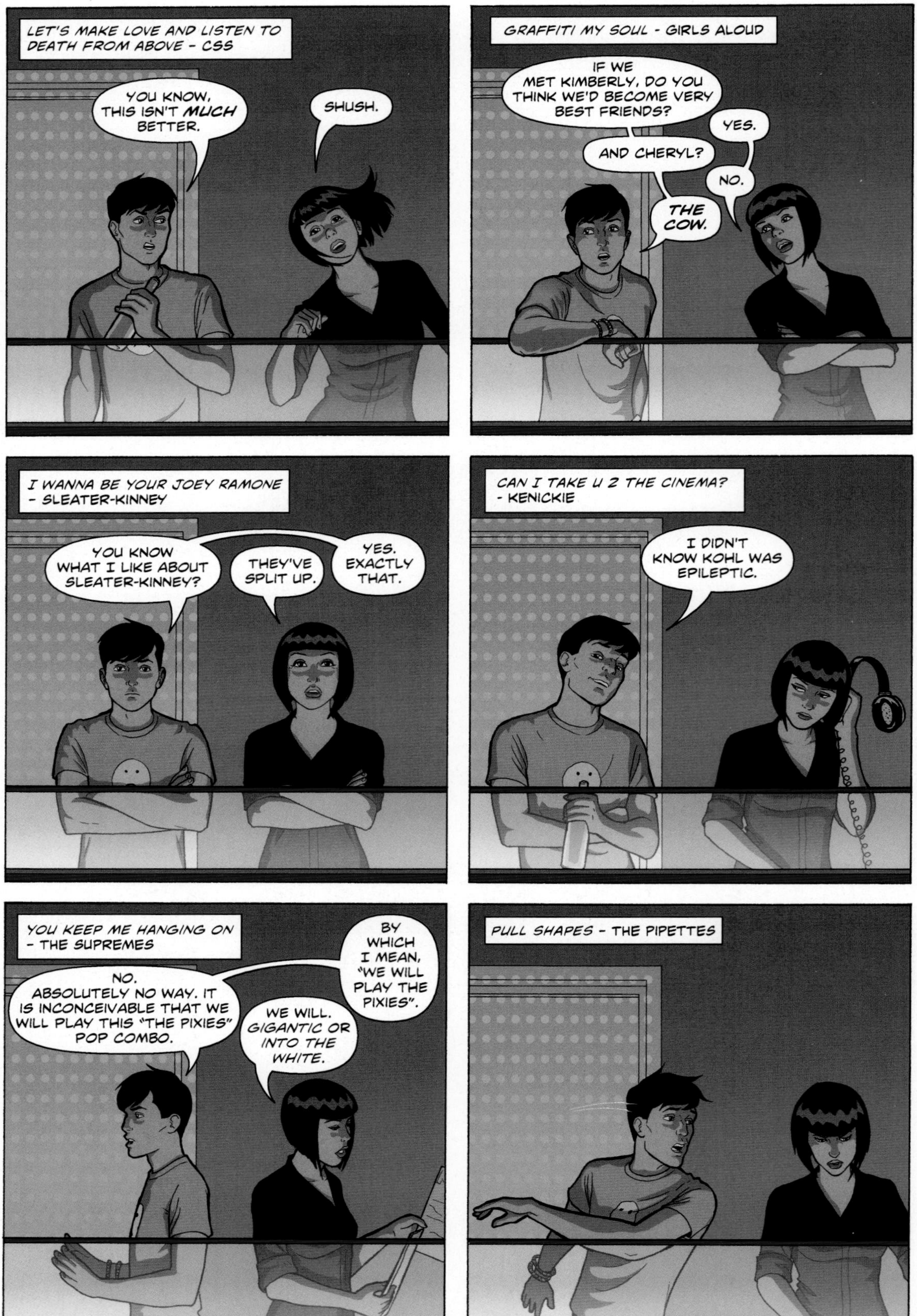
LET'S MAKE LOVE AND LISTEN TO DEATH FROM ABOVE – CSS
YOU KNOW, THIS ISN'T MUCH BETTER.
SHUSH.
GRAFFITI MY SOUL – GIRLS ALOUD
IF WE MET KIMBERLY, DO YOU THINK WE'D BECOME VERY BEST FRIENDS?
YES.
AND CHERYL?
NO.
THE COW.
I WANNA BE YOUR JOEY RAMONE – SLEATER-KINNEY
YOU KNOW WHAT I LIKE ABOUT SLEATER-KINNEY?
THEY'VE SPLIT UP.
YES. EXACTLY THAT.
CAN I TAKE U 2 THE CINEMA? – KENICKIE
I DIDN'T KNOW KOHL WAS EPILEPTIC.
YOU KEEP ME HANGING ON – THE SUPREMES
NO. ABSOLUTELY NO WAY. IT IS INCONCEIVABLE THAT WE WILL PLAY THIS "THE PIXIES" POP COMBO.
BY WHICH I MEAN, "WE WILL PLAY THE PIXIES".
WE WILL. GIGANTIC OR INTO THE WHITE.
PULL SHAPES – THE PIPETTES

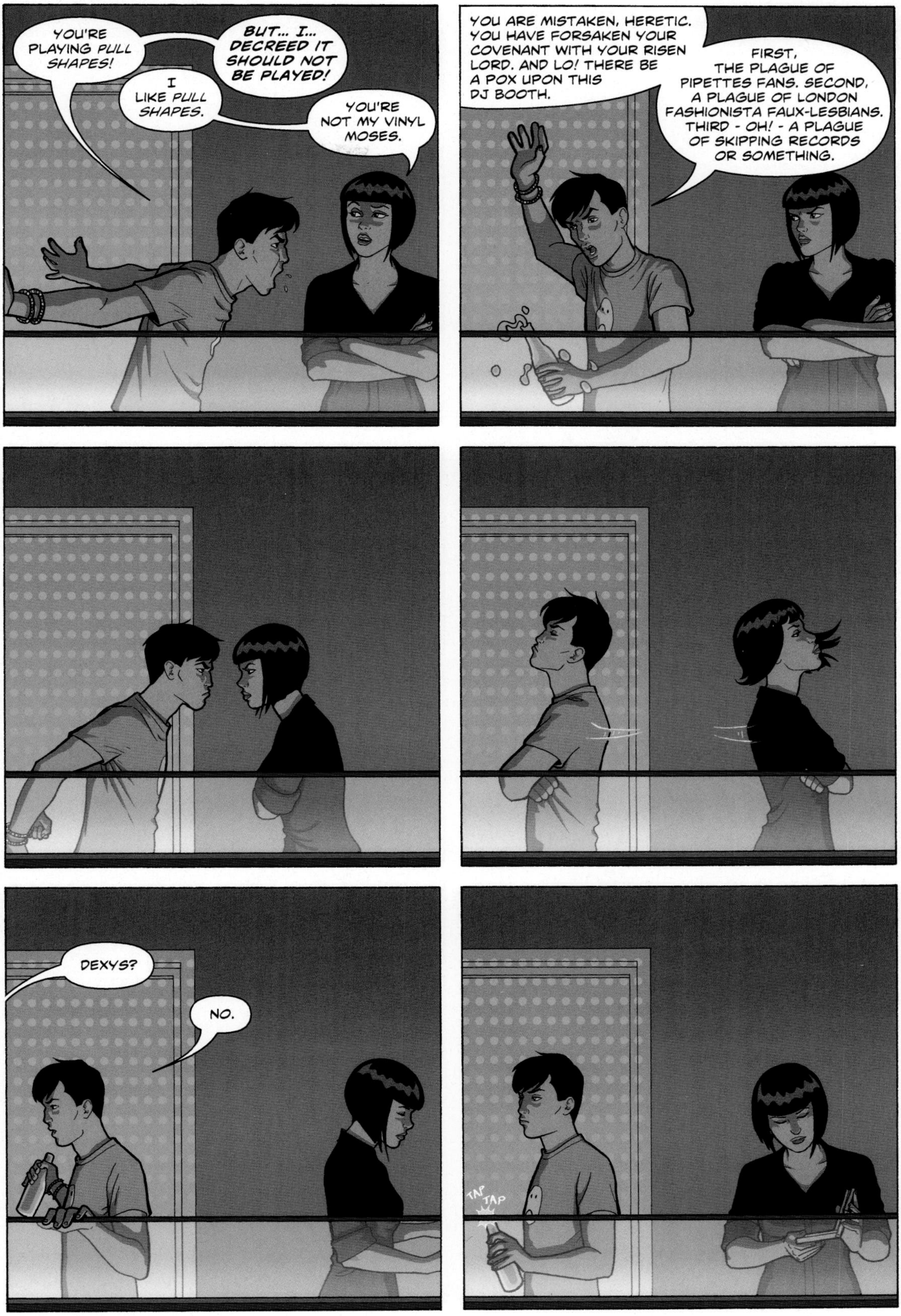
YOU'RE PLAYING PULL SHAPES!
BUT... I... DECREED IT SHOULD NOT BE PLAYED!
I LIKE PULL SHAPES.
YOU'RE NOT MY VINYL MOSES.
YOU ARE MISTAKEN, HERETIC. YOU HAVE FORSAKEN YOUR COVENANT WITH YOUR RISEN LORD. AND LO! THERE BE A POX UPON THIS DJ BOOTH.
FIRST, THE PLAGUE OF PIPETTES FANS. SECOND, A PLAGUE OF LONDON FASHIONISTA FAUX-LESBIANS. THIRD - OH! - A PLAGUE OF SKIPPING RECORDS OR SOMETHING.
DEXYS?
NO.
TAP TAP

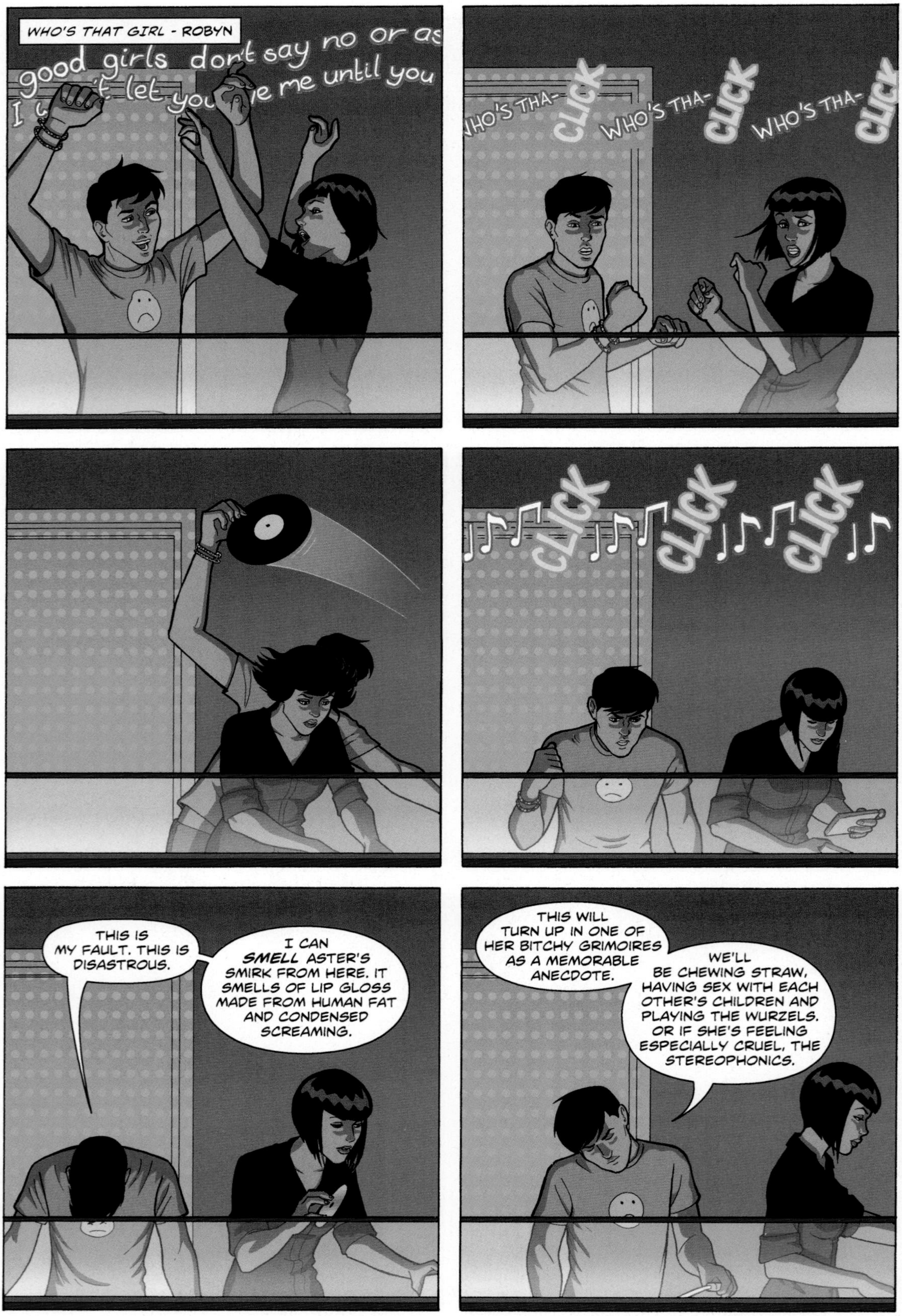
WHO'S THAT GIRL - ROBYN
good girls don't say no or as
WHO'S THA- CLICK WHO'S THA- CLICK WHO'S THA- CLICK
CLICK CLICK CLICK
THIS IS MY FAULT. THIS IS DISASTROUS.
I CAN *SMELL* ASTER'S SMIRK FROM HERE. IT SMELLS OF LIP GLOSS MADE FROM HUMAN FAT AND CONDENSED SCREAMING.
THIS WILL TURN UP IN ONE OF HER BITCHY GRIMOIRES AS A MEMORABLE ANECDOTE.
WE'LL BE CHEWING STRAW, HAVING SEX WITH EACH OTHER'S CHILDREN AND PLAYING THE WURZELS. OR IF SHE'S FEELING ESPECIALLY CRUEL, THE STEREOPHONICS.

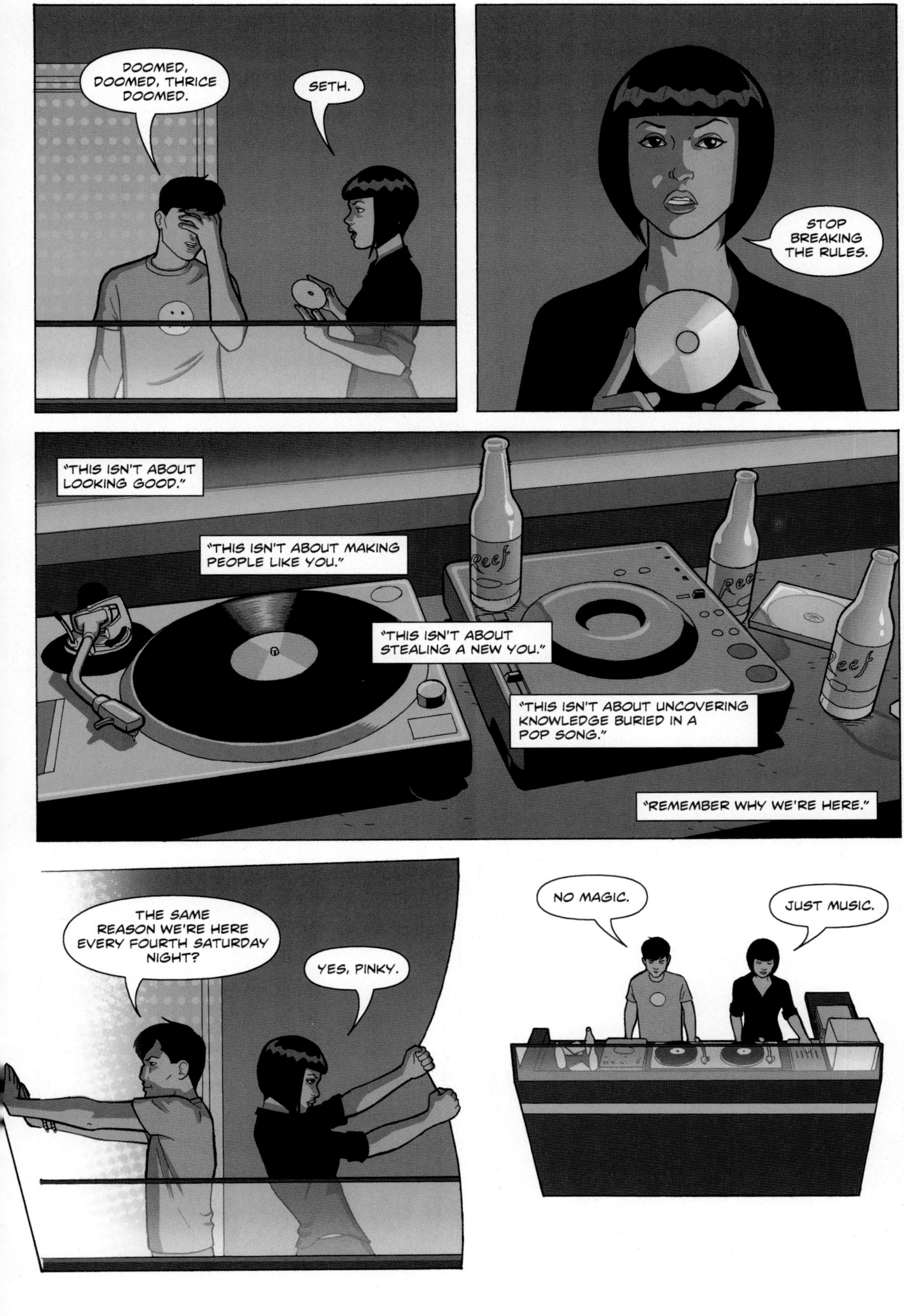
DOOMED, DOOMED, THRICE DOOMED.
SETH.
STOP BREAKING THE RULES.
"THIS ISN'T ABOUT LOOKING GOOD."
"THIS ISN'T ABOUT MAKING PEOPLE LIKE YOU."
"THIS ISN'T ABOUT STEALING A NEW YOU."
"THIS ISN'T ABOUT UNCOVERING KNOWLEDGE BURIED IN A POP SONG."
"REMEMBER WHY WE'RE HERE."
THE SAME REASON WE'RE HERE EVERY FOURTH SATURDAY NIGHT?
YES, PINKY.
NO MAGIC.
JUST MUSIC.

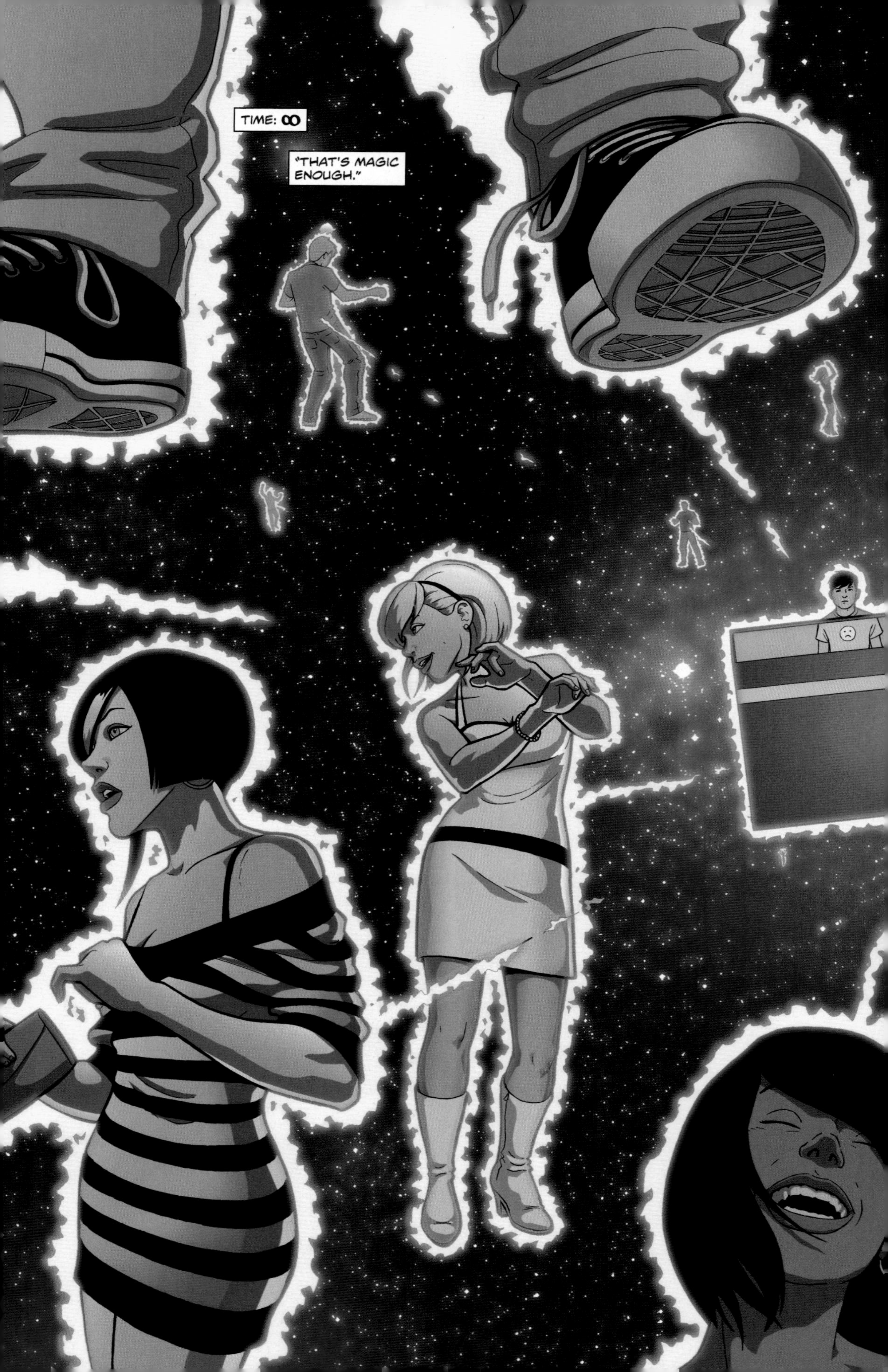
TIME: ∞
"THAT'S MAGIC ENOUGH."

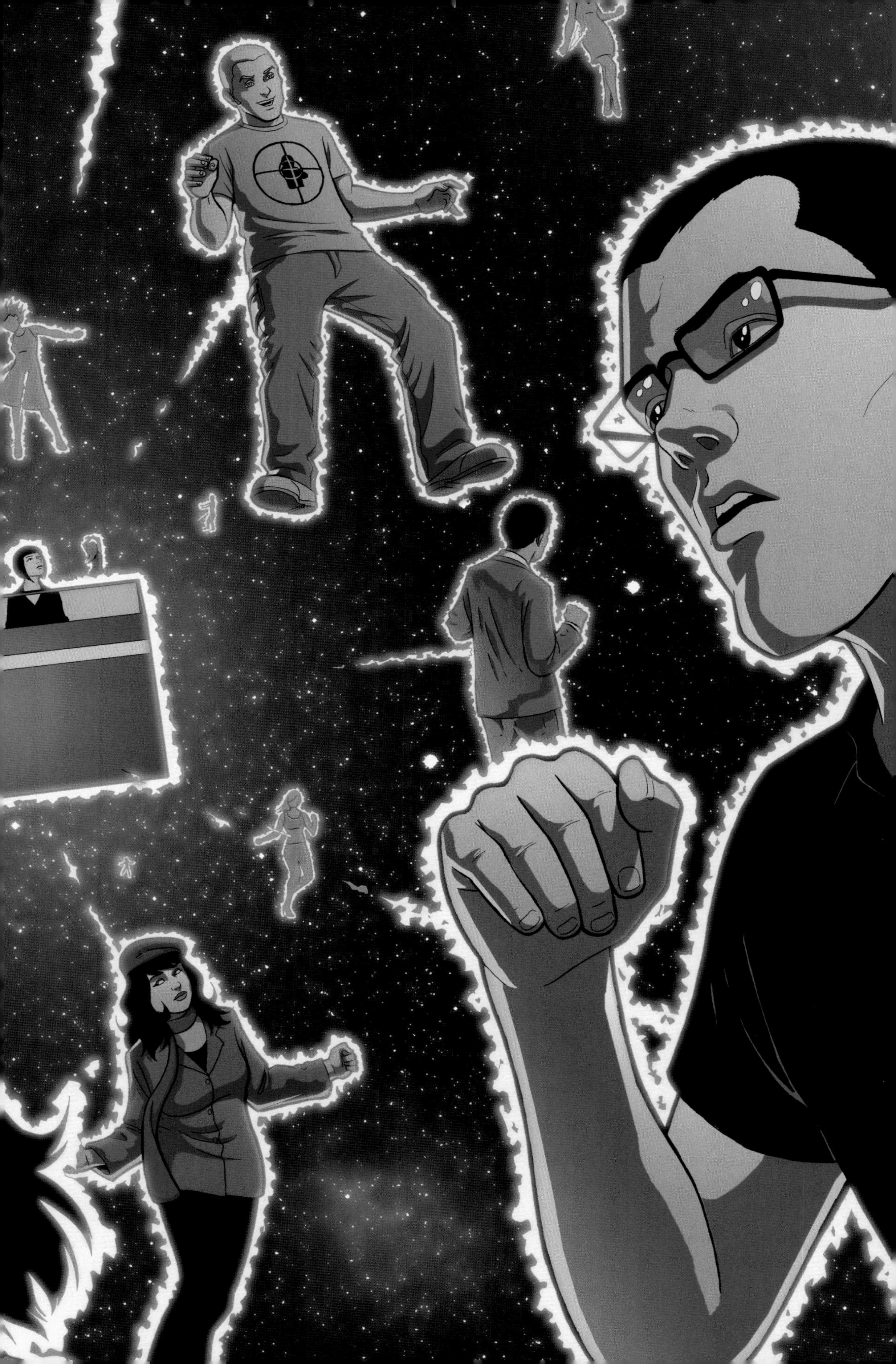

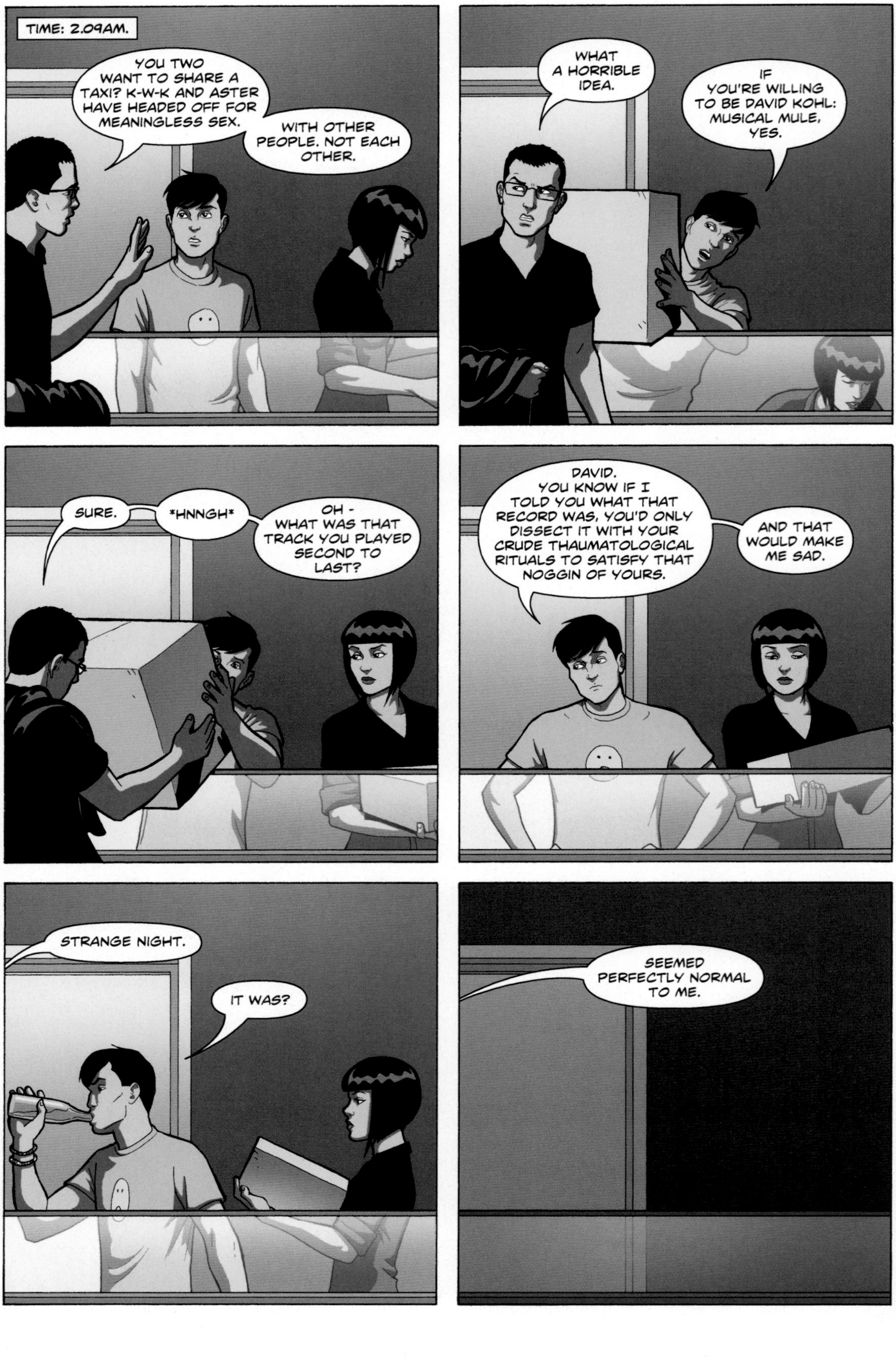
TIME: 2.09AM.
YOU TWO WANT TO SHARE A TAXI? K-W-K AND ASTER HAVE HEADED OFF FOR MEANINGLESS SEX.
WITH OTHER PEOPLE. NOT EACH OTHER.
WHAT A HORRIBLE IDEA.
IF YOU'RE WILLING TO BE DAVID KOHL: MUSICAL MULE, YES.
SURE.
HNNGH
OH - WHAT WAS THAT TRACK YOU PLAYED SECOND TO LAST?
DAVID. YOU KNOW IF I TOLD YOU WHAT THAT RECORD WAS, YOU'D ONLY DISSECT IT WITH YOUR CRUDE THAUMATOLOGICAL RITUALS TO SATISFY THAT NOGGIN OF YOURS.
AND THAT WOULD MAKE ME SAD.
STRANGE NIGHT.
IT WAS?
SEEMED PERFECTLY NORMAL TO ME.

PHONOGRAM

THE SINGLES CLUB

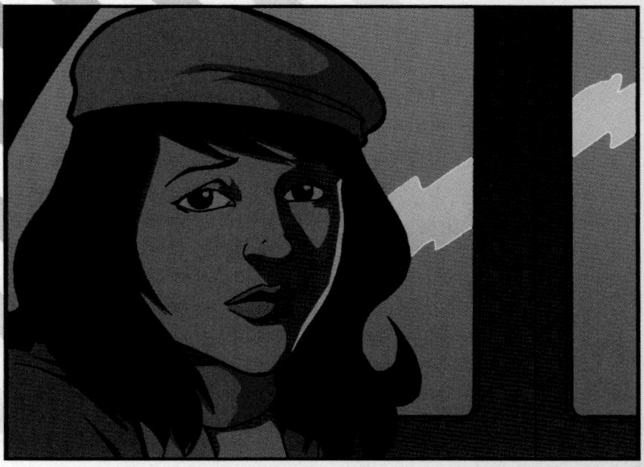

5. "LUST, ETC."

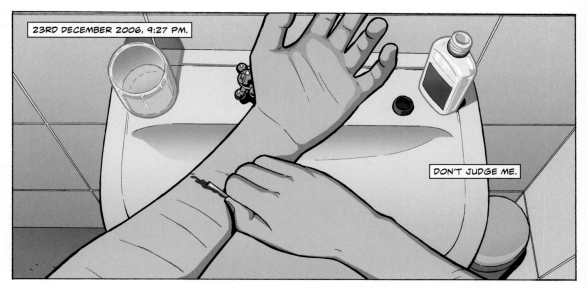

23RD DECEMBER 2006, 9:27 PM.

DON'T JUDGE ME.

"PEOPLE THINK I'M BEING PERVERSE ON PURPOSE."*

I'M NOT. I'M JUST ME. AND I'M WORKING ON THAT.

*Fulwood Babylon, Long Blondes

I'M A PHONOMANCER.

BUT DON'T BE CONFUSED.

THIS ISN'T MAGIC.

THIS IS THE FURTHEST THING AWAY FROM MAGIC.

THIS IS WHAT I'M RUNNING FROM.

THIS IS ME.

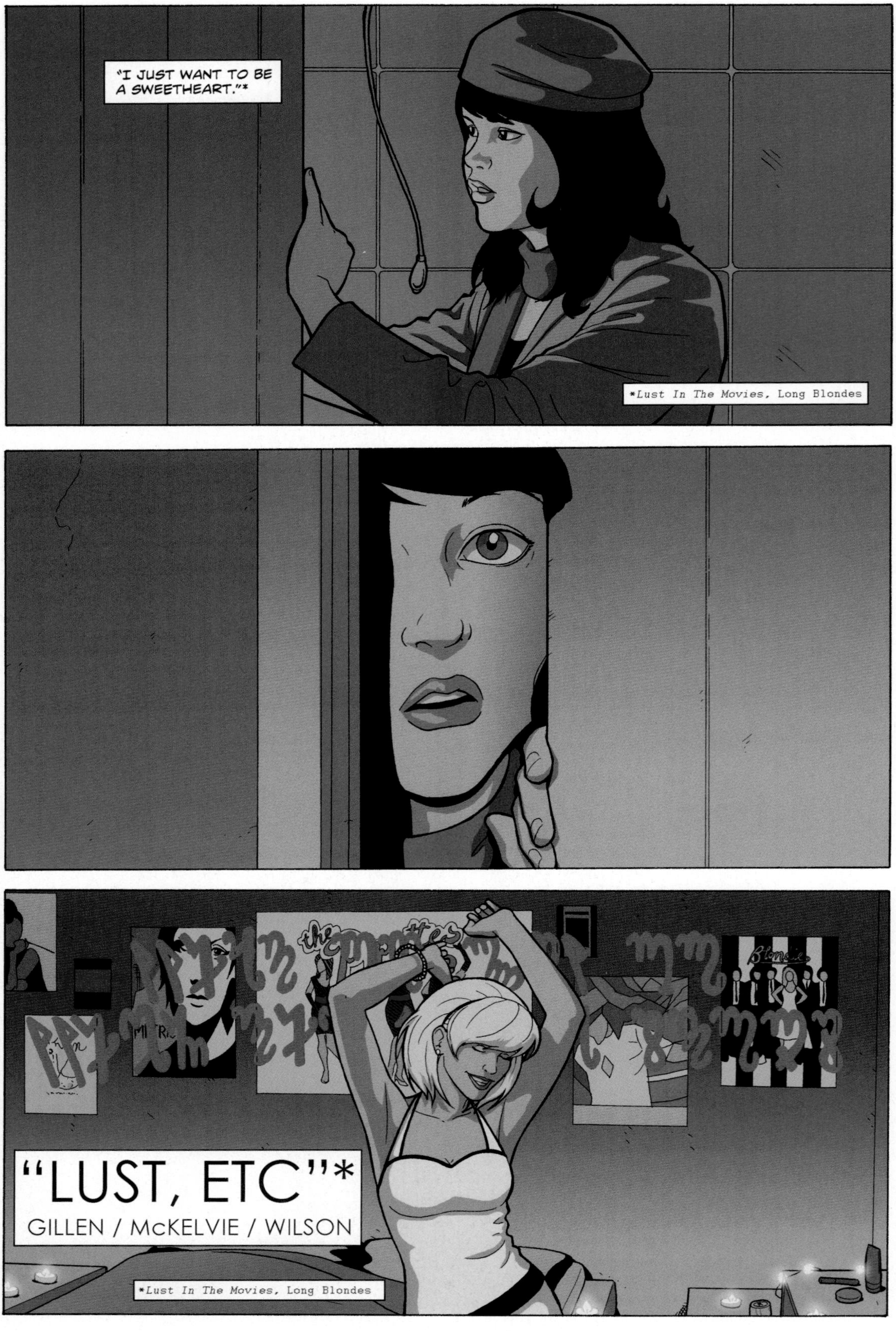
"I JUST WANT TO BE A SWEETHEART."*
*Lust In The Movies, Long Blondes
"LUST, ETC"*
GILLEN / McKELVIE / WILSON
*Lust In The Movies, Long Blondes

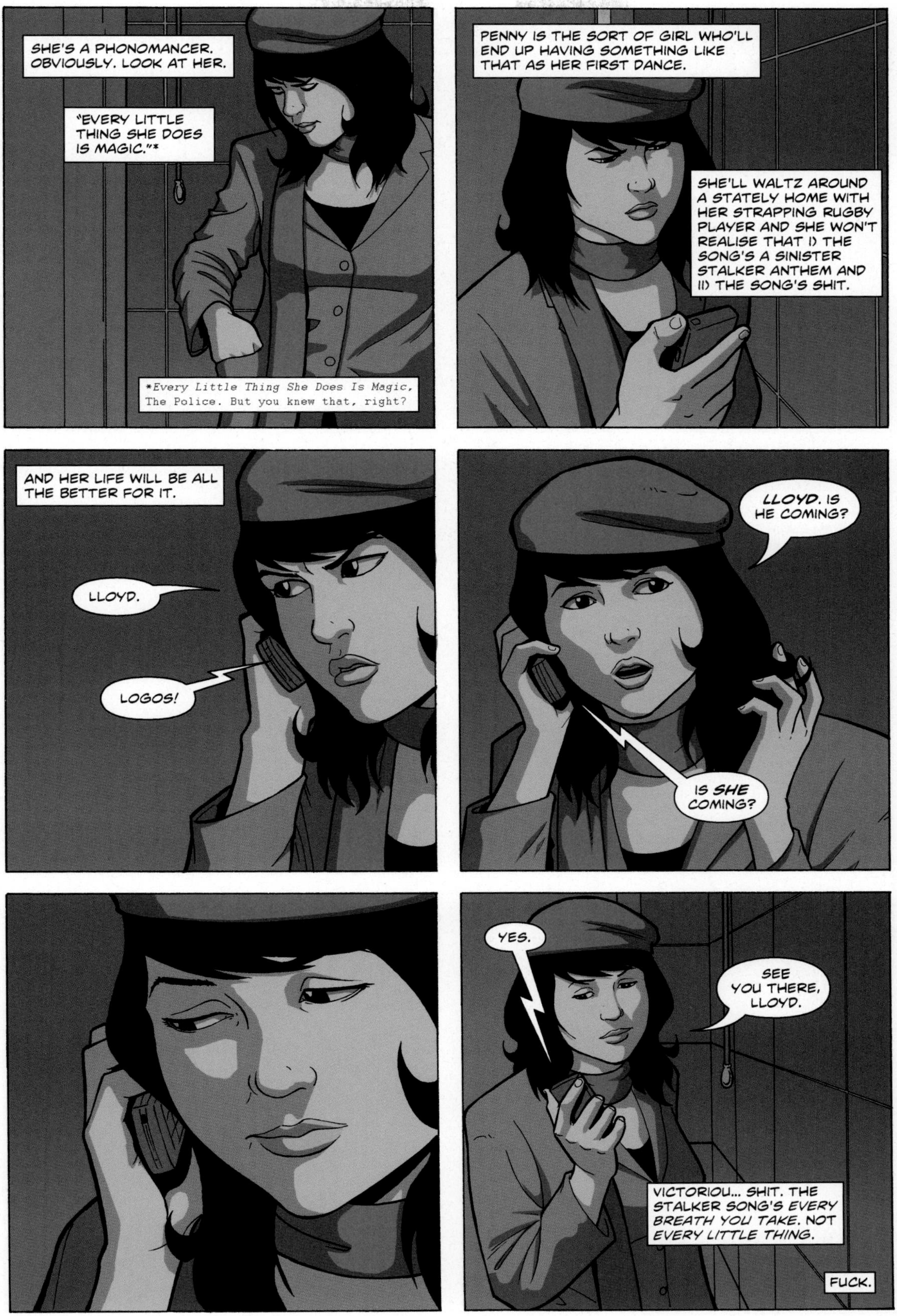
SHE'S A PHONOMANCER. OBVIOUSLY. LOOK AT HER.
"EVERY LITTLE THING SHE DOES IS MAGIC."*
*Every Little Thing She Does Is Magic, The Police. But you knew that, right?
PENNY IS THE SORT OF GIRL WHO'LL END UP HAVING SOMETHING LIKE THAT AS HER FIRST DANCE.
SHE'LL WALTZ AROUND A STATELY HOME WITH HER STRAPPING RUGBY PLAYER AND SHE WON'T REALISE THAT I) THE SONG'S A SINISTER STALKER ANTHEM AND II) THE SONG'S SHIT.
AND HER LIFE WILL BE ALL THE BETTER FOR IT.
LLOYD.
LOGOS!
LLOYD. IS HE COMING?
IS SHE COMING?
YES.
SEE YOU THERE, LLOYD.
VICTORIOU... SHIT. THE STALKER SONG'S EVERY BREATH YOU TAKE. NOT EVERY LITTLE THING.
FUCK.

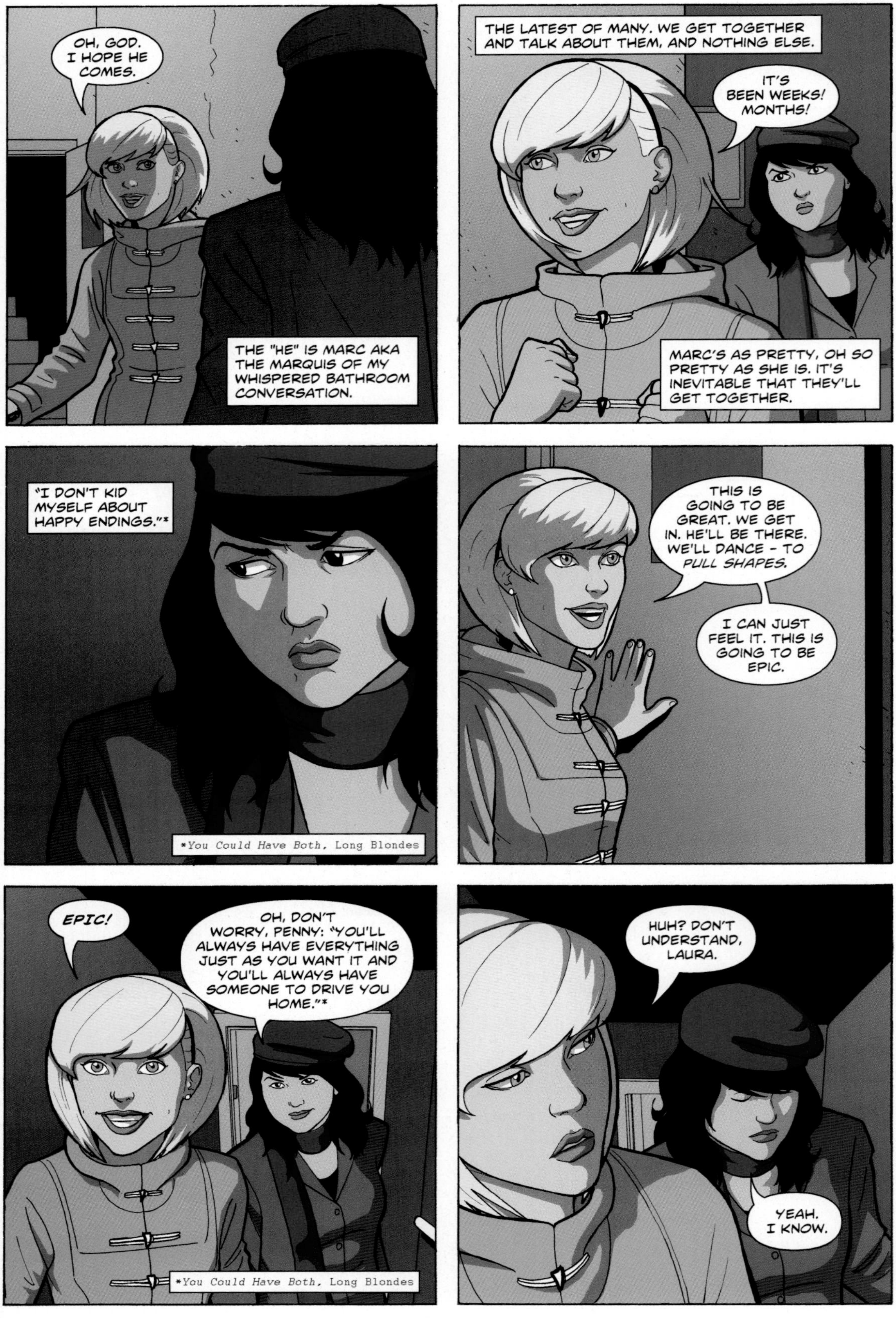
OH, GOD. I HOPE HE COMES.
THE "HE" IS MARC AKA THE MARQUIS OF MY WHISPERED BATHROOM CONVERSATION.
THE LATEST OF MANY. WE GET TOGETHER AND TALK ABOUT THEM, AND NOTHING ELSE.
IT'S BEEN WEEKS! MONTHS!
MARC'S AS PRETTY, OH SO PRETTY AS SHE IS. IT'S INEVITABLE THAT THEY'LL GET TOGETHER.
"I DON'T KID MYSELF ABOUT HAPPY ENDINGS."*
*You Could Have Both, Long Blondes
THIS IS GOING TO BE GREAT. WE GET IN. HE'LL BE THERE. WE'LL DANCE - TO PULL SHAPES.
I CAN JUST FEEL IT. THIS IS GOING TO BE EPIC.
EPIC!
OH, DON'T WORRY, PENNY: "YOU'LL ALWAYS HAVE EVERYTHING JUST AS YOU WANT IT AND YOU'LL ALWAYS HAVE SOMEONE TO DRIVE YOU HOME."*
*You Could Have Both, Long Blondes
HUH? DON'T UNDERSTAND, LAURA.
YEAH. I KNOW.

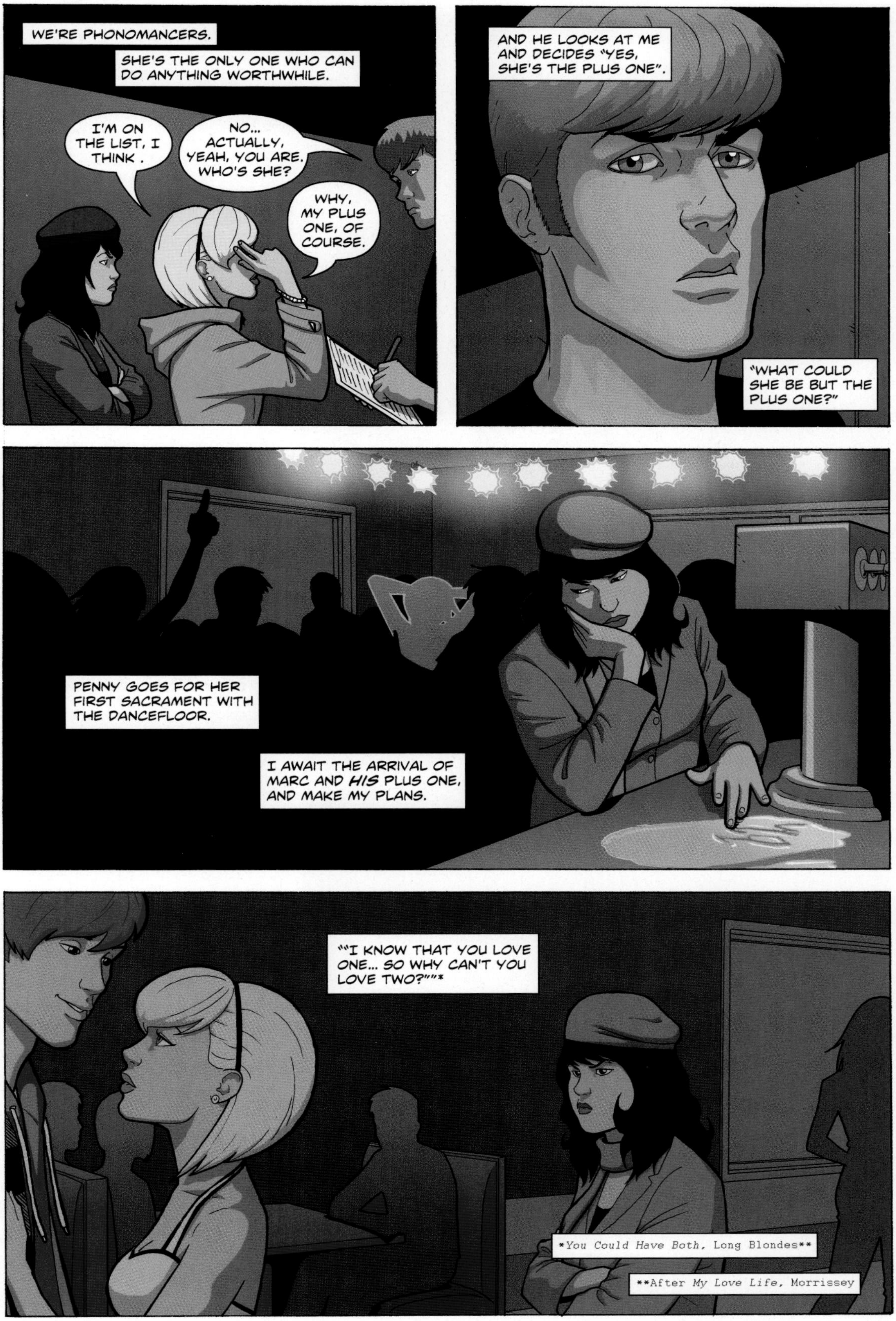
WE'RE PHONOMANCERS.
SHE'S THE ONLY ONE WHO CAN DO ANYTHING WORTHWHILE.
I'M ON THE LIST, I THINK .
NO... ACTUALLY, YEAH, YOU ARE. WHO'S SHE?
WHY, MY PLUS ONE, OF COURSE.
AND HE LOOKS AT ME AND DECIDES "YES, SHE'S THE PLUS ONE".
"WHAT COULD SHE BE BUT THE PLUS ONE?"
PENNY GOES FOR HER FIRST SACRAMENT WITH THE DANCEFLOOR.
I AWAIT THE ARRIVAL OF MARC AND *HIS* PLUS ONE, AND MAKE MY PLANS.
""I KNOW THAT YOU LOVE ONE... SO WHY CAN'T YOU LOVE TWO?""*
*You Could Have Both, Long Blondes**
**After *My Love Life*, Morrissey

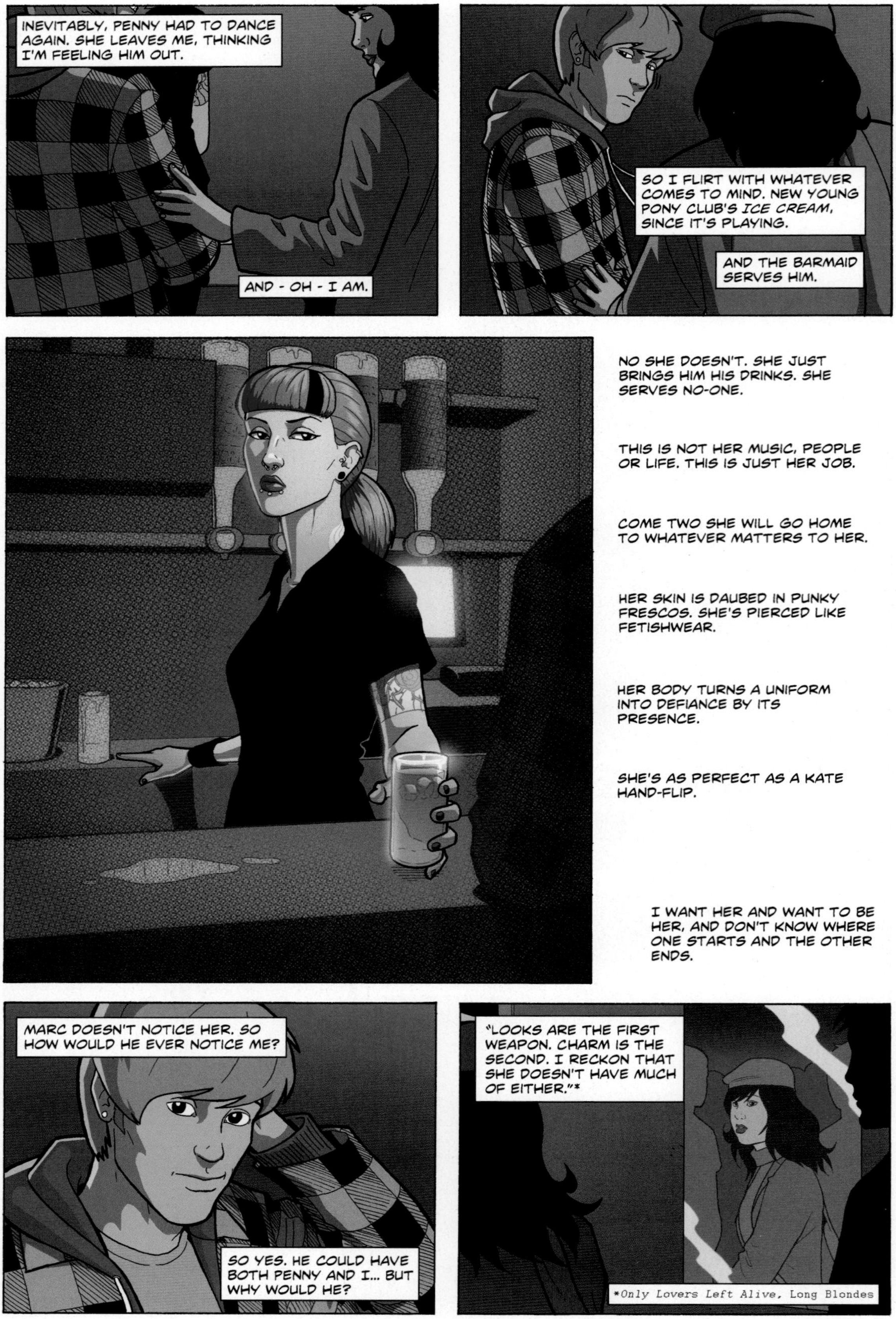
INEVITABLY, PENNY HAD TO DANCE AGAIN. SHE LEAVES ME, THINKING I'M FEELING HIM OUT.
AND - OH - I AM.
SO I FLIRT WITH WHATEVER COMES TO MIND. NEW YOUNG PONY CLUB'S *ICE CREAM*, SINCE IT'S PLAYING.
AND THE BARMAID SERVES HIM.
NO SHE DOESN'T. SHE JUST BRINGS HIM HIS DRINKS. SHE SERVES NO-ONE.
THIS IS NOT HER MUSIC, PEOPLE OR LIFE. THIS IS JUST HER JOB.
COME TWO SHE WILL GO HOME TO WHATEVER MATTERS TO HER.
HER SKIN IS DAUBED IN PUNKY FRESCOS. SHE'S PIERCED LIKE FETISHWEAR.
HER BODY TURNS A UNIFORM INTO DEFIANCE BY ITS PRESENCE.
SHE'S AS PERFECT AS A KATE HAND-FLIP.
I WANT HER AND WANT TO BE HER, AND DON'T KNOW WHERE ONE STARTS AND THE OTHER ENDS.
MARC DOESN'T NOTICE HER. SO HOW WOULD HE EVER NOTICE ME?
SO YES. HE COULD HAVE BOTH PENNY AND I... BUT WHY WOULD HE?
"LOOKS ARE THE FIRST WEAPON. CHARM IS THE SECOND. I RECKON THAT SHE DOESN'T HAVE MUCH OF EITHER."*
*Only Lovers Left Alive, Long Blondes

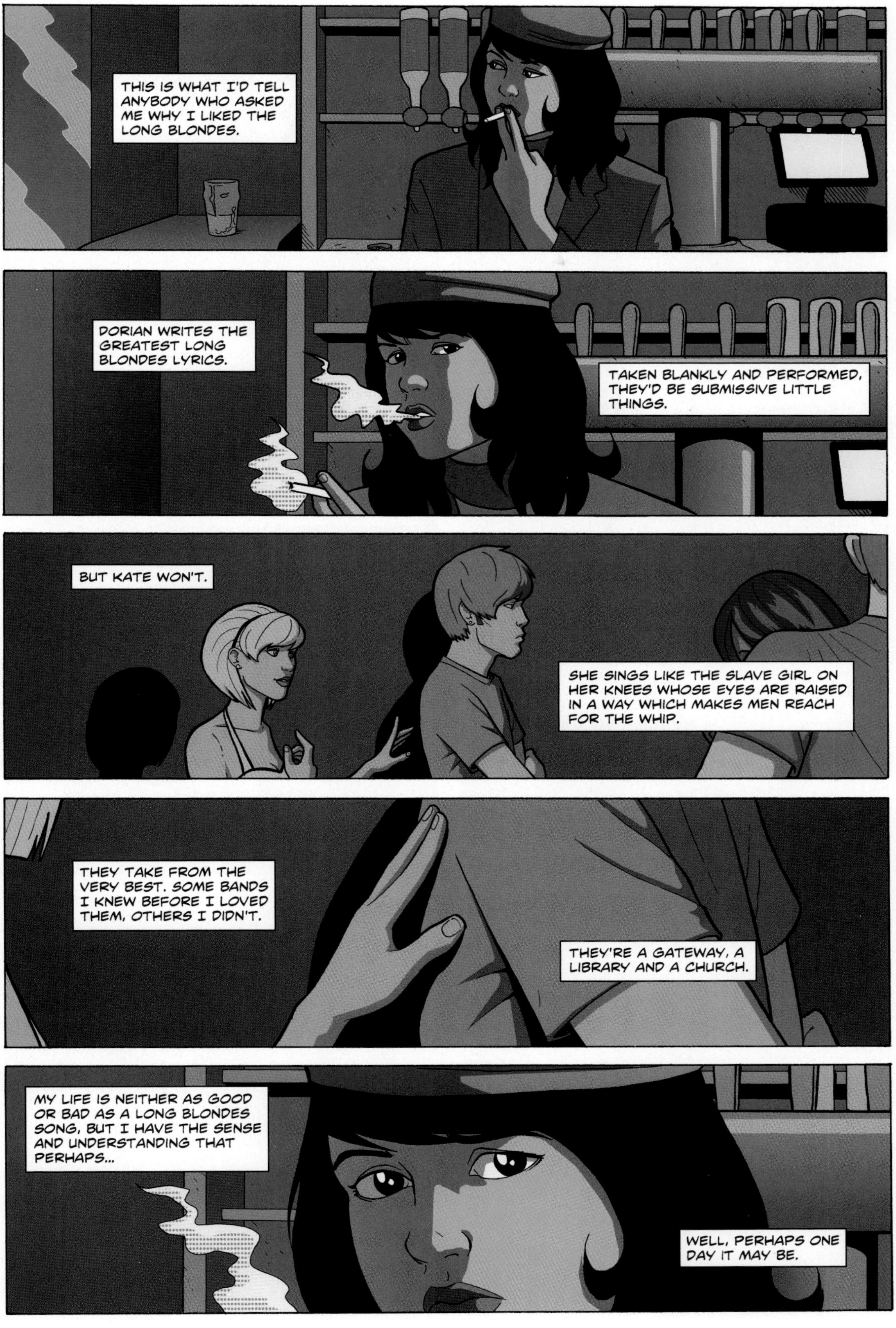
THIS IS WHAT I'D TELL ANYBODY WHO ASKED ME WHY I LIKED THE LONG BLONDES.
DORIAN WRITES THE GREATEST LONG BLONDES LYRICS.
TAKEN BLANKLY AND PERFORMED, THEY'D BE SUBMISSIVE LITTLE THINGS.
BUT KATE WON'T.
SHE SINGS LIKE THE SLAVE GIRL ON HER KNEES WHOSE EYES ARE RAISED IN A WAY WHICH MAKES MEN REACH FOR THE WHIP.
THEY TAKE FROM THE VERY BEST. SOME BANDS I KNEW BEFORE I LOVED THEM, OTHERS I DIDN'T.
THEY'RE A GATEWAY, A LIBRARY AND A CHURCH.
MY LIFE IS NEITHER AS GOOD OR BAD AS A LONG BLONDES SONG, BUT I HAVE THE SENSE AND UNDERSTANDING THAT PERHAPS...
WELL, PERHAPS ONE DAY IT MAY BE.

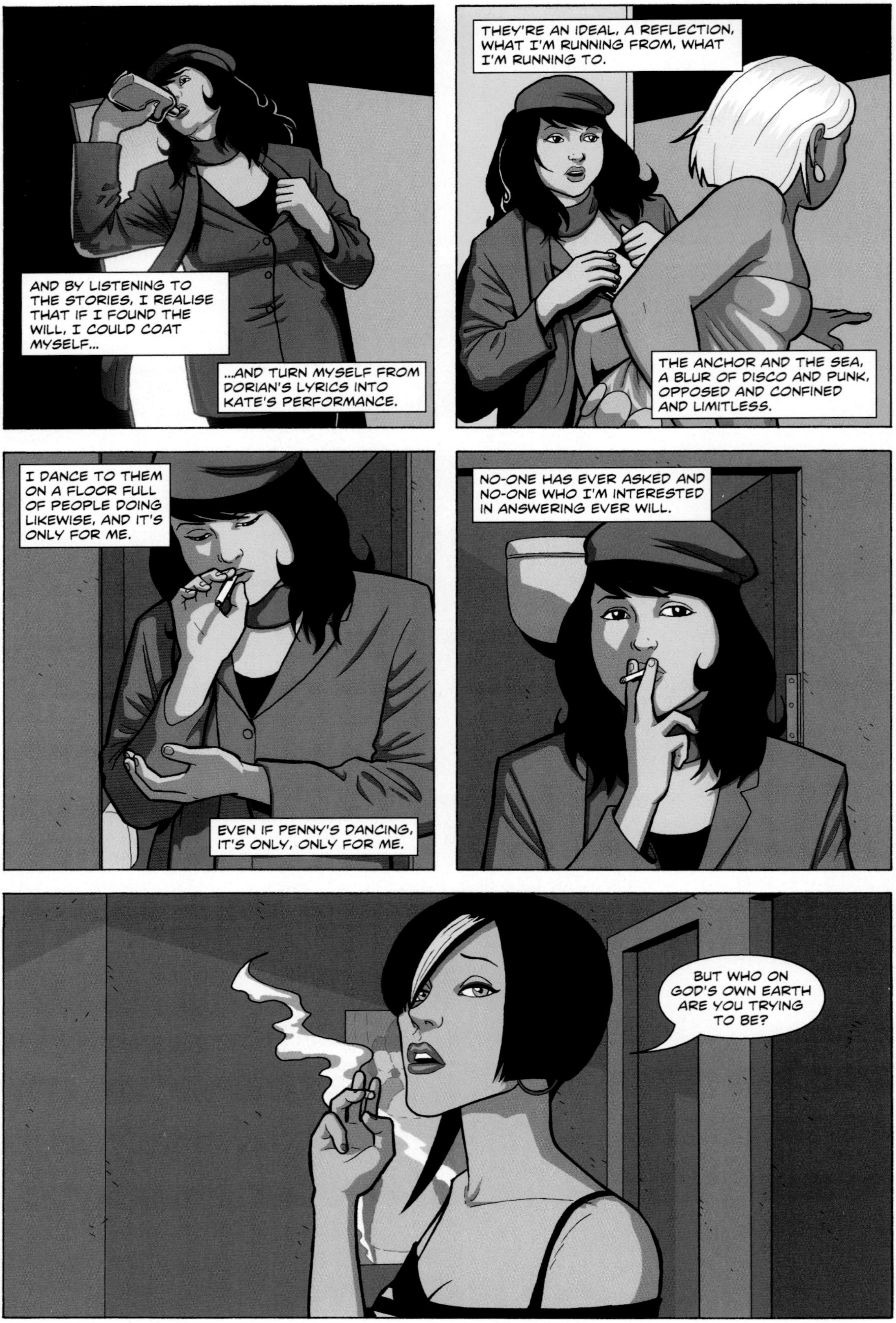
AND BY LISTENING TO THE STORIES, I REALISE THAT IF I FOUND THE WILL, I COULD COAT MYSELF...
...AND TURN MYSELF FROM DORIAN'S LYRICS INTO KATE'S PERFORMANCE.
THEY'RE AN IDEAL, A REFLECTION, WHAT I'M RUNNING FROM, WHAT I'M RUNNING TO.
THE ANCHOR AND THE SEA, A BLUR OF DISCO AND PUNK, OPPOSED AND CONFINED AND LIMITLESS.
I DANCE TO THEM ON A FLOOR FULL OF PEOPLE DOING LIKEWISE, AND IT'S ONLY FOR ME.
EVEN IF PENNY'S DANCING, IT'S ONLY, ONLY FOR ME.
NO-ONE HAS EVER ASKED AND NO-ONE WHO I'M INTERESTED IN ANSWERING EVER WILL.
BUT WHO ON GOD'S OWN EARTH ARE YOU TRYING TO BE?

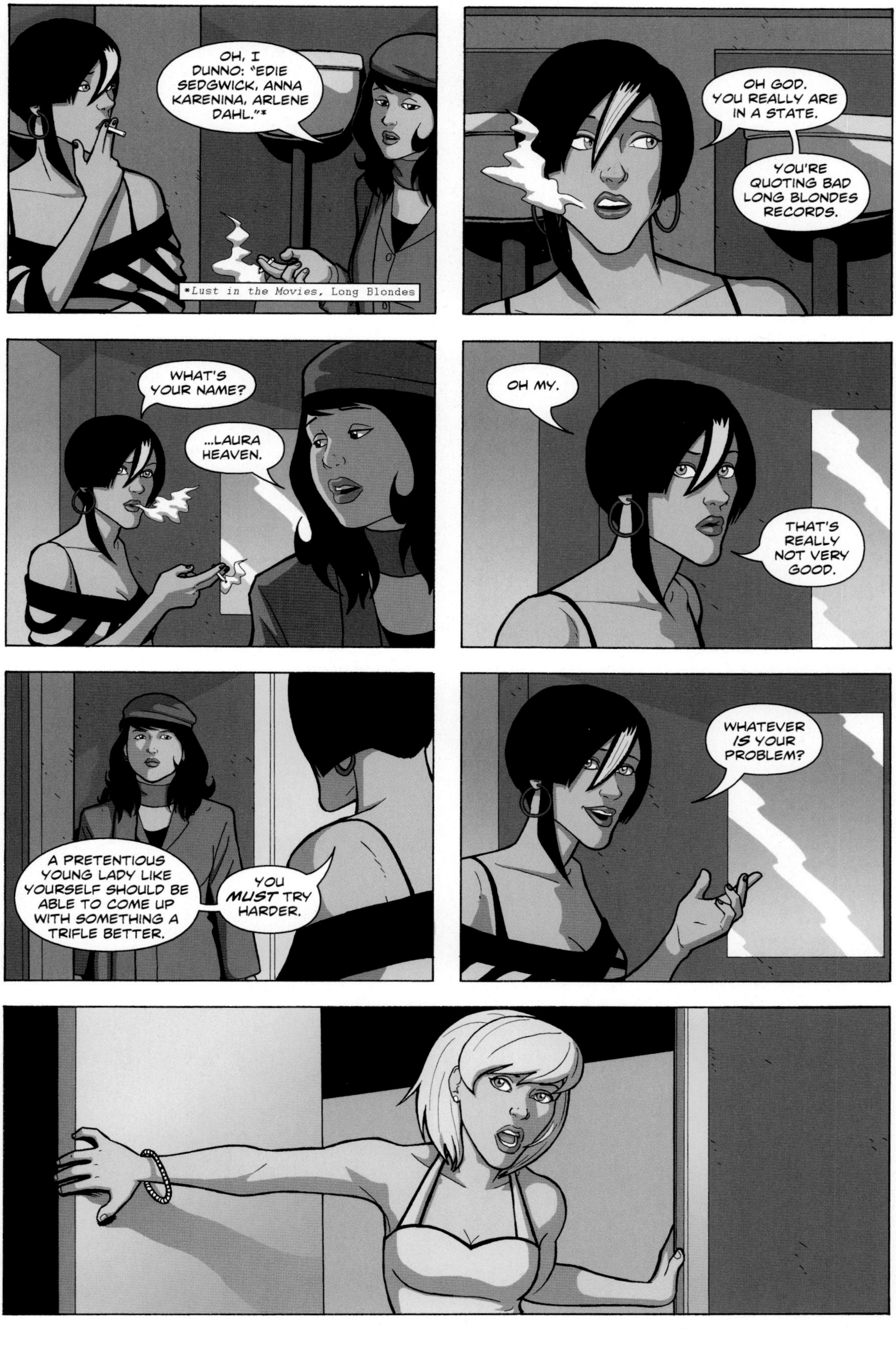
OH, I DUNNO: "EDIE SEDGWICK, ANNA KARENINA, ARLENE DAHL."*
*Lust in the Movies, Long Blondes
OH GOD. YOU REALLY ARE IN A STATE.
YOU'RE QUOTING BAD LONG BLONDES RECORDS.
WHAT'S YOUR NAME?
...LAURA HEAVEN.
OH MY.
THAT'S REALLY NOT VERY GOOD.
A PRETENTIOUS YOUNG LADY LIKE YOURSELF SHOULD BE ABLE TO COME UP WITH SOMETHING A TRIFLE BETTER.
YOU MUST TRY HARDER.
WHATEVER IS YOUR PROBLEM?

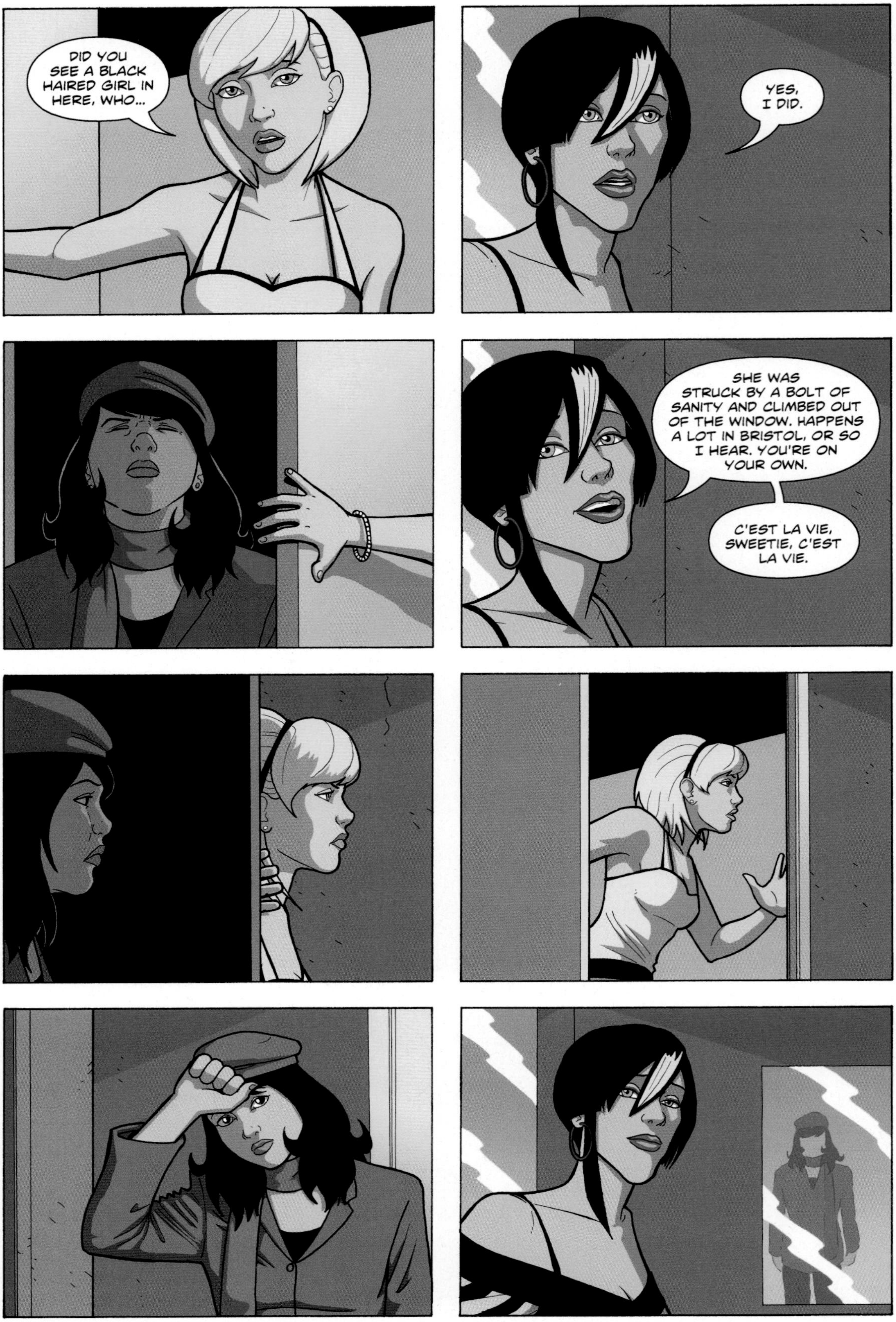
DID YOU SEE A BLACK HAIRED GIRL IN HERE, WHO...
YES, I DID.
SHE WAS STRUCK BY A BOLT OF SANITY AND CLIMBED OUT OF THE WINDOW. HAPPENS A LOT IN BRISTOL, OR SO I HEAR. YOU'RE ON YOUR OWN.
C'EST LA VIE, SWEETIE, C'EST LA VIE.

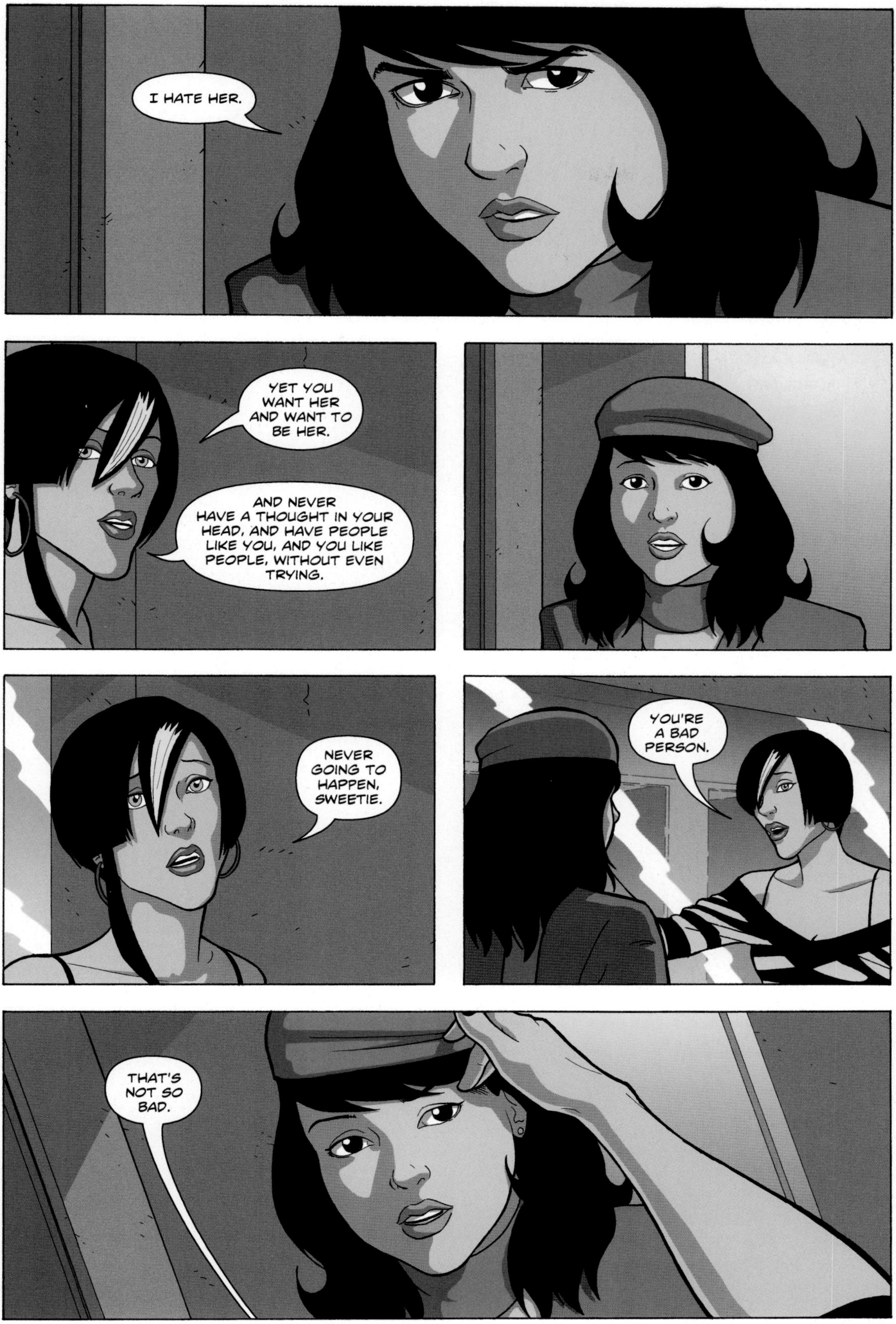
I HATE HER.
YET YOU WANT HER AND WANT TO BE HER.
AND NEVER HAVE A THOUGHT IN YOUR HEAD, AND HAVE PEOPLE LIKE YOU, AND YOU LIKE PEOPLE, WITHOUT EVEN TRYING.
NEVER GOING TO HAPPEN, SWEETIE.
YOU'RE A BAD PERSON.
THAT'S NOT SO BAD.

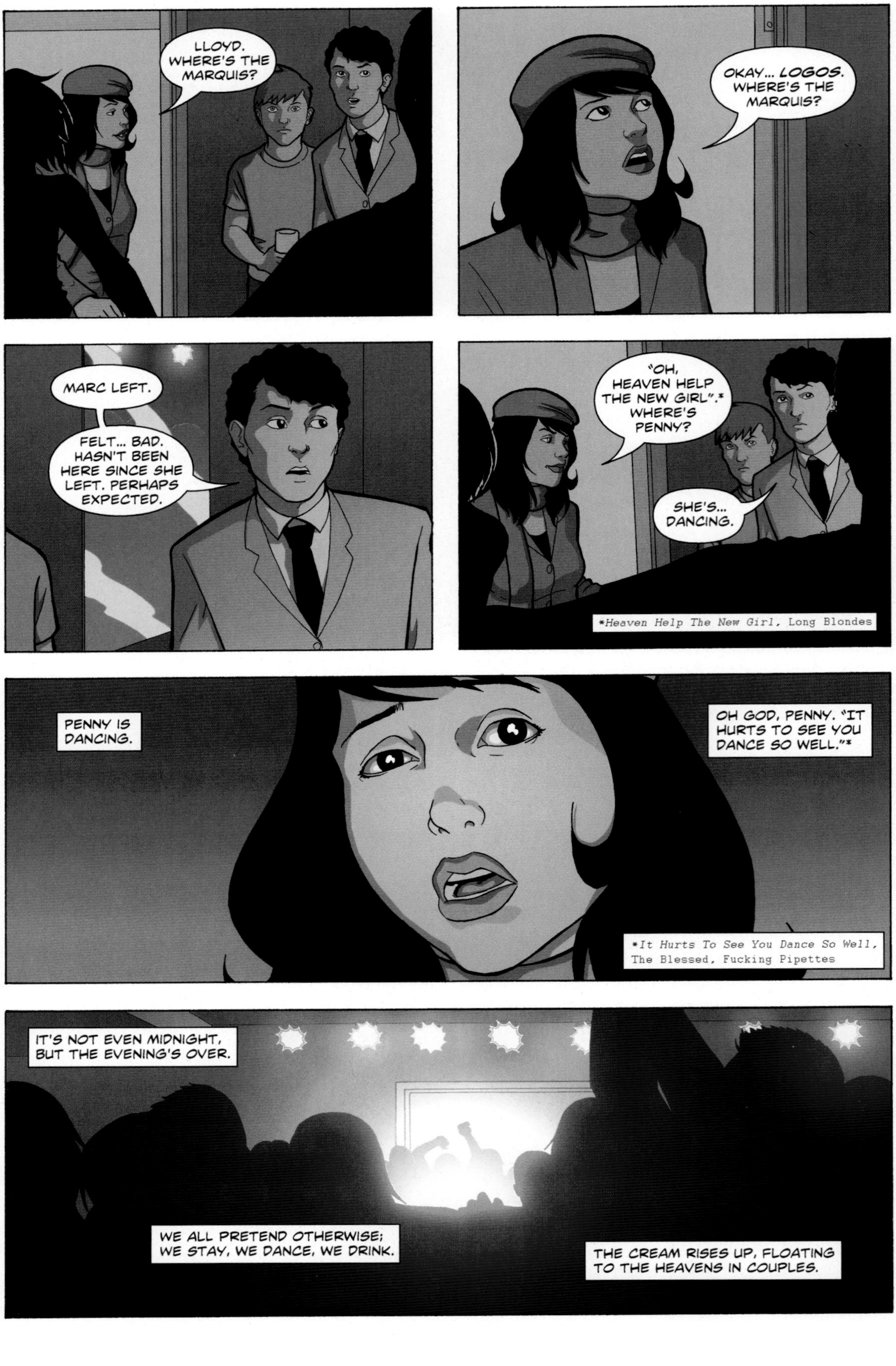
LLOYD. WHERE'S THE MARQUIS?
OKAY... *LOGOS.* WHERE'S THE MARQUIS?
MARC LEFT.
FELT... BAD. HASN'T BEEN HERE SINCE SHE LEFT. PERHAPS EXPECTED.
"OH, HEAVEN HELP THE NEW GIRL".* WHERE'S PENNY?
SHE'S... DANCING.
*Heaven Help The New Girl, Long Blondes
PENNY IS DANCING.
OH GOD, PENNY. "IT HURTS TO SEE YOU DANCE SO WELL."*
*It Hurts To See You Dance So Well, The Blessed, Fucking Pipettes
IT'S NOT EVEN MIDNIGHT, BUT THE EVENING'S OVER.
WE ALL PRETEND OTHERWISE; WE STAY, WE DANCE, WE DRINK.
THE CREAM RISES UP, FLOATING TO THE HEAVENS IN COUPLES.

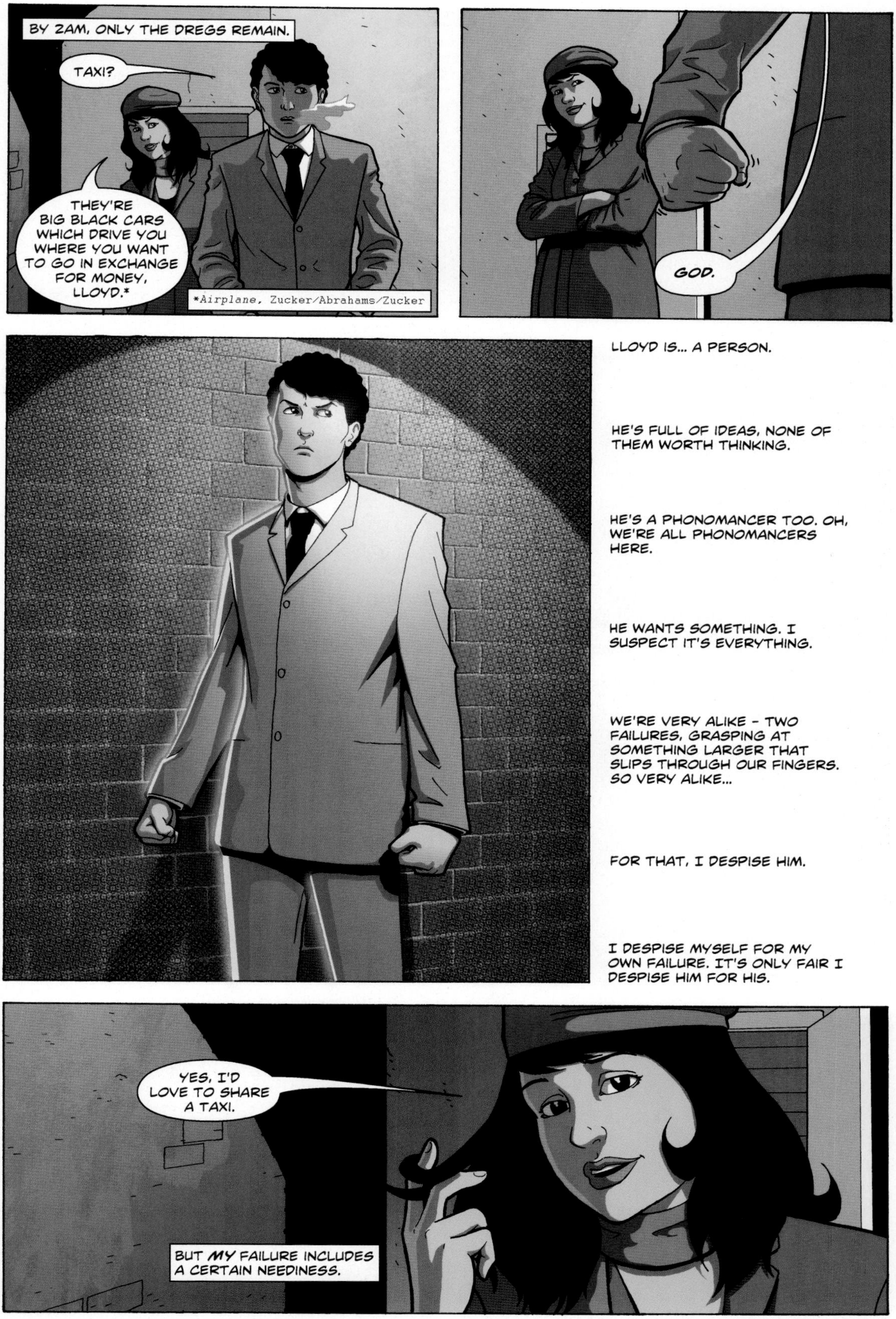
BY ZAM, ONLY THE DREGS REMAIN.
TAXI?
THEY'RE BIG BLACK CARS WHICH DRIVE YOU WHERE YOU WANT TO GO IN EXCHANGE FOR MONEY, LLOYD.*
*Airplane, Zucker/Abrahams/Zucker
GOD.
LLOYD IS... A PERSON.
HE'S FULL OF IDEAS, NONE OF THEM WORTH THINKING.
HE'S A PHONOMANCER TOO. OH, WE'RE ALL PHONOMANCERS HERE.
HE WANTS SOMETHING. I SUSPECT IT'S EVERYTHING.
WE'RE VERY ALIKE - TWO FAILURES, GRASPING AT SOMETHING LARGER THAT SLIPS THROUGH OUR FINGERS. SO VERY ALIKE...
FOR THAT, I DESPISE HIM.
I DESPISE MYSELF FOR MY OWN FAILURE. IT'S ONLY FAIR I DESPISE HIM FOR HIS.
YES, I'D LOVE TO SHARE A TAXI.
BUT MY FAILURE INCLUDES A CERTAIN NEEDINESS.

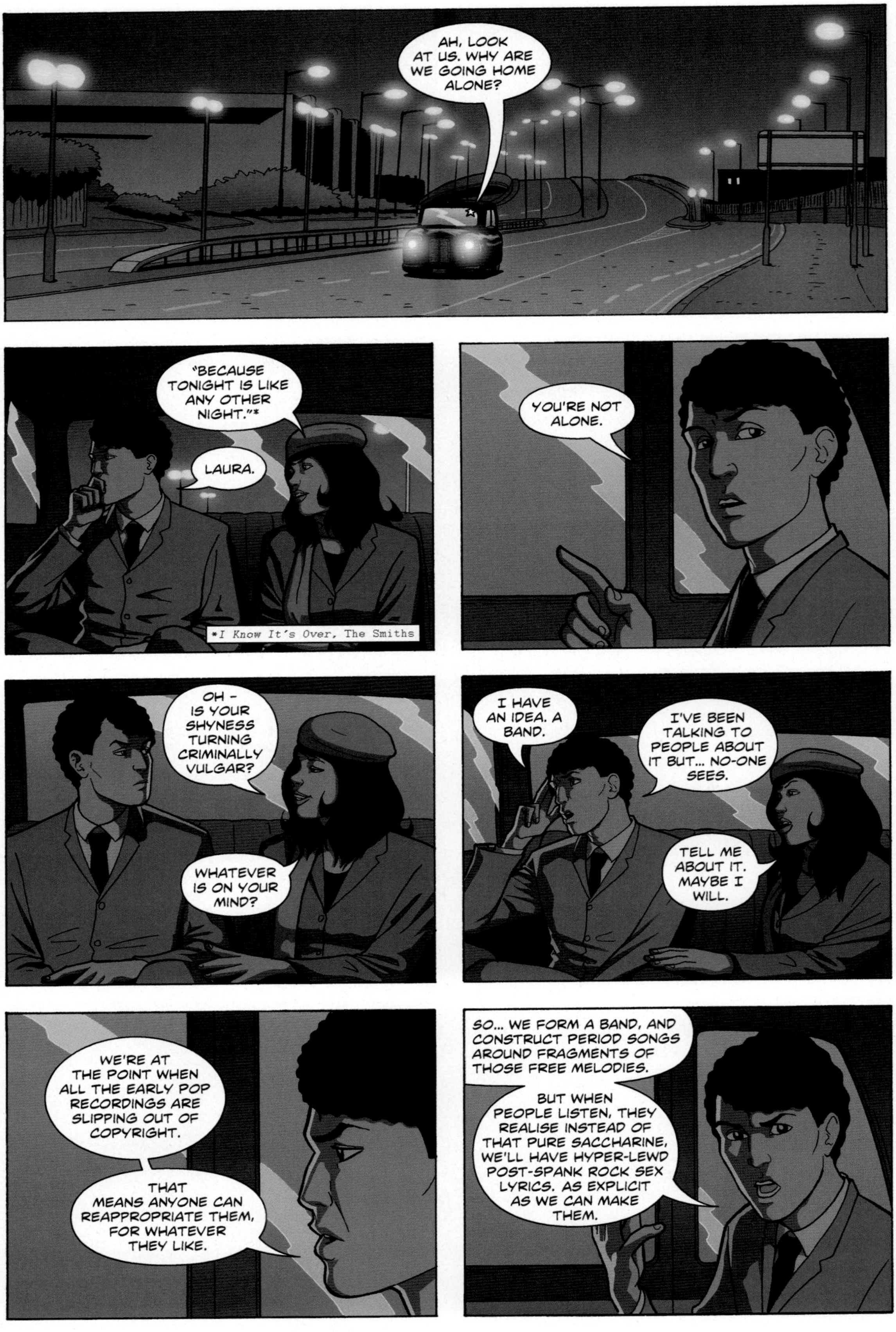
AH, LOOK AT US. WHY ARE WE GOING HOME ALONE?
"BECAUSE TONIGHT IS LIKE ANY OTHER NIGHT."*
LAURA.
*I Know It's Over, The Smiths
YOU'RE NOT ALONE.
OH - IS YOUR SHYNESS TURNING CRIMINALLY VULGAR?
WHATEVER IS ON YOUR MIND?
I HAVE AN IDEA. A BAND.
I'VE BEEN TALKING TO PEOPLE ABOUT IT BUT... NO-ONE SEES.
TELL ME ABOUT IT. MAYBE I WILL.
WE'RE AT THE POINT WHEN ALL THE EARLY POP RECORDINGS ARE SLIPPING OUT OF COPYRIGHT.
THAT MEANS ANYONE CAN REAPPROPRIATE THEM, FOR WHATEVER THEY LIKE.
SO... WE FORM A BAND, AND CONSTRUCT PERIOD SONGS AROUND FRAGMENTS OF THOSE FREE MELODIES.
BUT WHEN PEOPLE LISTEN, THEY REALISE INSTEAD OF THAT PURE SACCHARINE, WE'LL HAVE HYPER-LEWD POST-SPANK ROCK SEX LYRICS. AS EXPLICIT AS WE CAN MAKE THEM.

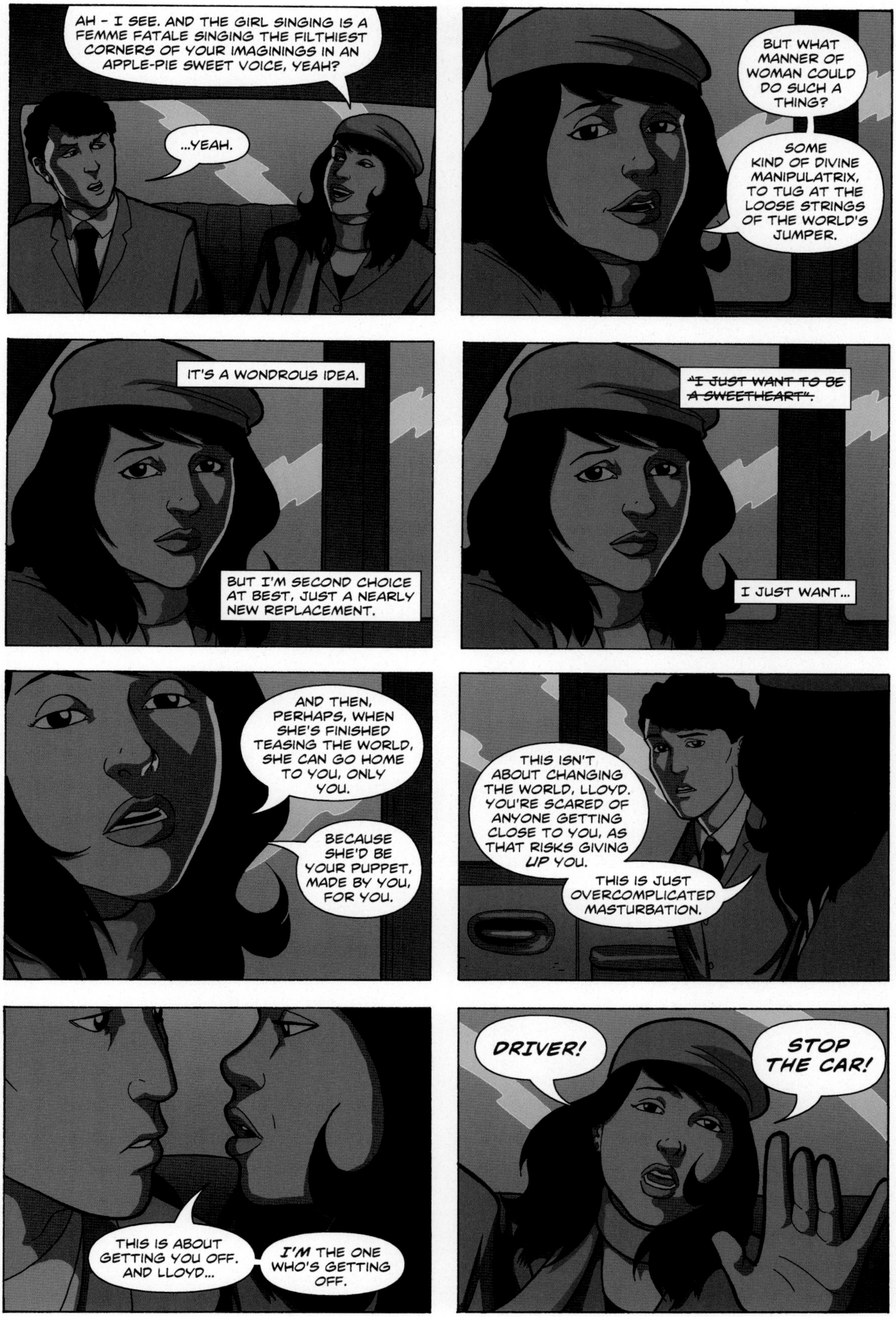
AH – I SEE. AND THE GIRL SINGING IS A FEMME FATALE SINGING THE FILTHIEST CORNERS OF YOUR IMAGININGS IN AN APPLE-PIE SWEET VOICE, YEAH?
...YEAH.
BUT WHAT MANNER OF WOMAN COULD DO SUCH A THING?
SOME KIND OF DIVINE MANIPULATRIX, TO TUG AT THE LOOSE STRINGS OF THE WORLD'S JUMPER.
IT'S A WONDROUS IDEA.
BUT I'M SECOND CHOICE AT BEST, JUST A NEARLY NEW REPLACEMENT.
~~"I JUST WANT TO BE A SWEETHEART".~~
I JUST WANT...
AND THEN, PERHAPS, WHEN SHE'S FINISHED TEASING THE WORLD, SHE CAN GO HOME TO YOU, ONLY YOU.
BECAUSE SHE'D BE YOUR PUPPET, MADE BY YOU, FOR YOU.
THIS ISN'T ABOUT CHANGING THE WORLD, LLOYD. YOU'RE SCARED OF ANYONE GETTING CLOSE TO YOU, AS THAT RISKS GIVING *UP* YOU.
THIS IS JUST OVERCOMPLICATED MASTURBATION.
THIS IS ABOUT GETTING YOU OFF. AND LLOYD...
I'M THE ONE WHO'S GETTING OFF.
DRIVER!
STOP THE CAR!

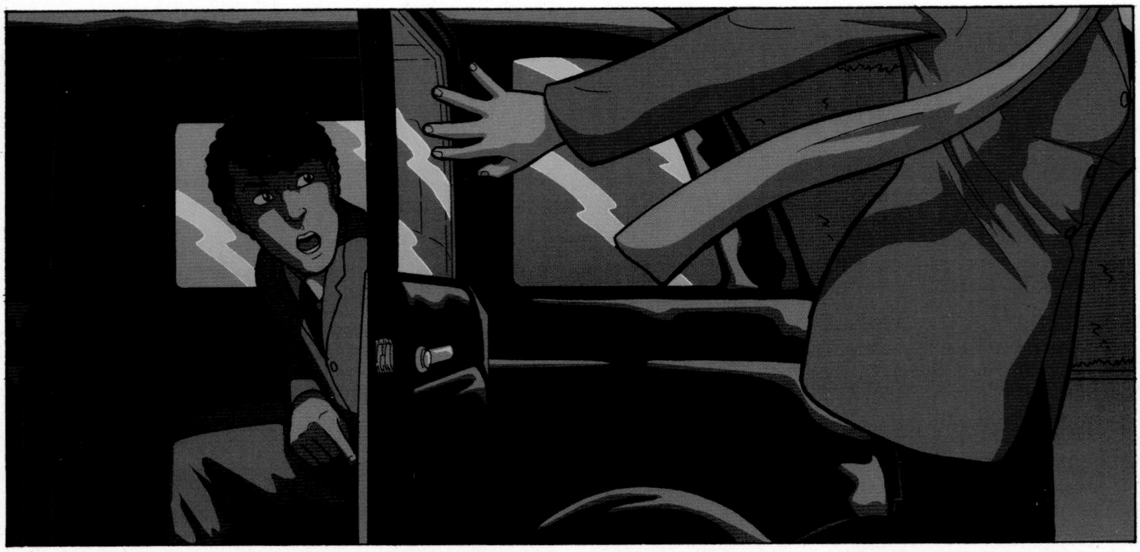

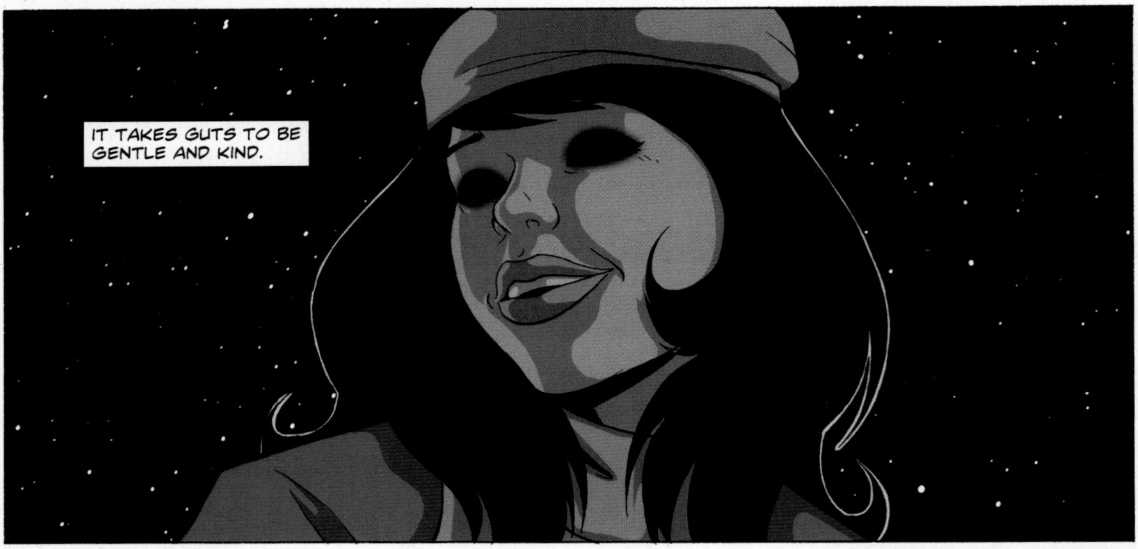
IT TAKES GUTS TO BE
GENTLE AND KIND.

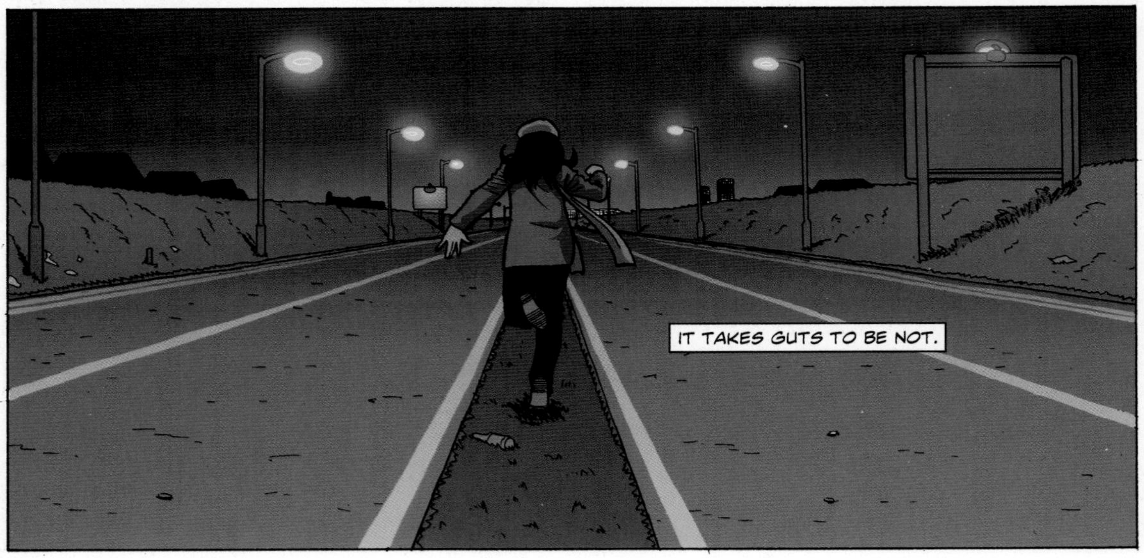
IT TAKES GUTS TO BE NOT.

PHONOGRAM

THE SINGLES CLUB

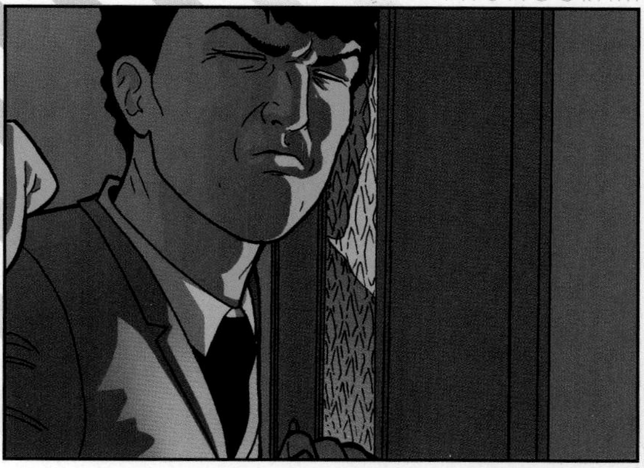

6. READY TO BE HEARTBROKEN

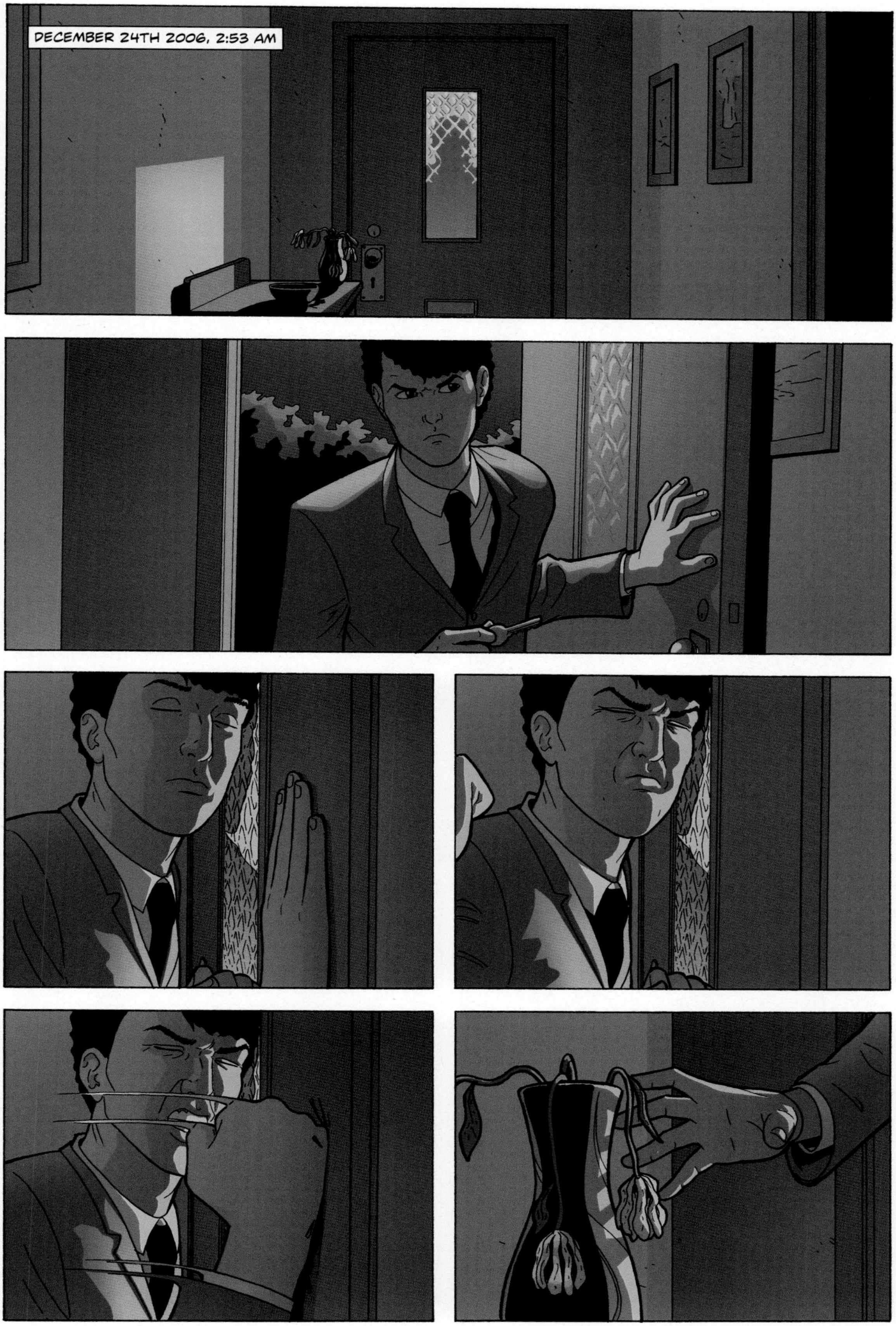
DECEMBER 24TH 2006, 2:53 AM

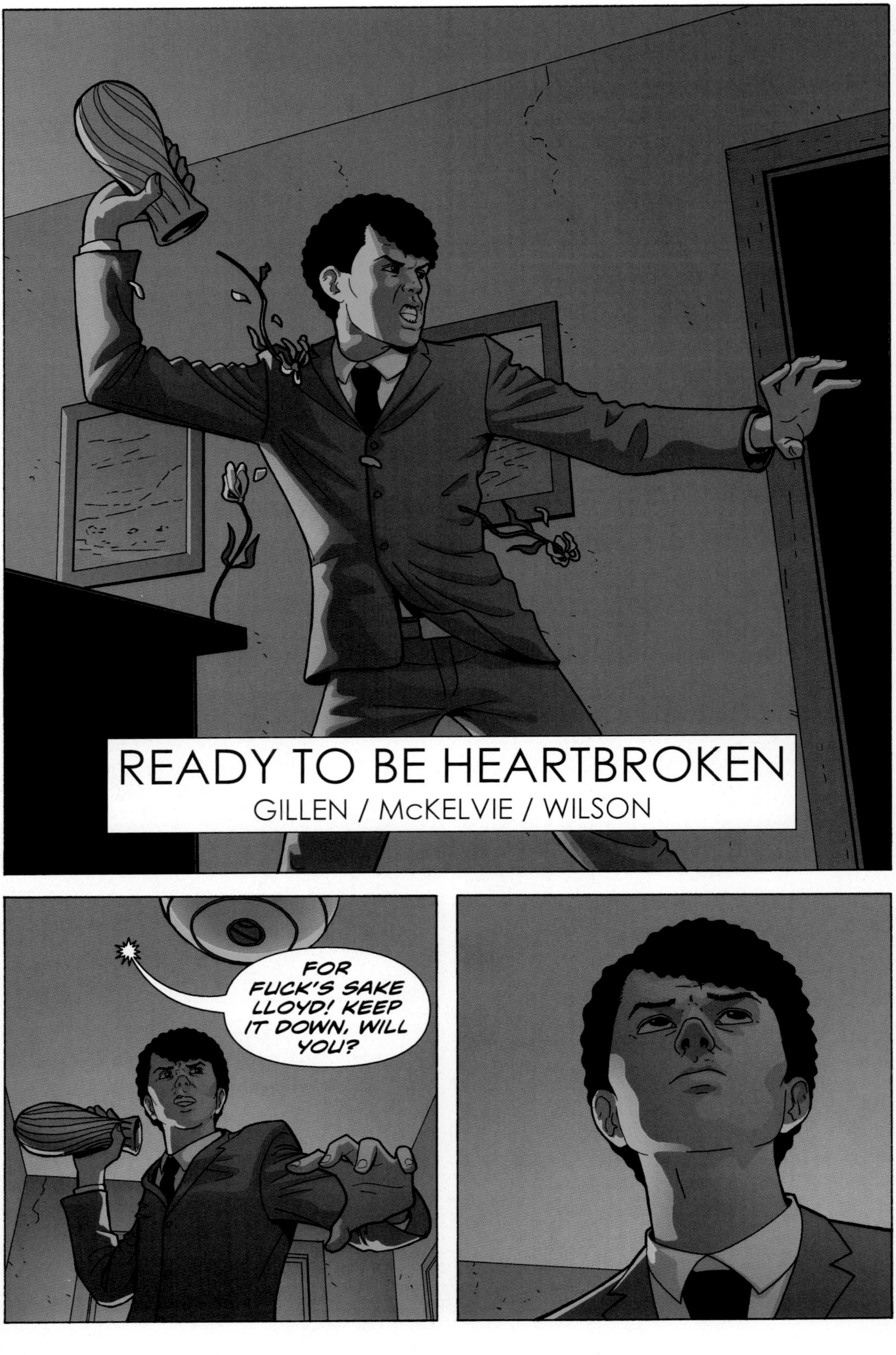
READY TO BE HEARTBROKEN
GILLEN / McKELVIE / WILSON
FOR FUCK'S SAKE LLOYD! KEEP IT DOWN, WILL YOU?

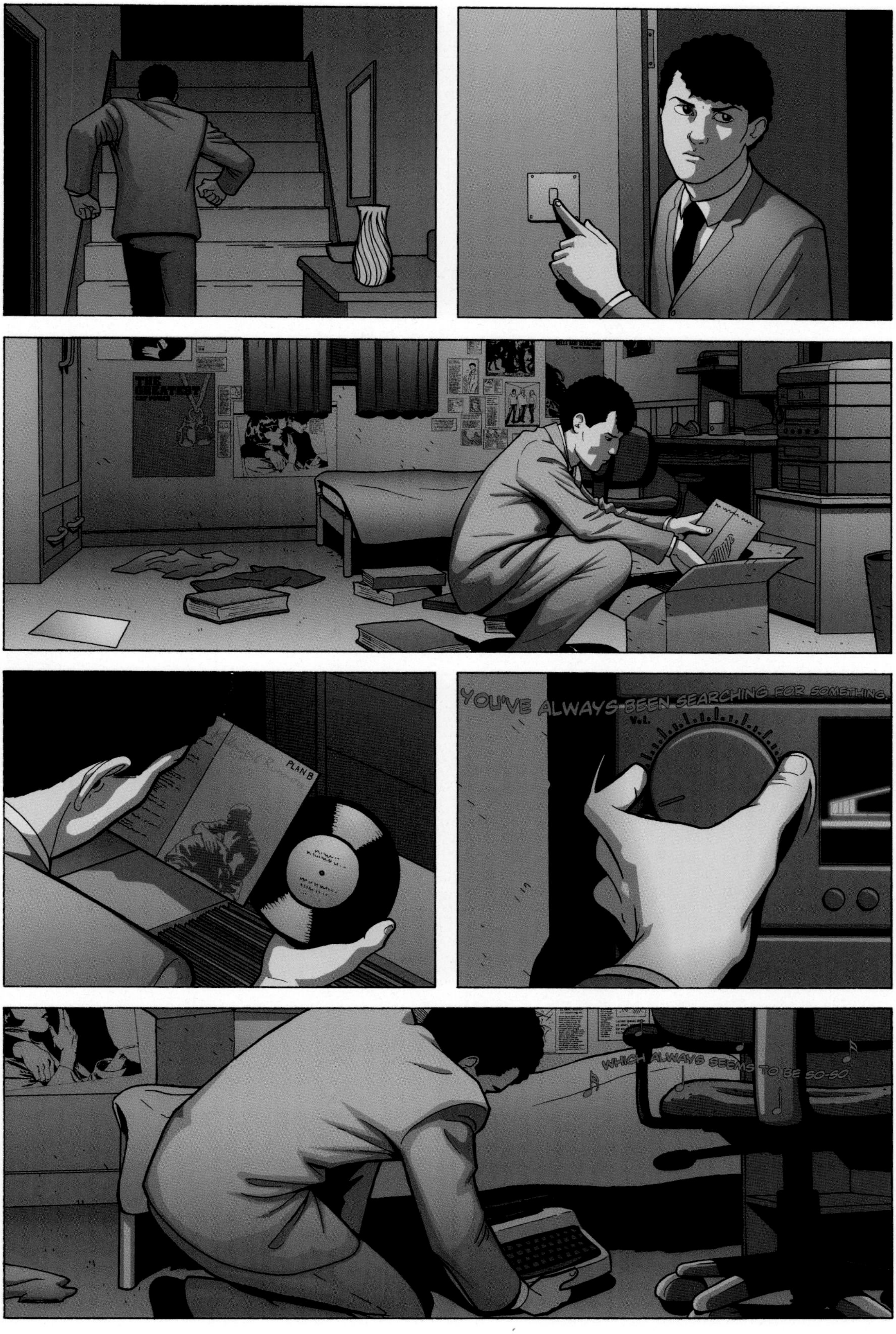
THE GREATEST
PLAN B
YOU'VE ALWAYS BEEN SEARCHING FOR SOMETHING.
Vol.
WHICH ALWAYS SEEMS TO BE SO-SO

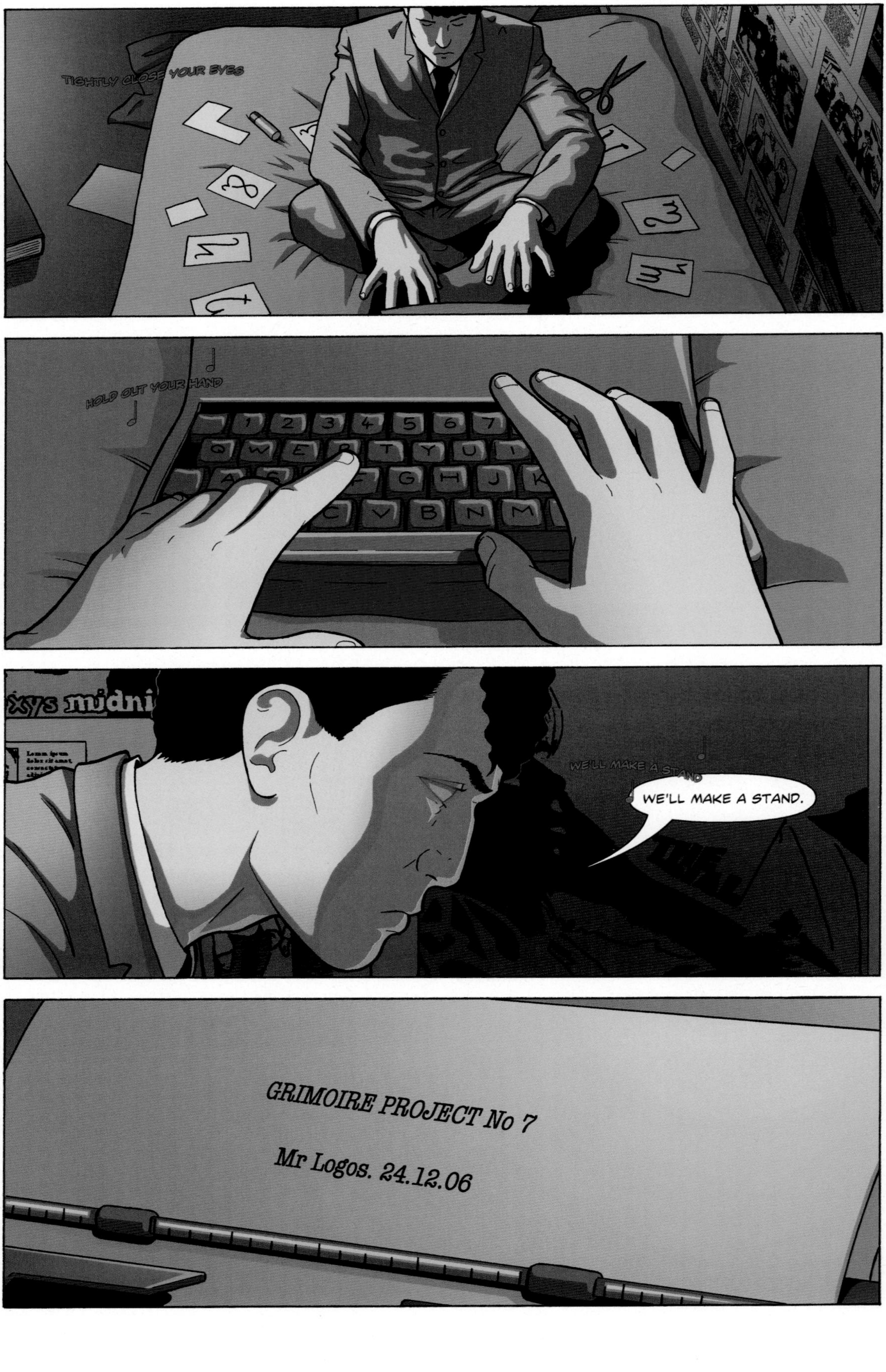
TIGHTLY CLOSE YOUR EYES
HOLD OUT YOUR HAND
WE'LL MAKE A STAND
WE'LL MAKE A STAND.
GRIMOIRE PROJECT No 7
Mr Logos. 24.12.06

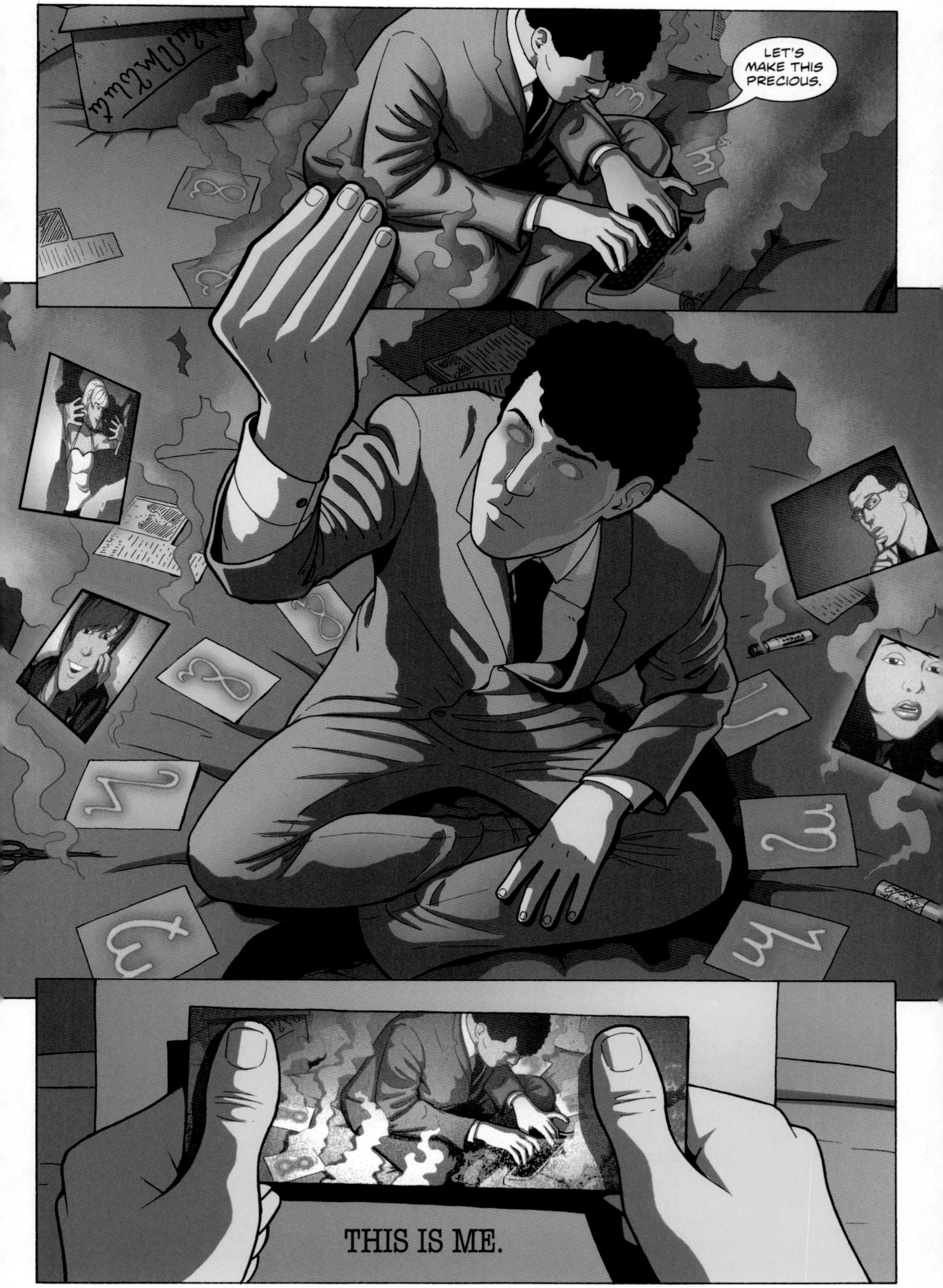
LET'S MAKE THIS PRECIOUS.
THIS IS ME.

GRIMOIRE PROJECT No. 7

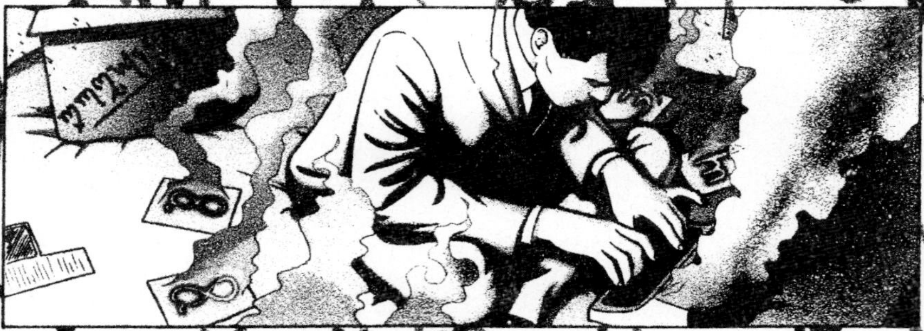

THIS IS ME.

You don't know me, but you will.

I turn to you seeking knowledge.

By exposing myself to you, I will find myself.

I will find something.

I refuse to admit there is no meaning here.

I will find meaning.

I will force it.

Music is Sublimated Emotion.

This Grimoire is Sublimated Thought.

MR LOGOS' PROBLEM OF THE DAY:

NO-ONE UNDERSTANDS ME

INCLUDING ME.

(And fuck you for thinking me emo)

(You have no idea of the meaning of the words you use)

(You have no ideas at all)

(And, by the way, I'm using capitals, not because I'm shouting. I'm using capitals as all lower-font is the typographical incarnation of faux-naif indie-dom and I am the furthest point away from that.)

(DYS?)

(Fooled you. DYS=Dys, city of Stix. No acronyms, no shortenings, no submission to the net malaise, no submission, compromise is the devil talking. He talks, I refuse to listen.)

LET'S MAKE THIS PRECIOUS:

THE MASTER PLAN (v2.79)

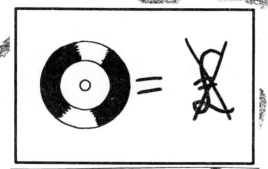

1) We're at the point when all the early pop recordings are slipping out of copyright.

RECORD
INDUSTRY

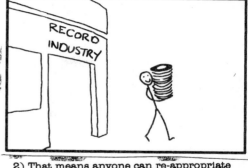

2) That means anyone can re-appropriate them, for whatever they like.

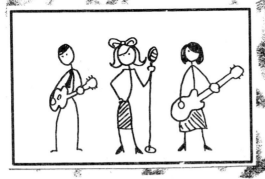

3) Form a band, and construct period songs around fragments of those free melodies.

XXX

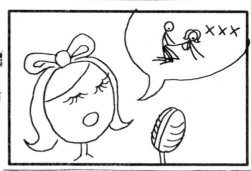

4) But when people listen, they realise instead of that pure saccharine, we'll have hyper-lewd Post-Spank-Rock sex lyrics.

XXX

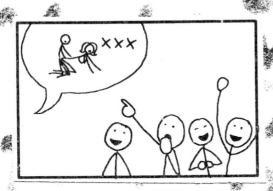

5) As explicit as we can make them.

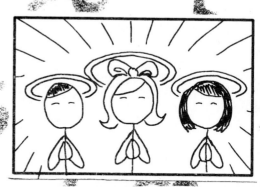

6) This expresses everything about the hypocrisies and perennial subtexts of pop music, and by doing so, we become Godheads.

Grimoire Project 7: Analysis of the response of others to The Master Plan. COntents:

DAVID KOHL INTERVIEW

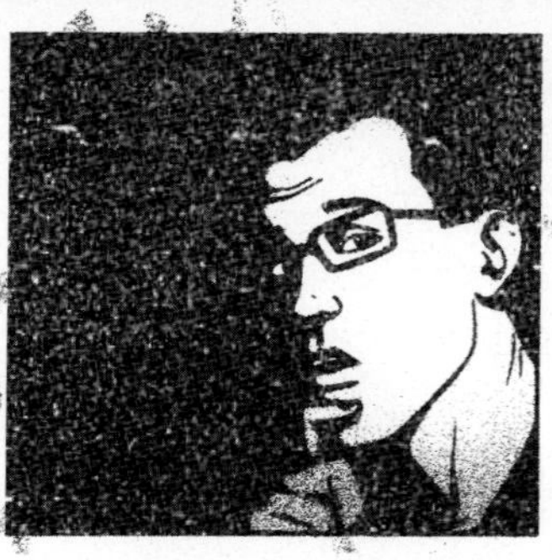

I saw David Kohl. I had to talk.

I'm not sure what I expected a man with a Goddess' blood on his hands to be like. More portentous, perhaps. Scarred by his experiences or scared of revenge, haunted by ~~rem~~ demons and the flickers of regret. None of that there. Odd flashes of intensity intermixed with lechery, our conversation was interrupted by his goonish friend bringing him drinks. I try and talk to him about the Britannia incident, but he laughs and dodged the issue. He mocked the works of the Adversary, claiming the hailing of the Fratellis as somewhat akin to the glorification of an abscess, mistaking pus for bonhomie. He seemed to approve of Dexys, though seemed to suggest I was missing something central from my understanding of the third album. Or similar. It was loud, and he talked fast and changed topic often.

Since he refuse to talk about his great work, I tried my own.

"I've had an idea. I was wondering what you make of it?"

"This isn't an idea about skinning members of Shitdisco and wearing them as Nu-rave suits?"

"No, of course not."

"Shame. Hit me."

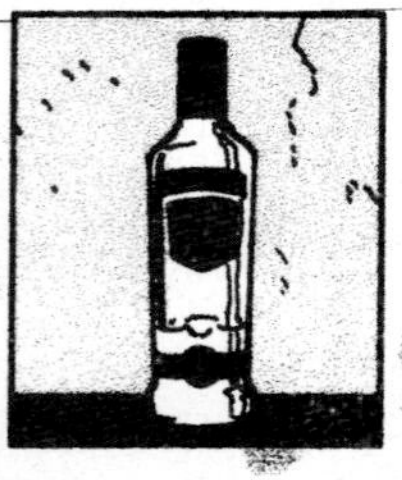

I tell him. He pauses, gestures for a break then orders another drink. I can't decide which disappointment cuts the deeper. That he drinks so much – I keep a bottle on the shelf, but solely as a reminder of my human weakness – or the way he so laviciously eyes the barmaid's jeans as she retreats. He's only human, it seems. I prompt him for his opinion. He grasps his head and squeezes it.

"You're onto something and I don't want to turn you away from it. It's.... not easy. But..."

He looks into space, sucks on his cigarette and sighs.

"You're sitting here, trying to write yourself into a better story, when a better story's all around you. I mean... you're a virgin, yeah?"

"I'm not", I lie, and hate myself for doing so.

"Whatever, he says, "Point being, whatever answers to your questions I give, are easy. There's no risk here. I can only tell you things you already know. You need to know stuff you don't."

He stops and looks over my shoulder.

"I mean, what story have you written yourself here? You've talked to me. Instead you could be... " he points, "Like that"

He points at Penny. She's dancing. He's right. He's right, and it isn't even her best of the night. That was earlier.

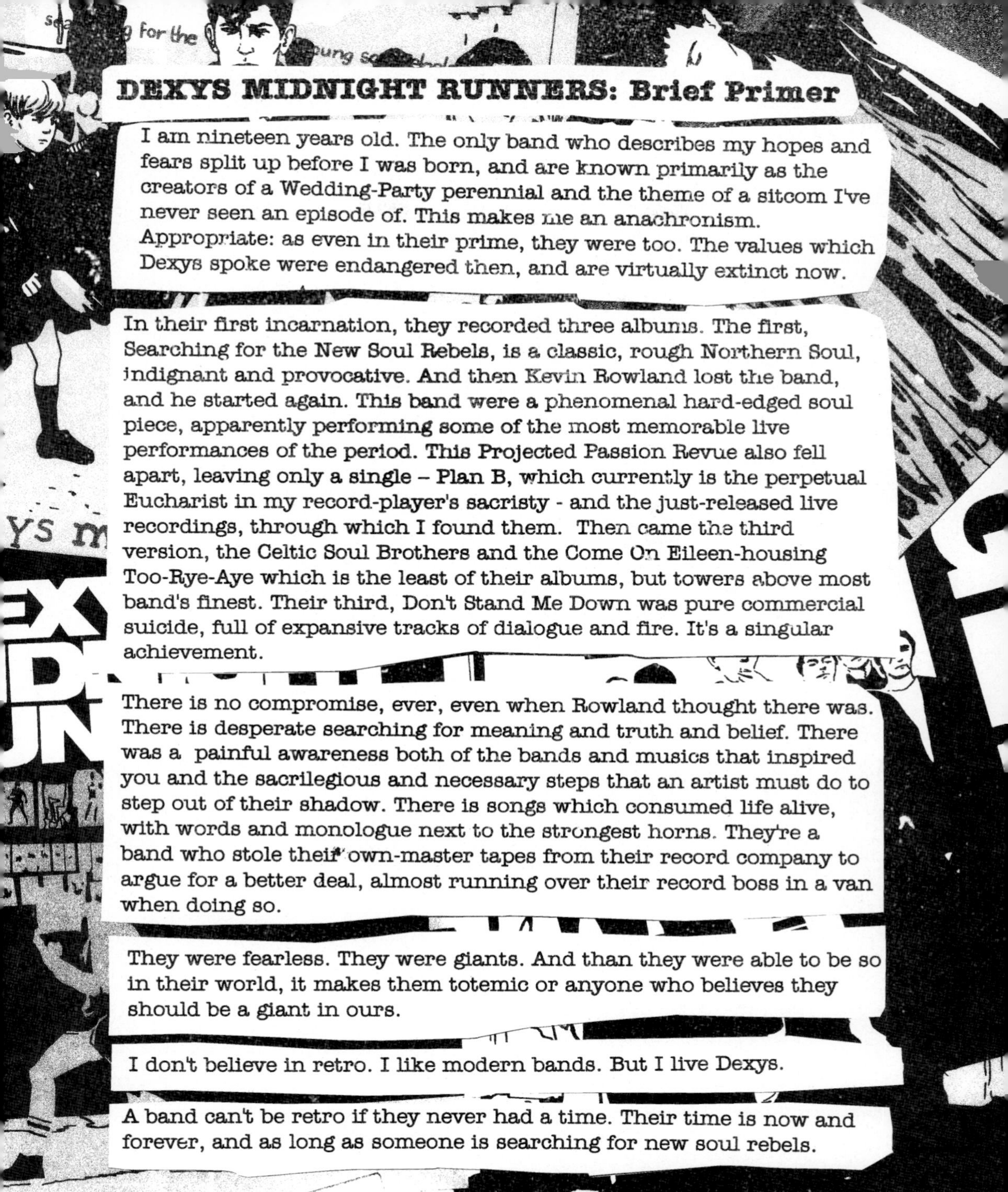

DEXYS MIDNIGHT RUNNERS: Brief Primer

I am nineteen years old. The only band who describes my hopes and fears split up before I was born, and are known primarily as the creators of a Wedding-Party perennial and the theme of a sitcom I've never seen an episode of. This makes me an anachronism. Appropriate: as even in their prime, they were too. The values which Dexys spoke were endangered then, and are virtually extinct now.

In their first incarnation, they recorded three albums. The first, Searching for the New Soul Rebels, is a classic, rough Northern Soul, indignant and provocative. And then Kevin Rowland lost the band, and he started again. This band were a phenomenal hard-edged soul piece, apparently performing some of the most memorable live performances of the period. This Projected Passion Revue also fell apart, leaving only a single – Plan B, which currently is the perpetual Eucharist in my record-player's sacristy - and the just-released live recordings, through which I found them. Then came the third version, the Celtic Soul Brothers and the Come On Eileen-housing Too-Rye-Aye which is the least of their albums, but towers above most band's finest. Their third, Don't Stand Me Down was pure commercial suicide, full of expansive tracks of dialogue and fire. It's a singular achievement.

There is no compromise, ever, even when Rowland thought there was. There is desperate searching for meaning and truth and belief. There was a painful awareness both of the bands and musics that inspired you and the sacrilegious and necessary steps that an artist must do to step out of their shadow. There is songs which consumed life alive, with words and monologue next to the strongest horns. They're a band who stole their own-master tapes from their record company to argue for a better deal, almost running over their record boss in a van when doing so.

They were fearless. They were giants. And than they were able to be so in their world, it makes them totemic or anyone who believes they should be a giant in ours.

I don't believe in retro. I like modern bands. But I live Dexys.

A band can't be retro if they never had a time. Their time is now and forever, and as long as someone is searching for new soul rebels.

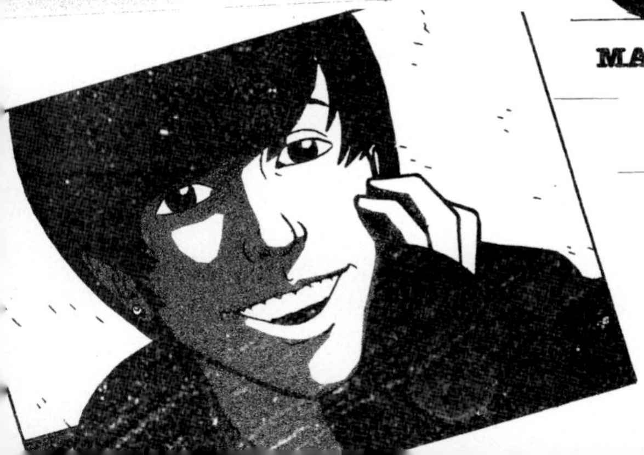

MARC'S RESPONSE TO THE MASTER PLAN:

He laughed.

Top 5 reasons why Marc is a coward

1) He hasn't gone to the club since She left.
2) ...
3) ...
4) He keeps on calling me Lloyd.
5) I mean, seriously, what is it with that?

PENNY'S RESPONSE TO THE MASTER PLAN

GAHK!

PASSION
DEVOTION
COMMITMENT
INTELLIGENCE

PASSION
DEVOTION
COMMITMENT
INTELLIGENCE

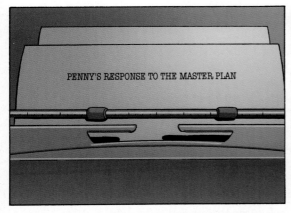

PENNY'S RESPONSE TO THE MASTER PLAN

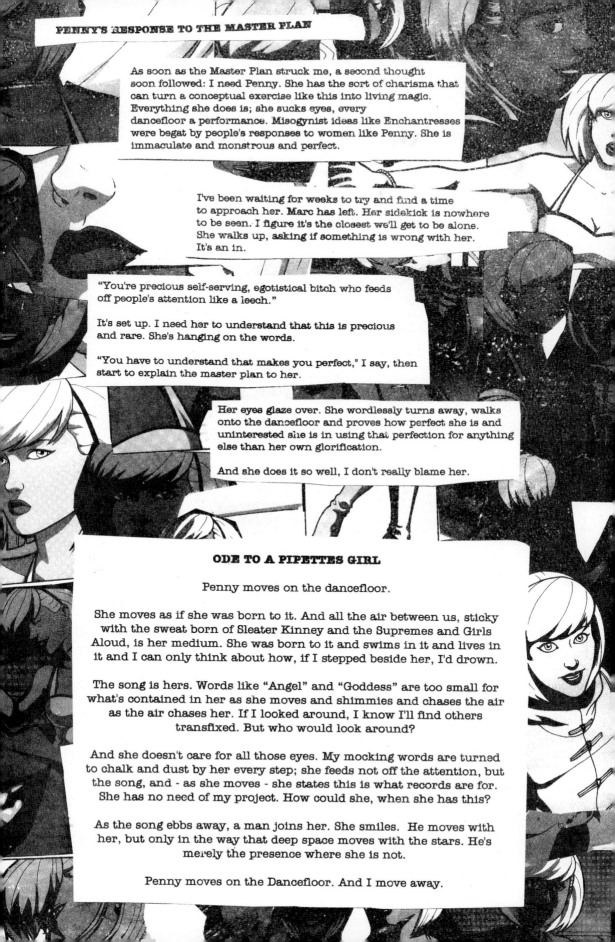

As soon as the Master Plan struck me, a second thought soon followed: I need Penny. She has the sort of charisma that can turn a conceptual exercise like this into living magic. Everything she does is; she sucks eyes, every dancefloor a performance. Misogynist ideas like Enchantresses were begat by people's responses to women like Penny. She is immaculate and monstrous and perfect.

I've been waiting for weeks to try and find a time to approach her. Marc has left. Her sidekick is nowhere to be seen. I figure it's the closest we'll get to be alone. She walks up, asking if something is wrong with her. It's an in.

"You're precious self-serving, egotistical bitch who feeds off people's attention like a leech."

It's set up. I need her to understand that this is precious and rare. She's hanging on the words.

"You have to understand that makes you perfect," I say, then start to explain the master plan to her.

Her eyes glaze over. She wordlessly turns away, walks onto the dancefloor and proves how perfect she is and uninterested she is in using that perfection for anything else than her own glorification.

And she does it so well, I don't really blame her.

ODE TO A PIPETTES GIRL

Penny moves on the dancefloor.

She moves as if she was born to it. And all the air between us, sticky with the sweat born of Sleater Kinney and the Supremes and Girls Aloud, is her medium. She was born to it and swims in it and lives in it and I can only think about how, if I stepped beside her, I'd drown.

The song is hers. Words like "Angel" and "Goddess" are too small for what's contained in her as she moves and shimmies and chases the air as the air chases her. If I looked around, I know I'll find others transfixed. But who would look around?

And she doesn't care for all those eyes. My mocking words are turned to chalk and dust by her every step; she feeds not off the attention, but the song, and - as she moves - she states this is what records are for. She has no need of my project. How could she, when she has this?

As the song ebbs away, a man joins her. She smiles. He moves with her, but only in the way that deep space moves with the stars. He's merely the presence where she is not.

Penny moves on the Dancefloor. And I move away.

LAURA'S RESPONSE TO THE MASTER PLAN

The taxi carries two people and their thoughts. If the driver knew exactly how much of the latter was crammed in, he'd have demanded an extra charge. Something breaks the moment. She thinks I'm flirting with her. I wasn't. I really wasn't. So I start to tell her of my plan, spinning off my practised line... and she pre-empts me. Her dark mind grasps it and elaborates beautifully. It's like the moment I hear about in bands when someone plays your song for the first time, and suddenly it takes wings and becomes something else – you hear it with new ears, and you understand that there's more here than what you brought, and there's an alchemy which makes all transcend. This is better than sex. We're so close, I think that perhaps it is sex.

And then, that close, she tells me what she thinks of the plan and

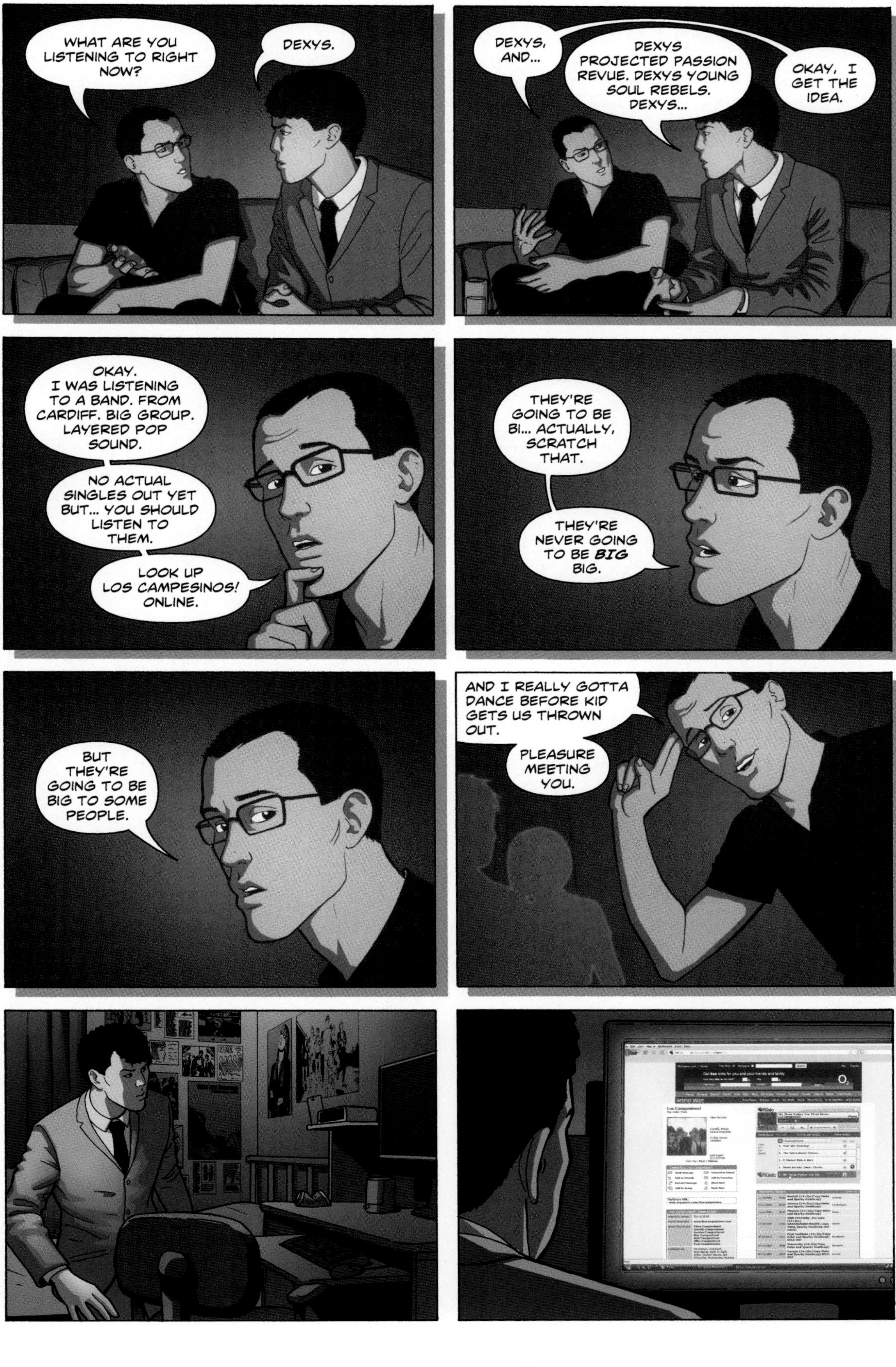
WHAT ARE YOU LISTENING TO RIGHT NOW?
DEXYS.
DEXYS, AND...
DEXYS PROJECTED PASSION REVUE. DEXYS YOUNG SOUL REBELS. DEXYS...
OKAY, I GET THE IDEA.
OKAY. I WAS LISTENING TO A BAND. FROM CARDIFF. BIG GROUP. LAYERED POP SOUND.
NO ACTUAL SINGLES OUT YET BUT... YOU SHOULD LISTEN TO THEM.
LOOK UP LOS CAMPESINOS! ONLINE.
THEY'RE GOING TO BE BI... ACTUALLY, SCRATCH THAT.
THEY'RE NEVER GOING TO BE *BIG* BIG.
BUT THEY'RE GOING TO BE BIG TO SOME PEOPLE.
AND I REALLY GOTTA DANCE BEFORE KID GETS US THROWN OUT.
PLEASURE MEETING YOU.

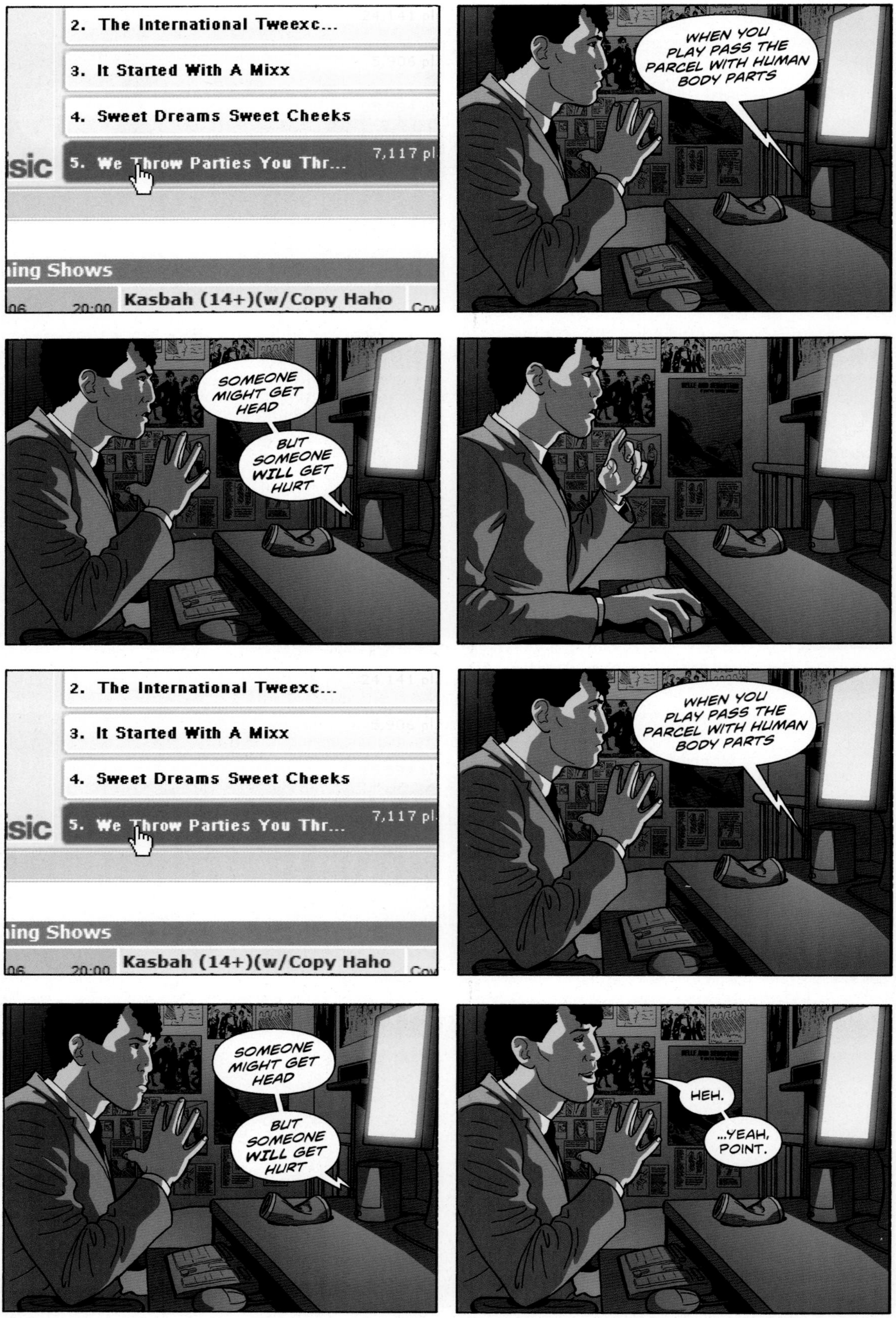
2. The International Tweexc...
3. It Started With A Mixx
4. Sweet Dreams Sweet Cheeks
5. We Throw Parties You Thr...
7,117
Kasbah (14+)(w/Copy Haho
20:00
WHEN YOU PLAY PASS THE PARCEL WITH HUMAN BODY PARTS
SOMEONE MIGHT GET HEAD
BUT SOMEONE WILL GET HURT
2. The International Tweexc...
3. It Started With A Mixx
4. Sweet Dreams Sweet Cheeks
5. We Throw Parties You Thr...
7,117
Kasbah (14+)(w/Copy Haho
20:00
WHEN YOU PLAY PASS THE PARCEL WITH HUMAN BODY PARTS
SOMEONE MIGHT GET HEAD
BUT SOMEONE WILL GET HURT
HEH.
...YEAH, POINT.

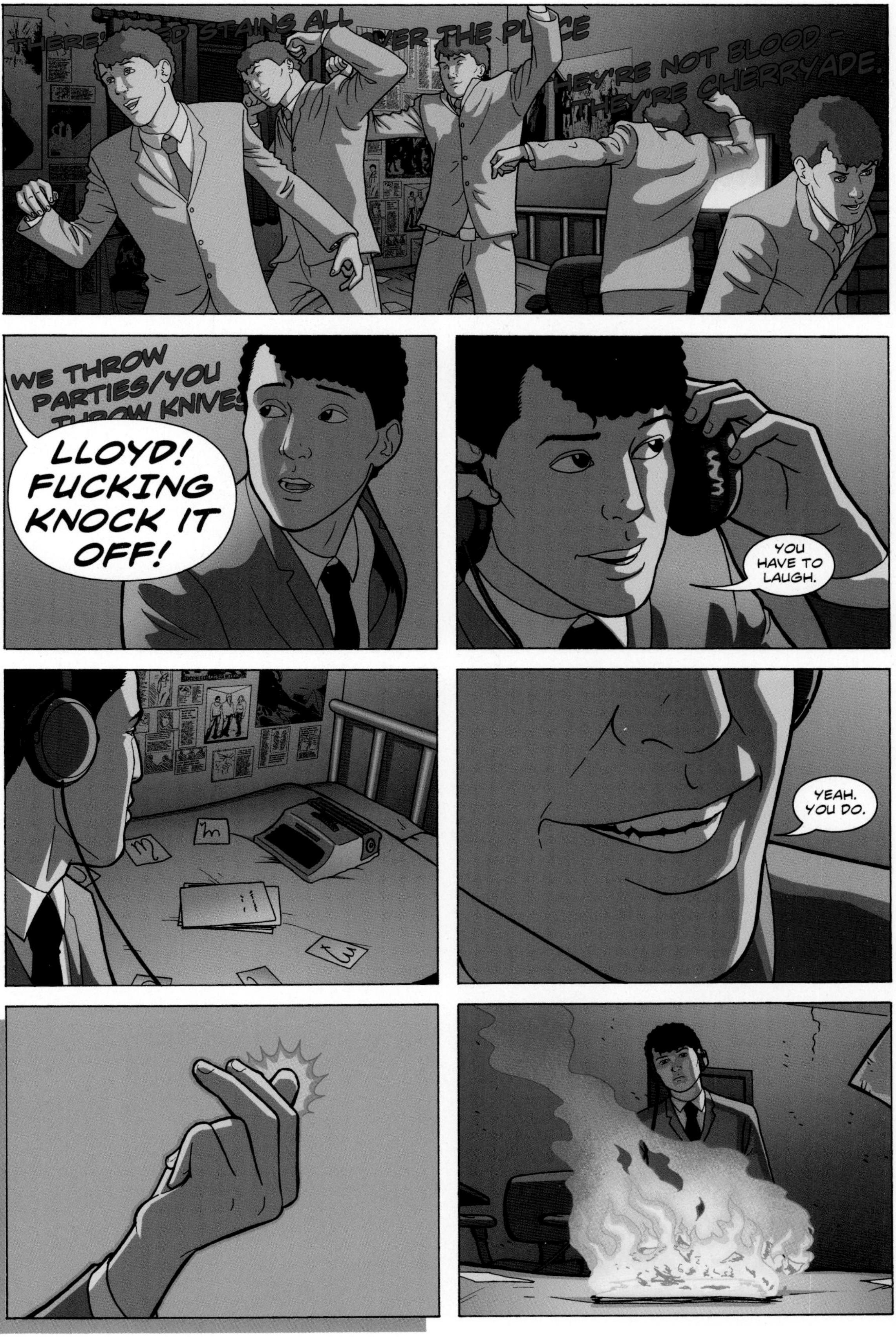

STAINS ALL
THEY'RE NOT BLOOD - THEY'RE CHERRYADE.
WE THROW PARTIES/YOU THROW KNIVES
LLOYD! FUCKING KNOCK IT OFF!
YOU HAVE TO LAUGH.
YEAH. YOU DO.

PLAN B.
MARC
AKA The Marquis
BLOOD AND CHERRYADE
Grimoire
VIII
MARC:
TELL ME WHAT YOU THINK.
L

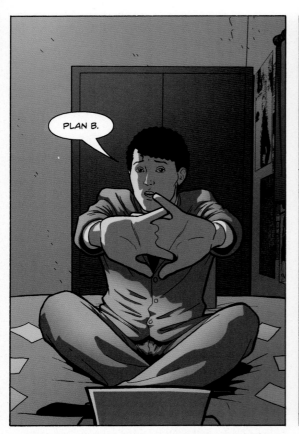

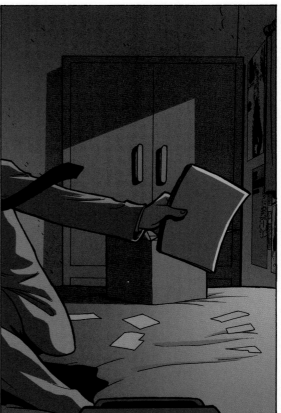

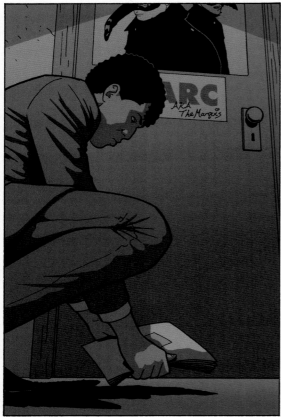

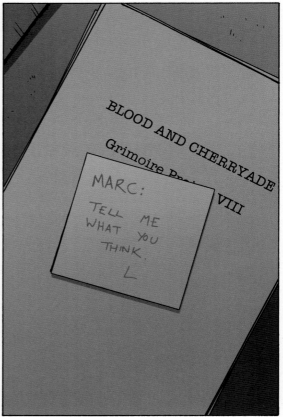

PHONOGRAM THE SINGLES CLUB

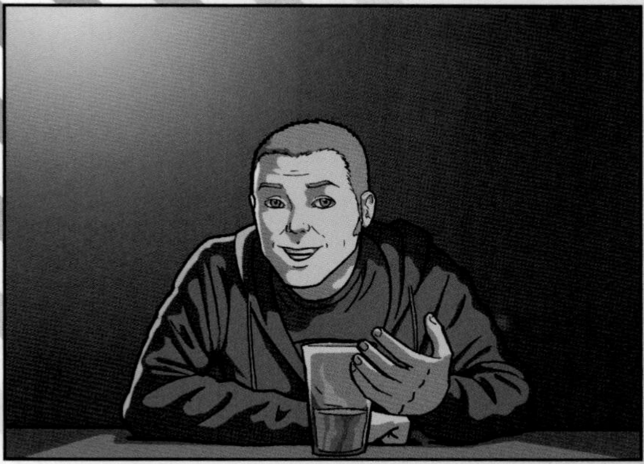

7. WOLF LIKE ME

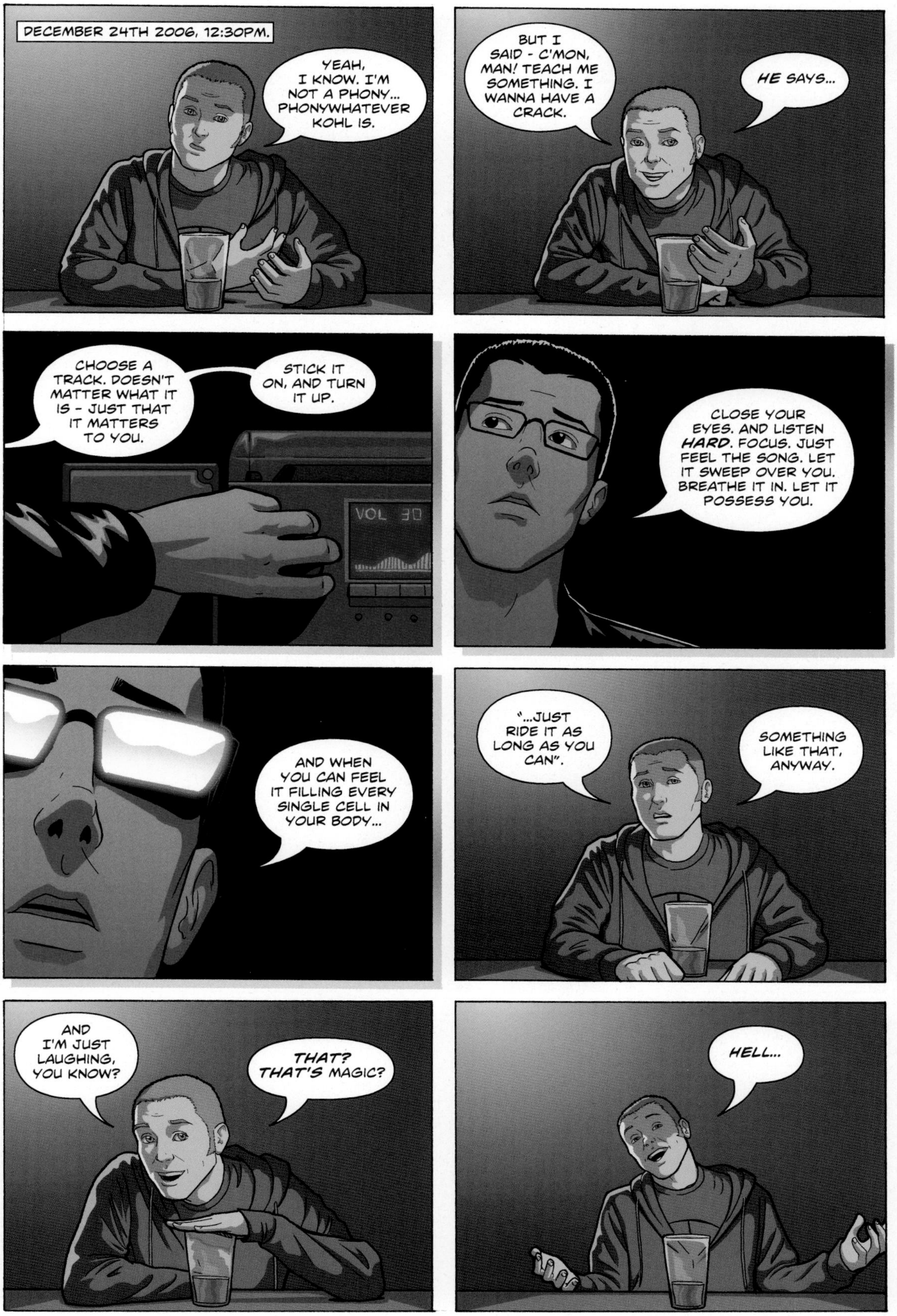
DECEMBER 24TH 2006, 12:30PM.
YEAH, I KNOW. I'M NOT A PHONY... PHONYWHATEVER KOHL IS.
BUT I SAID - C'MON, MAN! TEACH ME SOMETHING. I WANNA HAVE A CRACK.
HE SAYS...
CHOOSE A TRACK. DOESN'T MATTER WHAT IT IS - JUST THAT IT MATTERS TO YOU.
STICK IT ON, AND TURN IT UP.
VOL 30
CLOSE YOUR EYES. AND LISTEN ***HARD***. FOCUS. JUST FEEL THE SONG. LET IT SWEEP OVER YOU. BREATHE IT IN. LET IT POSSESS YOU.
AND WHEN YOU CAN FEEL IT FILLING EVERY SINGLE CELL IN YOUR BODY...
"...JUST RIDE IT AS LONG AS YOU CAN".
SOMETHING LIKE THAT, ANYWAY.
AND I'M JUST LAUGHING, YOU KNOW?
THAT? THAT'S MAGIC?
HELL...

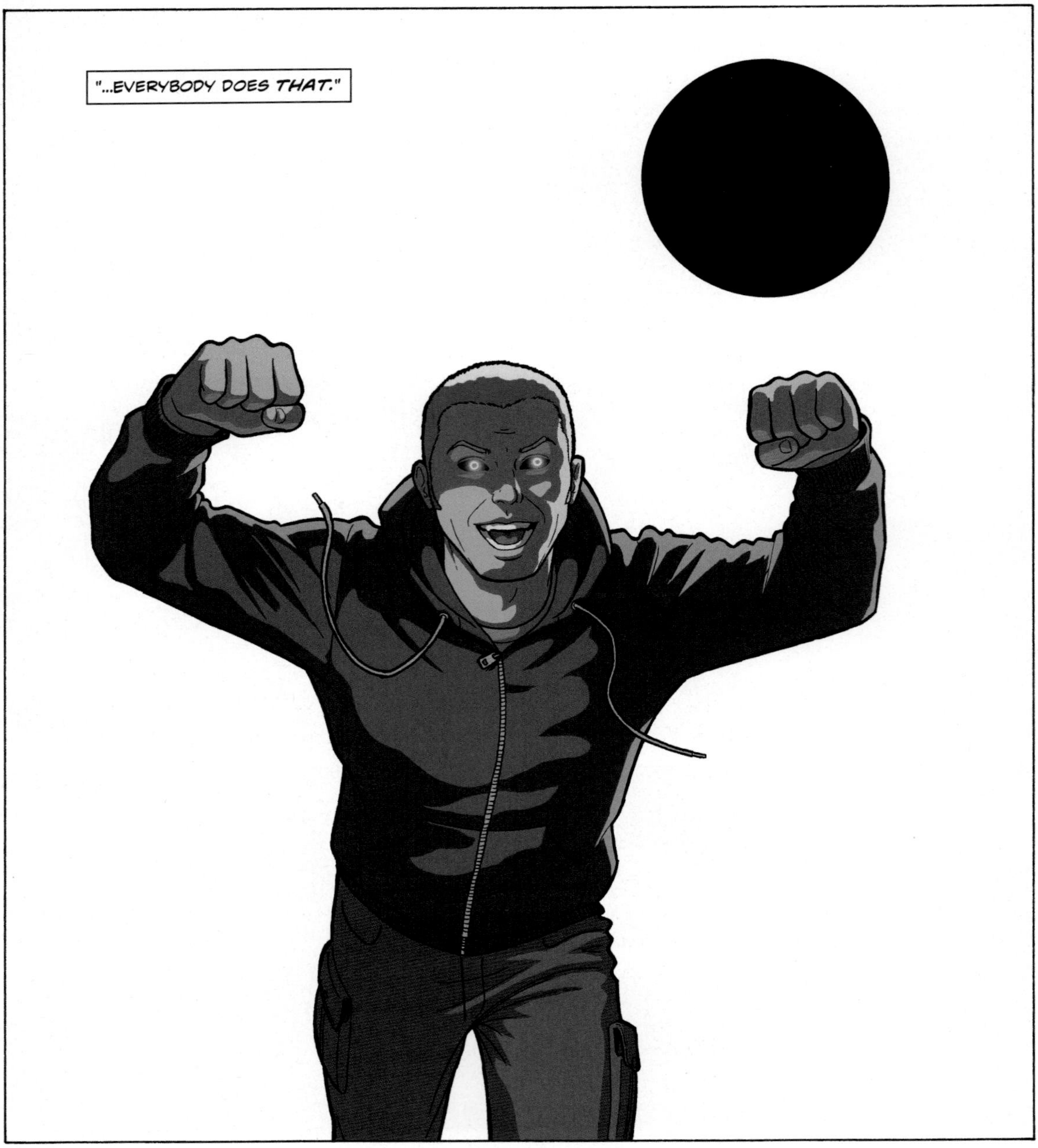
"...EVERYBODY DOES *THAT.*"

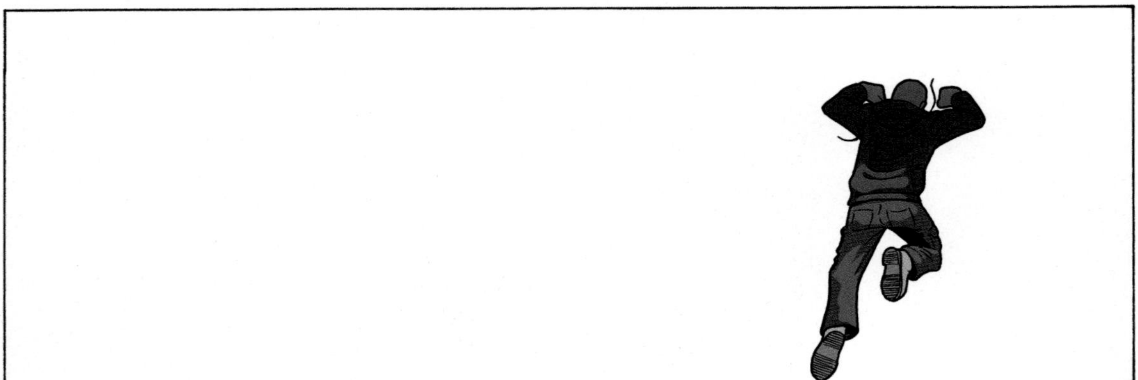

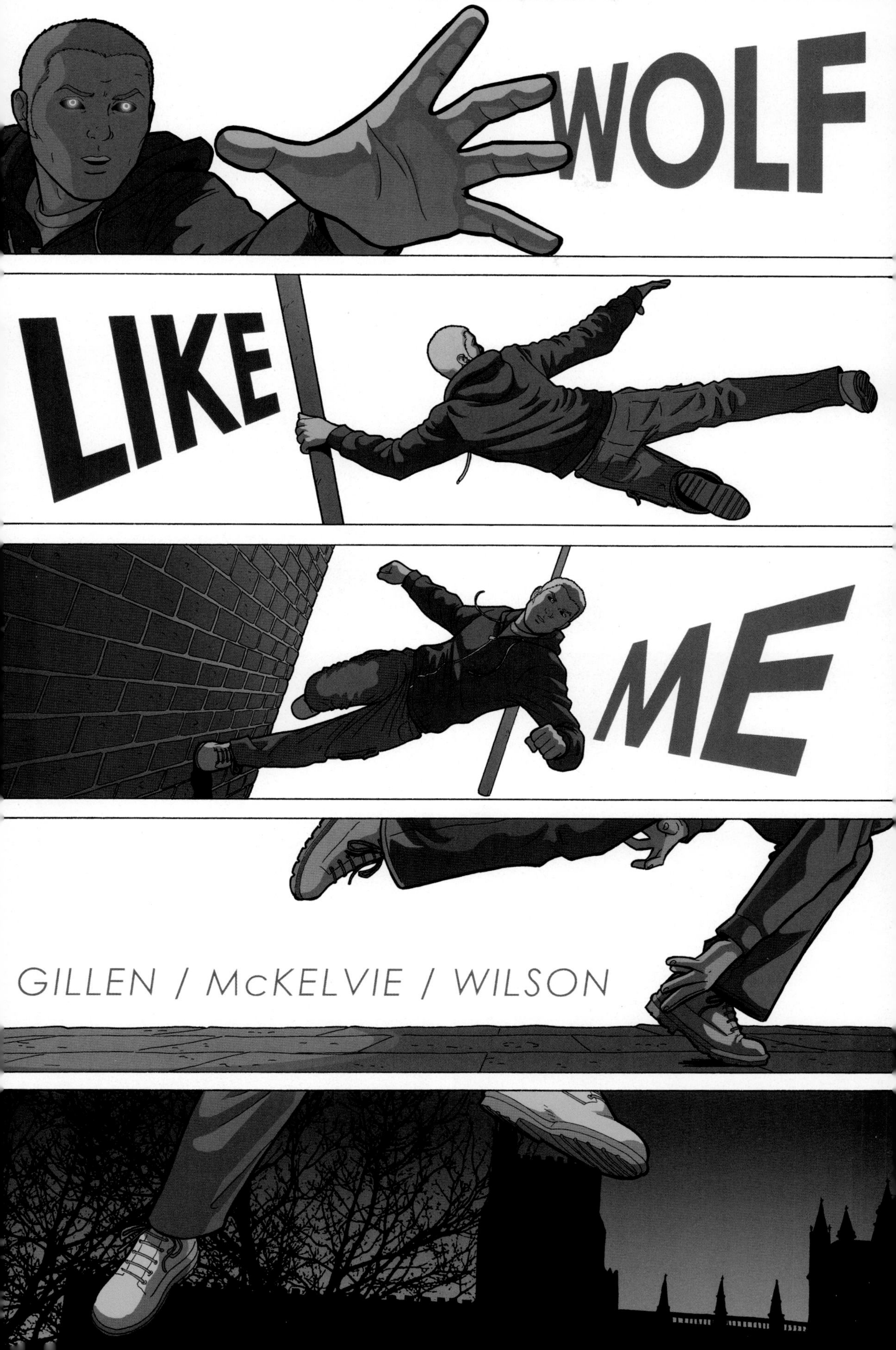
WOLF
LIKE
ME
GILLEN / McKELVIE / WILSON

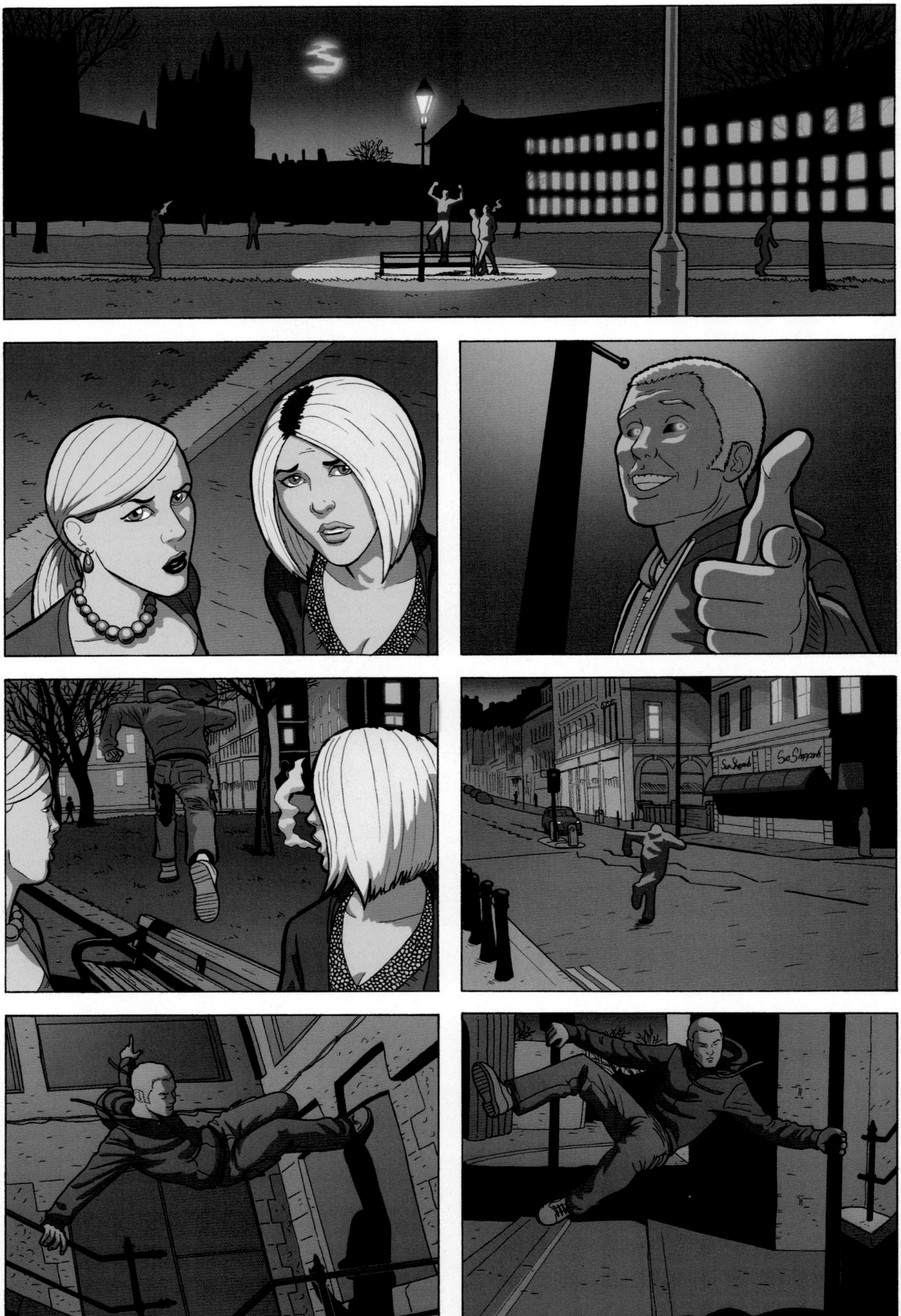

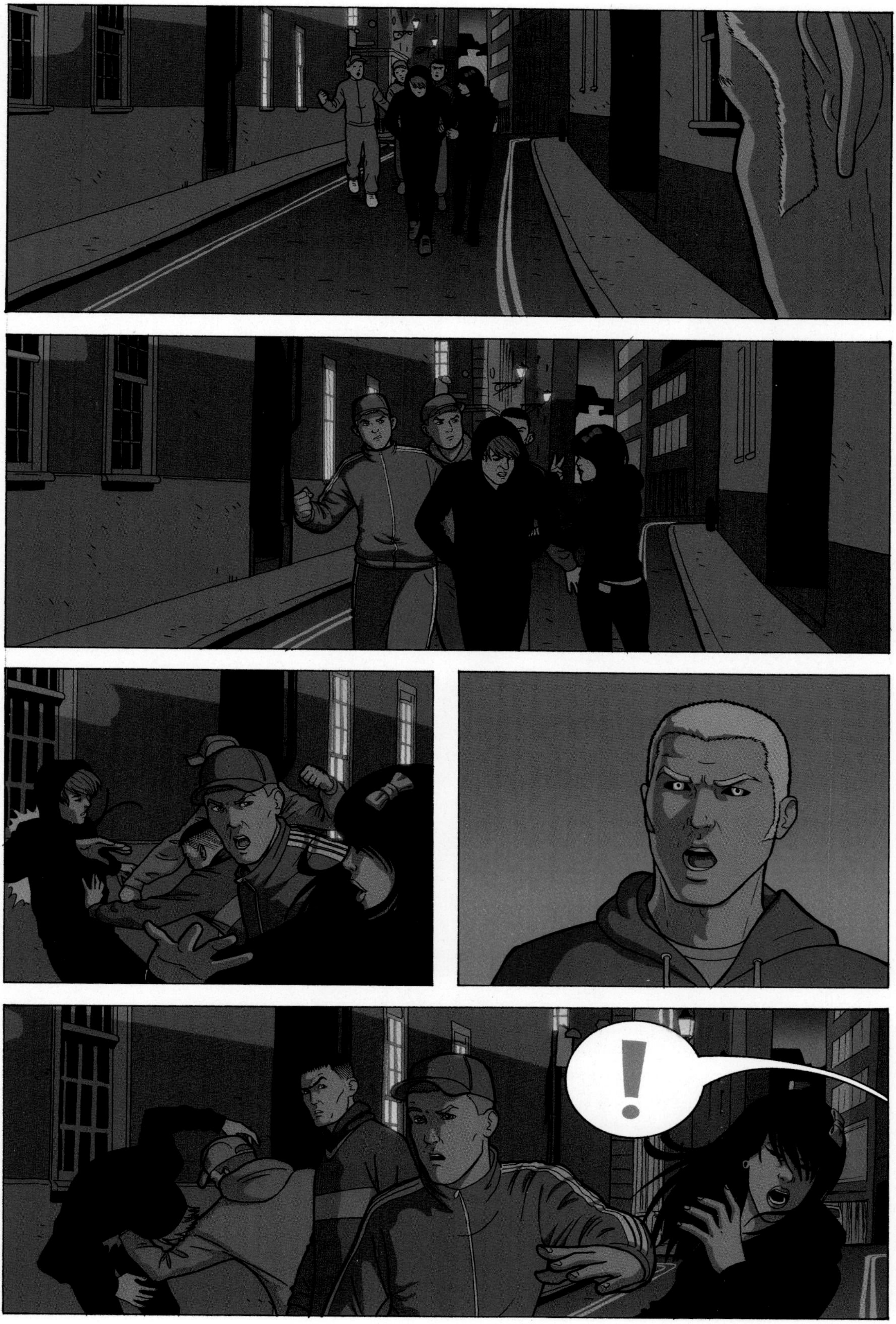
!

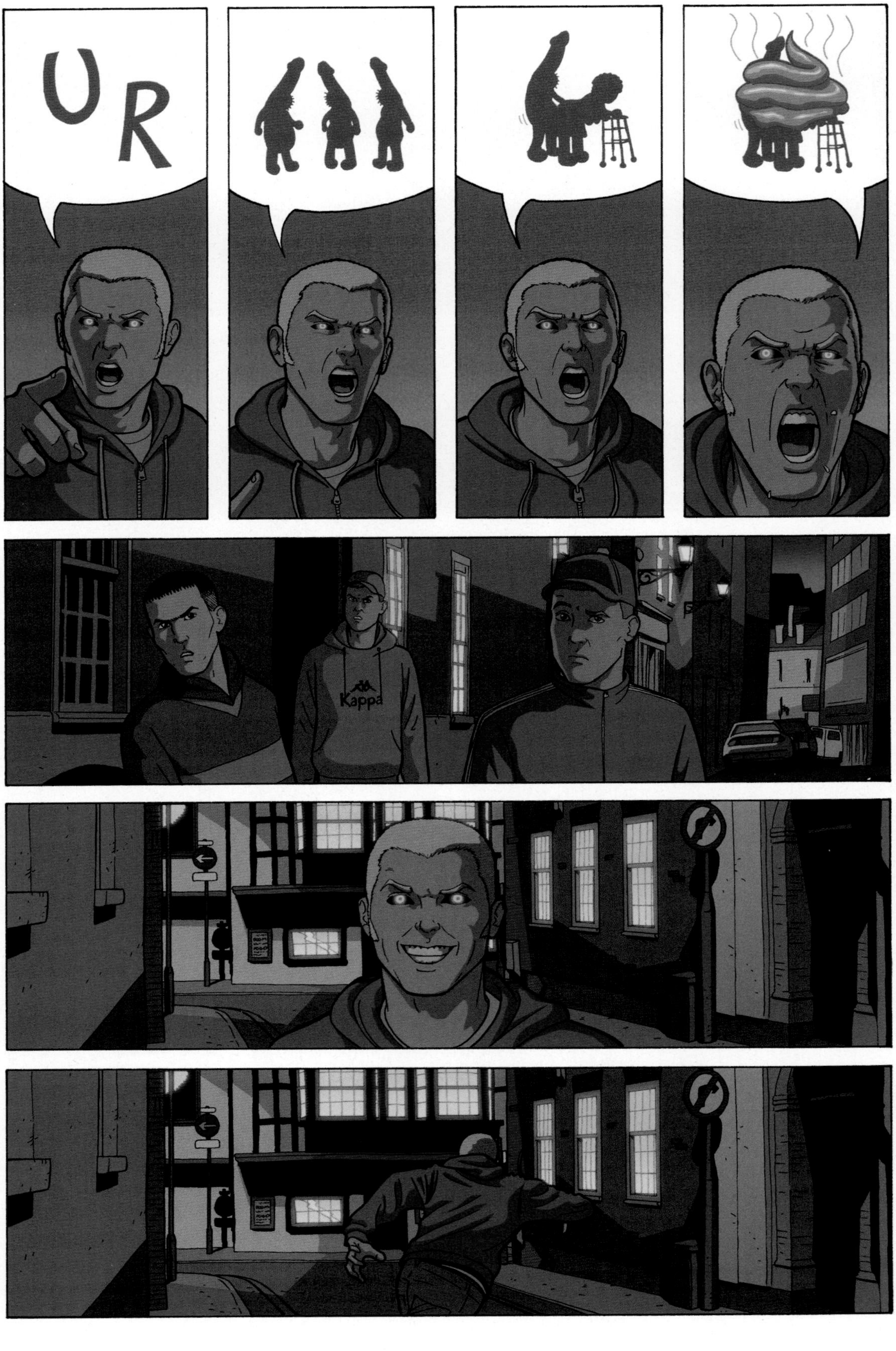

U R
Kappa

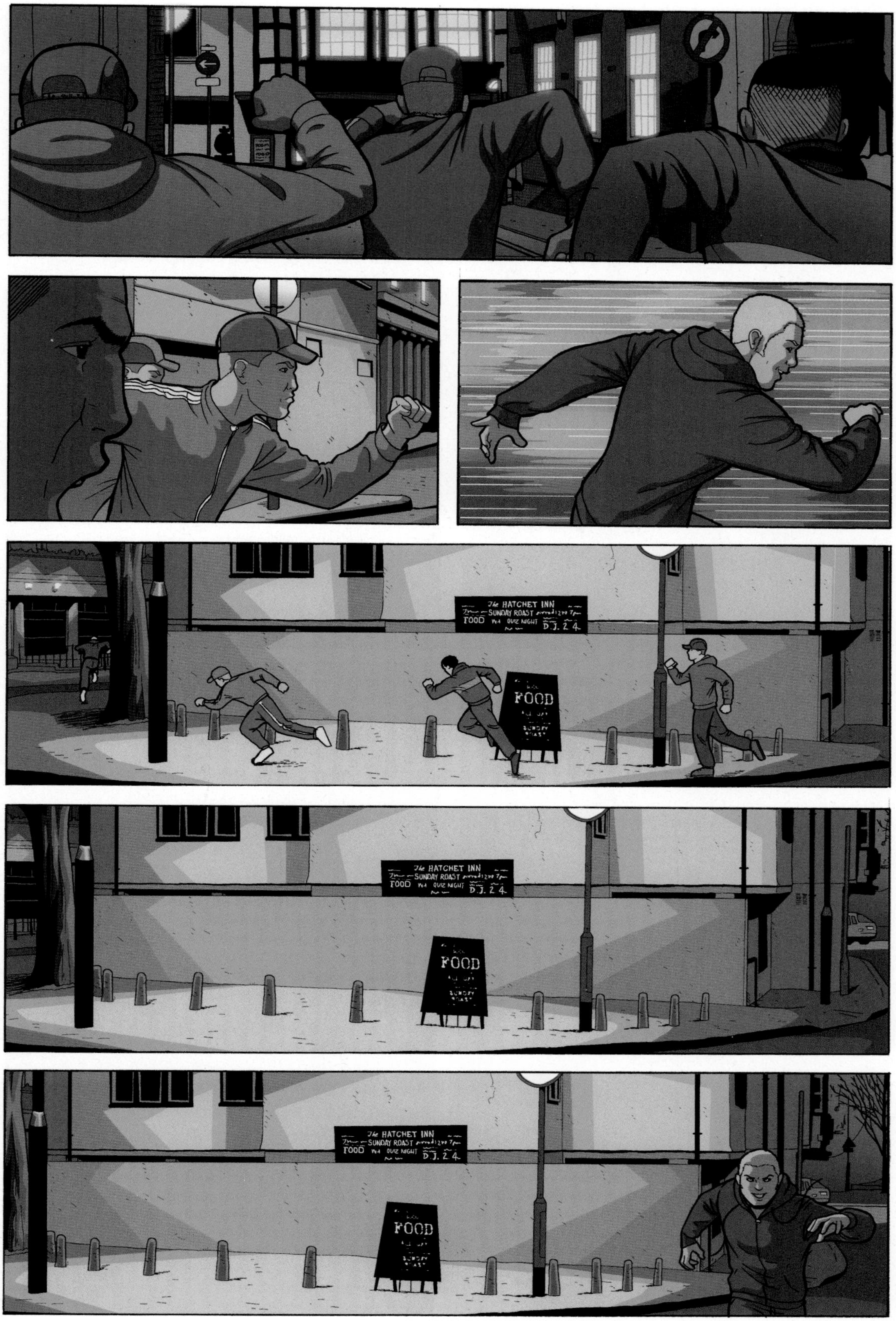
The HATCHET INN
SUNDAY ROAST
FOOD
QUIZ NIGHT
D.J.
FOOD

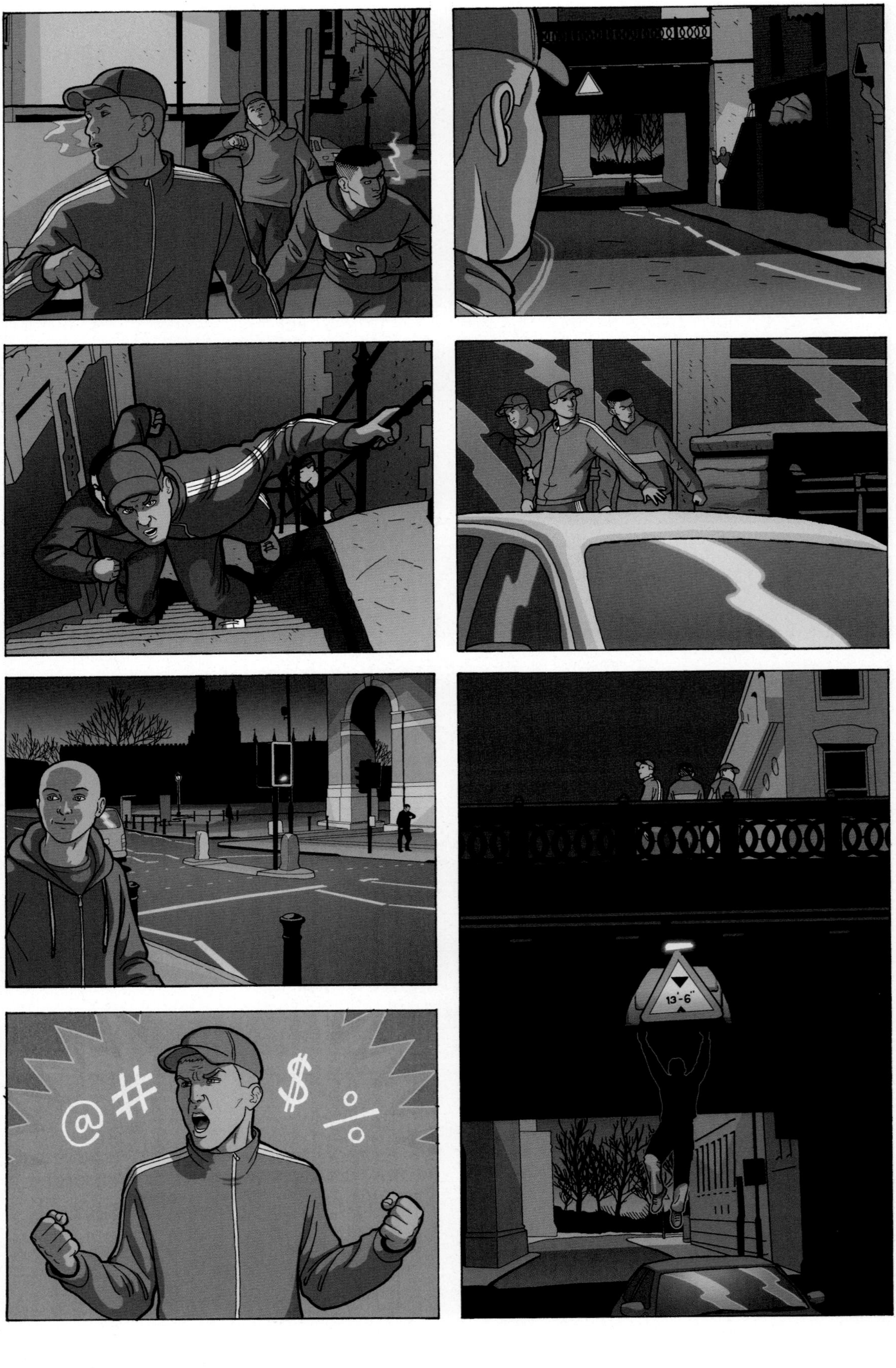
@#$÷
13'-6"

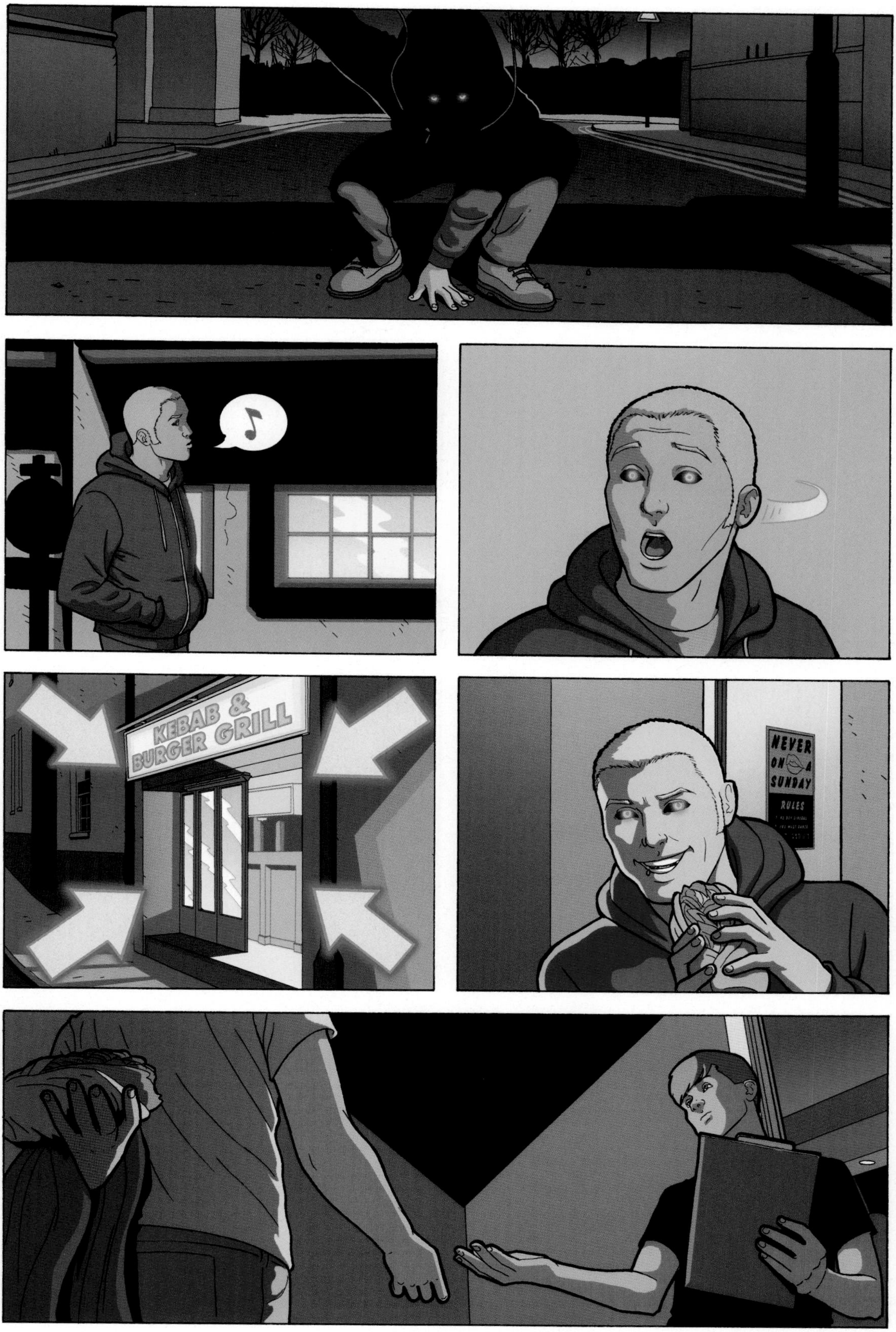
KEBAB &
BURGER GRILL
NEVER ON A SUNDAY
RULES

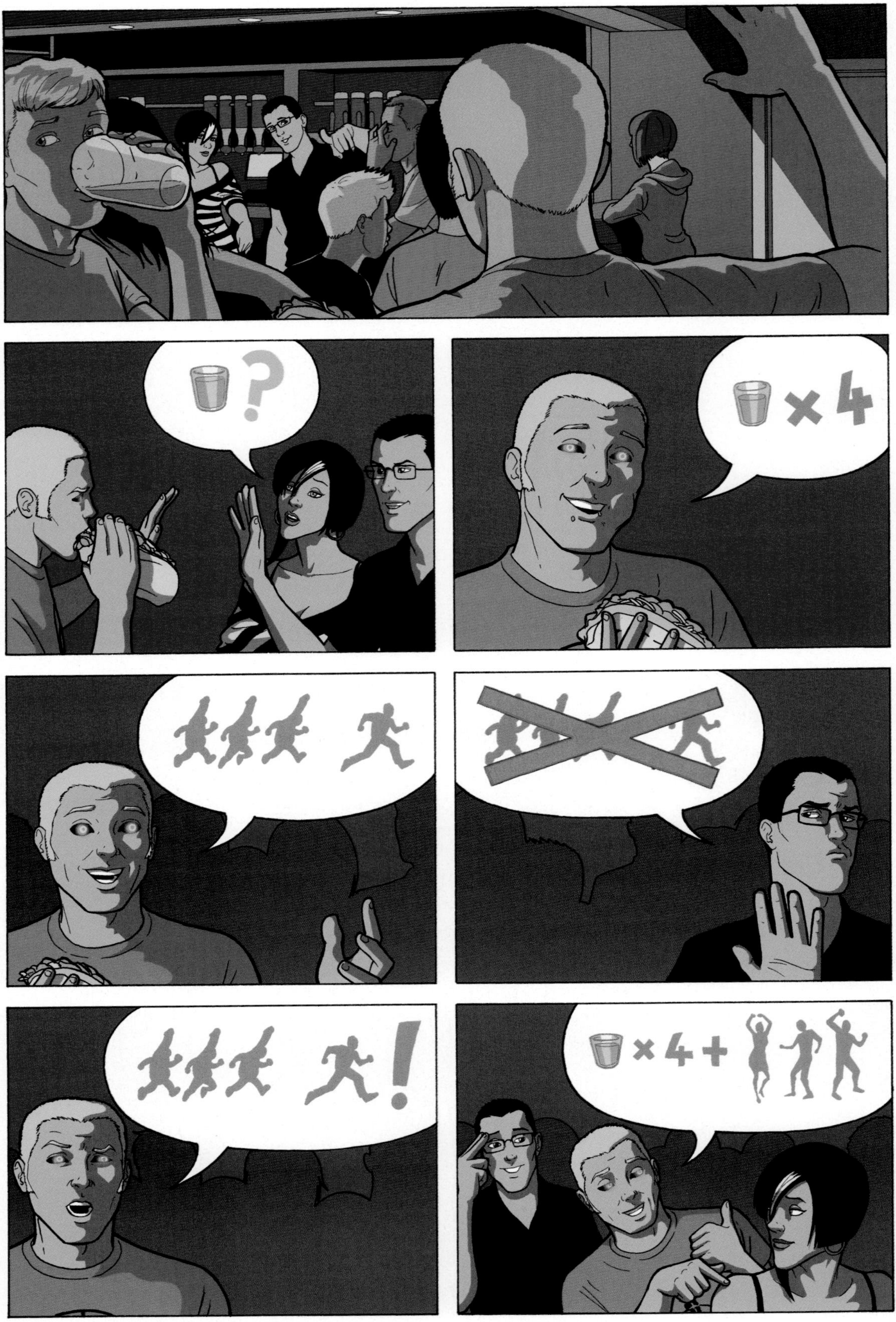
?
× 4
!
× 4 +

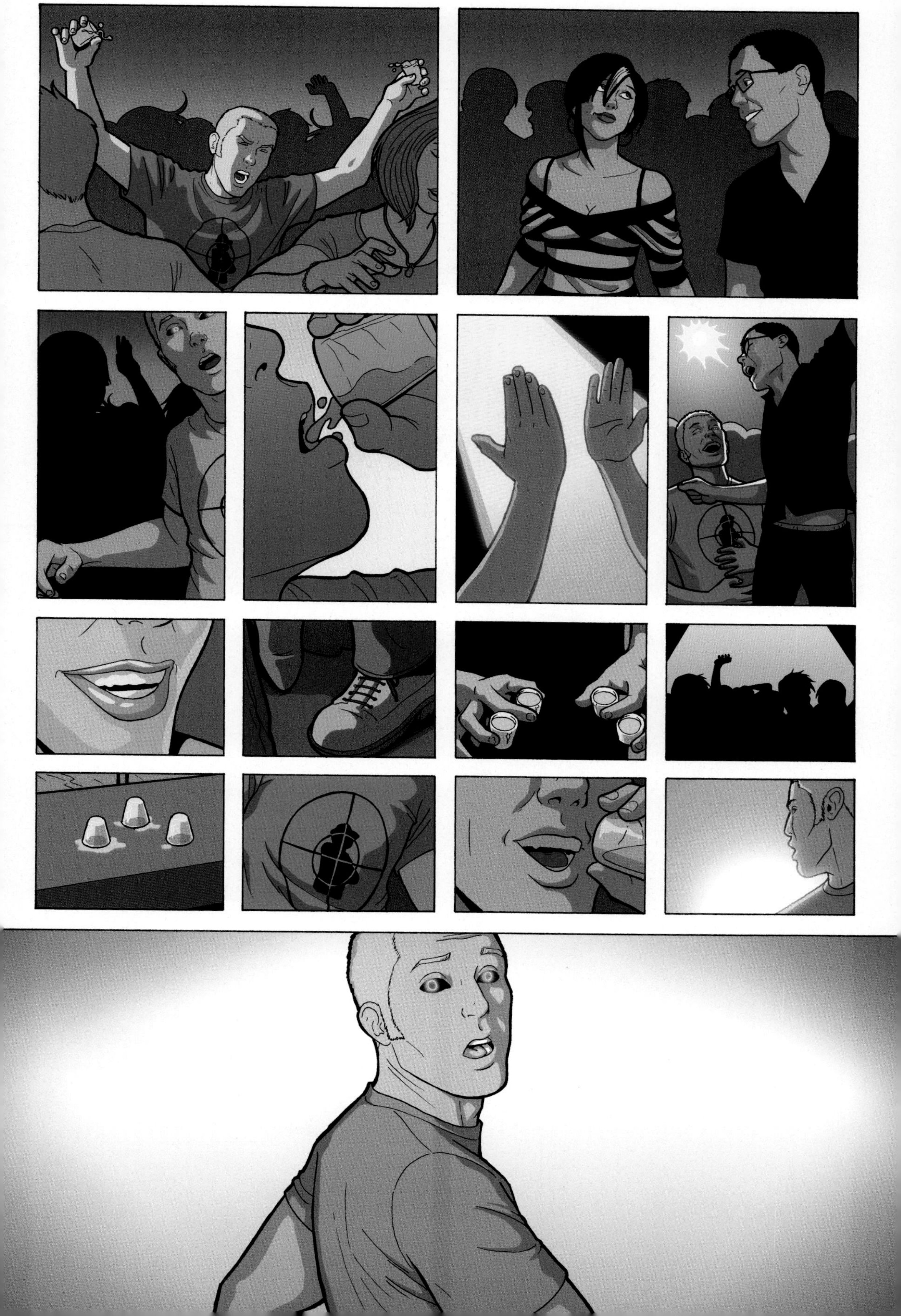

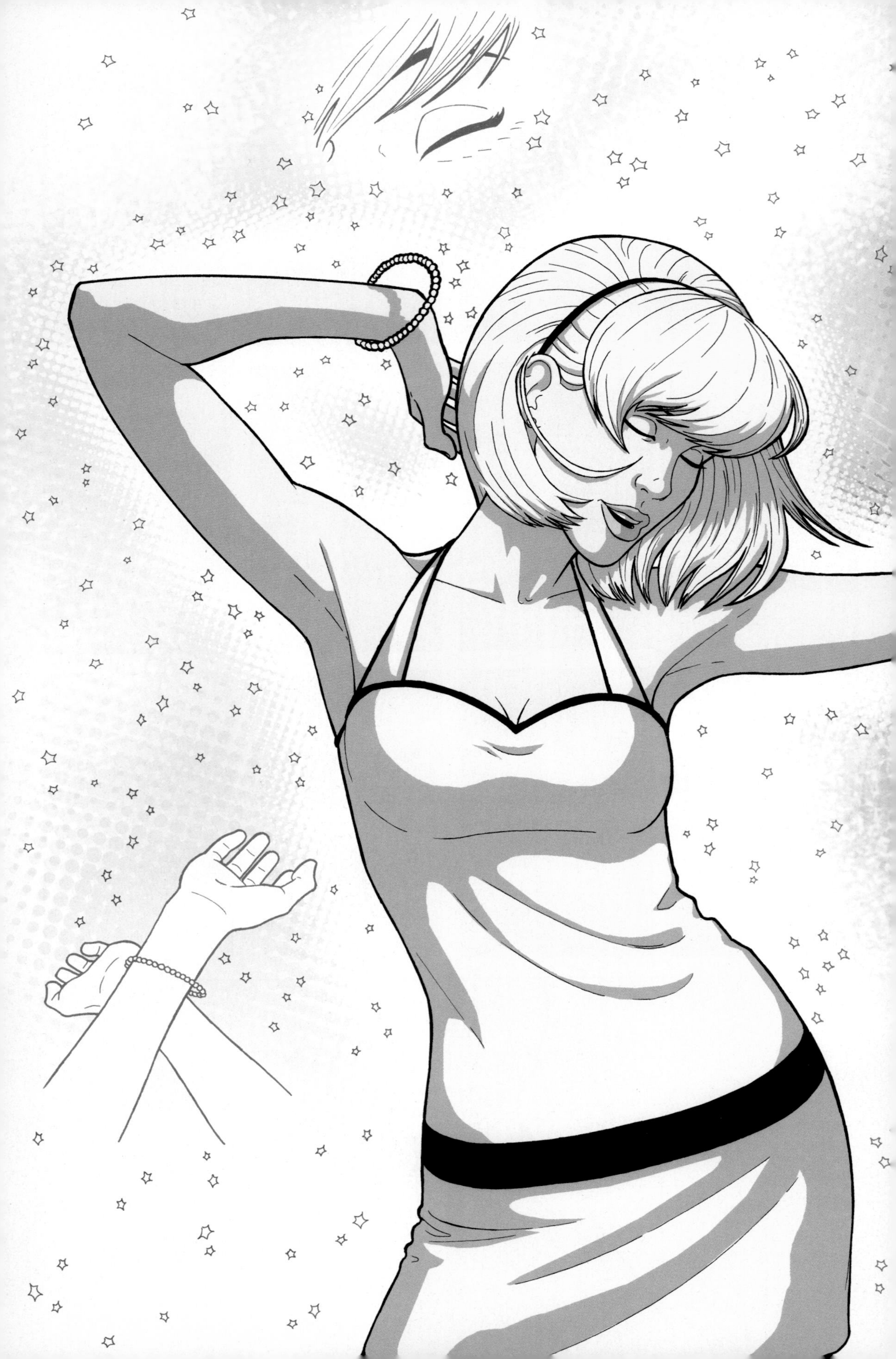

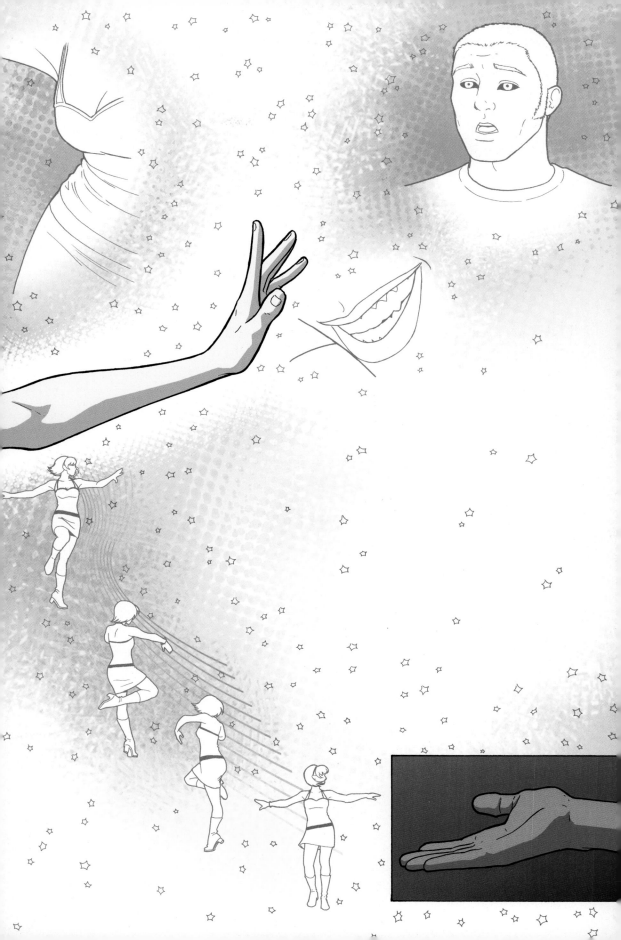

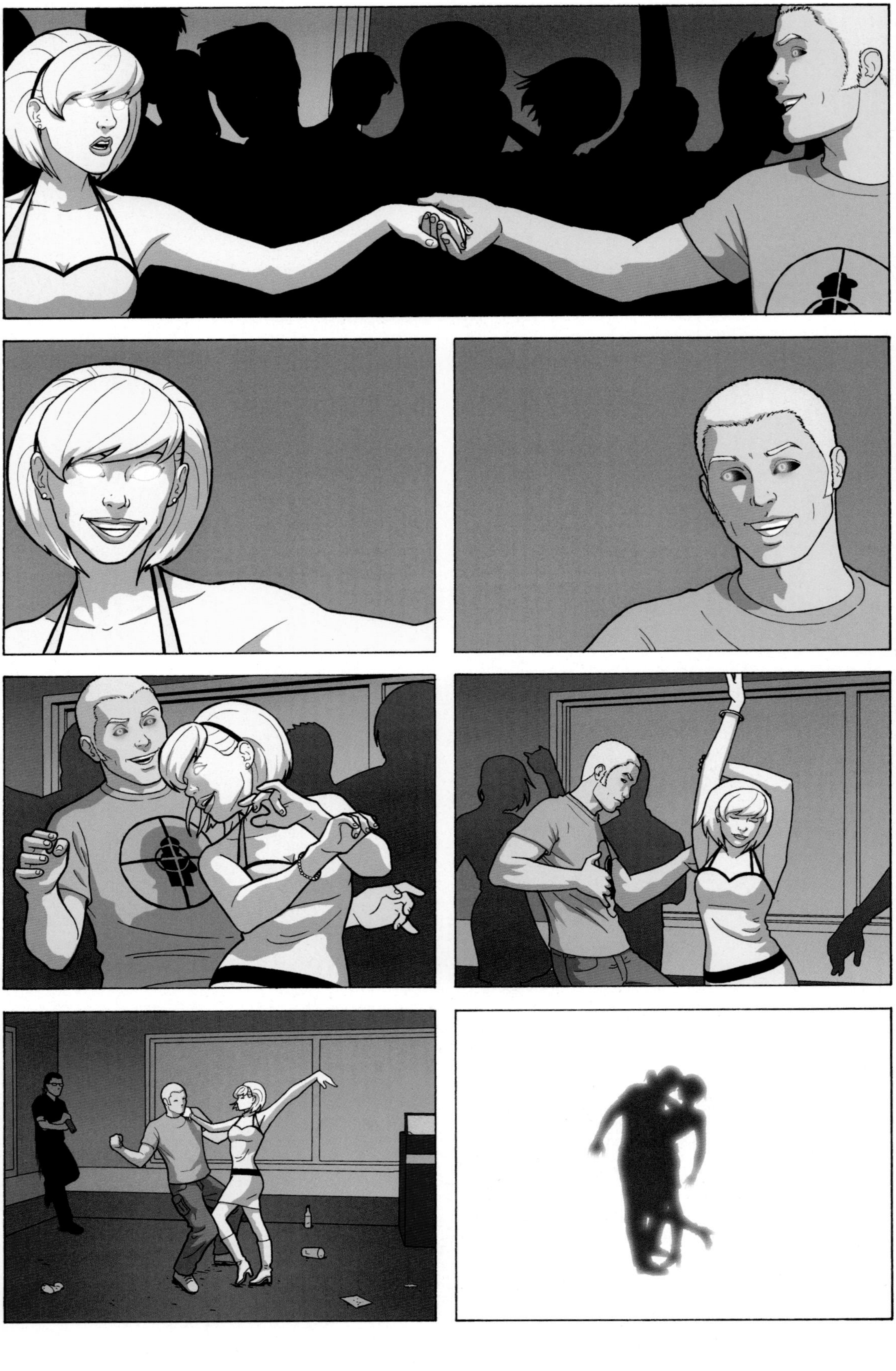

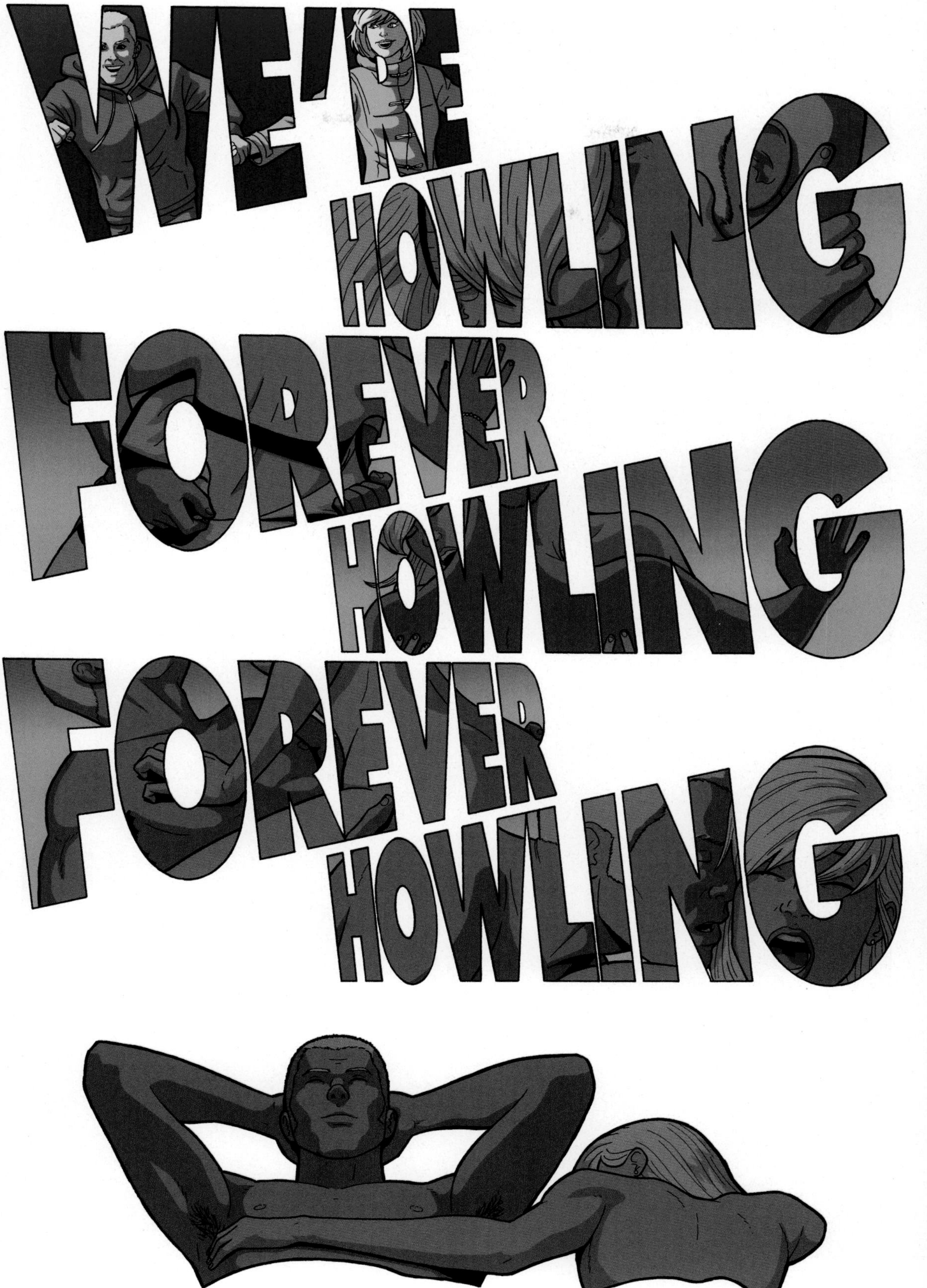
WE'RE
HOWLING
FOREVER
HOWLING
FOREVER
HOWLING

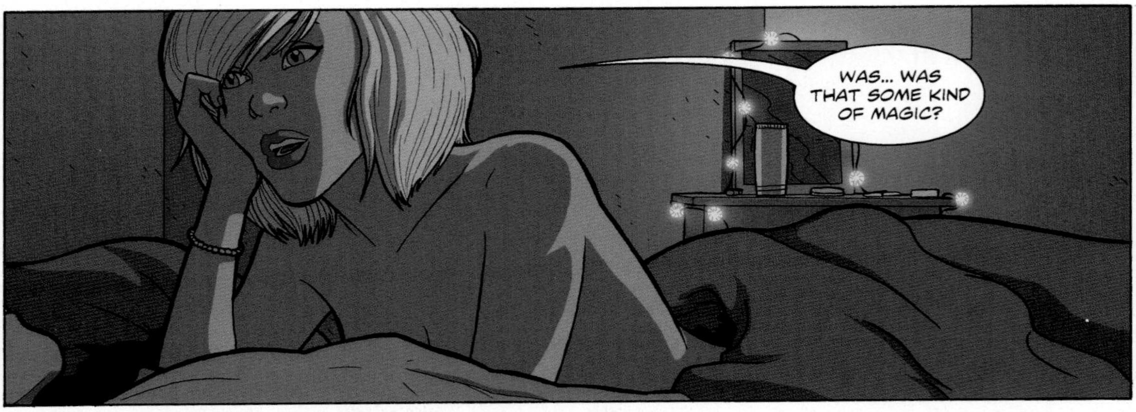
WAS... WAS THAT SOME KIND OF MAGIC?

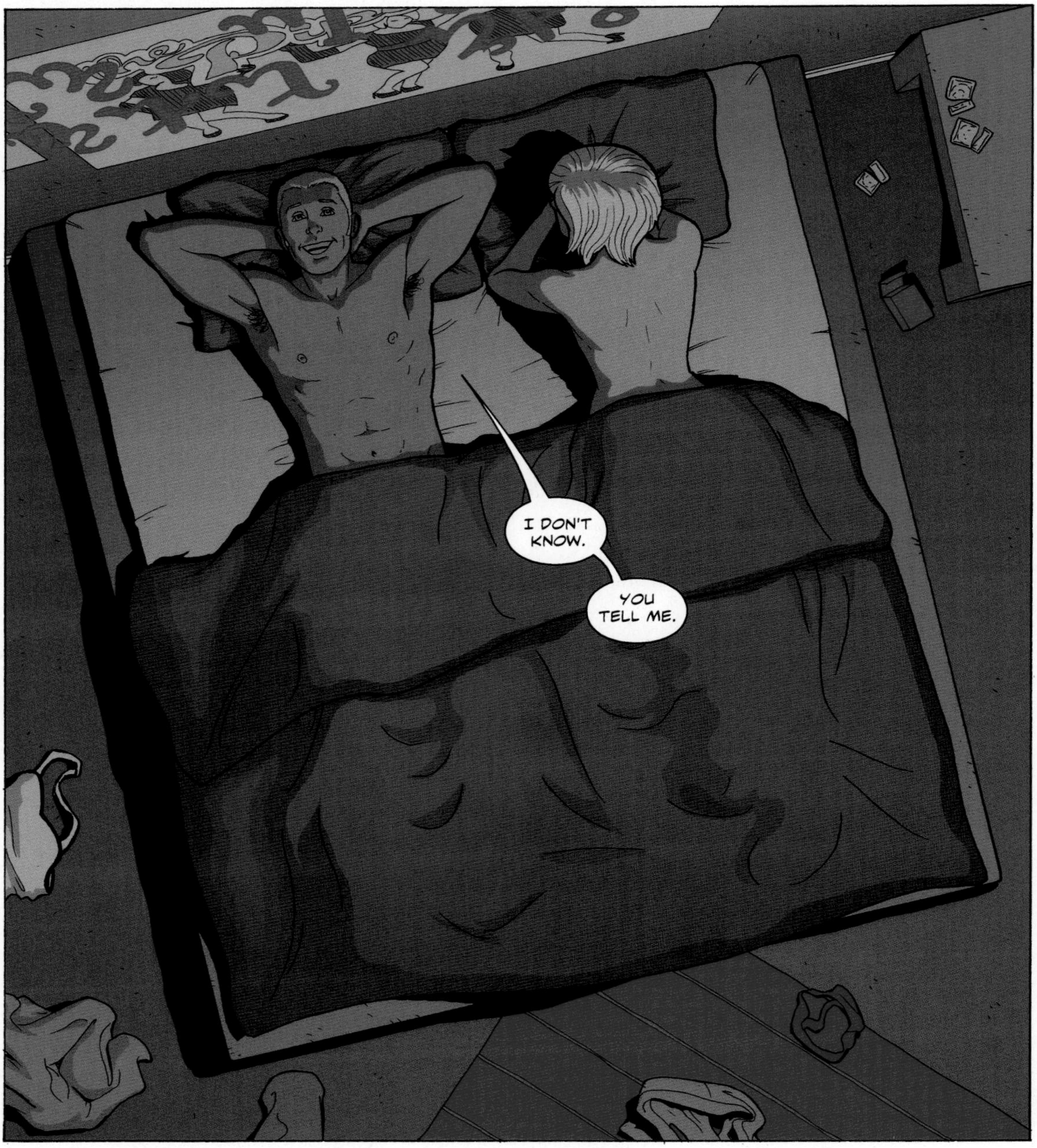
I DON'T KNOW.
YOU TELL ME.

GLOSSARY

Not necessary, but good to know, eh?

"4 minutes and 37 seconds of TV On the Radio": Well, it's the length of "Wolf Like Me" from *Return To Cookie Mountain*. Probably relevant.

Airplane: 70s parody film. Presumably one of her parents made Laura watch it. They fuck you up your mum and dad, etc.

Annie: The sort of 00s Norwegian pop Goddess that gets Seth Bingo all a-flutter. Start with *Anniemal*.

Arctic Monkeys: Social observation, garage-pop and massive sales. Of all the 00s NME hype bands, they're the one which you're kind of glad they made it. Period album would be their debut, *Whatever People Say I Am, That's What I'm Not.*

"Atlantis To Interzone": Klaxons' single, found on their *Myths of the Near Future*. Those Klaxons have totally read all the predictable boy-lit, and aren't afraid to let anyone know it. Well done them.

"Atomic": Blondie single, found on all their Best-ofs and playing 24-7 in the better part of your heart. It's an instant dance-floor.

Bath Moles: Not a David Attenborough special about elusive burrowing mammals, but a tiny club in Bath.

"Be My Baby": BOOM! BOOM-BOOM! TSCH! Spector-produced Ronnettes single with the drums that have launched a thousand indie-pop records.

"Beautiful Ones": Suede single from *Coming Up*. Enormously popular. Enormously hateful. The sort of shallow that gives "shallow" a bad name.

"Britannia": The Goddess of Britpop. Kohl got up to adventures involving her in the previous series, *Phonogram: Rue Britannia*. It's still available. Go order one. You'll like it. You've read it? Order another one. Money makes us hot.

Blondie: New Wave pop-awesomeness. If you want posturing points, start with *Parallel Lines*. If you just want a portable pop-altar, start with a *Best Of*. Ideally, do both.

"The Boiler": Single by the Specials AKA and Rhoda. That it was actually a Top 40 hit in the UK is a testament to the Special's enormous period fanbase. It's... well, not a dancefloor filler.

Busta: Busta Rhymes! Charismatic and mentalist rapper! Busta! Busta Rhymes! Woo Ha!! Woo Ha!! Er... start with *When Disaster Strikes...* if you were to choose an album, I think.

"Can I Take U 2 The Cinema?": Kenickie B-side. Hyper-adorable.

Chicks On Speed: Electroclash's answer to Bananarama. That is, awesome. Start with *Chicks On Speed Will Save Us All*, I think.

"Completely pointless endeavour...": Seth's mocking what Kohl got up to with Britannia in the last series. He's probably right.

Coolio: 90s West Coast rapper and... okay, I said this in the back matter of the individual issues, but he totally got his shoes stolen at a gig in my hometown. This threw me for weeks.

Crystal Castles: Screaming and bleeping faux-bitcore from Ontario. Period material would be *Alice Practice EP*, but that's all on their debut album *Crystal Castles*.

CSS: Cansei De Ser Sexy. Which is Portuguese for "In 2006, everyone fancied Lovefoxxx". Er... it's not, but it may as well have been.

"Dancing Queen": Abba's greatest single. Which is saying something. Start with *Abba Gold*. Though *The Visitors* is the one to own if you're trying to posture. Though trying to posture with Abba is always risky.

Dexys: Dexys Midnight Runners.

Dorian: Dorian Cox. Guitarist and main lyricist of The Long Blondes.

Dresden Dolls, The: Self-described Brechtian Punk Rock Cabaret. Which is the sort of thing you do to see if you can preempt someone just calling you goths. You can understand. The period album would be *Yes, Virginia...* but I'd start with their eponymous debut.

East 17: EVERYBODY IN THE HOUSE OF LOVE! Pre-ASBO early-90s pop.

Elastica: Wire-inspired Britpop. Recorded one album. No, they recorded one album. ONE ALBUM.

Emo: Emo, as a phrase, has a history which at least some people who feel proprietorship of the term feel the need to bring up when anyone uses the phrase like She is doing. Alas, it doesn't matter. They lost that war. Marc is being very emo.

"Every breath you take": A sinister stalker anthem by the Police.

"Every little thing she does is magic": Not a sinister stalker anthem by the Police.

"Everyday is Like Sunday": Nothing about stalking at all, by Morrissey. Also, splendid.

"Faster": From Manic Street Preachers' *The Holy Bible*. Grim and glorious hymn to personal autonomy.

Fratellis, The: Glaswegian Rock band. Period album is *Costello Music*. Kieron once saw them support the fragilely-experimental Young People in a tiny club, which is probably the least sensible pairing of bands he'd ever seen.

"Gangsta's Paradise": Coolio's ultrahit.

Garbage: Hyper-slick 90s pop-alternative. Always the precise sound of what a TV producer turns to when trying to signify a moody aggressiveness. An advertising jingle for wearing black. In other words, can be a lot of fun. We like *Garbage*.

"Gigantic": Pixies single about how awesome big cocks are.

Girls Aloud: Pretty much justify the reality-show 00s-pop treadmill singlehandedly. Period album would be *Chemistry*.

"Graffiti My Soul": Girls Aloud album track. S&M pop-sheen Prodigy, basically. From *What Will The Neighbours Say?*

Gossip: There was always a dance-element to their femme-punk radicialism. Period album is *Standing In The Way Of Control*.

"Got you all in check": WOO HA!! Splendid Busta Rhymes single.

Hard-fi: Sorta-Clash-influenced indie band. *Stars of CCTV* would still be the kinda-period album.

"It takes guts to be gentle and kind": And it does. From the Smith's "I Know It's Over" found on *The Queen Is Dead*.

"I can give you what you want. And... make your heart beat short": Laura's fumbling around with a line from the currently-playing New Young Pony Club's "Ice Cream".

"I got 5 On it": Luniz's 90s mega-hit-but-not-as-mega-as-Gangsta's-Paradise. Sinister and blissed.

"I Like A Boy In Uniform": SCHOOL UNIFORM! The Pipettes hymn to bisexuality wasn't actually their first single-release. Oh, *Seth*.

"I Wanna Be Your Joey Ramone": With the possible exception of "You're No Rock 'n' Roll Fun", Sleater-Kinney at their fluffiest. Found on *Call The Doctor*.

"It's a Vertical Expression Of Horizontal Desire...": George Bernard Shaw. And a good line to steal, if you're going to steal. And Laura certainly is.

"Ice Cream": New Young Pony Club single. Found on *Fantastic Playroom*. Agreeably slutty in a somewhat-clichéd manner. That's always one of the better ways to be agreeably slutty. Highly original agreeable sluttiness is kinda missing the point.

"Into The White": Pixies B-side. Kim Deal vocals. It's on a few Pixies *Best Ofs*.

Jam, The: What Paul Weller did first. We can't say anything mean about the Jam, because Image's publisher Eric Stephenson will hunt us down and decapitate us with a RAF-Mod-badge if we do so. I admit, rather than going to any one album, I'd start with a *Best Of* if you haven't touched them before.

Johnny Boy: The logical collision between the Manic Street Preachers and Saint Etienne. As such, commercially doomed. One album *Johnny Boy* and Kieron's single of the decade.

"Just A Song About Ping Pong": Operator Please's most known single. The Arcade Fire meets Bis, basically.

Kate: Kate Jackson. Long Blondes' singer. Laura's biting her style. It's 2006. Everyone bit Kate Jackson's style.

Kenickie: Simultaneously the answer to the general-knowledge question of "What band was Lauren Laverne in before turning to presenting?" and late-90s glitterkid godheads.

"Kisses...are... wasted...": "Your Kisses Are Wasted On Me". Not the Pipettes first single. But possibly their best.

Klaxons: London nu-rave and the contemporary NME-hype band. Everyone else in Kohl's list of Emily's ire is one too. Their *Myths of the Near Future* is actually a lot of fun.

Knife, The: Swedish electro. One of the very few bands which both Kieron and Jamie are properly devoted to. Period album is *Silent Shout*, but you'll want *Deep Cuts* too.

"Konichiwa Bitches": Splendidly self-aggrandizing Robyn single.

"Groove Is In the Heart": After some consideration, probably the greatest pop-single-as-actual-pop-single of our lifetime.

"Hot Topic": The potted-history of feminist pop-music you can dance to. In fact, you have to. Find on Le Tigre's *Le Tigre*.

Laura's Dialogue: As those who've got as far as chapter 5 will know, the vast majority of what Laura says is a quote. It's normally from the Long Blondes' – go and see their own entry to point at where you can explore 'em further. Any exceptions will be found elsewhere in this fine glossary.

"Let's Make Love And Listen To Death From Above": Cansei De Ser Sexy single. Shiny! The song is made of shiny!

"Let's make this our revolution...": Quote attributed to anarchist Emma Goldman. She didn't actually say it, but it's so awesome that you'd have to assume she'd be pleased with it anyway.

Libertines, The: Faded English romanticism. Can't stand them now. Couldn't stand them then, for that matter. Two albums, both of which you'd need to really get a handle on them. *Up The Bracket* and *The Libertines*.

"Libs": Libertines for people too lazy for those troublesome extra syllables.

"Line-up": Elastica single. Wire-like. In a "share the songwriting credits with Wire" sort of way.

Lloyd's Walls: Lots of bands, including Cat Power, Sonic Youth, Belle and Sebastian, The Make-up and magazine covers. The coded message is "Lloyd doesn't get out much".

Long Blondes, The: Sheffield's sadly-defunct most glamourous. Two real albums, the period one being *Someone To Drive You Home*. Their other referenced material will most easily be found on their singles-and-b-side-collection *Singles*. Only exception is "Fulwood Babylon" which you'll have to make do with locating on YouTube and/or Spotify. It's all worth doing so.

Los Campesinos!: Cardiff-formed gloriously over-verbal wall-of-sound indie-pop. If you've ever been tempted to write a manifesto about something only *you* deeply care about, then they're probably the band for you. Their early material Lloyd is listening to is collected on their *Sticking Fingers Into Sockets*.

Luniz, The: West-coast rap and makers of the eternal "I Got 5 On It", which you'll find on *Operation Stackola*.

"Maneater": Zombie-stomp of a Nelly Furtado single.

MCR: My Chemical Romance. If Team Phonogram had any sense, we'd have done an MCR-themed issue in a month when one of MCR singer's Gerald Way's splendid *Umbrella Academy* comic was released, and try and go for some crossover readership. Alas, we have no sense. As evidenced by us deciding to do *Phonogram*. Period album is *The Black Parade*.

Morrissey: 80s-titan of mope. I'd start with one of his Smiths albums. Namely, *The Queen Is Dead*.

Motown: Purrrrrrrrrrrrrrrrr.

"My Love Life": Morrissey single which the Long Blondes quoted in their "You Could Have Both" which we quote in... yes, we know.

New Young Pony Club: London electro-pop band. Period album: *Fantastic Playroom*. Sorry to be so boring, but I had to write about them every issue in the singles, and I've run out of funny things to say. SIGH.

Nu-Rave: Very late 2006.

Northern Uproar: Very late 1995. Except shitter than late 2006.

Oasis: Warring Mancunian brothers and whoever else they said were in the band, until they decided no one was. Well, until the next album, eh? Start with *Definitely Maybe*.

Operator Please: Australian punk-pop band formed to win high-school battle of the bands compo. Which sounds like the plot of a made-for-TV movie, but don't hold that against them. "Just a Song About Ping Pong" was actually early 2007, but Seth would have had it on promo. It's found on their *Yes Yes Vindictive*.

Penny's Walls: Klaxons, Blondie, Gossip, CSS and gig-posters torn off walls. The coded message is "Penny gets out a lot".

Pipettes, The: Brighton-based pop-manifesto band with a singer-turnover which makes the Sugababes look like a job for life. Period album would be *We Are The Pipettes*.

Pixies: The only band Kieron travelled to another country to see specifically. Aliens, inbreeding, bad-spanish, surf-guitar, heaven. Start with *Doolittle*.

Police, The: When not threatening the Fremen of Arrakis, Feyd-Rautha Harkonnen enjoyed forming new-wave reggae-influenced pop.

Projected Passion Revue: Dexys Midnight Runners Mrk 1.5. Only recorded a few singles before exploding, eventually reforming into the *Too Rye Aye*-era band. The singles, live material and a few radio sessions are collected into the really-quite-awesome *The Projected Passion Revue*. Worth believing in as much as Lloyd does.

"Protect Ya Ne...": "Protect Ya Neck" by the Wu Tang Clan, from their instant-classic *36 Chambers*.

"Plan B": One of the aforementioned Projected Passion Revue-era Dexys Midnight Runners singles. Lloyd will have dug to get a copy of it on vinyl.

"Pull Shapes": The Pipettes' purest statement of intent, basically.

"...Ready To Be Hearbroken": Shortened from "Lloyd, I'm Ready To Be Heartbroken" from Camera Obscura's *Let's Get Out Of This Country*. Answer song to Lloyd Cole and the Commotion's "Are You Ready To Be Heartbroken"?

"River Deep Mountain High": More Spector-wall-of-soundism with Ike and Tina. Except only really Tina, y'know?

Robyn: The sort of 00s Swedish pop Goddess that gets Seth Bingo all a-flutter. Except more so. Start with *Robyn*.

Rowland, Kevin: Troubled and inspiring Dexys vocalist and driving force.

"...Shyness turning criminally vulgar...": Referencing The Smiths' "How Soon Is Now?"

Sleater-Kinney: Olympia-formed now-defunct feminist-punk inspirations. Of all the band who tends to get joked about in *Phonogram*, this is the one I feel guilty about. Eventually I'll write someone who gives them their due. Until then, start with *Dig Me Out*.

Shitdisco: Nu-rave kinda thing. *Kingdom of Fear* was the album.

Smiths, The: Start with *The Queen Is Dead*. I'm not going to explain any more. Go listen. Now! Go! Shoo! Shoo! We'll wait for you.

Spank Rock: Agreeably obscene electro rap. Grab *YoYoYoYoYo*, as it's a lot of fun.

Specials, The: One of those tentpoles propping up British pop history. They opened the doors to more interesting things than existed before they did. That's one of the best things a band can do. Start anywhere, but I'd advise *More Specials* to get a picture of how unusual they were.

Stirnerian: Max Stirner. Extremely monomanical philosopher. Emily Aster doesn't spend all her time making sure her fringe is just so.

Stone Roses, The: Madchester They-could-have-been-a-contenders. Start with *The Stone Roses*.

Sugababes: Kind of the Dr Who of British Pop Music, in that one gets killed every few years and replaced with a budding new would-be star. Start with *One Touch*, which a compare-and-contrast to the present-day 'cubes will teach you lessons on the nature of pop.

Stereophonics: Oh, I can't be bothered. I get to write about the Supremes next. The Supremes! You wouldn't spend any effort on the Stereophonic's brand of welsh stadium-sized-pub rock if you got to write about the Supremes next.

Supremes, The: Diana Ross and the other two. BABY! BABY! WHERE DID OUR LOVE GO! And so on.

"The ban": Smoking in pubs was banned in the UK in 2007, so it was on people's minds.

"The theme to a sitcom...": The sitcom being Brush Strokes, which Dexys did the theme to.

"The Third Album": *Don't Stand Me Down*. One of the great commercial-suicide albums of all time, for the record.

Take That: The early 60s had The Beatles versus The Rolling Stones. The early 90s had Take That versus East 17. But hey! I'll take the 90s anyway.

Thekla: Bristol club. Actually on an enormous boat. Oddly charismatic.

"Wedding Party Perennial...": "Come On Eileen" which I suspect will be played at weddings until the end of time. Or, at least, I hope it will be.

"When you play pass the parcel...": Opening of Los Campesinos! "We Throw Parties, You Throw Knives". Found on *Sticking Fingers Into Sockets*.

"Who's That Girl?": Robyn's finest four minutes. A Knife-produced examination of confusion and that gap between you and them, wondering whether your shared love's enough mortar to fill the hole. And yeah, worth being that overwrought about.

"Woo-ha!!": GOT YOU ALL IN CHECK! It's the full title, but Kohl's being tediously anal by pointing it out.

"Wurzels, The": The premier Yokel-core artistes. Famously good lending schemes involving combine harvester keys.

"You Keep Me Hanging On": Supremes single. AN AWESOME SUPREMES SINGLE.

X-Ray Spex: Listening to X-Ray Spex in 2010 makes me think that X-Ray Spex were the only 70s punk band who really grasped the true horror of the future. Catch up with them with *Germ Free Adolescents*.

"Wolf Like Me": New York's TV On The Radio's most shamelessly upbeat moment. A welcome break from charting the progress of modern emotional and/or literal apocalypse. Find on *Return To Cookie Mountain*.

"Wine and bed and more and again": Rough paraphrasing a key refrain from Cansei De Ser Sexy's "Let's Make Love And Listen To Death From Above".

THE MAKING OF THE SINGLES CLUB

N.B. Please don't read this just after finishing the comic.

The following was passed from Kieron to Jamie at the Bristol con in May 2007. It was the first actual real document produced for The Singles Club, *and lays out the early ideas of where we were planning to take it. A lot of changes, but there's a lot of core elements which remain. It is presented here, with relatively few edits. Even for the embarrassing stuff.*

PHONOGRAM 2: CHRISTMAS SINGLE[1]
Dramatis Personae

PENNY B

The Golden Girl of the scene. Nineteen and – like everyone else in the comic - single. She's a fledgling Phonomancer, who primarily uses it to increase her own glamour. She's a beautiful and funny girl anyway, but is using dance based rituals to become even more dazzling. She means no harm by this. This means that she's probably the trickiest design in the whole comic. She's got to be beautiful, and someone who /uses/ her beauty (both magically and naturally) to influence people while /still/ being a sympathetic character. She's not a seductress. She doesn't make anyone do anything which hurts them for her advantage? She's someone who just radiates life, and likes being the centre of attention – in fact, since she's always been the centre of attention, doesn't realise that she *can't* be. Its her basal state. Her magical dancing is – for her – almost like putting on a show. It's her own little performance, her little art. The story is – basically – about making her realise it /is/ art. That is, it's not primarily for the audience. It's got to be for her.

In comics, the initial reference that comes to mind is Spider-man's Gwen Stacey. Not that I've ever read those comics, but it's /that/ sort of beauty. She's tall, slim and blonde, she brings to mind all sorts of metaphors about Nordic streams. She could probably be in a hair-care commercial. She's an enormous fan of retro-girl indie pop, especially The Pipettes. Appropriately, she dresses in 50s-60s style dresses, cut a few inches above the knee and mod-pop boots. All in white. Small jewellery on wrists and neckline to offset it. She's walked off the set of some old mod film, almost.

LAURA EVANS ("Laura Black")[2]

Laura has turned twenty; of the four younger characters in the series, she's the oldest. She doesn't really *like* that role, but she actively forces herself into it. She's masochistic in that way. And not really just that way – she has a tendency to torture herself emotionally and physically. Her primary urge is to become someone else – we meet Lloyd later, who wants to transform his environment. Laura turns that desire inwards. To this end, she's trying to ape other things she likes to force a change. She speaks primarily in quotes from other places – lyrics, writers, whatever. People sometimes get this, but mostly don't. Her efforts go unnoticed... while her friend pulls off dazzling magic which everyone loves. Laura is a bit embittered by this, but is really just as enamoured by her as everyone else: Laura is sexually confused. She's probably bi, and certainly has a long and slow burning crush on her friend.

(Laura is a mirror to Aster. While Emily wasn't exactly like Laura, there are a lot of similarities.)

Suitably, while Penny is a figure in white, Laura is her shadow. Her primary influence shows clearly – Laura is a passionate, devoted to the point of sociopathy fan of Kate Long Blonde. She has a similar glammy-punk-retro image. She's wearing a beret, and wears a scarf and antique fashion. The differences are telling though. While her beret and scarf can be a splash of colour – blue? - her clothes lean towards blacks and other darker hues. She's probably in trousers, if only because everyone else is leaning towards skirts. She is wearing a jacket though, which she never removes. Both for reasons of fashion and because she's secretly a cutter. The scarf is probably the main visual motif for her – rather than the short one, it's actually very long. Not quite Tom Baker Dr-Who, but it's a similarly striking visual motif. She wears a lot of make-up, modelled after Kate Long Blonde. She's shorter, plumper than the waif-like Penny – but not actively fat – and less attractive generally. She's the unattractive friend, and knows it.[3]

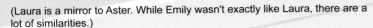

---

(1) I went back and forth between *Christmas Single* and *The Singles Club* for the title. I think I fell the right way.
(2) Laura Black changed to Laura Heaven shortly after writing this. Laura Black was shit. Laura Heaven is too, but Laura Black was shit the wrong way, if you see what I mean.
(3) Of course, in Jamie McKelvie world, "Less attractive" is relative.

LEE MARK LATHAM[4] (aka Marc, "The Marquis")

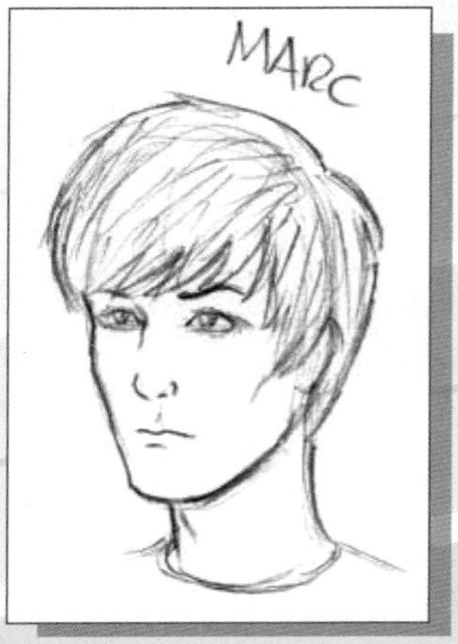
MARC

Lee is either just about to or just has just left his teens. Still – out of the four protagonists, he's probably the one who's most together... at least, he would have been a few months ago. He had a hectic two month affair with a girl (**THE GIRL**) which just redefined what he was expecting from life. She was a life-changing moment, and a skilled Phonomancer. He's literally haunted by memories of her – cursed by how good she was to be around, tied directly to the music. He can't get her out of his head, and it's an intense incarnation of this which powers most of his plot.

He's the best looking male character. I picture him actively pretty, with a splash of androgyny to him; he'll be wearing make-up, I dare say. In my head, I'm roughly basing his look off Patrick Wolf, with a similar dyed hair look to what he's got at the moment.

Shares a similar build too. Dresses fashionably. Musically, he leans towards more modern electro material – he loves the Knife, for example, something he'll share with Emily if they ever start talking (they don't). People often presume he's either gay or at least bi. He doesn't play up to this, but doesn't deny it either.

He's a minor Phonomancer, generally specialising with the pure hedonistic uses of the ability. Despite his successes – he's at least as good as Penny – he's very much a dilettante. He does well as he's not trying to do as hard a thing as either Lloyd or Laura. Neither Lloyd or Laura really understand this, so it grates with them. Long term, it's probable he won't be a Phonomancer for the rest of his life. It's something he'll probably drift out of, assuming he eventually shakes this curse...

He calls himself Marc. It's other people who call him the Marquis. He's one of the few people in *Phonogram* who've had an "honourific" applied to them, rather than choosing one. The name he's chosen, in fact, is slightly sleight.

LLOYD (aka Mr Logos)

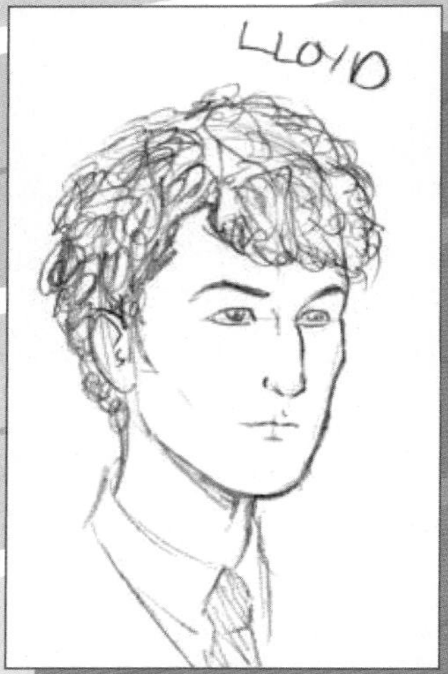
LLOYD

Lloyd is also at that nineteen/twenty boundary. He's a fledgling Phonomancer. While having more active success than Laura in actually making rituals works, what he's mainly doing is alienating himself from everyone else. This kind of suits him – Lloyd feels like an anachronism. While he likes many modern bands, in terms of his true touchstones he looks back at other people and movements... and mainly movements and people who were themselves anachronisms, even when they were active. He's an enormous Dexys fan, for example. He's driven by a puritanical desire not to compromise. He has very little sense of humour. And he desperately wants to change his life.

He's got two magic things he's concentrating on. One is his ritualistic fanzine/grimoire writing – looking for insight through music, and applying it to his own memories. The other is trying to get a band together, as a magical act. He believes he has a plan that if only people would follow, would change their lives. He's primarily here to try and recruit other characters into this plan. He also wants to sleep with Penny. Or maybe Laura. Maybe even Marc[5]. He'd like *someone*.

In short, Lloyd is ready to be heartbroken.

He's extremely tall and thin, over six-feet. He has tightly curling hair which may bring to mind him from the Kooks – a fact he despises almost as much as he hates the Kooks, but – out of sheer pig-mindedness refuses to make into a more fashionable look. I picture him in an almost mod-esque suit, almost certainly bought second hand, and in his head is meant to be a reference to the third-album Dexys' business/preppy image. He'll almost certainly have a few badges on his lapel.

He calls himself Mr Logos. No one else does.

In the same way Laura holds up a mirror to what Aster was a bit like when she was younger, Lloyd holds up a mirror to bits of Kohl. But we'll get to that.

(4) I have no idea why Marc's real name was Lee Mark Lathham at this point. It was probably a metaphor.
(5) I was playing with Lloyd's story about coming to terms with being gay for a long time. In the end, it didn't stick. Lloyd's sexuality is the least of his problems.

THE GIRL (aka She)

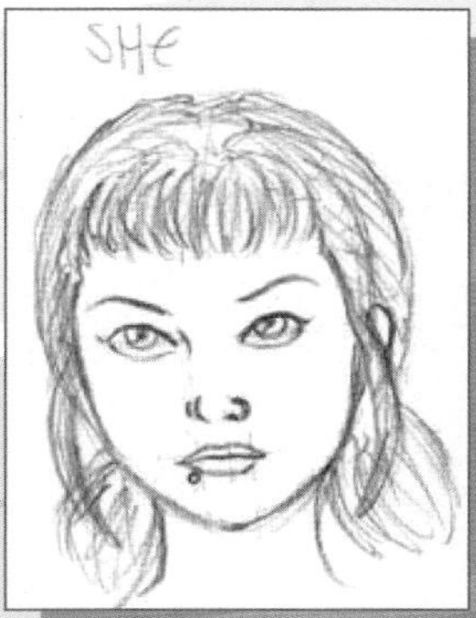
SHE

We're not giving her a name. She's referred to as "She" or "her" throughout. I may change my mind on this – I'm trying to make her mythic rather than just objectifying her, so we'll see how that turns out.

She's a Polish immigrant girl, and – by the seats of pants – an improvisational phonomancer (She's our first link to a less postmodern form of phonomancery – crazy folk using crazy Folk). Her role is to be every model of the strange, exotic, brilliant, life-affirming, sexy, tempestuous, slightly insane girl who you can't believe you're with all the time you were with her. She's not as classically beautiful as Penny, but the girl has a rampant sensuality. People should fancy her and she's both aware and fine with that.

Medium height, with an athletic – but not *slim* – figure. This comes to me now, and entirely randomly, but – of all the girls in the story, she has the best ass. I don't know why I know this. I just do**(6)**. Facially, her lips and eyes fight for dominance. She has a dusky complexion, and has dyed her dark hair a shock of something vibrant. In terms of clothes, it's a trouser and loose-shirt sort of thing – in my head, you'll get splash of Gogol Bordello to her.

That's probably the best reference for her. Confident, irresistible Gypsy Punk Girl.

SETH BINGO AND THE SILENT GIRL

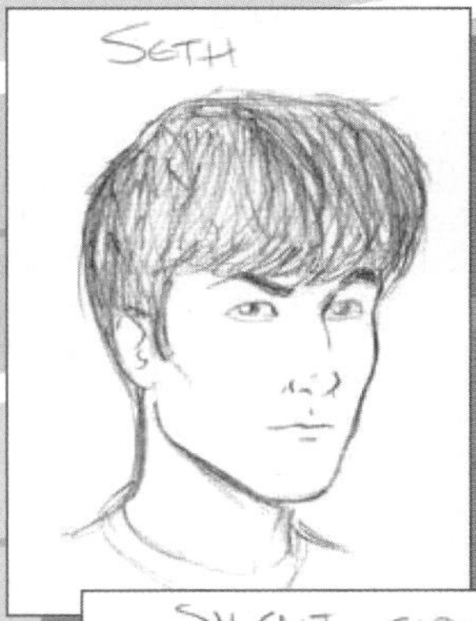
SETH

Dealt with together, as that's exactly what they are – at least, in this storyline. They're the two DJs of the night, and quite the pair.

Bingo is an old-time Phonomancer friend of David Kohl, now primarily living in London, DJing in Bristol for the night. Was once loosely affiliated with the coven, but split almost as soon as it was formed due to philosophical differences. He now loathes the circle and much of what it stands for – he hates Vox, Aster and Indie Dave (Aster most of all). Kohl, being a bit towards the edge of the coven, he treats better, but finds the whole adventures of Rue Britannia ludicrous. He's from a completely different tradition to anyone we've met so far – pure pop worship. He's narcissistic and solipsistic, capable of being blankly non-receptive and moody at a whim. Equally, he can be charming, funny and is a pretty talented phonomancer. He has a terrible tendency to speak of himself in a third person – also to explode apocalyptically on someone who fails some music-related taste-test. Don't you dare say Girls Aloud aren't a "real" band in his presence...

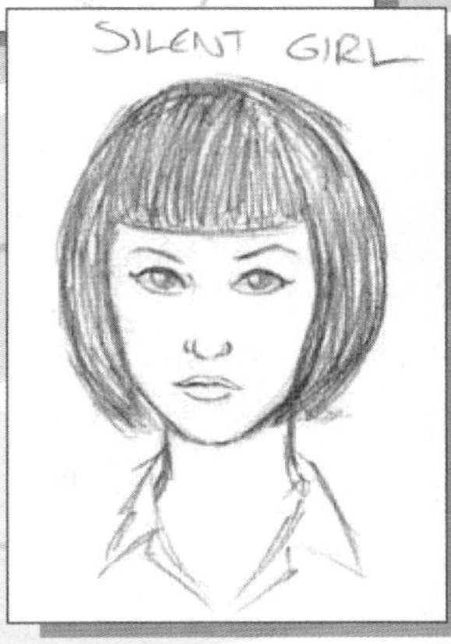
SILENT GIRL

The Silent Girl is exactly that. The Silent Girl at Bingo's side. She's never spoken to anyone else bar him, acting as some manner of enforcer. Bingo does the talking. She just stares and judges. People presume she's a phonomancer, but... well, who's to know? Some presume Bingo and Silent Girl are having sex. They're not. They just share an intense, private friendship. Bingo's solipsistic – but its a solipsism of **two**.

Physically, Seth is short and thin, but not unattractive. He's prettier than Kohl, for example, but has a relative sharp delicacy to his features that prevents either true handsomeness or genuine extreme-pretty boy. You could describe him looking rat-like, but that'll be a little harsh. If he's a rat, he's a pretty one. A couple of years younger than Kohl, he dresses even younger. His hair is tousled into a classic indie-kid fringe which hangs over his forehead. He likes alcopops. He is primarily clothed in skinny-fit T-shirts which most would presume to be ironic but really very much aren't: modern pop bands like Girls Aloud, for example. He could have a backpack. He could have random Japanese esoterica. You may want to add some chunky Japanese jewellry to the look, or perhaps some Hello-Kitty designed stuff. He could even be wearing shades, but I suspect we don't want to lose his eyes**(7)**.

Silent Girl is even shorter, and a good mix between being petite and curvy; she's openly attractive, and always perfectly groomed. She's the model of an indie-girl; think the hotter style of Belle and Sebastian fan with a splash of the Hello-Kittyisms. I picture her in a dress, but an elegant skirt/shirt combo would do. She's inching towards her mid/late twenties, just old enough to get comfortable in herself with none of the insecurity we'll see in some of the younger female cast. She spends most of her time, with other people there, just staring, blankly. She has an ability to make almost everyone else feel small, as if they may not measure up to her standards. She doesn't smile, at least to anyone else who isn't Bingo (The episode which is based around this pair, we reveal she's exactly the same as everyone else in their closed little universe). A dark brunette, straight hair, cut in a curving bob, probably. Lightly applied make-up. That sort of heart-shaped face – for some reason, this brings to mind Sophie Ellis Bextor, which isn't a bad model, if thinking about in her theaudience days.

(6) I still don't know. Semiotics are funny sometimes. I'm going to do a lecture on The Semiotics Of Ass one day. Anyway, this didn't matter, as due to our oppressive eight panel grid, you were lucky to know whether a character had legs, let alone whether they were attractive down there or not.

(7) Yeah, losing the eyes would be bad, but I still love the original Seth Bingo sketch with them.

Now for three people we've met before...

DAVID KOHL

Kohl, as is his wont, hasn't changed physically at all. He keeps as close to that iconic resonance – black, black, blackity-black – as he can. Possible exception – he may be wearing converses. Tonight, after · all, is a dancing night.

EMILY ASTER

Aster – much to her horror – finds herself at an Indie-night. She didn't really realise it would be an indie-night of THIS variety before heading out, so isn't dressed in something that fits in too well. It's clubbing gear for her. Being Emily, she'll have something new which we haven't seen her in before. I suspect this look will need to be openly slutty – the sort of microskirt that Mira enjoys wearing in the Duloks even[8], but twisted into Emily's style. She may have changed her hair since *Rue Britannia* – it is, after all, set nearly a year after the last one. Anything fashionable towards the arse end of last year would be perfect – that sort of contemporary history look is very important with her. Picking up a fashion/music mag like Dazed & Confused from December and taking something directly may be profitable.

KOHL FOR HEIGHT COMPARISON

CHERYL KIMBERLEY NADINE NICOLA SARAH

KID-WITH-KNIFE

Kid-with-Knife remains Kid-with-Knife. Never change, kid, never change. We'll probably see him slip out of his hoodie at some point. Beneath it, he's wearing a simple, well-cut T-shirt. We can probably see his necklace at some point, which has an arrow-head on. Never actually saw that in last series. Well, another time, eh?

THE PLAYLIST

The key events of *The Singles Club* happen in around an hour at the club. The following playlist basically acts like the click-track for the whole *Singles Club*, keeping it in time, or at least vaguely coherent. Careful examination of this with the issues will reveal that there's some panel transitions in the main comic actually are far longer than they appear. They are! They totally are. Comics are sneaky like that.

Blondie – "Atomic"
Ike & Tina Turner – "River Deep Mountain High"
Nelly Furtado – "Maneater"
Crystal Castles – "Air War"
New Young Pony Club – "Ice Cream"
Salt-N-Pepa – "Push It"
Johnny Boy – "You are the Generation that bought more shoes and you get what you Deserve"
Cansei De Ser Sexy – "Let's Make Love And Listen To Death From Above"
Girls Aloud – "Graffiti My Soul"
Sleater-Kinney – "I Wanna Be Your Joey Ramone"
Kenickie – "Can I Take U 2 The Cinema"
The Supremes – "You Keep Me Hangin' On"
The Pipettes – "Pull Shapes"
Robyn – "Who's That Girl? "
The Knife – "We Share Our Mothers' Health"
Elastica – "Line Up", "Who's That Girl?"

(8) London comedy-pop sensations. Jamie is namechecked in their "Octopus In Love" from Children Of The Sea. Immortality, of a sort.

REFERENCE PHOTOS

Here are some samples of the background work we used in the book. The photos here are for the scenes in issue 7. Kieron took them, which is why they are often wonky/of the floor/not actually a photo of the background I needed. With the aid of Google Street View, I managed to piece it all together. ***- JM***

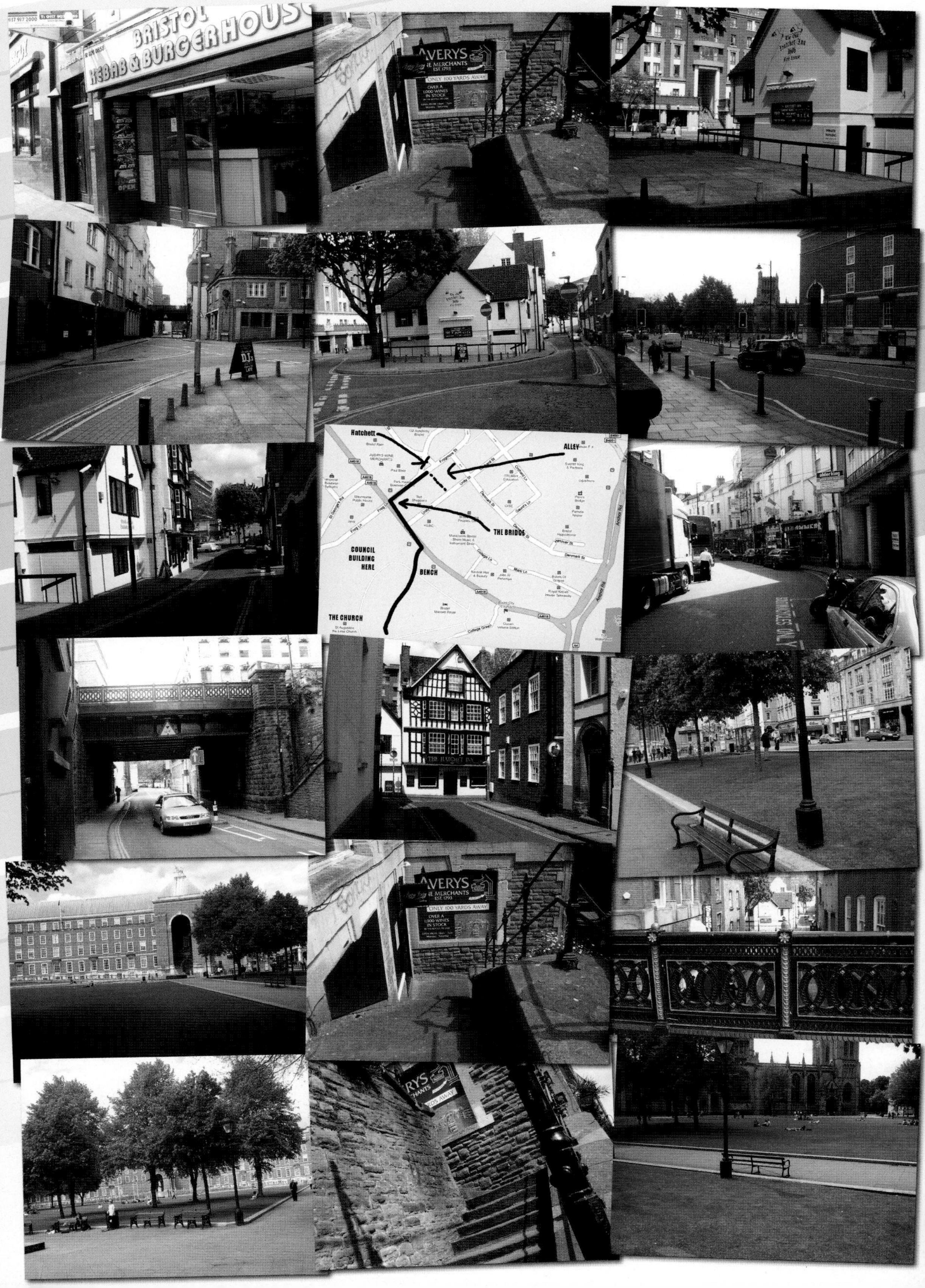

BRISTOL
KEBAB & BURGER HOUSE
AVERYS
WINE MERCHANTS
EST. 1793
ONLY 100 YARDS AWAY
OVER A
1,000 WINES
IN STOCK
Hatchett
ALLEY
THE BRIDGE
COUNCIL
BUILDING
HERE
BENCH
THE CHURCH
THE HATCHET INN

3D MODELS

I built a 3D model of the club in Google Sketchup so that I could keep it consistent throughout the series. By moving the camera around the model, I could plan out the angles I wanted to use in the comic. ***- JM***

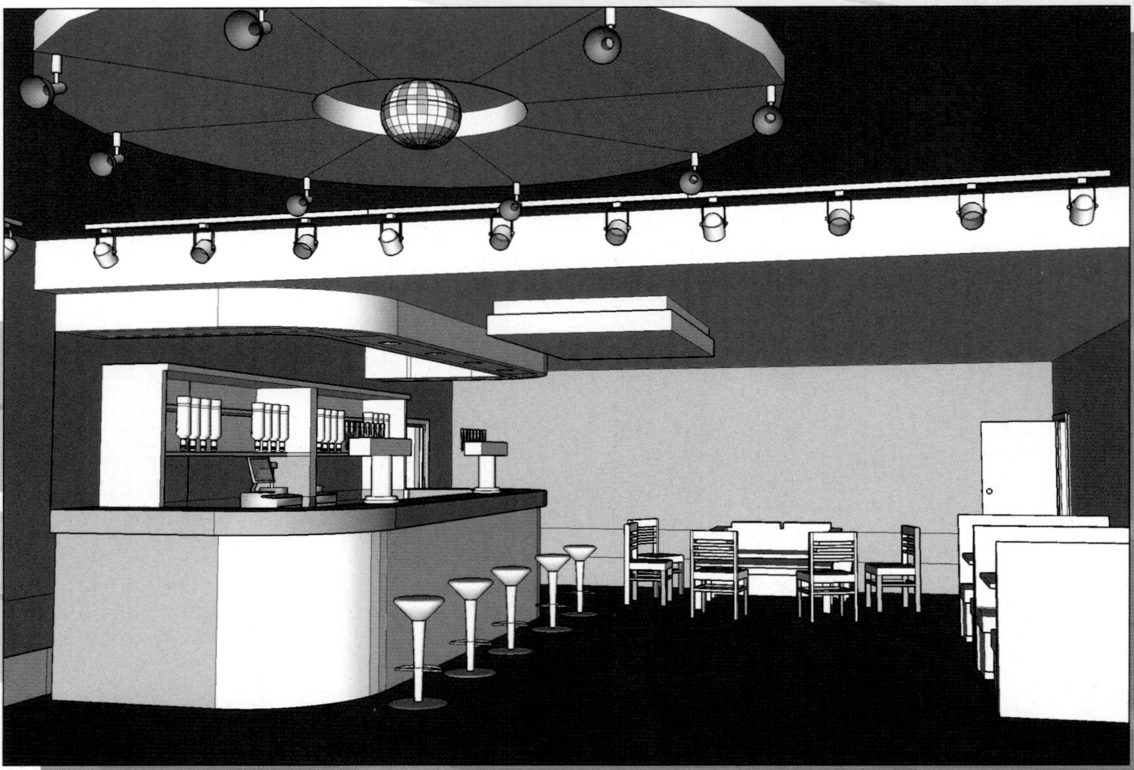

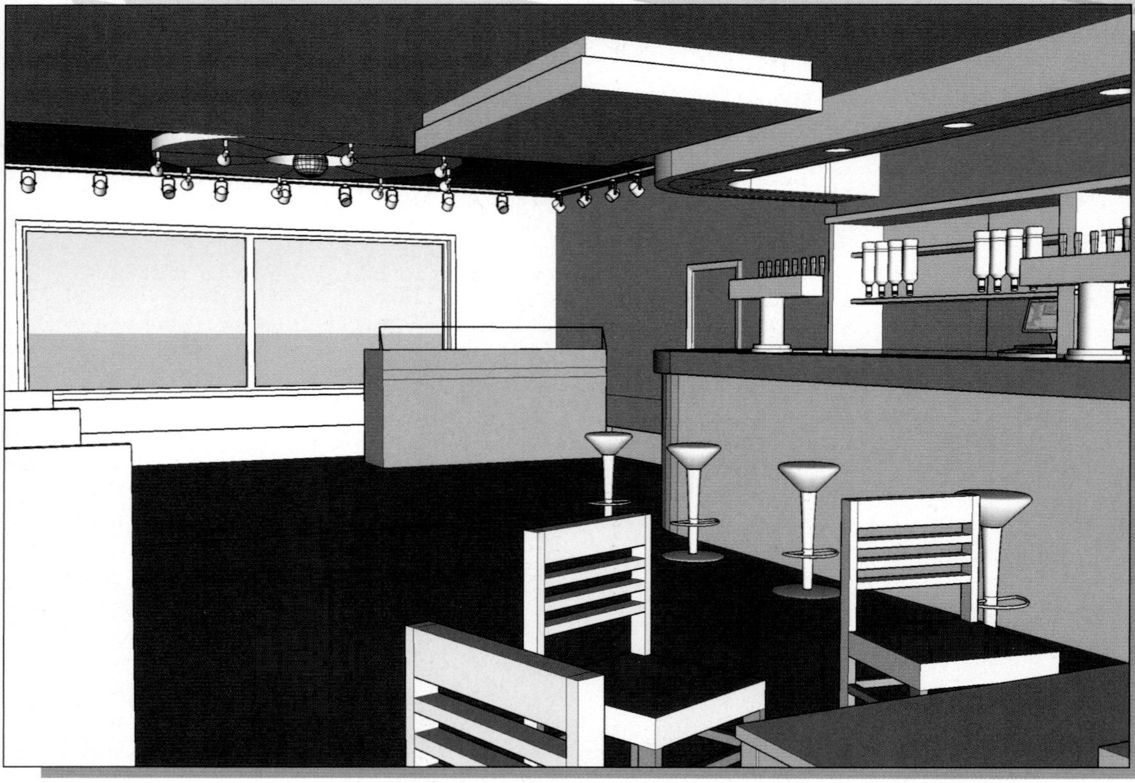

GENERAL INSANITY:

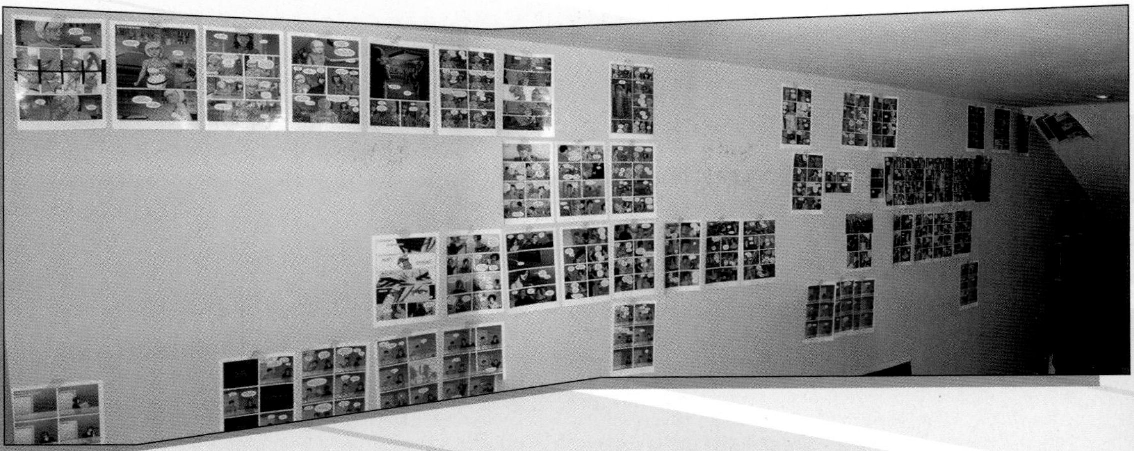

JAMIE'S PICTURE OF THE ARRANGED WALL

About halfway through the series, it became necessary for me to chart the movements of the people in the background of each scene, so that it would all match up when you're reading the scene from the point of view of a different character. To that end, I cut up copies of all the issues I had and put them up in chronological order on my wall, so I could see who was where at any given point. It lasted about two months before it started feeling very opressive and I had to rip it down. ***- JM***

CUTTING STUFF FOR THE ZINE ISSUE

To get the proper zine-effect for the issue, we gathered in Jamie's flat with glue, scissors and glitter and set to work. I don't think I've ever felt as sinister as I did with a pile of inexpertly cut-out Penny's heads at my feet. **- KG**

I've never seen Kieron happier than when he was cutting up bits of paper. Ever the zine kid. ***- JM***

METHOD DRINKING

I generally write most of the first draft of any *Phonogram* script drunk, and then edit it into shape sober (i.e. I edit a lot). About half way through writing *The Singles Club*, I had a little brain wave. As well as my usual routine of obsessively listening to the records the characters would like, I'd become a *method drinker*. In other words, drink whatever the character I'm writing would be drinking. For example, when dealing with Laura, I'd be throwing back neat swigs of the cheapest vodka from the corner shop – which was fantastic motivation to get a move on with the issue, just so I could stop drinking the foul stuff. This had a few unforeseen consequences. For example, when getting alco-popped up for Seth and Silent Girl's issue, I didn't realise the enormous bottles of cheap stuff were actually highly caffeinated. As such, I spent most of the night twitching with chemical energy. I never said I was smart. ***- KG***

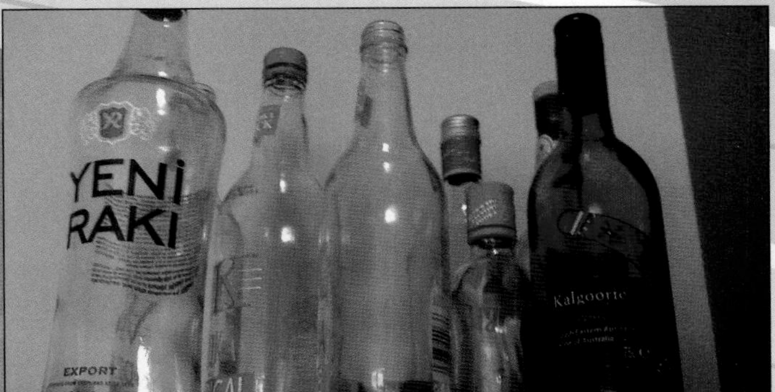
YENİ
RAKI

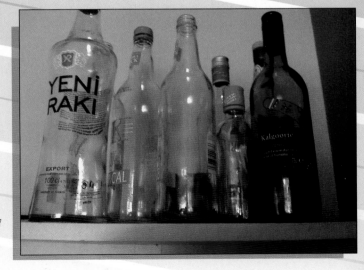

FROM SCRIPT TO PAGE:

PAGE 3

XX **(1)**
OO
XX
OO

3.1
We're just behind the vase, back on its place on the side. Lloyd's replaced it there. We're looking down the hall, away from the door, watching the shape of Lloyd move away from us, almost at a march.

NO DIALOGUE

3.2
From inside Lloyd's Room. He's in the doorway, turning on the lightswitch. He looks determined now, looking about the room.

NO DIALOGUE

3.3
Wide shot which we'll use to basically establish the room. It's a cluttered place. It's someone who does anything other than tidy up. Essential items: A computer, a bed, a record system – and actually a record system, as in Vinyl. He keeps his vinyl in the box.

Here, we have Lloyd crouching by the Music system, flicking through the Vinyl.
Posters and Flyers are on the wall. Bits of newspaper clippings, pulled out of the papers. Some of them have been edited into improvised collages. As you do the room, I can throw names at you. We've seen a girl's bedroom. This is very much a boy's - and a boy like Lloyd.

EDIT: Later, the following mail was sent:

You know, his walls actually say a lot about the guy:
Dexys - probably album sleeves which he's bought cheap, and stuck up.
Arcade Fire (SERIOUS YOUNG MAN!)
Cat Power (The Greatest, possibly)
Something B&S. Possibly earlier period - Tigermilk or if You're Feeling Sinister
Beruit.
Joanna Newson - probably Ys
Something by the Make-up: - go through for Album covers, but the iconic photo on the wikipedia page would work
Sleater Kinney
Sonic Youth (Goo cover)
Antony & The Johnsons

Oddly, I think he would have once like Art Brut before he got TOO SERIOUS, so I'm tempted by have something by it on there which he's half forgotten. He's the guy who'd actually rip off covers of magazines, cut out photos, clippings, so don't feel limited to actual posters.

NO DIALOGUE

3.4
From behind him, crouching by the record player. He's just pulled a single from its sleeve. It's a vintage copy of the Dexys single, Plan B. This was from Dexys Mrk 2, who never released an album, existing between Dexys Mrk 1 (Geno) and Dexys Mrk 2 (Come on Eileen). Phonomantically speaking, it's a rare artifact. It looks like this: http://tinyurl.com/yzvftb8

We can see the volume dial on the stylus here. It's about mid-high on the full range.

NO DIALOGUE

3.5
Close on Lloyd's hand, turning the volume to about as low as it goes. This is, of course, the opposite of the TURN IT UP which we kind of expect here. Also, practical. Also, a little nod towards a Dexys Record, Let's Make This Precious' urging to not turn up the record. Also, because it's the middle of the night, and Lloyd is cursed with being considerate.

RECORD: You've always been searching for something. **(2)**

3.6
Lloyd reaching beneath his bed, pulling out a typewriter. There's already a medium-sized cardboard box full of junk that's been put on top of the bed. There's probably some rolls of paper and similar sticking out – he box is decorated in scrawled Theban -PRECIOUS

RECORD: But everything seems so so-so

(1) This is my page tablature, something only I do, and I only do it on *Phonogram* nowadays. It's a basic map of the page when they're grids. There's more complicated codes when the grids get funnier, but this is a basic one X is a panel. OO is a merged panel.
(2) When working for Marvel, I normally actually capitalise my dialogue. But you have to pay me THE TALL MARVEL DOLLAR to go through ALT-C U-ing it all in Open Office. Jamie isn't worth it.

PENCILS

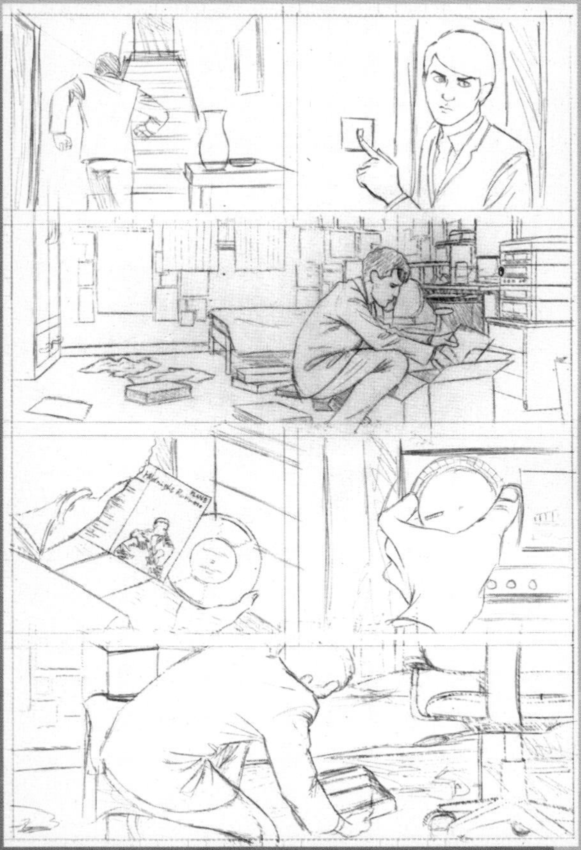

INKS

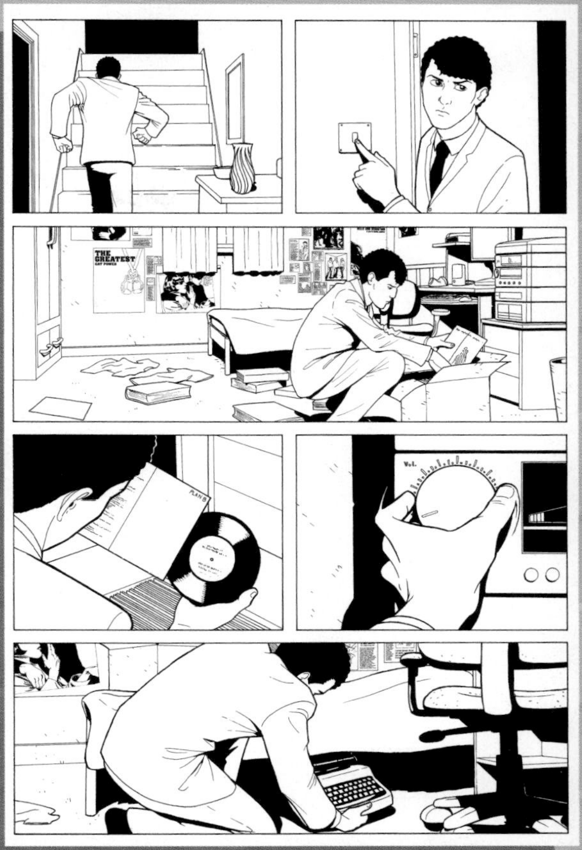
THE GREATEST
PLAN B
Vol.

FLATS

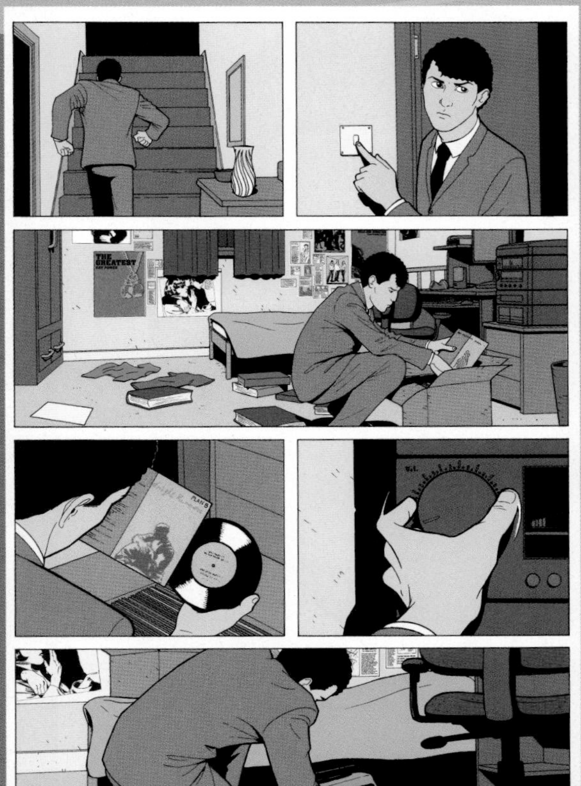
THE GREATEST
PLAN B
Vol.

COLOURS

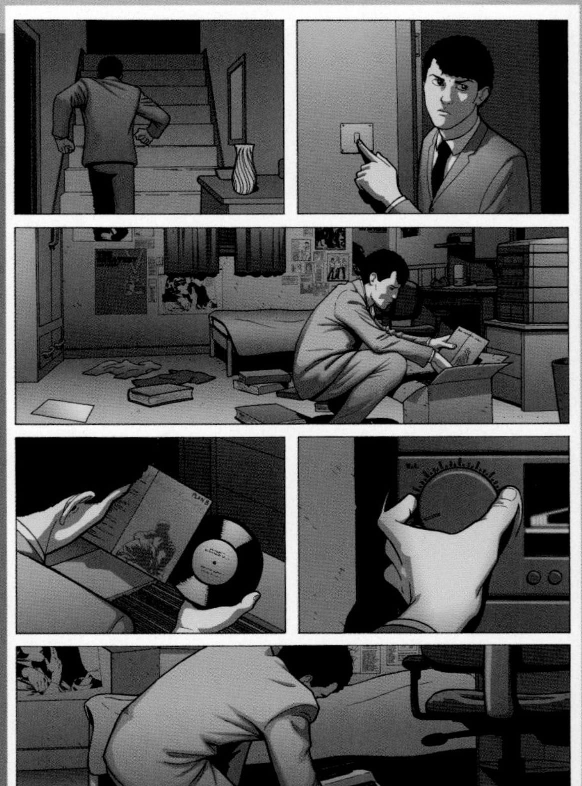
Vol.

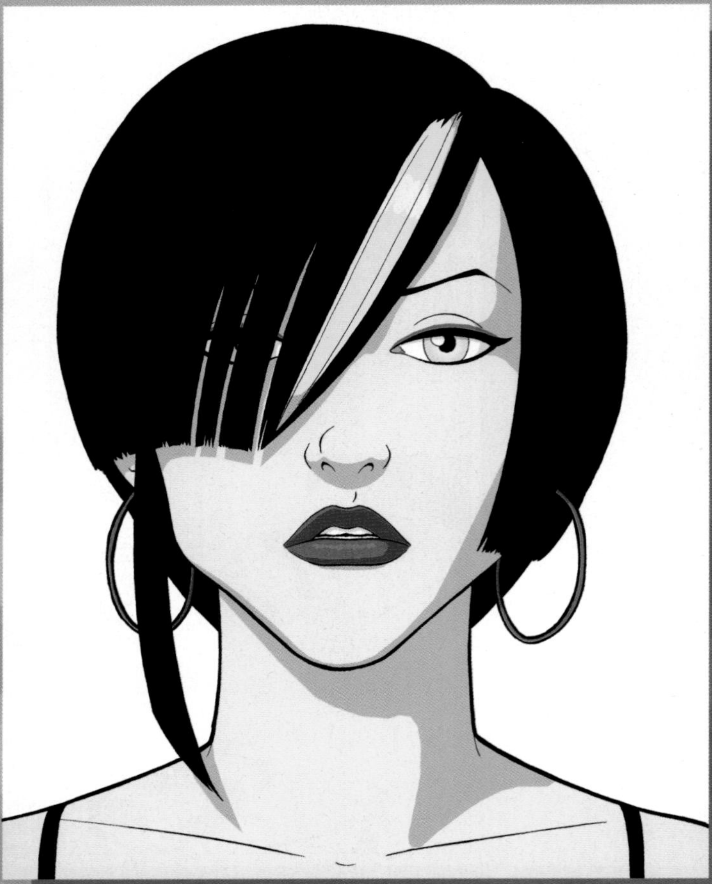

EMILY AND CLAIRE

To make the cover for the third issue, Jamie did these two fine faces, and then composted the pair to make the final image - which you'll see in a few pages. The idea of the covers was to make them look reminiscent of club-flyers, and the Emily issue worked particularly well - it turned up in a fairly extensive list of covers of the year at Comics Foundry. We reprint the full images here, to show them off. Also allow you to cut them out and make your own Emily and Claire finger puppets. Yes, it'll ruin the book, but then you can buy another one to replace it and we can have more of your money. ***- KG***

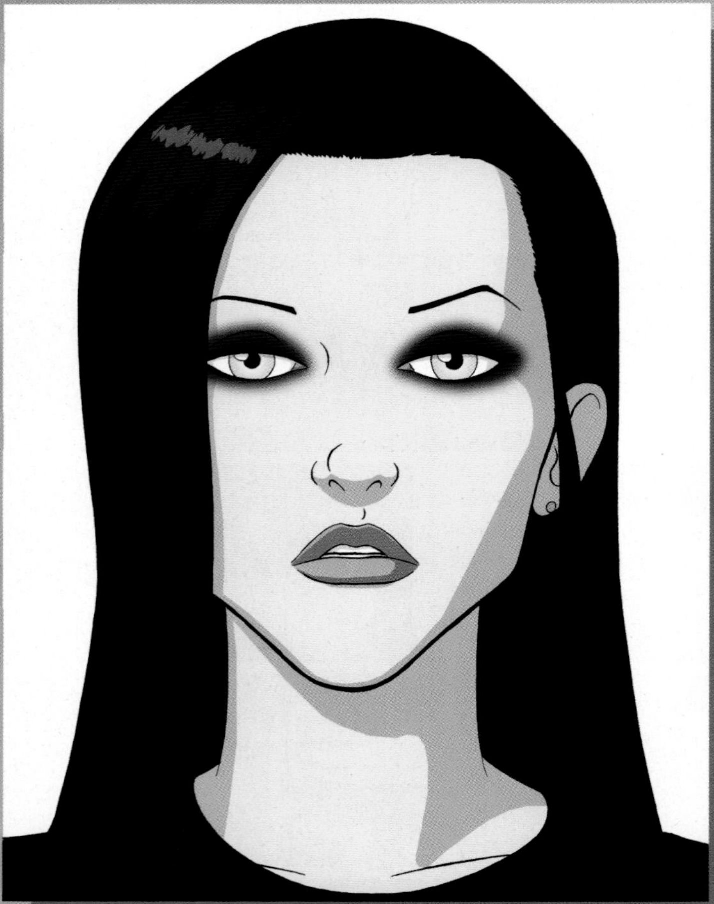

PHONOGRAM: THE ZINE:

This warmed our cold, black hearts. Matthew Sheret of London comics group We Are Words And Pictures *(http://wearewordsandpictures.com/)* curated a limited edition *Phonogram* fanzine (*"PHONOGRAM VS. THE FANS"* in the ATP-festival style). Lots of art and text contributions from the readers, and this frankly disturbing cover from Jamie. **- *KG***

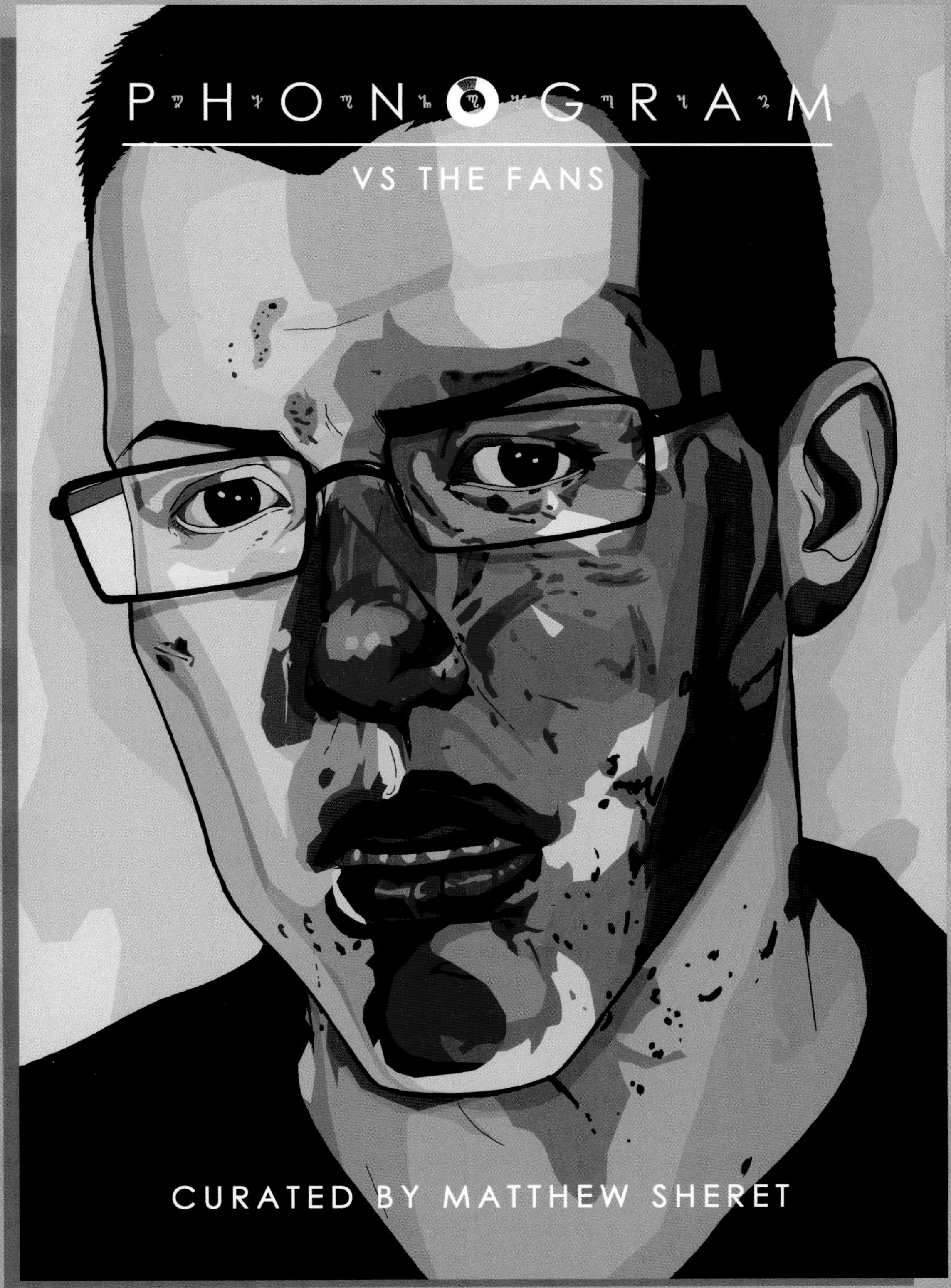
PHONOGRAM
VS THE FANS
CURATED BY MATTHEW SHERET

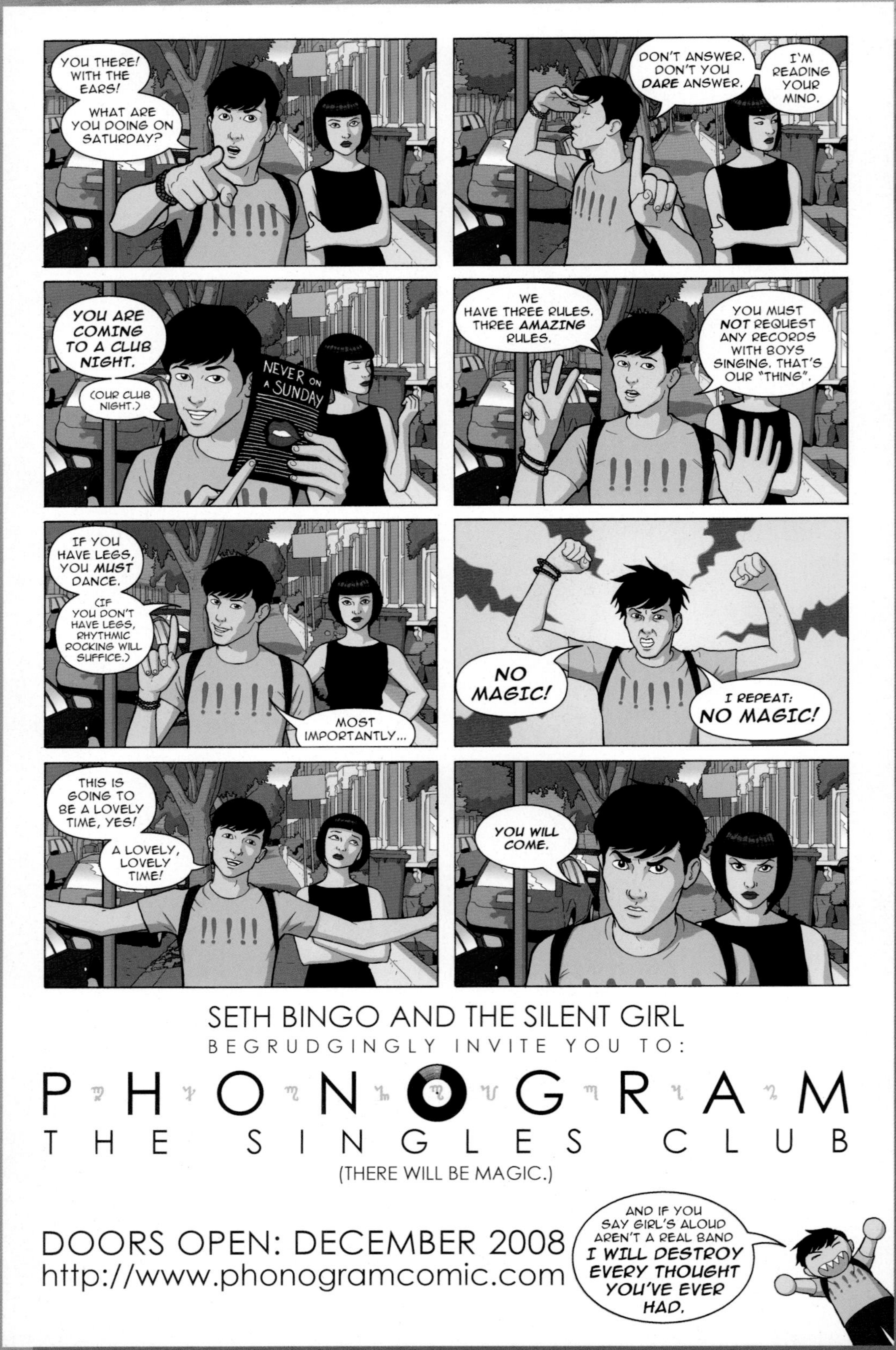
YOU THERE! WITH THE EARS!
WHAT ARE YOU DOING ON SATURDAY?
DON'T ANSWER. DON'T YOU DARE ANSWER.
I'M READING YOUR MIND.
YOU ARE COMING TO A CLUB NIGHT.
(OUR CLUB NIGHT.)
NEVER ON A SUNDAY
WE HAVE THREE RULES. THREE AMAZING RULES.
YOU MUST NOT REQUEST ANY RECORDS WITH BOYS SINGING. THAT'S OUR "THING".
IF YOU HAVE LEGS, YOU MUST DANCE.
(IF YOU DON'T HAVE LEGS, RHYTHMIC ROCKING WILL SUFFICE.)
MOST IMPORTANTLY...
NO MAGIC!
I REPEAT: NO MAGIC!
THIS IS GOING TO BE A LOVELY TIME, YES!
A LOVELY, LOVELY TIME!
YOU WILL COME.
SETH BINGO AND THE SILENT GIRL
BEGRUDGINGLY INVITE YOU TO:
PHONOGRAM
THE SINGLES CLUB
(THERE WILL BE MAGIC.)
DOORS OPEN: DECEMBER 2008
http://www.phonogramcomic.com
AND IF YOU SAY GIRL'S ALOUD AREN'T A REAL BAND I WILL DESTROY EVERY THOUGHT YOU'VE EVER HAD.

THE ADVERT

We got our mileage out of this. We made it as a promo piece and lobbed it online. We used it as a physical postcard and gave it out at conventions. We stuck it on the back of every issue, to introduce the series concept in a relatively pithy way. And we're re-printing it here. It seemed to go down well, as a marketing object. It's clearly one of the things which contributed towards *Phonogram: The Singles Club* being the huge commercial success that it was. ***- KG***

COVER GALLERY

A gallery of covers. Like, obv.

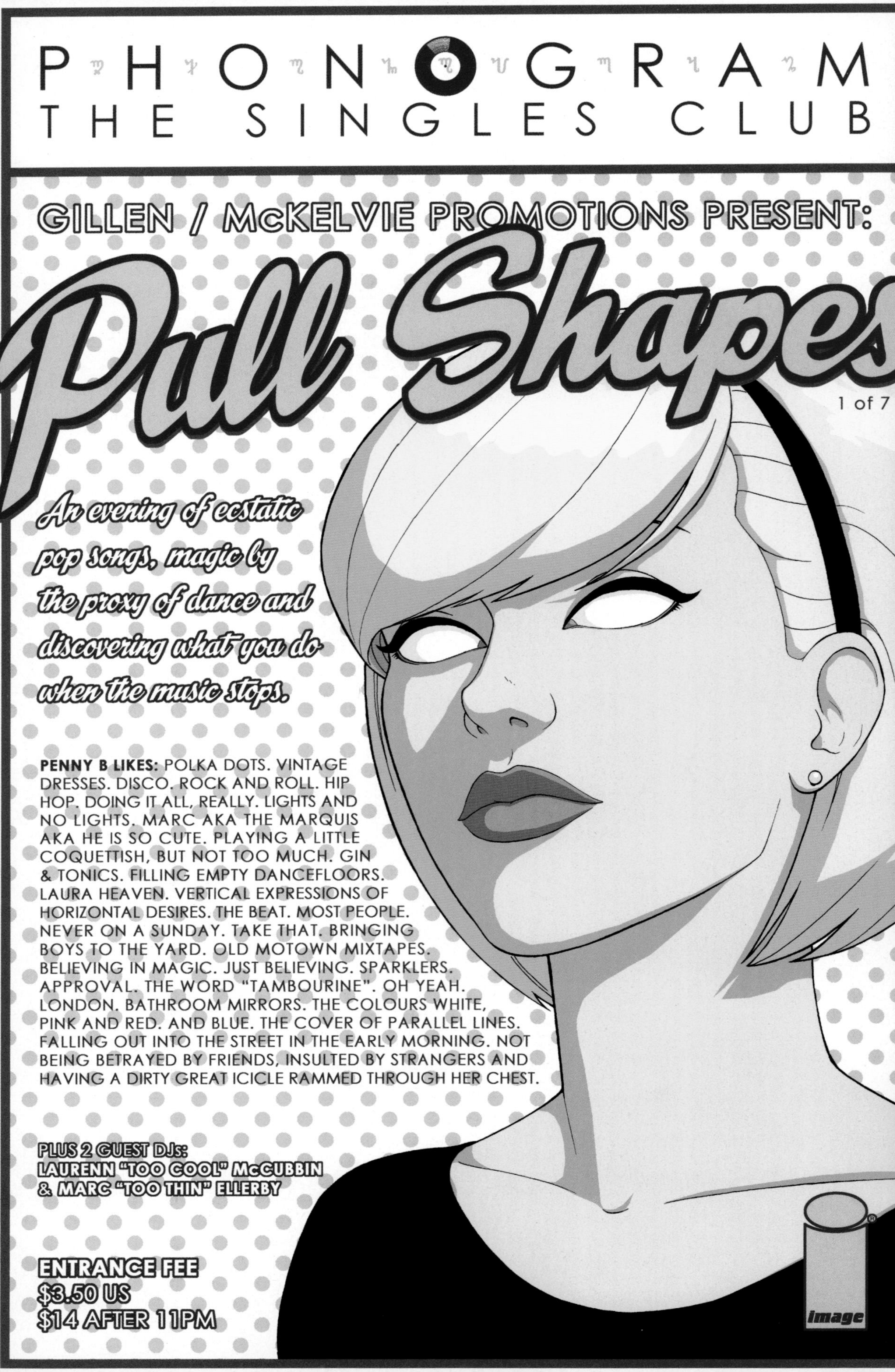
PHONOGRAM
THE SINGLES CLUB
GILLEN / McKELVIE PROMOTIONS PRESENT:
Pull Shapes
1 of 7
An evening of ecstatic pop songs, magic by the proxy of dance and discovering what you do when the music stops.
PENNY B LIKES: POLKA DOTS. VINTAGE DRESSES. DISCO. ROCK AND ROLL. HIP HOP. DOING IT ALL, REALLY. LIGHTS AND NO LIGHTS. MARC AKA THE MARQUIS AKA HE IS SO CUTE. PLAYING A LITTLE COQUETTISH, BUT NOT TOO MUCH. GIN & TONICS. FILLING EMPTY DANCEFLOORS. LAURA HEAVEN. VERTICAL EXPRESSIONS OF HORIZONTAL DESIRES. THE BEAT. MOST PEOPLE. NEVER ON A SUNDAY. TAKE THAT. BRINGING BOYS TO THE YARD. OLD MOTOWN MIXTAPES. BELIEVING IN MAGIC. JUST BELIEVING. SPARKLERS. APPROVAL. THE WORD "TAMBOURINE". OH YEAH. LONDON. BATHROOM MIRRORS. THE COLOURS WHITE, PINK AND RED. AND BLUE. THE COVER OF PARALLEL LINES. FALLING OUT INTO THE STREET IN THE EARLY MORNING. NOT BEING BETRAYED BY FRIENDS, INSULTED BY STRANGERS AND HAVING A DIRTY GREAT ICICLE RAMMED THROUGH HER CHEST.
PLUS 2 GUEST DJs:
LAURENN "TOO COOL" McCUBBIN
& MARC "TOO THIN" ELLERBY
ENTRANCE FEE
$3.50 US
$14 AFTER 11PM
image

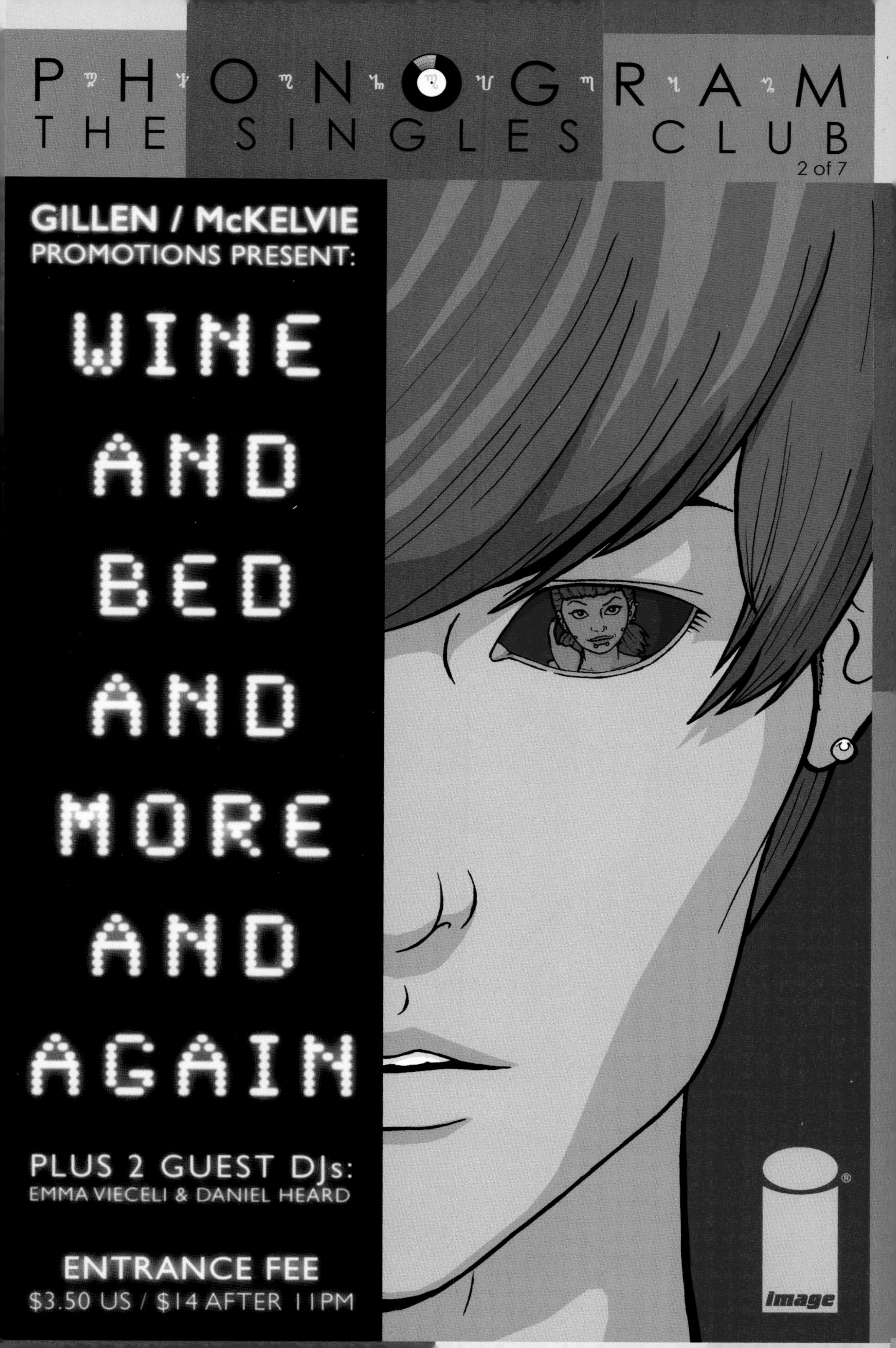
PHONOGRAM
THE SINGLES CLUB
2 of 7
GILLEN / McKELVIE
PROMOTIONS PRESENT:
WINE AND BED AND MORE AND AGAIN
PLUS 2 GUEST DJs:
EMMA VIECELI & DANIEL HEARD
ENTRANCE FEE
$3.50 US / $14 AFTER 11PM
image

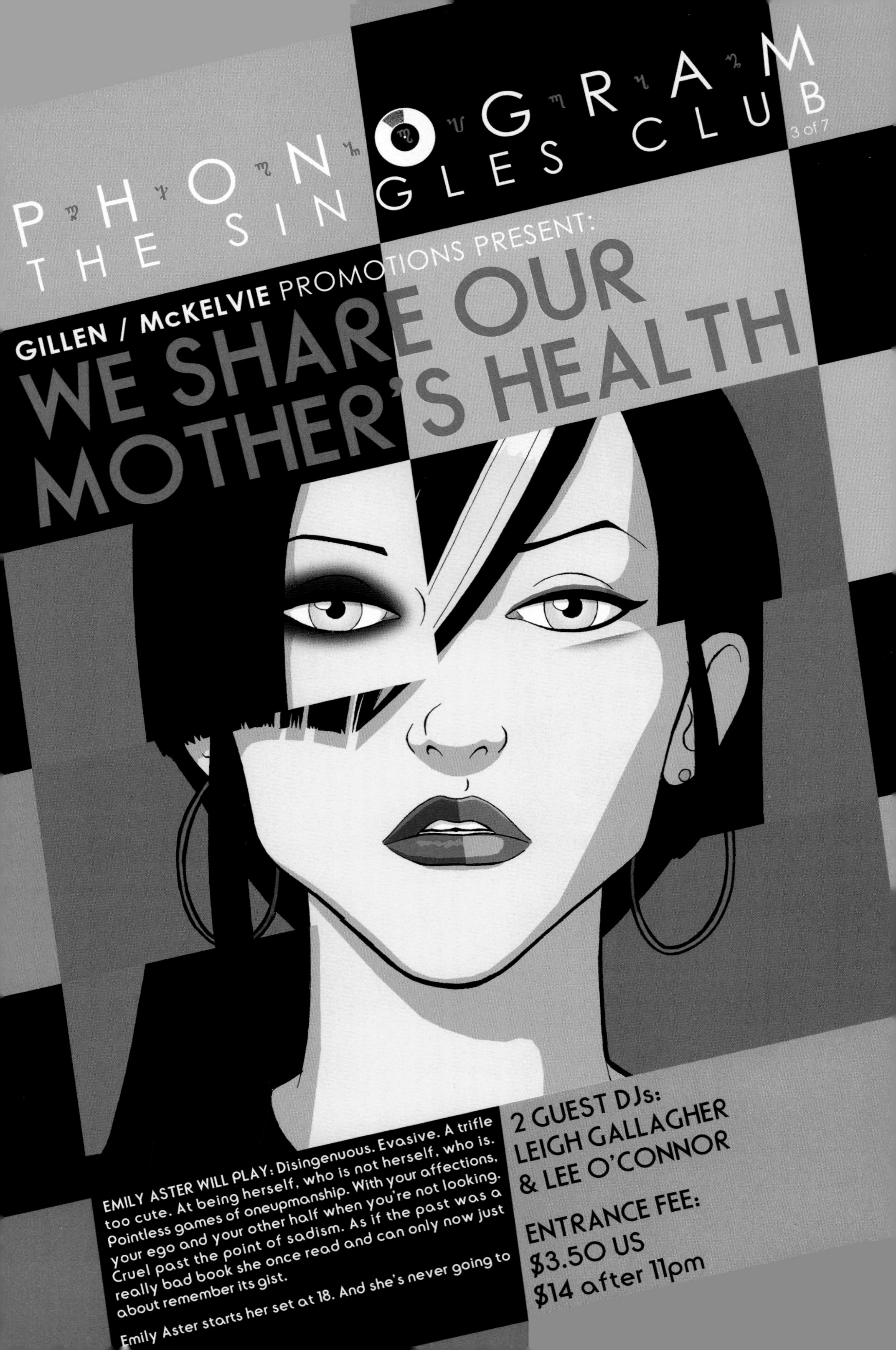

PHONOGRAM
THE SINGLES CLUB
3 of 7
GILLEN / McKELVIE PROMOTIONS PRESENT:
WE SHARE OUR MOTHER'S HEALTH
EMILY ASTER WILL PLAY: Disingenuous. Evasive. A trifle too cute. At being herself, who is not herself, who is. Pointless games of oneupmanship. With your affections, your ego and your other half when you're not looking. Cruel past the point of sadism. As if the past was a really bad book she once read and can only now just about remember its gist.
Emily Aster starts her set at 18. And she's never going to
2 GUEST DJs:
LEIGH GALLAGHER
& LEE O'CONNOR
ENTRANCE FEE:
$3.50 US
$14 after 11pm

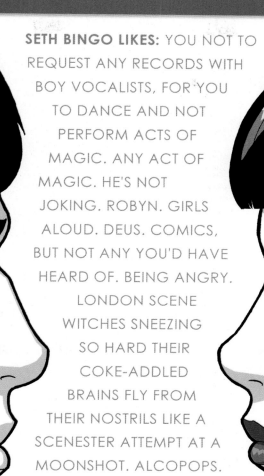

PHONOGRAM
THE SINGLES CLUB

SETH BINGO LIKES: YOU NOT TO REQUEST ANY RECORDS WITH BOY VOCALISTS, FOR YOU TO DANCE AND NOT PERFORM ACTS OF MAGIC. ANY ACT OF MAGIC. HE'S NOT JOKING. ROBYN. GIRLS ALOUD. DEUS. COMICS, BUT NOT ANY YOU'D HAVE HEARD OF. BEING ANGRY. LONDON SCENE WITCHES SNEEZING SO HARD THEIR COKE-ADDLED BRAINS FLY FROM THEIR NOSTRILS LIKE A SCENESTER ATTEMPT AT A MOONSHOT. ALCOPOPS. SILENT GIRL, MOSTLY. VIDEOGAMES OF THE LATE EIGHT-BIT AND EARLY SIXTEEN-BIT PERIOD. PRETTY LADIES. GAY CLUBS. JAPAN. TURNING MUSIC UP YOU WANT TO TURN DOWN. LAUGHING AT PEOPLE. MAKING PEOPLE HAPPY. NO, REALLY. **SILENT GIRL LIKES:** ... **SETH BINGO HATES:** YOU.

GUEST DJS
DAVID LAFUENTE &
CHARITY LARRISON

GILLEN / McKELVIE PROMOTIONS PRESENT

KONICHIWA BITCHES

4 of 7

ENTRANCE FEE $3.50 US / $14 AFTER 11PM

image®

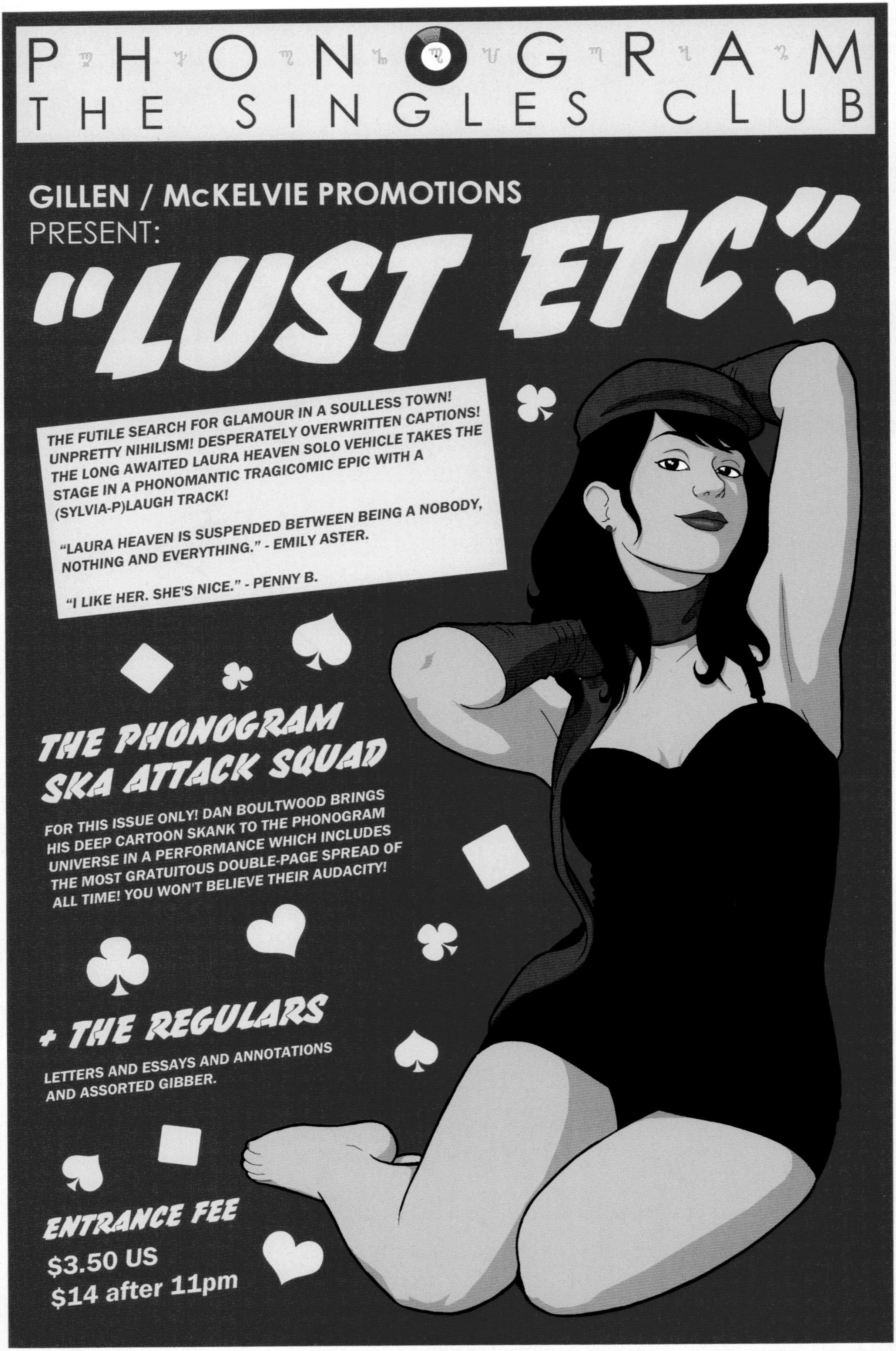

PHONOGRAM
THE SINGLES CLUB
GILLEN / McKELVIE PROMOTIONS
PRESENT:
"LUST ETC"
THE FUTILE SEARCH FOR GLAMOUR IN A SOULLESS TOWN! UNPRETTY NIHILISM! DESPERATELY OVERWRITTEN CAPTIONS! THE LONG AWAITED LAURA HEAVEN SOLO VEHICLE TAKES THE STAGE IN A PHONOMANTIC TRAGICOMIC EPIC WITH A (SYLVIA-P)LAUGH TRACK!
"LAURA HEAVEN IS SUSPENDED BETWEEN BEING A NOBODY, NOTHING AND EVERYTHING." - EMILY ASTER.
"I LIKE HER. SHE'S NICE." - PENNY B.
THE PHONOGRAM SKA ATTACK SQUAD
FOR THIS ISSUE ONLY! DAN BOULTWOOD BRINGS HIS DEEP CARTOON SKANK TO THE PHONOGRAM UNIVERSE IN A PERFORMANCE WHICH INCLUDES THE MOST GRATUITOUS DOUBLE-PAGE SPREAD OF ALL TIME! YOU WON'T BELIEVE THEIR AUDACITY!
+ THE REGULARS
LETTERS AND ESSAYS AND ANNOTATIONS AND ASSORTED GIBBER.
ENTRANCE FEE
$3.50 US
$14 after 11pm

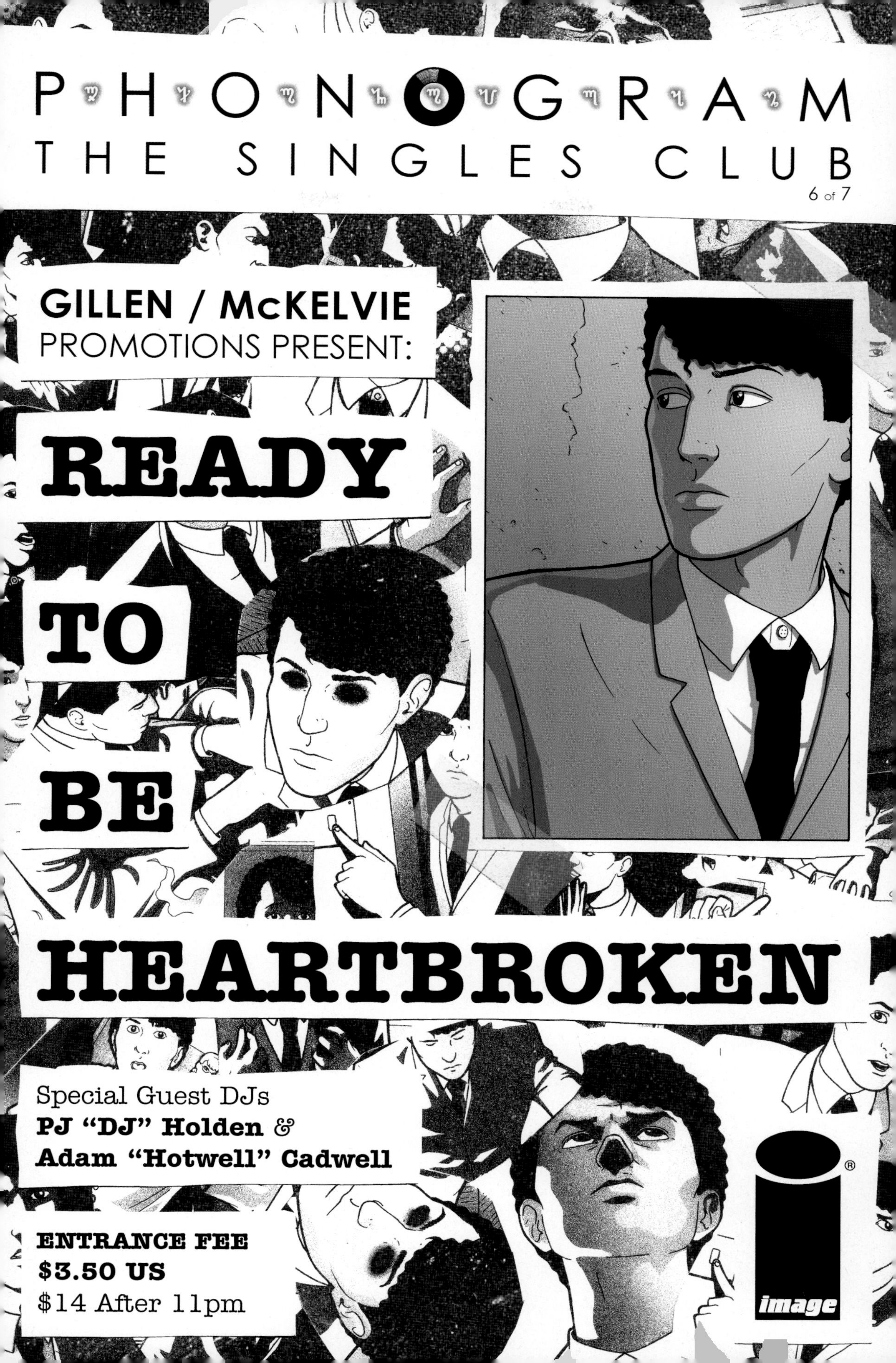
PHONOGRAM
THE SINGLES CLUB
6 of 7
GILLEN / McKELVIE
PROMOTIONS PRESENT:
READY
TO
BE
HEARTBROKEN
Special Guest DJs
PJ "DJ" Holden &
Adam "Hotwell" Cadwell
ENTRANCE FEE
$3.50 US
$14 After 11pm
image

PHONOGRAM
THE SINGLES CLUB

7 of 7

WOLF
LIKE
ME

GILLEN / McKELVIE PROMOTIONS PRESENT
A WILD NIGHT OUT FEATURING **4 GUEST DJs:**
NIKKI COOK / BECKY CLOONAN / ANDY BLOOR
SEAN AZZOPARDI

ENTRANCE FEE $3.50 US / $14 after 11pm

image